CW01151710

Freeing My Alpha

Book 2 of *My Shy Alpha*

RIVER KAI

RIVER KAI

Freeing My Alpha

Book 2 of *My Shy Alpha*
THE STEAMY SHIFTER ROMANCE SERIES

Copyright ©2024 River Kai Art.

All rights reserved.
riverkaiart.com

This is a work of fiction. The story, all names, characters, organizations, and incidents portrayed in this novel are from the author's imagination or used fictitiously.

No part of this publication may be reproduced, distributed, or transmitted in any form or by any means without the prior written permission of the publisher, except as permitted by U.S. copyright law.

Edited by Kayla Vokolek
Cover and Illustrations by River Kai

ISBN (eBook): 979-8-9900293-2-3
ISBN (Paperback): 979-8-9900293-3-0
ISBN (Hardback): 979-8-9900293-4-7

Library of Congress Control Number: 2024908426

Our books may be purchased in bulk for promotional, educational, or business use. Please contact your local bookseller, or send a request to River Kai Art at riverkaiart.com/wholesale or PO Box 1414, Wilsonville, OR 97070.

First edition, June 2024

10 9 8 7 6 5 4 3 2 1

Riverwolf Fantasy Press
The Fantasy Romance Imprint of River Kai Art

To all those grieving
what could've been.

You matter,
you are loved,
and you belong here.

1

Rainn has me hooked arm in arm, skipping ahead of me. "Run with me, Luna! Noah told me you're fast!"

Now I understand why Noah told me to wear my hiking boots. Dousing ourselves with mud before we've seen a single Lycan child, Rainn and I burst into laughter as we blast through dense thickets, a collection of little leaves gripping our long hair. My mate's younger sister glances over her shoulder, and the brightness in her eyes stirs warmth in my chest. I never had a doting younger sister, but with just that look, I feel like I do.

Rainn pulls me to a stop, crashing into my torso with a hard hug. "Oh, your scent just got sweeter than ever. I love you too, Luna."

"I— I love you too… too?" My world spins as I struggle to keep up with Rainn's affection downpour—all within the first three minutes since we said hello.

I'm not Greenfield Pack's Luna—not yet, at least—but loving words from pack members like Rainn make me feel like I've long-earned the title of the pack's maternal protector. And even though I'm only part Lycan, instincts well up inside me whenever a pack member huddles up to me. I wish I could hug everyone here all at once.

Rainn's smile widens as she pulls back. "Don't worry, you don't have to say a single thing—not when your scent is so honest. I love that about Noah too."

As Rainn takes off, still gripping my hand, I laugh through my watery eyes. She's so different from her shy, stoic brother, but so similar at her core: her wolf is ever-present in a curious, unbothered ball of energy.

"Ever since you asked to hang out with me and help out with my class, I've been so excited that I couldn't sleep!" Rainn shakes her head, laughing at herself. "I can't wait for you to meet everyone. They've been asking me all week about you."

"They have?" I'm smiling, but nerves blast through my guts.

I have no idea what Lycans teach their kids in the Greenfield Forest School, but from what Noah and Rainn explained, it's more of a daycare for homeschooled wolves, many of whom have been expelled from human schools for wolflike behaviors.

My preschool student, Andy, has been on my mind nonstop; his biting incident helped me recognize a new slew of wolfy misunderstandings in school. As future Luna, I want to make sure Greenfield Pack kids can access free education, but even more so as an educator.

I'm mildly terrified of what I might discover today. I asked Noah about a few standards of human early education, and his eyebrows formed into a deep scrunch.

"They're wolves," he said. "They learn some of that, but they need to learn how to hunt, survive, and protect their family and pack, first and foremost. Everything else isn't as vital for Lycans as it is for humans."

My chest tensed, protective instincts bubbling to the surface. "But they have human forms too. They need reading, math, and science skills, or else they'll be even more segregated from human society."

Noah's resulting, earth-shattering concern surprised me. My sweet, shy Alpha sat with his head in his hands for over an hour, and I could only pull him out of it by promising him I'd take a look at the curriculum in person—and that I trust him and his pack to know what's right for their needs.

Today, I only want to observe. My top Alpha mate and his little sister are proud of their Greenfield Forest School, and I wouldn't dare drag down Rainn's teaching style. My degree is in human education, not Lycan. Maybe the pups really do have a passable amount of literacy, numeracy, and science literacy.

Right on cue, a pup bursts from the bushes, stealing Rainn

from my grasp with a tackle. I scream, but Rainn laughs, rolling across the forest floor with the child in her arms and popping back up to her feet. The pup nuzzles into her chest, giggling as Rainn vigorously rubs his back.

"My little Alpha! You are getting *so* good at prowling!" Rainn beams.

The pup screeches through his excitement, squeezing her as hard as his little arms can manage in a display of pure pride and joy.

That's when Rainn kisses his forehead, over and over. I release a sharp gasp.

Rainn whips her head around, meeting my eyes with dilated pupils. "What's wrong?"

I'm too stunned to speak out loud, resorting to the telepathic mindlink we share with Greenfield pack members. *You kissed him.*

Rainn's shoulders loosen. She breaks into her usual reassuring smile, setting down the Alpha boy. *Of course I kissed him. I'm his daytime mom. And so are you for today!*

I want to smile along with her, but my stomach churns. *What do their parents think about that?*

They expect me to love on them! Wolves need a sense of community to grow up strong, and everyone trusts each other to help raise every pup as their own.

My heart tugs at the thought of Noah being raised like this. Feeling loved from all angles. I'm tempted to melt at the thought, but I can't shake the human fears I know too well.

No one's worried they might fall into the wrong hands?

Rainn laughs. *Oh, no. At the first predatory hint in their scent, we handle those wolves with our fangs. No one's getting to our babies here. Especially not under Noah.*

I wring my hands, still uneasy. I know it's different for them, but for whatever reason, I'm drowning in culture shock. But if Noah and I have a baby someday, does this mean they'll grow up feeling safer than I feel now? That they have a better chance in this world? I bite my lip, staving off a giddy smile. It feels too good to be true.

A flood of pups trickles in through the forest, brawling,

scrambling up trees, and face-planting into the fresh mud stirred up from last night's downpour.

"One, two, three, eyes on me!" Rainn shouts.

So some things are the same.

Or maybe just this one thing.

Every single wild eye zips to Rainn and me in a millisecond. Their laser focus tempts me to take a step back. The pups might be in a disastrous state of leaves, mud, and scratches, but every pup awaits Rainn's direction no matter how young, better focused than a crowd of adult human teachers in our board meetings. Survival instincts emanate from them, as well as a gentle, wafting glow of eager curiosity in their scents.

Now that they're frozen, I do a quick mental check of everyone present, memorizing who I'm accountable for today. The longer I stare, the more pups I spot: tucked behind each other, infants wrapped into their older siblings' arms, and just the tops of heads and eyes poking through bushes.

Rainn smiles at me before turning back to her class. "I brought someone *very* special with me today."

The class's focus zips to me. They take a collective deep breath, and I feel like it's the first day of my teaching career all over again, shuffling where I stand as I overthink my nervous smile. All it takes is one little wolf to scream "Luna," and a deluge of little ones pour onto the path, latching onto my legs and hopping all around me.

I burst into heavy laughter. "Oh, my goodness! Look at all of you sweet pups!"

But there's no true way to express my vibrating excitement, flowing so strongly through my body that it aches. These aren't just any pups, these are our pack's pups.

Greenfield Pack is one huge family. Rainn isn't the only one to tell me everyone treats each other like their own dearest loved ones, regardless of if they've met before.

But carrying the Greenfield family name signifies something deeper: these little ones are Noah's. *Ours.*

I hug them back on instinct, gathering as many squirming bodies into my arms as I can hold. My wolf zooms in rapid circles through our bond. *I love them! I love them!*

Noah doesn't mindlink anything—our bond tells me he's running in wolf form, and therefore, full wolf brain—but his wolf certainly notices mine. He's on the prowl at the perimeter, somewhere to the southwest; our bond tugs my heart toward him like a compass. His heart aches with longing, and I assume it's because he's desperate to meet with Rainn and me in an hour, as planned. I have a feeling he'll show up even sooner.

My heart picks up the pace. What will Noah be like, surrounded by all these pups? Will his playful wolf be in charge, or his steady, quiet pillar of a personality, soothing these pups into tranquility?

"Here you go!" A little voice cries out, depositing a literal infant into my arms.

I gasp. "Oh, *my*— Who is this?"

"Sarah!" Bright, beaming eyes of an older sibling greet me above a tooth-gapped grin. "She likes your scent."

My heart flips over itself as baby Sarah burrows her face into my chest, her arms flailing with excitement that she hasn't figured out how to control yet.

"Oh, God, she's so— They're *all* so—" Nothing can describe my love for the curious eyes around me. I look to Rainn for help, my heart threatening to overflow.

"Okay, okay!" Rainn laughs, shooing pups off me. "We can take turns nuzzling our Luna throughout the day, or else we won't have enough time to play with her."

With that, they scurry off, affectionately brushing our sides on their way. Many pups cling to one other instead, nuzzling one other's faces and glomping into heavy hugs in greeting.

I've never seen anything like it. Most of the workweek, I have to stop my human kids from harassing each other too much, not from consensually cuddling too much. My hands shake as I adjust Sarah in my arms, nestling her in a tender cradle when she whines for deeper touch.

Overwhelming instinct takes over, and before I can stop myself, I'm nuzzling her chubby cheek. I freeze the second I realize what I'm doing, but Sarah explodes into a squealing bundle of happiness, her full gums on display.

My heart splits open from how quickly she expands it. It's not just her unbearable cuteness, but her warm, delighted scent.

There's a hint of wonder in every fleeting waft of it, but most of all, there's a deep, hungry love for me as her current caregiver. I can't slow my rapid breath.

Goddess, I can't take this, Noah mindlinks. *I need to see you in action.*

2

I can't bear to respond, flustered to my core. By the time I can pry my eyes off Sarah's adorable marshmallow cheeks, Rainn has taken off down the path, leading the little ones with brisk strides. She doesn't bother looking back despite a few stragglers. But as they keep their eyes trained on me instead, I realize they're waiting, keeping me looped into the pack.

"Thank you for waiting, pups! Let's get going so we don't miss anything Teacher Rainn says."

With a gasp, the pups scramble over a massive fallen log, darting after Rainn. I laugh, enamored by their excitement. That alone tells me Rainn's classes are priceless. Best of all, Sarah lets out a gurgly laugh with me.

"It's all so exciting, isn't it, Sarah?" I giggle along with her, rubbing her little back in my palm. My heart races as she gazes into my eyes in pure trust, releasing another wave of flowery, happy baby scent.

We catch up to Rainn, stilling ourselves with the hush of the surrounding pups. They're focused on Rainn's point.

"Can someone tell me what this is?"

"A footprint!" A little voice shouts from the bushes behind Rainn.

She smiles. "Yes! What type of footprint?"

"Deer," says a chorus of high voices.

"Excellent! Can any of my littles tell me what else they notice? How long ago did our deer visit this part of the forest, and where did they go?"

A few pups around six– to seven-years-old jump eagerly with

their hands up, and Rainn laughs. "I know you know, my big loves. Let the little ones respond first."

The little ones are extra little today, the closest toddler seemingly just reaching three. She gapes in frozen silence, only glancing between Rainn and me with her eyes.

"Tell me what your nose notices." As Rainn taps her nose's tip, her lowered voice hushes the group. Our collective silence draws out the sound of the gentle air current, wind billowing our clothes and rustling the leafy overgrowth.

Little pups stoop to sniff the deer hoof impression in the fresh mud. Each time another pup rushes over, they smash their own prints in the mud, collectively smearing each other's backs as they topple over one another. Some return to the bushes and trees, attempting to peek over the tops of everyone's heads.

One tiny pup in particular wobbles, popping upright too quickly. I catch her just in time, but Rainn grants her a beaming smile, widening the little one's eyes. The toddler sucks her thumb, using her free hand to point behind the group.

Rainn claps rapidly, letting out a sharp giggle. "Yes! Oh, Goddess, yes! You are *so* good at this, Chels! That's exactly where the deer went!"

The little one breaks into a breathy smile, proudness emanating from her form as she claps for herself. It tears my heart from my chest with overwhelming affection, begging me to squeeze her little cheeks.

But as the rest of the pups chime in, discovering together how many hours ago the deer passed through these trees, I slump into myself.

These tiny Lycan children can track scents effortlessly. I don't know how to pick out a scent, let alone decipher what portion of the scent would tell me its age.

I gasp, startled from my thoughts by Sarah's sudden mouthing of my chest. She wriggles in my arms, her breath speeding into an anxious pant when she realizes I'm not rushing to breastfeed her.

"O-oh, uh—" My cheeks burn hot as Rainn meets my eyes.

"Oops, someone's hungry!" Rainn opens her arms for Sarah, but not after whipping a breast from her tank top.

My jaw drops, feeling like I've been dropped off in another

country for the day—not because she's breastfeeding, but because she's a teacher feeding a stranger's child from her body.

But the pups continue to discuss the deer tracks, and Sarah latches on, everyone behaving as if this is normal. Sarah suckles away as Rainn holds her one-armed, squatting back down with the rest of the class, but I'm left standing with my head still spinning.

Rainn does a double take, breaking into a giggle. *Oh, yeah. I forgot to mention I gave birth to Sarah about six months ago.* All I can do is gape. Rainn adjusts Sarah, stroking her head as Sarah gulps ravenous mouthfuls of milk. *Between us, I'm happy to be a teacher-mom for thousands of kids and carry pups for those who can't.* Rainn winks. *Plus, this way I can get a full night's sleep.*

My brain catches up with what Rainn just disclosed, connecting Sarah's doe-brown eyes to Rainn's gorgeous features.

Rainn, I had no idea you were a surrogate!

With a happy nod, Rainn kisses Sarah's head. *And I'm slowly getting myself ready to carry another pup for a new family, hopefully by next year. That little one—climbing the tree with those cute little pin curls—he was the first pup I carried.*

My heartstrings strum as I follow Rainn's nod, finding a toddler with a bright, gummy smile holding hands with who must be his best friend. They rescue a fat worm together, depositing it into the bushes before it can be stepped on. It reminds me of Amy and me; Amy always admired how I could notice all the little details in the world, long before we knew why my brain works like it does. But Noah's little sister was the one who granted this boy life. The more I look at his sharp features, softened only by round cheeks and an elated smile, the more he looks like a tiny, cheerful Noah.

I'm torn. On one hand, I'm staring into a possible future I've always wanted. On the other, I know in my heart that Noah didn't have the freedom this little one does. I felt it the second we bonded: something dark and brooding, poisoning the depths of Noah's emotions.

But today's pups of Greenfield seem different. Rainn not only created this safety for her students, but also brought two of them to life. I look back at her with newfound wonder. The sun's glow ignites Rainn's profile as it peeks through the forest canopy, giving her an added air of royalty.

"Teacher Rainn, you're the coolest woman I've ever met," I whisper.

She gasps, dissolving into blushing laughter. But the pups chime in, patting her arms and tugging on her clothes.

"You are!" One of the older pups shouts.

A little one stands on her toes, pushing through the crowd to mold herself to Rainn's side. "I-I love you!"

Rainn's laughter brightens, filling the forest with more open love than I've witnessed in another teacher. But I know the feeling well. They really are our daytime kids.

Which is also why my attention zips behind me, pulled by pure instinct. "Where are you all off to?"

"Tracking the deer!" A distant voice cries.

But another head pops out of an even farther bush. "Not me! I smell Alpha Noah!"

This gathers everyone's attention. Before we can stop them, pups spill into the thickets, darting away from us. It ignites a primal fear in my chest, but Rainn calmly pulls herself upright, lifting Sarah over her shoulder to burp her. Her tranquility relaxes my shoulders, especially as she smiles adoringly at her class.

"Alpha Noah, huh? Well, who can tell me how long ago he scouted this section of the forest for his daily check?"

My heart races at the thought, still unable to grasp how my regal mate exists. The first time I saw him shift for a perimeter run, bristling with focus, every bone in my body trusted the territory he protects. I never felt safe in this winding forest growing up, but Noah's presence changed everything for me.

"Alright, Teacher Luna, here she is." Rainn plops a milk-drunk Sarah back into my arms.

Sarah's eyes droop with satisfaction. I erupt into adoring, silent giggles, overcome with Sarah's smacking lips.

But by the time I can sort her wispy hair back into order, I get the sense we're no longer standing back from the crowd.

I gasp as little noses sniff the air around me, a pile-up of bodies gathering at my feet. "Oh, my— What do we smell, now?"

"We *told* you. Alpha Noah!" A pup shakes his head as if that's the most obvious answer in the world.

I sputter out laughter. "I did say goodbye to him recently, so I'm sure I do smell like—"

Words escape me as pups swarm my personal space, sniffing my legs in a voracious wolf pile until I nearly topple over. Rainn steadies me, but the pups' laughter rises throughout the forest, spurring me into contagious giggles. Self-control lapses from there; we're all cracking up, excited to share this space together.

Until a scent catches my nose: the sweetest, most endearing hint of cinnamon and sugar I've ever smelled.

I lift my head, feeling new eyes on me.

Noah and I lock stares.

Our bond spikes with such heavy emotion that I suck in a startled breath. Every single pup freezes, following my gaze.

Noah hasn't expressly said he *wants* to have kids. Whenever we've talked about it, it's been surrounding my desires, not his. It sounds like he generally plans to have them in his lifetime. I just don't know if he feels the same deep, unshakeable desire to raise them, or if it's just a social expectation placed on him. And I don't think I'll feel okay with planning to have a baby until he makes it clear.

His gaze is so powerful that my knees feel weak. Leaves pepper his dark hair thrown to one side, and his clothes strain around his broad shoulders, telling me he's newly shifted into his human form and still bristling with energy from his scouting run.

But those sharp, stoic eyes aren't their usual teal; they're stark yellow.

His wolf has shown up to greet us.

No one dares to move, awaiting the top Alpha's cue. But he can't seem to move either. Heavy emotion ripples over his brow, his eyes locked on my form like he's craving to absorb the picture I paint. I look down at the little ones at my feet and Sarah in my arms, warm, chubby pups squished against me from every angle. Noah must've seen us interacting the whole time.

Or maybe there's even more to it. Noah mentioned he's bonded deeply with not just me, but every single Greenfield pack member. Does this mean he felt us celebrating our excitement together until his wolf couldn't resist checking for himself? Could he feel these pups' laughter in his heart, sharing it with us too? I love that thought so much that my chest aches, stealing my breath until it becomes uneven bursts.

The youngest pup can't contain herself, throwing her tiny arms in the air with a delighted screech. Noah melts into a grin wide enough to show off his sharp incisors, and the forest fills with screams and laughter as the pups sprint to their Alpha. Well, not just sprint to him—they *launch* themselves at him, thrusting their bodies into the air with full confidence he'll catch them.

Rainn bursts into a cackle. "There's one... Two... Three, four, five! Six!"

Noah's eyes widen, but his smile turns mischievous. He snatches up every airborne pup until his sturdy arms spill over with too many pups to hold. They crawl across his biceps and shoulders, overtaking him until he crumbles beneath them around nineteen, sputtering into deep belly laughter that even I can rarely rouse from him.

And I'm stuck standing here, cuddling Sarah against my throbbing heart as my brain restarts. I don't think I'll ever be able to process the vision in front of me, more gorgeous than anything I've imagined our lives to become together.

Noah doesn't just like kids, he *loves* them.

But does he want to dedicate every waking hour to kids as a parent? That's a whole separate question, forcing me to swallow my excitement.

Rainn finally catches her breath, pulling pup after pup off Noah with rapid precision only for them to run right pack and pounce on the pile. "Alright, enough, enough! You found him already!"

Rainn herds the pups back into the clearing around the deer tracks, but some kids stick by Noah, their hands miniature against his wide palms. They tug on him with all their might, and he chuckles, unmoving as if he's only brushed by a light breeze.

When he meets my eyes, his genuine, erupting smile flips my heart.

"Hi." His soft, deep voice rumbles through my chest, and we're not even touching.

"Hi," I breathe.

His eyes fall to Sarah in my arms, tracking my thumb softly rubbing her as she drifts deeper into sleep. But Noah's gaze stirs my scent into a mushy, sweet explosion, begging me to tackle my mate with a hard kiss. Instead, I bite my bottom lip, unsure how else to contain myself. Noah's eyes brighten as he breaks into a wider smile.

"Are you joining our lesson or not, Alpha Noah? You're our biggest distraction today." Rainn crosses her arms with a grin.

Noah pulls his focus from me with a chuckle. "Okay, okay, I'm joining the lesson for today."

The pups around us cheer, and Noah and I laugh. He allows them to guide him toward the clearing, widening his stance to dodge the pups cluttering his feet.

Before I can follow after them, multiple pups stop Noah; they turn around, extending their hands for me.

Noah and I meet eyes and smile.

But there's an extra warmth and giddiness in our bond that wasn't there before, giving my heart a workout.

As our class settles onto a rare patch of dry leaves beneath a heavy canopy, Rainn's bright voice enraptures everyone's attention.

So far, Rainn has managed to include every core subject in her lesson while keeping it hands-on, and I can tell the pups genuinely care about her teachings. Some pups climb trees as they listen, fiddling with bugs, sticks, or leaves, but I know better than to think they're distracted. Rainn seems to understand that every kid is different, allowing them to pay attention in their own ways.

Noah and I might actually be the only ones having trouble focusing; I can't stop feeling the eyes on my right cheek.

Biting the inside of my cheek, I stop myself from erupting into anxious, excited giggles. The different, novel sensation in our bond only grows with my smile, expanding by the second in my chest.

Everything in me wants to pounce on my mate.

For now, I settle on teasing him.

Just when I nod along to Rainn's question, I shoot Noah a quick glance to catch him staring. His focus zips back to Rainn, but excitement sparks in our bond, loving the silent game of chase. I hold my breath, containing my laugh.

But Noah's eyes drift back to me. They're stark yellow, just like his shifted wolf.

My stomach flips. He's more excited than I thought.

His eyes glide down my body, tracing the baby still nestled in my arms, then dart back to my face. His breath heightens, and then I feel it: an uncontainable ache spills from Noah, sharpening his breath.

I have to swallow twice, my throat constricting with emotion.

Noah hasn't said a word, but I can feel the answer I'm looking for. I just can't believe it's real. That my life actually brought me here after so much disappointment around this very subject.

When Noah found our class today, he wasn't just adoring how sweet it was to see me interacting with kids; he was agonizing over the thought of us and our kids, just like I was.

But is now the right time?

I can't bear to keep looking into Noah's eyes, my heart racing out of control and dampening my palms. I duck my head, busying my focus on delicately wiping Sarah's drool before it slips down her squishy cheek.

"Would you like to answer this question for us, Alpha Noah?" Rainn asks.

Noah's back straightens. "I, uh— What was the question, again?"

His little sister sighs, and the pups erupt into quiet giggles.

Rainn shakes her head with a laugh. "Alright pups, I think we all need a change of pace. Let's continue our hike."

Noah gives Rainn an apologetic smile. She sticks her tongue out at him and they both laugh.

As Noah helps me to my feet, he forces his stare off me. It might look like he's just busy analyzing the pups crowding his legs, but I can feel the muffled desperation in his wolf's core to tackle my antsy wolf.

"Follow your teacher," Noah softly says to the pups crowding us.

I'm surprised how well they listen, darting after Rainn without complaint. Although, they are looking back at Noah with absolute awe in their eyes. Or no, maybe they're looking at me too?

Multiple pups slip their arms around one other, glancing at Noah's arm over my shoulder. They refocus on their lesson with brighter smiles, pride lifting their chests as they not only mimic Noah, but also me, their future Luna. It stirs something in me I thought I could patiently wait for.

Noah does a double take at me, breaking into a wide smile. "What is it?"

"Nothing." I bite back a smile. "It's just, we're getting to live out our wishes to share a childhood. I feel like I went back in time to take a class with you in the forest, and—"

I break into giggles at Noah's wide, overjoyed grin, unable to speak another word. He leans in, putting a protective hand on my forearm cradling Sarah as he leans in to nuzzle my cheek.

"I'm loving every second too," he whispers.

Goddess, help me. Sarah looks even more like him now that they're side by side, and he's holding her and me in his arms like we're his. My heart falls over itself until I'm unable to keep looking at my sweet mate.

Rainn guides us down a small trail on the clearing's edge. A line of curious pups hops into her footsteps in the mud.

"We're nearing the portion of the forest with extra poison oak. You all remember how to identify it, right?"

"Right," a chorus of proud voices chimes after Rainn.

"Good! Let's steer clear and warn each other if we spot it."

I smile, my heart lifting. Dad left me with the skills to recognize Greenfield Forest flora too. With how haphazardly these pups roam the forest, I can see why they already needed to memorize how to avoid poison oak so early.

"Can someone help me find the next set of footprints for our deer?" Rainn asks.

My eyes zip to the forest floor, scouring the mud beneath the leaves. But then Rainn adds, "Use your nose only!"

My stomach sinks. Noah glances back as my feet slow, and I try to smile.

But I don't know how to do this. Toddlers track wild deer with their noses all around us with no problem. Maybe I could too, but I have no idea where to start. I was never taught.

You okay? Noah mindlinks. We're striding ahead, Noah's focus remaining on the pups as he gives them encouraging nods. "Good job, Beta, that's exactly it," he murmurs, drawing a wide grin onto a little boy's face.

My heart flips. Before today, I could only imagine how sweetly Noah would treat our children, but this is giving me a clearer glimpse that's so delightful, I almost can't stand it.

But as his eyes flicker to mine, they're still greener than usual. "You okay?" He tries out loud this time.

I drop my head, hiding my flushed cheeks. "Sorry. I'm okay. I just remembered something."

"Yeah?" He draws closer, hugging me against his side.

The wind gushes through the trees, ruffling leaves and pups' hair as far as I can see. They're covered in mud, but they're also all smiling.

"Yeah," I whisper. "I used to love playing in the dirt."

Noah breaks into the widest smile possible, dissolving all my flustered nerves. We break into soft giggles, huddling in closer. "Goddess, I can imagine you getting your tiny hands all muddy."

I laugh. "I loved it. But my mom didn't."

Noah tilts his head, studying my expression. I'm still smiling, but there's no denying the tumultuous ache from my side of our bond.

Maybe classifying my situation as "never taught" is putting it too lightly. The more I think about it, the more I realize life trained me into not only a subservient woman but also as little of a Lycan as possible. Every curious, wolflike childhood memory ended in shame.

Rainn calls out, "Over here, everyone!"

Noah and I follow the pups to Rainn. A part of me is dying to participate, but to do so, I'll have to ask how to track scents in the first place, and that sounds humiliating.

These pups entrust their lives to Noah and me with full faith we'll keep them safe. But how can I when I can't sniff out danger unless it's shoved in my face?

As Rainn explains the intricacies of scent tracking, my eyes gloss over. My heart races and my chest burns, embarrassment sinking me further into Noah's side without me realizing it.

But a soft nudge on my shoulder guides me away from the group. Hurrying away while the pups are distracted, Noah and I stop behind a nearby boulder.

I look up to find Noah's gentle smile. When I can't fully smile back, he doesn't pressure me for answers: he sends me a wave of his soothing scent. My shoulders soften, but I'm tempted to cry.

Fuck, no, I am crying. One look at my mate splits my heart open, my tears falling within mere seconds of staring into his knowing eyes. I suck in a tight breath, tilting my head back to keep my tears from dripping on Sarah.

"Hey, it's okay, gorgeous," Noah whispers. I bite my lip, shaking my head no, but he wipes my tears with his big thumbs, retaining his smile. "It is, sweet Omega. Here, let me hold her, and I'll show you what to do."

I suck back tears, stirring Sarah awake. Before she can melt into fussy tears with me, Noah bundles her into one arm. I cover my mouth, but I bust out laughing through my tears anyway; Sarah looks so small against Noah's chest that it looks like he's tucking a football into one arm.

His eyes widen. "What? Am I doing something wrong?"

"No, not necessarily." I laugh. "She just looks like a little mushy pile of baby clothes when you hold her like that."

Noah shuffles Sarah over his shoulder. Planting one massive palm over such a tiny back, Noah flips my heart with his bright grin. "Better?"

I giggle as silently as I can, sneaking behind Noah's shoulder to check Sarah's expression. After a quick rub over her eyes, Sarah flops in complete trust of Noah, her cheek squished against his shoulder and leaving her lips to hang open.

"Oh, Noah, she's..." I bite my lips. *She's totally asleep.*

My heart stops when Noah peeks over Sarah's head to meet my eyes. For a second, I feel like I'm looking far into the future. My eyes are still watering, but this time I'm smiling.

"Come here." His low, rumbling whisper sends a warm buzz through my stomach. "Look right here with me, and tell me what you see."

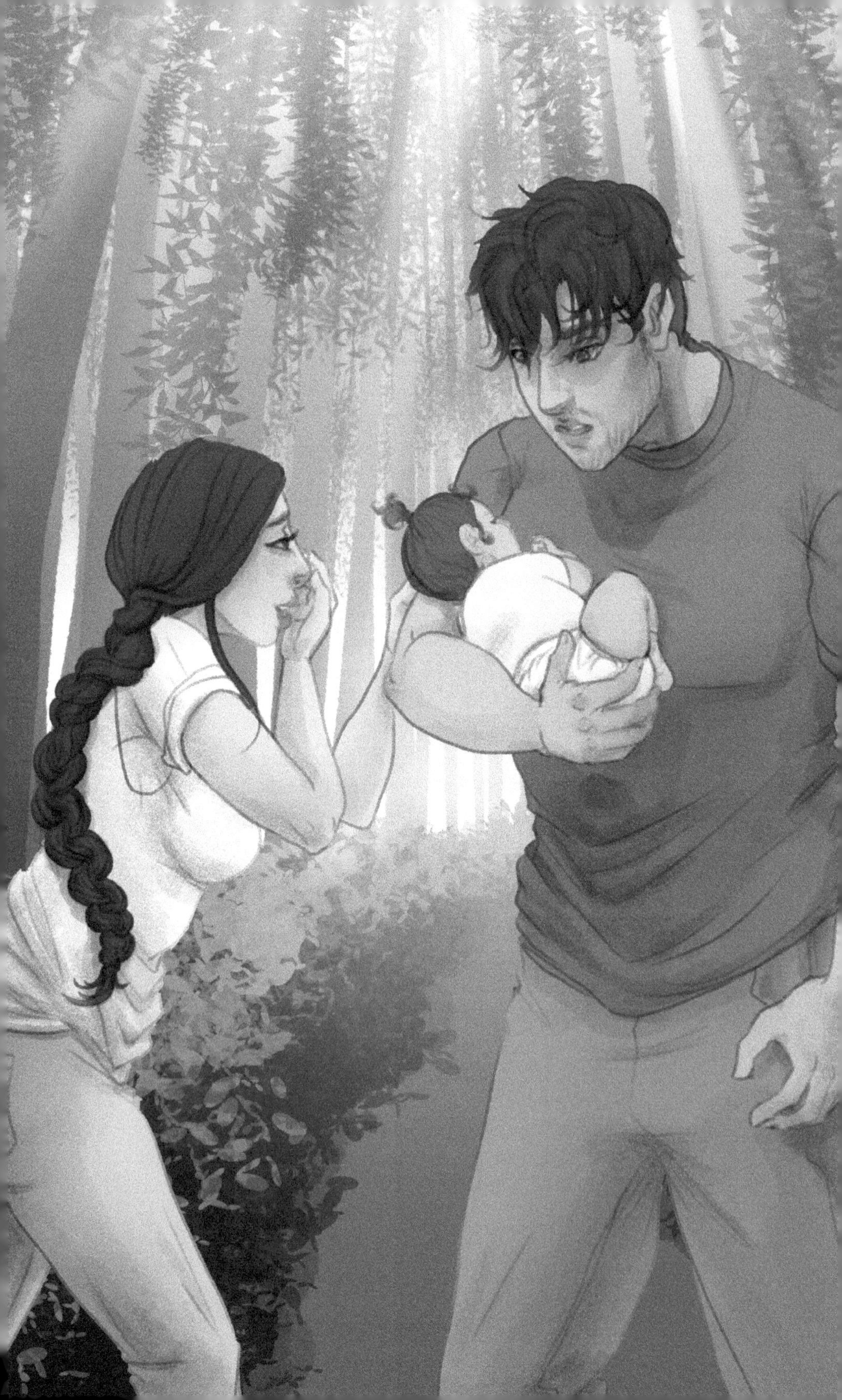

Deflating a little once I remember why Noah took Sarah from me in the first place, I follow Noah's point to the boulder beside us. It's covered in moss, bugs, leaves, and more—so much that I can't pinpoint a majority of the details on it.

I'm not smiling anymore. The more I look, the more overwhelmed I become.

Noah rubs my back. "There's no wrong answer. What's the first thing you noticed?"

I clear the tears from my throat, standing up straighter. "Moss."

"Hell yeah, there's a lot of moss. That shit's endless, and so many different kinds are mixed into each clump that it's a complete mindfuck, right?"

I sputter out a laugh. "Shh, they have little wolf ears."

He slaps a hand over his mouth, glancing at the pups behind us. When he turns back to face me with wide eyes, my cheeks hurt from smiling. Noah breaks into delighted giggles, kissing my wet cheek.

"It's overwhelming though, right?" He asks.

I bite my lips as my stomach knots into my spine.

God, why is this hitting me so hard? All I can do is nod to keep from crying more.

Noah gives me rapid shoulder rubs. "You're not alone in that. It's super overwhelming for *all* wolves. Especially before they're given any tools."

This captures every atom of my attention. I dare to look into Noah's eyes, no longer concerned about how mortified I am. Does he mean this struggle is common? That all Lycans start out feeling lost?

Noah gives me a soft smile, drawing me in for a side hug. "You wanna know what I think is happening?"

I nod, glancing up at him. He gives me a heavy forehead kiss before pulling away, allowing me to stand on my own.

Noah gestures across the rock. "There's so much clouding your attention that when you try to track scents, it's all flooding you at once. No one sat down with you and told you how to zoom in." Noah holds his hand out for me, drawing me closer until our noses are a mere inch from the boulder's surface.

Adjusting my hand in his, Noah uses my pointer finger to

trace the moss. Dozens of little textural bumps ruffle beneath my finger pad, reminding me a patch of moss isn't just one plant, it's *thousands*.

Noah's deep voice is hushed beside my cheek. "How could anyone expect to notice just one of these little tiny plants when they're all the way zoomed out, and with a huge boulder full of life blocking their nose?"

What started out as embarrassment blooms into intense fascination. I grip Noah's hand, guiding him against me until we're hip to hip. "So I can zoom in with my nose? How?"

He grins. "You absolutely can. Stay right here."

As Noah backs away, he turns just before he's immersed in a crowd of pups. He crouches beside one of them, tugged by the sleeve by an excited pup with the most starstruck smile on her face. Noah's adoring smile warms my heart from here.

Do you remember how I smell? Noah mindlinks.

Yes, I say immediately.

Can you describe it to me? Give me as much detail as possible.

I close my eyes, remembering all I can about Noah's scent. *You smell... sweet. Not like cookies, but like love.*

That was cheesier than I meant for it to be. When I open my eyes, Noah's cheeks are bright red. I cover my mouth to silence my laughter.

W-what else, other than sweet? He asks.

I clear my throat, turning around. *I— Well, you smell... fiery, sometimes? But then it can be stronger depending on your mood. Like when we have sex, you smell spicy. I don't know how else to explain it, other than that it burns me up from the inside out.*

Noah doesn't respond to this.

His golden stare peeks through the crowd of pups, dropping my heart to my knees.

The wind carries numerous scents, but now that I'm paying attention to Noah's, his scent sticks out like it's screaming. I perk up with a smile. *Actually, that's how you smell now.*

Noah watches me take a deep, slow inhale of his scent, his eyes fixated on my form. The longer he watches, the clearer I can smell him.

"Alpha Noah, your scent hurts my eyes!" One kid whines.

Noah abruptly stands, turning away. "Sorry. I need to take a walk."

Rainn is red-faced through suppressed laughter as her brother plops Sarah in her arms and makes a beeline for the bushes. When Rainn and I meet wide eyes, we erupt into giggles.

I'm sorry, love. I didn't mean to torture you, I mindlink Noah.

No, you're fine. I can't contain my goddamn wolf around you and these precious pups.

My heart flips, forcing me to clamp both palms over my scent glands. I shuffle my feet through the forest groundcover, unsure where to go or what to do with myself. Pups continue to mill about, searching the immediate area for more deer tracks, but I wouldn't be surprised if they complained about my scent too, any second now.

Noah's soft chuckling rumbles in the distance. *Goddess, you're so cute.*

I bite my lip, turning every way. Noah is nowhere in sight. *Are you watching me?*

Yes. Come find me, using your nose. You have a hang of my scent now, right?

My heart thumps, partly at my wolf's excitement to chase her mate. But can I really do it?

I don't know; maybe I can, or maybe I can't. All I know is that I really want to.

Okay, Alpha. I'll try.

Noah's excitement only rises as my wolf crouches in our bond, her wagging tail doing nothing to conceal herself. As I draw another deep inhale through my nose, I'm met with so many scents that my brain pounds in my skull. Clasping my forehead with a wince, I close my eyes.

You can do it. Think about what I smell like, Noah mindlinks. *Try smaller, faster sniffs rather than deep, big ones.*

I exhale hard, clearing all distractions from my mind. My memory fills in a phantom sweetness, doing its best to mock Noah's scent. Or, wait, no. Maybe I smell a hint of it?

My lungs flex through every inhale, instinct taking over as Noah's scent shines brighter in my mind's eye.

Am I doing it? Am I tracking him?

Taking a few steps to my right, I sniff faster now. I feel ridiculous, but I can't stop myself. Something primal within me has unlocked, and I've never craved Noah's scent more. Pups swirl around my feet, watching me with curious, focused eyes, but I can't spare them more than a glance. My feet move faster, kicking up leaves as I ignore all spatial awareness to push through a wide thicket.

A faint crinkle of leaves sends my system into full alert. With a sharp turn of my head, I'm face-to-face with Noah. Except to my surprise, he's just as shocked as I am—and he's covering both his mouth and scent gland to block his scent.

Before I can stop myself, I break into a proud grin.

And I'm tackled into the thicket.

I scream through a laugh, my limbs too weak to defend myself from Noah's kisses all over my cheeks.

"You did it! You did it so fast that I had to make it harder for you, and you *still* did it!" Noah laughs.

My eyes water, but I'm smiling wider than I have all day. Scents are so much stronger now, and I still have a slight headache, but I haven't felt this excited over my own accomplishments since I lowered my OCD diagnostic test scores to subclinical levels. I'm almost embarrassed as pups trample around us, adding to our wolfpile over my childish accomplishment, but as their laughter flutters through the forest canopies, Noah's smile shines so bright that his eyes squint. My heart couldn't be happier.

Until a sharp, stagnant scent passes my nose. Furrowing my brows, I alert Noah's wolf without meaning to. He pulls me to my feet in seconds, his joyous smile erased. I feel awful for it.

But Noah tucks pups against him, searching my eyes. "What do you smell?"

I swallow hard, struggling to catch my breath. "I think it's—Well, I don't know—" I sniff again, but Noah shakes his head.

"Don't overanalyze it. Trust your wolf. Something's wrong, and I believe you."

Rainn rushes to our side, her sharp eyes just as serious as Noah's. But the longer we sit in one place, the stronger the scent becomes.

"I think it's a few Alphas," I say.

3

Noah closes his eyes, taking a deep breath. When he opens them again, his eyes are stark yellow. "You're right."

Before he can flip around, seven burly men stream from the forest thickets behind Noah, setting their sights on us. Not a single pup makes a sound, cramming themselves behind Noah's protective form as Rainn huddles into my side. Her frantic glances over pup heads as she counts them beneath her breath sends my heart into overdrive, all her ease from earlier erased.

Are these pack members? Wait, they have to be, otherwise Noah would've chased them from Greenfield. Even still, they look furious. How concerned should I be for our safety? I shuffle a few pups behind me, reassuring two little ones who grip my thighs with my hands on their heads.

The men still haven't said anything. I'm on the verge of panic; we can't stop all of them if they attack, not with this many pups to protect.

But our Alpha doesn't panic.

Noah crosses his arms. "Class is in session. I'm not available."

A pale, muscled man with auburn hair flashes a sharp smile, his semi-shifted incisors on display. He comes to a halt ten feet from us, leaning one shoulder against a tree before crossing his arms to mirror Noah. "We didn't want to have to interrupt playtime either. Unfortunately, you've left us no choice."

The bearded, scowling man to his left doesn't look as relaxed. "Let's get to it. I'm wasting my lunch break for this, and we have urgent demands for our family's safety that require your attention."

Noah nods, motioning to a clearing about 30 feet to our left. As Noah strides toward it, the Alphas follow without complaint.

Rainn and Aliya, feel free to continue class. They won't bother the pups, Noah mindlinks.

Rainn meets my eyes, fear creasing her forehead. As she herds the pups away, I can't bring myself to follow.

My head is fuzzy and my knees weak. I don't like something about those Alphas' scents. Noah walks further from me by the millisecond, and the sight of his back turned gnaws at my stomach.

Before I can stop myself, my wolf takes charge: I scamper back to Noah's side.

His sharp stare meets my face over his shoulder. Yellow irises flip my heart.

"Our future Luna is joining us?" The grinning Alpha asks. Except he's not really asking; his eyes sweep my body before I've even had a chance to say hello.

Noah puts himself between us with his next step, tucking me into his side. My guts churn, but Noah's voice is still calm. "Of course she is. She's your future Luna. Show her respect."

The Alpha laughs. "Of course, Alpha Noah. I'll be a true gentleman, at your request."

"That wasn't a request. It was an order."

I don't want to say hello anymore. We walk in silence, and I burrow deeper into Noah's side.

Are you okay? I ask.

Yes, I know these guys. Which is why I'm more worried about you. They're extremely sexist, so the second you feel too uncomfortable or triggered, please allow yourself to leave. Noah's jaws tighten. *But you have to walk when you go, Omega. Absolutely do* not *run.*

I swallow hard. All those years Mom warned me to never run from a wolf, was she actually warning me about *Alpha* Lycans in particular?

One of the silent Alphas meets my eyes, and I shrink. He must smell my petrified scent. Now that I've figured out how to track Noah's scent, it's easier to single out others. These guys and their grungy, angry scents didn't come to praise Noah's leadership skills.

As we come to a stop in the open clearing, putting distance between our two groups, I can breathe a little deeper.

Noah releases my side, his arms crossing back over his chest. "Alright, Alphas. What's on your mind?"

"It's been three years since you signed the Fair Territory Act into law, and it's still far from fair. Things are becoming unsustainable," the auburn-haired Alpha says.

My eyebrows furrow. I have no idea what that law entails, but its title doesn't sound bad.

But Noah's heaving sigh only tenses the Alphas' shoulders. His voice is low and commanding. "No matter how many times you return to debate this with me, I will not take any land away from Omegas or Betas in favor of Alphas. Every wolf has their equal share. That has been, and still is, my final word on the Fair Territory Act."

A man with dark brown hair speaks up. His voice is as shaky as his trembling, rapid hand gestures. "But there's nothing 'fair' about it. You should know this. Alphas are naturally superior, and a large majority of us are mated to Omegas and Betas that rely on us. We can't protect them without more resources for our bigger, stronger bodies. You're taking away from everyone by taking away from Alphas."

Noah shakes his head. "I haven't *taken* anything from you. I'm refusing to give you an unfair advantage just because of your pheromones."

"Unfair? How is it unfair when, biologically, we—"

"No sex is superior. We are all Lycans," Noah says.

The Alphas meet eyes, shaking their heads. The largest of them has been silent this entire time, but as he steps forward, I'm tempted to step back; he's a little wider than Noah, and almost as tall, his hazel, brooding eyes not sparing me a single glance.

When he speaks, there's a subtle growl behind each deep syllable. "It's no wonder other packs think we're weak. You let so many Rogues in that our Omega population exploded. Do the math. Alpha allocations are only getting smaller."

"I don't know who told you that, but again, nothing of yours is shrinking. The math is that everyone who joins our pack is provided for. We're sheltering refugees of all sexes in the

Community Center temporarily, and unfortunately, yes, things are getting crowded there. If you'd like to help us construct new housing, I'd be happy to direct your applications to Dave. We can even give you provision bonuses in return if a bigger share is what you're looking for."

The man shakes his head. "You're avoiding the subject. We're talking about Rogues invading our pack due to your weak influence around 'Omega abuse,' giving Omegas a pass just because they're Omegas. But all Rogues are *Rogues*, Alpha. Not refugees."

Noah uncrosses his arms, standing taller. The Alphas freeze at the sight. But as acid burns through my veins, I can't stop myself.

"Are you seriously implying these Omegas all lied about their abuse, just for an excuse to *invade* your land?" I ask.

With my angry, pointed stare, the men remain silent.

"Do you know how painful it must've been for these Omegas to have to question their mate bonds in the first place? Their abusive mates forced them to defy what they must've hoped was the Moon Goddess's blessing, crushing their hearts when they're left hurt instead of loved. Then, in order to escape, their souls have to be literally ripped apart. There's nothing easy about how any refugees got here."

The Alphas fidget a little, but not a single one of them meets my eyes more than a glance.

Except the man with auburn hair.

He laughs. "Now, that's a reach, Luna. It's unfortunate that a few of them have struggled, but a vast majority haven't—"

Noah huffs out a dark, interrupting laugh. "Wow, that sounds so much better. So basically all of these abuse survivors are faking it, except a rare few that aren't master-manipulators? What a fucking joke, man."

"You don't need to be a dick. This is a serious issue," the auburn-haired Alpha snaps.

"Yeah? But you're telling me that based on conspiratorial bullshit, I should exile pack members I've already vetted. If that's not a big fucking joke, then you agree you're threatening the livelihood of other pack members, and we've got a bigger problem here. And it's not with Rogues. I hate to break it to you for the millionth time, but they already belong here."

Spittle escapes the Alpha's lips as his face blazes red. "I'm not talking about them all, just some. Enough to make a sizable dent in what you *owe* us."

With his smile erased, the Alpha's bared fangs look even longer. It sets my blood on fire. My wolf howls to run.

But Noah's hand settles on my back. A gentle sweep of his fingertips soothes my pounding heart, but it's not enough. The Alpha eyes me, and I swear I can feel his gaze burning my skin. I almost wish he had that snarky grin back.

"Big mistake." Noah steps in front of me with a growl. "Do *not* intimidate your future Luna."

My heart flips. I grip the back of Noah's shirt, afraid of what he'll do. But to my surprise, his show of dominance makes the Alphas relax, their focus turning to the trees or floor—anything but Noah's stoic stare.

The auburn-haired Alpha sighs. "Alright, whatever. Here's the thing, man. We're cramped, so what the hell are you doing about it?"

"The Community Center is cramped, not our territory. It's one of the largest in the US."

"You won't claim more land? We'd help you fight for it."

Noah somehow grows larger, his chest expanding with each breath. "That will never be an option. This is its maximum size. I refuse to wage unnecessary wars with our neighbors to make it any larger, and I disagree with the packs causing so many Rogues to flee in the first place, so a merger is off the table. We can comfortably house our new pack members with proper materials and time. There will be no bloodshed."

The Alpha scoffs. "But it's an Alpha's Goddess-given right to dominate—"

"Fuck, no. There will be *no* bloodshed, especially not in the name of Alpha domination. Do you understand me?"

The auburn-haired Alpha stares deep into Noah's eyes, and every bird silences for miles. I hold my breath, afraid the slightest movement will set them all off.

But the auburn-haired Alpha drops his head with a scowl. "I understand, Alpha."

As I struggle to catch my breath, my eyes race between the

Alphas. Noah's wolf stands guard over mine in our bond, and his human form tucks me tighter behind his back.

He must've seen it coming: from behind Noah's back, I recognize the dark brown-haired Alpha's growling tone as he invades Noah's personal bubble. "What are you so afraid of? That one day soon, you'll have to face the truth from the Alphas around you? That if you try to expand Greenfield territory, the other pack leaders will find out you're more Omega-like than some Omegas we know? Are you afraid they'll hunt you down, or deep down, do you think it's rightfully so, because this isn't your true place, *Alpha?*"

All I can do is gape wide-eyed into Noah's back. What the hell is this Alpha talking about? If their philosophy is that Alphas are defined by pure-blooded muscle, no one is more Alpha than my mate. But for whatever reason, Noah's wolf bristles, baring his teeth in defense.

I grip his shirt tighter. Noah was right, this is triggering; they sound exactly like Steven, but the Lycan version. And if these Alphas are like Steven, unpredictability is in their nature. I'm afraid they'll be set off at whatever Noah says next. What should I do? Should I mindlink Yasmine? Dave?

No, Noah acted like this ambush was normal. He'll know what to do, won't he?

God, does Noah have to deal with aggression like this *every day?*

But as Noah's wolf expands, his human form stands as tall as he can. His next words are quiet, but I can hear his dark grin in his deep voice. "Alright, so what if I really was an Omega?"

Noah steps forward, out of my hands. With one step, all seven Alphas take three steps back.

"You can't handle being smaller than an Omega? Weaker than one?"

I grip my heart as it pounds harder and faster than I've ever felt it.

I was wrong: Noah was slouching. He's at least three inches taller than the bearded Alpha, and with his muscles tensed, he's twice as wide. My mate backs multiple large men into the thickets with just two steps.

The auburn-haired Alpha swallows hard. "No. We'll never tolerate being dominated by one. That's an insult to our genetics and intellige—"

"*Enough*," Noah growls.

We all hold our breaths, blinking rapidly as Noah's Alpha musk burns our eyes.

"You've wasted my morning spouting sexist shit. Get the fuck out of my sight."

The Alphas don't take another breath before turning their backs to Noah, shuffling through the leaves in retreat. But they don't leave without a few mutterings.

"Sexist, what the fuck?"

"Dude, maybe he really isn't an Alpha."

Noah laughs, but his unenthused tone is chilling. "Uh-huh, whatever. Challenge me face-to-face if you really want to prove those superior genetics."

A few of the Alphas look back. But with one glance at Noah's fanged grin, they shut up and scurry away.

I can't be relieved. I grip Noah's taut bicep, placing one hand over his heart. The poor organ races beneath my palm.

"God, what is their problem?" I breathe. "Are you okay?"

Noah sighs, closing his eyes. He takes a deep breath. And another. When he speaks, he shakes his head. "More or less."

With a hand on my back, Noah guides me back to Rainn, leaving the Alphas in the distance with large strides. I struggle to follow after him on my short legs, but Noah's steps only stretch wider. His voice is even, but agitation charges through our bond.

"These Alpha-domination asshats show up every now and then, but I don't want you to think this is widely accepted behavior in Greenfield. It's just that there's so many of us in our pack that some ignorant Lycans are bound to show up."

"That makes sense," I say.

Noah huffs. His words race faster with every sentence. "I wish it didn't. Everyone's entitled to opinions, sure, but I don't tolerate when those opinions harm the lives of other pack members."

My stomach rolls. "Are they mainly against Omegas? It sounded a lot like classic human misogyny, but I don't really know if it's right to compare Omegas to human women or not."

Noah bites his lip, mulling over my words for longer than I expected him to; normally he answers my questions about Lycans in a heartbeat. But with another harsh huff, Noah's anxiety spikes in our bond. "Remember how I told you that I believe pheromones are more based around personality and emotions, and that other wolves don't really agree with me?"

"Yes, back when we first met. I know it's not the same thing as gender identity for humans, but it still made me relieved that I could introduce you to Kira without worrying about her safety as a trans woman."

Noah blinks a few times before giving me a weak smile. "O-oh. That's comforting to hear, actually." He pulls me closer, his grip tight on my hand. "Traditionally, we were taught our wolf sexes are hard-wired as an Alpha, Beta, or Omega based on our dominant pheromones. It's implied that most cis men are born Alphas, most cis women are born Omegas, and most intersex people are born Betas, and each one has certain expectations on how they're traditionally supposed to behave. But I really don't agree with that; everyone's just so different. Pheromones go up and down constantly depending on how we feel, and since the traditional belief also relies on Alpha strength being a genetic superiority thing, it rubs me the wrong way."

My heart drops. I almost don't know what to say, especially as the pieces fall into place: Noah is far more trapped into his pack leadership role than I realized. I knew he was watching his back for dominance challenge attacks at any moment, but he's also having to monitor his every miniscule behavior that might appear socially as weakness—as in, a sign he has Omega in him. Would he express more of his sensitive traits out in the open if he wasn't in this top Alpha role?

No wonder those Alphas were giving him a hard time about not asserting dominance; they can't understand why any Alpha would deny what they see as an inborn superiority.

The further my emotions dip into fear, the tighter Noah's shoulders tense. "Anyway, these guys take those traditional beliefs to another extreme, saying shit like they said today about their 'Goddess-given right to dominate.' As someone who has lived with Omegas my whole life, that's just fucking gross."

"That really is." My voice is soft despite my chaotic thought overload. It doesn't feel like the right time to tell Noah that the more he describes this Alpha domination thing, the more familiar it sounds—like Steven's thoughts on his God-given right as a man to reign over me as a woman.

But Noah is far too worked up to notice my hesitation. "Between us, I have these guys classified as a cult in my personal database. They're small, not much more than 10 or 15 extremist Alphas, but I have my eye on them. I really didn't want you to have to hear that shit. Fuck—"

"Noah." The sharpness of my voice stops Noah in his tracks. He faces me, wide-eyed and breathless. I comb his choppy hair back into order, running my shaky fingers through it. "Are you really okay?"

He shrugs, his forehead creasing. "I-I don't know. I'm really worried that could've made you feel less safe here. I find that—U-upsetting."

I can't help myself, breaking into a sad smile. "I still feel safe."

"You do?"

"Of course, love. Especially hearing you verbally kick their asses by standing in your truth. I love you to pieces." I smile as Noah relaxes, drawing me to his chest. Breathing in his protective scent blankets peace over me. I loosen just enough to release my innermost thoughts. "These concepts aren't new to me, anyway. They sound a lot like a Lycan version of Steven."

Noah's arms tense.

Before I can blink, he steps back from me, gripping his forehead.

But he doesn't say anything.

"Noah? I'm sorry, I didn't mean to be an extra downer—" I reach for him, but I gasp. Yellow eyes stare back, his wolf on full alert.

"Do you think he's an Alpha-domination Lycan?" He rasps. "He could be in one of those shitty neighboring packs, just like I've been worried about."

I shake my head. Not because I don't believe Noah, but because I don't want to. The thought of Steven morphing into a giant, raging beast sends my nervous system reeling, my vision fading into black and white.

"Fuck, I'm sorry." Noah grabs my cheeks. "Breathe. Keep breathing. You're safe. I'm right here with you, and we're safe."

I take slower, shaky breaths, clinging to Noah's shirt. Within a minute, my heart settles. Dropping my forehead against Noah's chest, I rapidly shake my head, accidentally letting a thought-clearing compulsion slip through.

But as a new thought crosses my mind, I perk up. "Wait, he has to be human. Wouldn't Amy have noticed Steven's pheromones on me if he was an Alpha Lycan?"

Noah deflates.

Oh, God. By the sinking ache in our bond, I'm terrified of what he'll say next.

Noah's forehead ripples. "Not necessarily. I'm honestly impressed you could smell those Alphas. Maybe it's because you were already tracking my Alpha pheromones, but I didn't notice them at first because a lot of hunting Alphas use scent-blocking drugs. It's a common practice."

My heart ticks into my throat. "What? Why would they need to do that? No, why would they be allowed to? Wouldn't that help them get away with crimes?"

Noah sighs. "Yeah, but barring all Alphas from their meds would be discriminatory too. It's available freely for Lycans with overpowering pheromones, just like rut suppressants. A lot of Lycans are hell-bent on not having to rely on human society to survive, and they use scent blockers to hunt for food because, honestly, we reek—just like the pups told me today. So even if those Alphas weren't actively hunting, I don't have time to prove they aren't planning to, and they'll usually catch a squirrel or something if I try."

Within a millisecond, my mind creates an exhaustive list of ways power-hungry Alphas could abuse this substance. Prey doesn't have to be limited to small game. It could look like other Omega Lycans. I'm a small, unprepared animal too.

With my heart hammering faster and faster, I clutch Noah's sleeve. "Let's talk about something else."

"Aliya—"

"Has there really been territory allocation debates from so many extra Rogues?" I cut Noah off. I know I'm giving into my PTSD's avoidance tactics by changing the subject, but I can't help it. My mind isn't in a good place to keep talking about anything else severely triggering today.

Noah sighs, kissing the top of my head. "Yeah, I've been really stressed. I don't know what to do because more and more Rogues are hearing we're a sanctuary every year, and they're mostly Omegas since they hear rumors that we're a sanctuary when most packs have Alphas that treat Omegas like… Well, like shit."

I bite my lip, closing my eyes. I guess I chose the most triggering question possible.

Noah groans, squeezing me to his chest. "I'm so sorry you had to see that. Fuck, you were so happy, and—"

"No, Noah, I hate that you have to see this too, and that you're so stressed. How can I help?"

"Just keep your heart and mind safe for me, please. I don't want you to have to be exposed to more of their bullshit if it becomes too triggering."

I pull back, meeting Noah's eyes. "But something in this is triggering for you too, isn't it? I can feel it."

Noah can't hold my gaze, zipping his focus to the trees beside us. He chews on his lip, his forehead knotted. "I-I— I guess so."

A twinge of his pain stings my heart. I pull Noah closer, craving to soothe him. "Then that's exactly what I find so admirable about what you're doing to help others who have been through horrible things too. There's really no way to avoid all triggers, so I'd rather let them pass through me as they come. In the meantime, I can show up for our pack, just like you do."

Noah frowns. "You and I both know there's a point where triggers become too strong that it doesn't work to power through. I'm not sure that's healthy or okay to do to yourself."

"Well I'm still okay, right? I'm not great, but I'm okay." I stroke his hand, and Noah gives me the biggest puppy dog eyes. "Let me decide what's safe for me, and I'll let you know if it's too much. You can't do that for me."

"O-okay, you're right. Sorry."

"It's okay. I get it; I don't want to watch you hurting either." I plant a soft kiss on his cheek. "But right now, I want to prepare myself to be a trustworthy, safe Luna by your side someday. So far, I don't know as much as you do about how this all works. That's not very Luna-like."

A smile finally breaks through Noah's worried frown. He takes a few breaths, stifling his prancing wolf at the thought of me becoming Luna. I giggle, and Noah drops his head with a grin.

"T-then maybe we can show you around the Community Center. It was a huge relief for Rainn and I when you offered to give us your thoughts on the Forest School, so maybe you could also check out how things are for the Rogues?" He runs his hands down my arms before slipping his fingers into mine. "I have a feeling they'll trust you to hear how everything really is for them. Most Rogue Omegas are skittish around Alphas, so all they'll tell me is that things are perfect, which is absolutely not true. I wish it was, but I know it's not."

My heart throbs, imagining myself being there for other Omegas—Omegas who have been hurt before, like I have. I could make a difference for them, being the person I needed back then. That feels more Luna-like than anything I've ever imagined myself doing.

"Yes," I breathe. "Yes, I'd *love* to." I grip Noah's hands. "But are you sure they'll feel okay around me?"

Noah's forehead softens with his shy laugh. "Oh, absolutely. Talking to you can make anyone feel safe."

I breathe through Noah's words as endorphins chime throughout my heart. "That's how I felt from the moment I met you."

Rainn's voice echoes throughout the trees nearby, chatting with the pups now that the danger has passed, but I don't turn to spot them; I'm too busy gazing deep into Noah's eyes. He melts as he stares back, every fear in our bond washing away.

Noah's big fingers weave into the back of my hair, drawing me close. As our lips meet, my heart lifts above the trees, imagining what we could create together. It might not feel completely safe here now, but with Noah's guidance, I trust it can happen. It will, and I want to play a role in getting us there.

4

"I need to talk to you about something shitty," Noah mutters as he tucks his towel around his bare waist.

I halt in place, my hairbrush combed halfway through my hair. "Okay, what is it?"

We meet eyes in the bathroom mirror, but Noah looks more uncomfortable by the second. I set down my brush, spinning around to face him directly.

Droplets spill from Noah's hair like a timer counting the seconds. The only sound in the room is the buzzing fan over our heads, still pumping out damp air from our hot bath.

It's been over a week since we were ambushed by Alpha-domination cultists, but Noah has been quieter ever since. Tenser. I haven't had much of a chance to ask him about it; we've hardly had alone time together with how busy he's been. Thankfully, it's finally Saturday. But with me looking at him face-to-face, Noah's shoulders raise.

I rub his arm. "Hey, what's wrong?"

"I just— I don't ever know how to bring this up. I feel bad bringing it up."

I sigh, dropping my hand. "This is about Steven, isn't it?"

Noah meets my eyes again, hurt racing across his features.

I pull him over to the toilet seat, plopping myself on the closed lid. Then I pat my lap. "Come sit."

Noah lifts one eyebrow, unable to suppress a smile. "Sweet Omega, I don't think—"

"Don't you dare call me tiny, you big, sweet Alpha."

Noah's soft laugh lightens my spirits by miles.

With a tug on his hand, I convince Noah to hover-sit in my lap. I burst out laughing. "You have to actually put some weight on me!"

"No," he laughs, shaking out a few droplets from his hair and spraying my face.

I scream-giggle, burrowing my face between his shoulder blades.

With my arms wrapped around his waist, we sit in silence. But after 30 seconds, Noah scoops me up, switching our positions.

"Fine, I give up," I laugh. "But don't think you're upsetting me just by saying his name. Part of what I've worked on with Jenny in therapy is speaking words out loud, treating words and thoughts like words and thoughts, not like real-life dangers to avoid. It's helped."

Noah nods, kissing my shoulder. "O-okay, that's good to hear."

"So what about Steven did you want to ask?"

Noah's eyebrows flinch when I say Steven's name. "I still think my questions could be *extremely* triggering."

I clear my throat, dropping my eyes to my hands. I'm tempted to pick at my nails. "Are you talking about the break-in?"

Noah rapidly shakes his head, but this time his water-flinging doesn't make me laugh. His stare clings to the bathroom tile, avoiding my face. "No, not about any particular acute trauma. I don't want you to relive that moment unless you have to."

The sharp silence between us makes my heart race. Somehow, I'm touched.

I'm also relieved; I don't really want Noah thinking too much about the exact details of the break-in. He probably wants to hear them, at least once, and I know his thoughts aren't in my control. But for now, the thought of anyone I know imagining me in that state makes me feel weak all over again.

I'd never call another person in my shoes "weak," but this was Steven's goal. He knew I felt like an exception, and he exploited it. To his credit, he was an excellent manipulator of my brain. I still find little pieces of his teachings in the background of my thoughts.

Recounting every detail from that day makes me feel like raw meat, baring my sore spots for someone to chew off a devastating chunk of me. I don't trust people anymore.

Then I met Noah. Over the past three months, I've bared my soul to him more than anyone I've ever met.

Everything has changed. Maybe my judgments about my "weaknesses" can continue to change too.

As my mate anxiously runs his hands up my sides, I relax into his chest.

"I trust you," I whisper. "I know I haven't told you everything about what he did to me that day, but I want to. Someday soon."

Noah drops his forehead against my shoulder, wrapping his arms around me. His breath is sharp but quiet, flexing his built chest against my back.

After a minute-long hug, Noah's deep voice rumbles even quieter against my shoulder blades. "Basically, I've been thinking a lot about us having kids."

My heart flips. That wasn't what I was expecting to hear.

I open my mouth to speak, but I'm too shocked at what's dying to come out on instinct: me too. All day, every day.

But Noah trudges on, picking up speed. "Ever since you told me you felt like you're being watched, it hurts to think about. I know it's a PTSD thing for you, and all these asshole Alpha cultists aren't helping, but it's also because you don't know where *he* is. I don't want you to have to feel like you have to watch your back for the rest of your life, not in Greenfield. Not in your own fucking home. Especially not while you're pregnant, or while you're taking care of our kids. That's not fair to you at all, not when I might be able to do something about it."

I bite my lip. My eyes are already watering, partly from Noah's agitated Alpha musk, but mainly from how startling it still is to experience Noah's compassion while I'm recalling Steven's heartlessness.

"Noah, I don't want you to have to—"

"No, not 'have' to." He breathes hard against my back, shaking his head. "I can't *stand* that no one fucking listened to you. I want to be that authority figure in your community who listens. The one who believes you."

I bite my lips, no longer able to stifle tears. Dropping my head, my shoulders shake as my expression warps.

Noah's head pops up. His balled-up hands in my lap soften to caress my abdomen. "Fuck, I'm sorry…"

"No," I suck back tears, smiling. "Thank you."

Cupping Noah's cheeks, I drop my forehead against his. We close our eyes, breathing through the humming emotional overwhelm in our bond.

But the longer we sit in silence, the more my heart aches too much to ignore. When I open my eyes, Noah's are already open.

He tucks my damp hair over my shoulder, replacing its wet chill with his overheated palm on my neck. "What are you thinking?"

My eyelids flutter at his gentle, sweet brushing on my mark— the scar he left on my sensitive scent gland to symbolize our bonded souls. A loving wash of his concern warms my heart through our shared emotions, but it also makes my chest ache worse.

This beautiful soul staring back has suffered immensely too. Fear spikes our bond around triggers I'm slowly noticing over time, but mainly when he's not home with me. I know he hides them, and I don't think it's solely because he's afraid to show his pain.

I think no one believed or protected Noah either. The thought scalds my heart.

Of course he's guarded. Why wouldn't he be? When no one else shows you they're safe, you do everything you can to survive—alone.

I sort Noah's hair, biting back tears. "It's just— What about you? Aren't you still going to be uncomfortable that whoever hurt you just as badly is still out there too?"

Noah traces my eyes. Instinct stifles my breath as he analyzes me.

For a second, I don't recognize him. All his emotions have been washed away.

Then he taps on my side. "I need to stand."

I hop off his lap immediately, my eyes wide. "I'm sorry, I didn't mean to—"

He gives me a soft smile before throwing his shirt collar over his head, disappearing into the fabric. "Don't be sorry. You didn't do anything wrong, sweet Omega."

When he pulls his head through the collar, his back remains to me. Noah hurriedly throws on the boxers and worn black jeans from his clean clothes pile beside the sink, his agitation rising by the second in our bond. Then he reaches for the door handle.

Fuck, I hit a major sore spot. With my experience, there's no mistaking what just happened; Noah is in the throes of hyperarousal from PTSD, his emergency alert systems thrusting into overdrive. I've described it to Jenny as sprinting in place, giving me urgency to scream or run, but terrifying me that I'll hurt myself out of panic from how heavily the fear wracks my heart until I'm begging for it all to end already. I doubt Noah wants to be confined in this small, humid bathroom.

I stick close to Noah, but not too close, allowing him space to breathe. I didn't expect this reaction, and I'm not sure he expected it either. I haven't breached the subject of Noah's monster since he disclosed a tiny piece of trauma in his den, but I know he's worked on this in Prolonged Exposure therapy—as in, his trauma is *massive*.

He's worked hard in therapy, I'm sure, but I also know sometimes it's too raw to fully work on. Or even if it's worked on, trauma never truly disappears. Every time there's another trigger, there's a potential setback.

I just hope Noah will be okay.

Squeezing my fingers over and over again to self-soothe, I follow Noah past his living room. I've never seen him this triggered before, so I'm not sure what to expect. What type of symptoms his PTSD presents itself as. It's eerie: I genuinely can't feel *anything* from his side of our bond, so maybe he's dissociating.

But when we reach Noah's kitchen, he pulls out a barstool for me. I track him across the kitchen as he rolls his shoulders out, but it's almost like I'm watching a silent movie of his usual morning routine—like we weren't just talking, at all. After a few quick circles of his arms, he opens a drawer at the end of his kitchen cabinets and fetches a black pen and a white lined notepad.

Noah sets the notepad on the countertop beside me, leaning

heavily into the rich brown wooden block. After a few silent seconds, I swallow hard, unable to stifle my worries.

Noah glances at me in passing, but he does a double-take when he sees my face. "Hey, it's okay. Really."

He drops his pen, reaching across the countertop with an open palm. I place my hand in his. He smiles softly, but there's a visible, cavernous crack in his stoic mask, a horrendous pain seeping through the sudden grayish exhaustion around his eyes. It tears at my stomach, acid stinging my throat.

Noah runs his thumb over my knuckles, softening his voice. "Do you not believe me? If I seem upset, I'm not upset at you. None of this is your fault. It's— It's Barrett's."

I swallow hard. Noah's the one who can't say Steven's name, opting for using Steven's last name, "Barrett," instead. What if I'm triggering Noah worse than I realize?

Wait, that's right: we were supposed to be talking about Noah's abuser now, not mine. Did Noah just deflect me?

I know it's not the same as Steven's deflections, but I can't calm my racing heart: in the past, deflections were my warning sign. If I challenged Steven's avoidance of an important topic, I'd be the one to pay for it.

This is where I'd usually follow Steven's cue to keep myself safe, but this isn't Steven. Noah is holding my hand, looking into my eyes for answers. I have to give him a chance.

"That's not how I saw what just happened." I settle onto the barstool, keeping my tone gentle. "I brought up something sensitive, and I'm worried I triggered you badly."

"Oh… Oh." Noah bites the end of his pen, his brows furrowing. After a few seconds of staring into the distance, Noah drops the pen to the countertop with a massive sigh. "No, you were fine. I just don't know how to solve that either. I don't know what to say that's not a huge fucking disappointment that might make you lose faith in me because there's—" His breath hitches. Noah swallows hard like his throat ran dry. "There's not a single thing I can fucking do about that situation, but— But I know I'm good at tracking, so please don't think I can't help you, it's just— This one's—" Noah smashes his face in his palms, breathing hard into them. "This one's different."

My heart burns. Noah's emotions are slowly returning to my awareness, and they're too much to bear. What the hell happened that feels so unfixable to my powerful mate?

Noah takes a deep, shuddering breath as his wolf frantically paces across our bond. "But at least I haven't tried to track down Barrett yet. There's still hope there. I swear, there's hope."

I'm nauseous. "You want to track him? And then what?"

He shrugs, keeping his forehead in his palms. "File that restraining order, for one."

My heart leaps. I mentioned my rejected restraining order to Noah *one* single time.

Revealing bloodshot, weary eyes, Noah tilts his head, blinking at the blank lined paper between us. "But if he's a Lycan, I can do a lot more."

My stomach growls, and Noah lifts an eyebrow. He breaks into a smile, but I shake my head, unable to laugh.

"I don't like this. I don't know what you're thinking, and I'm starting to get triggered, myself."

Noah rounds the counter to sit on the barstool beside me, his smile erased. "I'm not thinking about anything I'm not saying aloud. I just *can't*—"

He drops my stare, taking a shuddering breath. God, the way he just croaked out that last word physically hurt my nerves with the pain it carried. When he speaks again, he hides the ache in his voice with a flattened tone.

"I can't stomach telling you about what I've failed to do in the past, or why I failed at it. That's why I'm extra weird. I'm sorry."

Rubbing Noah's arm feels like a pathetic attempt at comfort, but I'm unable to find the right words. I don't know enough to know what's true, but I doubt Noah failed at anything. That sounds more like his disorder making him extra harsh toward himself.

Noah doesn't seem to notice I haven't spoken, his knee bouncing as he returns to rubbing his head. "But if Steven is a Lycan, I can put word out that he's not allowed around our Omegas, our women, or any of our ally packs. That's the least I should do, other than locking him up for what he did to you if he takes a single step onto our territory."

My heart races just as quickly as Noah's pacing wolf. Noah isn't just telling me he'll take me seriously, he's *acting* on his words. I don't know how to process it.

A strange guilt creeps in, warning me I'm taking too much space. Soon enough, Noah could get sick of my bullshit, just like Steven, so I shouldn't put any extra stress on Noah. To stay safe, I have to keep the peace.

But with my intensifying emotions, Noah's eyes glow yellow. "He'll be a rightful outcast, and assumed guilty far quicker if he ever pulls anything even close to harassment of anyone else. I *can't* let that happen to any of us again, Aliya. I *won't*."

His breath shakes through every word, but now I certainly feel something; his anger in our bond is just as strong as my heartache. I'm so grateful for him, but I know Noah's wolf well enough to recognize he's been weird lately: brooding and quiet for his usually excitable puppy-self.

I suck in a sharp breath. This might finally be it; what Noah is doing for me is exactly what he needs someone to do for him.

But fuck, I can't. I don't have the skills to track his monster, let alone prevent them from hurting anyone else. Even if I was stronger, I wouldn't know where to begin. I don't have the resources or skills to protect Noah. He's the one teaching me how to function like other Lycans in the first place. Who am I to think I can solve this massive, terrifying problem for him?

Pathetic tears prick my eyes. I feel so small, so feeble.

For now, my wolf reminds me.

There's still one person I might be able to stop.

I straighten in my seat, grabbing the pen and notepad. "Alright, ask me anything you might need to know about Steven, and I'll write it down."

Relaying Steven's identifying details has been too much to stomach at once, so between binging movies together, Noah stepping out to solve a minor issue at the border, and my unexpected, trauma-exhausted nap on the couch, we've managed to gather a small list in a mix of our handwriting.

- Name: Steven Barrett
- Identifying features: blonde, light brown eyes, probably human, 6'1", runner, lean, athletic, toned
- Hometown: Westview
- Family members: Stacey and John → parents, Aaron → older brother in WA

  Note: Steven felt betrayed by his mom for kicking his dad out when they were kids because he felt like he had to become the parent way too early on in life to make ends meet and didn't have a real childhood, so I never met any of them

- Job/Workplace: 5 years ago, he was working at Chestnut Real Estate → address: 406 Chestnut Rd, Westview, OR 97139

- controlling
- jealous

I've ended up on the carpet, fiddling with the strands. Noah tucks his massive form between the couch and coffee table just to settle against my side. "Alright, are you ready for the hardest questions?"

My smile fades. I take a deep, shuddering breath. "Yes."

As agreed upon, we'll roll through Noah's questions about Steven's core beliefs quickly. My heart pounds faster by the second, my anticipatory anxiety spiking. What if I can't handle it as much as I think I can?

Maybe I can't, I tell myself. I can't be certain.

My stomach gurgles.

"If you had to pick one thing you heard the most, what was his top belief about male superiority?" Noah asks quietly.

My focus flickers across the carpet, struggling to sum up years of Steven's indoctrination. But Noah and I planned to rapid-fire speak without allowing OCD or PTSD to tag team too long, and it's proving necessary; both disorders pour doubts into my mind. What if I made all this up? What if I was wrong about feeling harmed, and Steven was right about everything—that I was a delusional, whiny girl?

But in my heart, I know the truth.

My voice shakes as I spout it. "Everything went back to one thing with him: that men are inherently owed many things, and not giving it to them was unjustified, especially as a woman."

I huff through the silence. I expect Noah to write something down, but his notepad remains stationed in his lap.

And his tender eyes remain on me. "You okay?"

I nod, giving him a soft, quick smile. "Keep going."

He glances between my eyes. "What would he do if you challenged those beliefs?"

Anxiety burns my veins, so I pick at my nails. "He'd make it really personal. Saying stuff like how I like to make everything about me, or that women complicate the simplest things."

Noah frowns. "So he'd shift the blame? Would he always make it about your gender or sex, or was it all different personal things about you?"

I open my mouth to say it wasn't always about gender or sex, but then I shut it again. "Actually, now that you say that, I think it was both. He'd dig at little things I'd do wrong, and it felt so personal, but from a distance, I can connect them all to things he found irritating about women, in general. I walked away from that relationship feeling like trash, not just because of what he did, but because I felt like trash as a woman."

A flicker of hurt races over Noah's features. He places his hand over mine. "Do you still feel like trash?"

My heart flips. I wriggle where I sit, uncomfortable with my answer. Eventually, I spit it out. "Only when I think about that day he broke in."

With that, Noah scribbles additions to his notes at the bottom of our list, his jaw clenched hard enough to bulge a vein across his temple.

- generally a wimpy ass coward
- classic abuser:
  - judgmental, hyper-critical
  - lack of morals around how to treat others: highly objectifying.
  - manipulative, word-twister
  - demands power, control, and dominance, especially over women ✱✱✱
  - doesn't like to face problems head on
    ↳ could use to our advantage when confronting him

✱✱✱ fixated on beliefs to the point of violence
↳ proof of potential to hurt others

Once he's done, Noah allows me to take the notepad from his hands. I suck in a shaky breath in anticipation of how I'll respond, but this list feels surprisingly neutral.

It's more than the list; I was afraid of serious trauma fallout within myself from today's continually triggering conversation, but the more we've written down, the lighter I've felt. And I know why.

With one glance at my mate beside me—his brooding stare tracing the ceiling as if it'll help him solve this puzzle—I truly feel it: I feel believed.

Cupping my hand around my mouth does nothing to stop a sob from escaping. Noah jolts upright. Within seconds, I'm tucked into his lap, my chest squeezed against his in a tight embrace.

"I'm so sorry," Noah whispers.

The ache in his heart pangs through me. I squeeze him back twice as hard.

"No, it feels like you're saving her," I say. "That version of me who felt so alone and scared that day."

"Fuck." Noah's watery whisper tugs at my chest's core. He kisses the top of my head, but I can feel his lips quivering as his breath shudders through fresh tears. "She wasn't trash."

Whimpering through another sob, I grip Noah as hard as I can.

We hold each other in silence until our tears run out. After what must be an hour of nuzzling, tracing each other's features, and gentle massages of each other's arms and backs, Noah and I shift into a smiling exhaustion.

It's weird; I couldn't imagine smiling after spending a whole day working through past traumas. But the longer I gaze into Noah's adoring eyes in front of me, the less I can stop myself from giggling. He laughs, wrapping me in his arms until I hum through the endorphins from his deep, satiating squeeze.

"Fuck, you're too cute. How did I get smushed down here with you, sweet Omega? I don't remember." Noah whispers. His smile widens as I purr against his chest.

"You're right, I don't remember us choosing to be sandwiched between the couch and coffee table either, but I love it. What started this whole thing again?"

Noah chuckles. "Just your annoying mate's paranoia kicking in, or something."

Then my eyes snap wide open.

No, this all started because Noah was thinking about having kids with me.

As I gape at him, Noah's eyebrows raise higher and higher. "W-what?"

"You've been—" I bite my lips. I never thought I'd be able to say this to someone. My heartbeat thrums into my ears. "You've been thinking about having a baby with me?"

5

Noah ducks his head, breaking into the sweetest, shiest smile. "O-oh. Yeah, I have thought about it. A lot."

I dissolve into uncontainable giggles. It terrifies me for a second: I don't want to celebrate a promise for future kids too early. Not again.

But I can't stop myself. With how sweet and shy Noah looks, laughter spills out of me, filling my parents' old living room with my excitement.

Noah takes breath after breath, in an apparent struggle to speak, until he exhales hard, dropping his stare. "*Fuck*. I keep imagining you with Sarah in your arms during Rainn's class. And her little heart, it felt so happy, and I—" Noah exhales hard again, shaking his head. "I can't believe how lucky I got. That you might— You might w-want that— with me."

I grip my heart to keep it from bursting. When Noah glances at me, anxiety creases his features, but I can't suppress the deep, elated grin from erupting from me. We break into shy laughter, dropping our foreheads together.

"I can't believe *you* might want that with me," I say.

"I do," he whispers. He can't look at me, but he said it.

"Noah," I whisper.

He peeks up at me. We stare into each other's eyes, forehead to forehead. Neither of us speak, but it's not silent; our anxious breaths tangle between us, heating my cheeks.

"I *really* do too." My voice shakes, but my confession rips through me, excitement and nerves sending my nervous system through the roof.

"I know, I— I can feel it. B-but I also get the sense you've put a lot of thought into it," Noah mutters. "Having kids and how you want to raise them, I mean."

All I can do is nod. I don't know where to start. How much excitement might be too much? What if I scare him away?

But Noah can't bear to look at me. "I-I don't know, I'm a little nervous about that. Not because I haven't thought about it, but after the whole Forest School thing, I realized how much I don't know about what human kids need to learn. When you find out what I'm like raising kids, I'll probably seem a little— I don't know. Immature."

I sit back, cupping his cheeks in my hands. "What I've seen of you around kids hasn't been immature. Far from it. You're their favorite role model in the world, and an absolute sweetheart to them."

He ducks his head, burrowing into my neck before breaking into shy giggles. "Don't compliment me to my face."

I sputter out a laugh. "Noah, I'm serious! You don't need to have the same knowledge as me. It's all about what we bring to the table together, right?"

Noah sucks in a heavy breath, then holds it. My words catch up to me, heating my cheeks. I groan, burrowing my head into Noah's shoulder.

"You're giving me cute aggression," Noah growls. He squeezes me hard, and I bust out laughing. "Teach me something about parenting, Miss Matsuoka. Please. Before I eat you."

I laugh even harder, digging my nose into his mark until he squirms away from me. We meet eyes with beaming smiles and bright red cheeks, and I love every second of it. I feel so wholly present.

My voice comes out shy and shaky. "Actually, I do have a few books about a few different parenting styles."

Noah's eyes widen. "Shit, see? There are styles? With definitions?"

I laugh, kissing his cheek. "Yeah, but I— Um— We don't have to strictly use any of them." My heart flutters, still so unaccustomed to discussing this possibility with a partner. I can feel Noah's pointed stare on my cheek, but I unruffle my button-up, standing from his lap. "But defining each style was helpful for me to categorize different belief systems in my head. I already know I work better with a goal in mind, so I like to pull my favorite morals from each style to create my own personal style—For teaching, at least. I can show you my favorite books."

Noah stands, straightening above me in excitement. "Wait, what do you mean by a goal? A goal about how to act as you teach them, or what morals to teach them?"

I clasp my hands, working out my thumb in an attempt to cope with Noah's gorgeous stare. Is it just me, or is he as excited as I am about having a baby? God, is this real? I'm not used to being this happy.

Shit, what did he ask me?

I clear my throat. "Sort of both. My goals are focused on what I'd like to teach kids about the world. I want to show up for them with compassion and my own morals to help them through life."

Noah's pure, grinning excitement melts into something new that I can't name. Heated, pointed stares roam across my body. "Show me."

Taking Noah's hand, I can't stop myself from grinning as I guide him to my bedroom bookcase. He joins me on the carpet, grabbing each book from my hands as I continue to pull them out—until we're left with a giant stack that has Noah chuckling beneath his breath.

When I meet his eyes, he's beaming. "I had no idea you had so many parenting books."

My heart flips at his soft, delighted murmurs. I shuffle through my bookcase, unable to hold eye contact as I gather the two remaining titles. "W-well, part of it was for teaching."

"No, don't hide your excitement. I love it. You're about to kill me with how fucking cute you are right now."

I laugh, dropping my portion of the stack onto the bed. Once we have them all spread out between us, we sit facing each other on my unmade blankets.

But I don't have to hand Noah the books that matter most; he rifles through the stack, pinpointing the one with a thick bundle of sticky tabs poking from the pages.

My heart pounds into my ears. It's a book by one of my favorite

Early Childhood professors, detailing how to raise kids with full belief in kids' intentions to be good. That when they're "bad," it's a sign they need support meeting one or more basic needs.

But before Noah opens the book, I put my hand over the cover. Noah looks up, surprised.

"I don't want to push my ideologies on you," I say. "I had plenty of time to research this, so please, don't feel like you have to copy me or decide this right away."

"But these are the ones that sound the best to you, right?"

When I nod, Noah bites back a smile.

"Then I really want to know what you think sounds good. I trust your judgment."

The silence burns between us.

Until Noah sets the book aside. "Here's a better idea: how about you tell me what goals you have in mind, instead? And I can tell you what I want to be like as a parent too— Or, well, I might have a clearer idea of what I don't want to do."

My heart flips. "Okay."

We shuffle our sitting positions, facing each other with straightened, alert backs.

But neither of us speaks. We break into sudden, blushing laughter, and Noah buries his face in the hand I left on my knee.

"I-I'll start," he mutters into the back of my hand.

My eyebrows raise. I thought I'd have to be the one to get my shy Alpha to speak after I took my turn, but his wolf paces in our bond, preparing himself to be vulnerable with me.

"All I know is, I d-don't want to ever, ever hit my kids. I don't even want to yell at them. I guess if I had to sum it up, I-I don't want to believe it's my job to scare them into behaving."

My stomach flutters. I've never heard someone put it so plainly before. "God, exactly. I don't want to do any of those, either."

"Your turn." He smiles against my fingers, and I laugh.

How did he stomach this? I'm quivering where I sit, half from excitement and half from raw fear. But this fear is beautiful; it's reminding me this is something I care about most.

"I guess one thing I've thought about a lot is that I want to help my kids to not only express their emotions with words, but to also identify their feelings through physical and mental cues.

I feel like our generation missed out on that, and it's something that worries me for my students."

Noah nods with furrowed brows. "Fuck, yeah, you're right. That one might be more of your wheelhouse. I really suck at it still."

"I don't think so." Running my fingers through Noah's hair, I can't stop smiling. "You've shared some really vulnerable things with me in our cuddle balls, my shy Alpha."

Noah laughs, rubbing his forehead against the back of my wrist. "That's because I'm more open with you than anyone. Either way, I'd love to get better at expressing how I'm feeling so I can teach them alongside you."

He kisses my fingers, but I can hardly feel it over the elation vibrating through my chest. He's saying "them," as in *our* future kids.

With a hum, Noah lifts his head. "I have another: I want to try not to expect their lives to look a certain way."

"What do you mean?"

Noah sits back on one hand, clinging to mine with the other, but he's still feeling too shy to look at me. He studies my ceiling, rousing my heart muscles with his soothing, deep voice. "I don't know how to phrase it, exactly. Just that I don't want to tell them who or what they are, I guess. I felt a lot of pressure as an Alpha, growing up. I don't want that for them. I don't want them to think we'd be disappointed if they turn out— Well, different."

I can tell Noah is tense, even without his wolf pacing in our bond: his shoulders are practically up to his ears. This desire means a lot to him.

Scooting closer, I gently rub the back of his hand. "My shy Alpha, I *love* that idea."

When we meet eyes, a spark zaps from my heart to my gut. We break into instant, contagious smiles. And with that, Noah breaks into giggles.

I laugh. "What is it?"

Noah can't stop giggling. "Nothing. I just haven't seen you so excited before. It's making me extra happy."

My heart swells, threatening to burst. At the same time, it aches. I take a deep breath through my pounding heart muscles, preparing myself to admit the truth. "I've never had a partner to share this excitement with before."

Noah gazes deep into my eyes, giving me a pained sigh. But when his hand releases mine to land on my hip, his thumb tracing over my hip bone, we grow extra quiet.

His touch holds more meaning than I expected it to. Someday soon, he could be pulling me to him by the hips with the intention of getting me pregnant.

My heart flips into my throat at the mere thought. I flush to my neck, no longer able to hold Noah's focused stare. But as my yearning scent floods the room to meet Noah's rising Alpha musk, I bite my lips, unsure what to do with myself. Does this mean he wants to try soon-soon? Maybe I'm not actually ready if I can't even look into his eyes.

But I want to be. I dare to peek back up at him. The second I meet his shy, flustered stare, his hair tousled over one eyebrow as he ducks his chin, I melt in adoration. Stroking his chest, I do my best to extend my soothing scent.

Instead of calming Noah's breath, his chest rises faster beneath my fingertips.

Noah's quiet huff breaks the silence. We meet eyes, and his irises are vibrant again—his wolf demanding to be front and center in our bond. Our sudden, sexual desire heightens, building upon itself until there's no way to ignore it. Even before either of us speaks, the intention is clear; there's nowhere else for our affection to go except in a fit of passionate sex.

Noah clears his throat. "Do you want to—"

"Yes," I blurt out.

6

Noah pulls me into his lap. He's done so a million times, but I suddenly feel like I'm back in college, ready to frantically strip and get right to it for the first time with no clue foreplay exists.

But instead of kissing me, Noah rushes in with a heavy hug. I let out a small breath from the impact, but my eyes flutter in bliss as he gives my whole body a satiating, tight squeeze.

"I love you," he whispers. "I don't know what to do with myself again."

Wrapping my arms around him, I kiss the permanent mark I left on his neck, loving the pleasure-induced thrill it stirs in our bond. "You don't have to do anything. I love you too, just like this."

Keeping his torso tight against mine, Noah only leans back with his head. Our noses brush as Noah's golden eyes meet my stare.

"I want you," Noah whispers against my lips.

My stomach flips. He doesn't usually say things like that. I think he avoids it to overprotect me from feeling pressured to have sex, but I know Noah, and he only wants me if I want him back. And every piece of me wants him too.

As I crash my lips against his, his hands tighten against my waist, and I've never craved him more. It's wild how rapidly my body responds to him lately; I can physically feel my cervix lifting toward my belly button, every internal muscle preparing for Noah to enter me. I gasp for air between kisses, unable to catch my breath with how good it feels to be against him, my skin buzzing everywhere we meet.

Noah leans forward, carrying my weight until I'm safely nestled into the pillows behind me. Staring up at him, I tug his shirt off, and he unbuttons mine. My heart only hammers harder as he unlatches my front-fastening bra, leaving me bare with my clothes splayed at my sides.

But as he strips my pants, Noah freezes.

"What?" I ask, still breathless.

Noah clears his throat, opening his mouth to speak. He flattens his palm against my abdomen, dropping my heartbeat into my belly. I gasp at how sensitive my stomach feels beneath his gentle hands, especially now that there's meaning applied to it. Noah's sharp gaze snaps to my face. When we meet eyes, he hurriedly moves his palm to my thigh.

"What's wrong?" My voice shakes through my exhale.

"W-well, I just realized— I initiated, but I wasn't clear about *what* I initiated, so—"

I suck in a tight breath. He's right: I said "yes," to sex, but did he mean sex without a condom?

"I mean, I—" I bite my lip, unsure what to say.

How do you decide when it's the right time to bring a whole new life into the world? God, am I a horrible person for thinking I have the power to decide that? Is this a god complex?

"Hey," Noah whispers. My attention zips back to him. With one glance into his stable eyes, I melt into the pillows. Noah softly smiles. "There you go. There's no pressure. We've got time."

I prop myself on my elbows. "But I'm not sure I'll know when it's time."

Noah's concern flickers in our bond. "If it's not an immediate yes, I'm not comfortable with pushing it."

I frown. "I'm not sure if I've told you this before, but OCD is called 'the doubt disorder.' No matter how hard I try, I'll doubt everything, forever, since I can't find absolute certainty in almost anything."

Noah's eyes widen. "Oh, shit, I wasn't thinking about that. I'm sorry." Biting his lips, Noah runs his hands down my sides. "T-then what do you think would be better? I mean, an immediate yes might not be a good merit, but maybe what I meant was more like I don't want to ignore your human side. I've been aware from the start that my culture would be moving *way* too fast compared to how you were raised. I'll be here for months, *years*, ready to do this with you, and I want us both to feel prepared."

I grip Noah's arms, desperate to keep feeling his hands on me. My heart hasn't pounded so hard in weeks, unaccustomed to discussing these possibilities with him after we settled into a gentle balance. "You're right. I want this to be intentional and well thought-out too, especially since it won't be our baby's choice to be born, it'll be ours to be parents. This is totally, completely on us. We'll be choosing to dedicate the rest of our lives to them."

"Y-yeah, I— Yeah. Exactly. It's a massive decision." Noah chews on his bottom lip, studying my face. I can't quite read what he's thinking, and it only makes my heart hammer harder.

Noah's eyes widen, watching me open and close my mouth with heavy, anxious breaths. I laugh through my embarrassment at his quirked eyebrow, gripping fistfuls of the sheets beneath my sides.

"Do *you* want it now?" I blurt out. "Even after talking about all these scary responsibilities and commitments?"

My mate fidgets over me with a hard swallow. His cheeks are still flushed, but a massive burst of shyness erupts in our bond, darkening them another shade. "I'm right there with you in terms of wants, but— But I don't mind waiting either."

I gape beneath Noah as the reason for his sudden flood of shyness becomes clear; when we met, he might've played this off as something he'd want someday, but I think becoming a father is a deeply ingrained life dream for Noah too. Which means now that he's found me, he's *been* ready, and it's not just to please me.

The go-ahead relies on me.

I spread my knees, considering it. My scent blossoms with my thoughts, imagining Noah inside me with nothing between us.

But as Noah's eyes suddenly shift into yellow, he blinks hard. A waft of his Alpha musk forces me to wince through its sharp sting, and Noah jerks back from me. "Wait, I— I feel weird."

My heart kicks into a sprint as I cup his burning cheeks, searching him all over for what's wrong. "Weird? Like how?"

He shuts his eyes tight, but his hands squeeze my hips. No, wait, they're drifting lower. Okay, he's gripping fistfuls of my ass...

and dragging his nose across my jugular to scent the sensitive gland on my neck.

I shiver. "Noah?"

His voice comes out as a half-shifted growl. "You smell good. You want me to get you pregnant so badly. Every instinct in me is begging me to knot you."

"Oh— Oh, my God—" I gasp as Noah's tongue works my scent gland, pleasuring the erogenous zone until each lick echoes across my pussy. "Noah, are you rutting?"

My system races for an entirely different reason now. I hug Noah close, doing my best to stay calm as his scent erupts around me, drawing out every lustful molecule in my body. With one hard press of his erection against my core, I huff against his cheek. This only encourages Noah.

"Fuck, I can't—" He growls deeper, rubbing on me faster until I squirm. "I can't stop it from getting stronger. Maybe it's from talking about getting you pregnant, but now— Fuck, that's all I can think about."

Admittedly, I find that painfully arousing. But I know Noah is severely uncomfortable when he ruts.

He's been scared of hurting me during sex since the day we met, especially after learning about my previous trauma. Flashes of his fear in our bond convince me to pull back from his affections. He's ever-obedient of my consent, remaining stationed on my bed, but I've left the poor Alpha to pant in place, gripping the sheets as his cock uncontrollably flexes.

Stepping off the bed to hide my hips against the side of the mattress, I stroke Noah's wild hair out of his eyes. "You're okay. I'm right here to help you."

My heart aches as Noah slips into fear.

His expression warps as he suppresses his wolf. "I-I hate rutting. I d-*don't* want to do anything you don't want me to do. What if my stupid wolf breaks the condom a-again?"

I run my fingertips down the scarred mark I left on his neck. Noah freezes, and I give him a soft smile. "He's not stupid, first of all. He's my favorite wolf in the world, and an absolute sweetheart that never fails to make me so, *so* excited about life." Noah sucks in a deep breath as if he's finally coming up for air. I hum in approval, giving his mark a few more circles. It must feel as good as I hoped; he groans, gripping his cock as it drips.

Stooping to meet his eye-level, I regain his focus. "And second of all, he might break it, or he might not. I can't promise one way or another. Either way, I'm not scared of you or your primal side, gorgeous. I'm giving you my consent to mate me tonight, and I trust you'll listen if I change my mind and tell you to stop."

He groans, gripping my hips. "I love you too much. I want your pups."

I bite my lip, ignoring my wolf rolling over for him in our bond. Fetching a condom from my bedside drawer, I take Noah's flexing shaft into my hands. "I love you too, Alpha. And that's not what we agreed on doing today before this happened, so we're going to wait a little longer, okay?"

He pulls me closer, nuzzling deep into my neck with a frustrated growl. "Fuck, you're right, but I can smell how badly you want it. I'm sorry I can't give it to you."

My breath shakes as warmth pools in my groin, accompanied by a heavy flex of my core. His pheromones are designed to throw me into heat, but I promised Noah the next time he rutted, I'd be there for him like he always is for me.

He's been able to help me stave off almost all discomfort from my latest heats, keeping them short by dropping everything to mate me through them the second I feel one coming on. Noah's rutting usually ignites from my heat, disappearing naturally through our mating sessions.

His sudden rutting today may be different than our usual timing, but I'm not worried; since I happened to be here at the onset, it'll be far easier for us to lessen his rut to a measured hum without any need for rut-suppressant drugs. We'll just have to continue mating until his wolf decides he's knotted me enough to potentially impregnate me.

The trick will be to convince his primal side that he was successful despite using protection, just like we have to do with my pesky wolf.

Drawing Noah's lips off my mark, I hold his sweet face in my palms. Stark yellow irises stare back. He's craving me, I can smell it, but he adores me just as heavily. Just his eager, trusting stare flushes me down to my neck.

I soften my voice. "I've got you. I'm going to put this condom on you, then lay myself on the bed. The harder you fight it, the worse you feel, so I want you to let yourself go with me and enjoy yourself as usual, okay? Let's make it fun together."

Noah holds stock-still as I step away from him, my pillow in hand to place at the bottom of the bed. He tracks every movement, so I turn my back, giving him a good look at my ass as I strip my panties.

Peeking at him over my shoulder sends a thrill up my core. He's still eyeing me, but he's not staring at my bare ass. He's staring straight into my eyes.

The room floods with his Alpha musk, stinging my nose, but I make the mistake of inhaling as much of its enticing scent as I can. Concern flickers across Noah's face as I twist my hips, my knees dipping as his pheromones hit extra hard. I cling to the end of the mattress, catching my breath through aching pulses between my legs.

With a deep, growling hum, Noah tenses, ready to pounce. But he stops himself with a quick jerk of his muscles, sticking in place. "Fuck."

"You're okay. I want this too." Stationing my pillow under my hips, I lay back on the foot of my bed, my cheeks burning. No matter how long I've known Noah, I'm still not used to his dirty wolf's thoughts during sex, but I want to slowly meet him there over time. It takes every ounce of confidence I can muster to say, "I'm ready for you."

With my knees lifted and opened at my sides, I've shifted Noah's stare from aching to ravenous.

His wolf's little stomps in our bond tell me he's dying to race over, but his human form doesn't move. He's practically vibrating in place.

Biting back a laugh, I open my arms up for him. "Come here, Alpha—"

Smashing me into the mattress in a flash of his warm, copper skin, Noah growls over me. I sputter out a laugh through our heated kiss, but it quickly turns into rapid, frantic gasps; Noah's fingers glide down my soaked labia, effortlessly slipping into me to curl against my G-spot. I let out a deep moan beyond my control, widening my legs for more.

Noah groans. "Fuck, you weren't lying. You smell like you want it heavy today. Do you?"

All I can do is nod; I can't even choke out a yes as he mates my clenching pussy with a third finger. My heart races into my throat as Noah's palm rocks faster, pressing my clit between each tender, internal rub. My knees are no longer at my shoulders, squirming at Noah's sides as he palpates my deepest nerve, already bringing me seconds away from orgasming.

But just before I come, Noah slips his hand out. I gasp at the sudden exit.

Noah pins me with his electric stare. "Sorry. Too rough?"

I huff through every word, struggling to catch my breath. "No. Keep going."

As Noah steps forward, coating himself in my leftover fluid on his fingers, I lift my hips automatically; I know I'll have to if I want him to fit in me. He's so swollen that when I grip him, he's too stiff to give a true squeeze. Noah shudders, curling over me on the bed.

"Poor Alpha," I whisper. Dragging his tip over my core flares Noah's eyes into an even brighter yellow, spiking anticipatory anxiety into my throat. Digging my heels into the bed's edge, I lay back, straightening my hips to align with my torso. "Okay, love. Come here—"

Noah wraps his big arm around my waist, and I'm cut off by my sharp gasp as he enters me. Just his tip makes me flex around him, my legs shaking at how full I feel.

"You okay, Omega?" Noah rocks back, his heavy-lidded eyes roaming my face above open, indulgent lips. I can feel how good he feels in our bond, so I don't know how he's not crumbling like I am. Dropping limp against the mattress, all I can do is moan, using my feet on his ass to urge him inside me. Noah pushes deeper with his next thrust, as requested, breathing in my reaction.

He's so thick that my eyelashes flutter from how satiated I

feel, waves of tingles flickering up my chest. I'm left squirming beneath him, my knees popping up to give him better access.

Noah purrs in response, pumping a little deeper. "You're doing so well, Omega."

My moan comes out louder, and Noah smiles. Desperation clouds my thoughts as Noah slows, opting for heavier pulses against my cervix until my back arches.

He frowns. "You're stressed."

I can hardly speak, trapped on the edge. "I was already so close, so now—"

He growls, pushing himself higher over me. It tilts my hips over the pillow, allowing his pelvis to rock against my clit.

Every nerve between my legs ignites. Noah kisses me, but I moan between every breath beneath him, digging my fingers into his back. But Noah doesn't stay looking at me. When I catch him watching us mate in the mirror at the foot of my bed, a rush of shyness stifles my breath.

But Noah drops more of his weight on me, intensifying the internal massage he's thrusting out of me. I sputter out an uncontainable moan at how luxurious it feels, my thighs quivering at his sides.

Purring, Noah kisses my neck. "Good girl. Don't hold those sounds in. Let me hear them."

With one palm on the back of my pelvis, Noah tightens my hips against him, rubbing my clit back and forth as he mates me faster. Wet sounds fill the room from Noah's friction inside my dripping pussy, but they're nowhere near as loud as my rising breath, speeding so quickly that I choke out a hefty moan.

"There you go. Fuck, you're doing so good."

Holy shit, I don't know if he's riling me up on purpose, but he's so direct today. My cheeks burn hot, but his words double the pressure he's kneading into my cervix, curling my toes. I smash my lips into Noah's, and Noah deepens his cuddling thrust. Every inch of my body feels coated in him, his arms encompassing me now that both his knees on the bed spread my legs wider.

Alpha, imagine you're bare inside me, I mindlink. *Picture it clearly for me, gorgeous.*

As I break into high, loud whines of moans, Noah's eyes roll back. His wolf must love the thought of knotting me tonight with nothing between us; he drops his jaw, drool coating his fangs as if they're preparing to bite. The thought of him re-marking me kickstarts my orgasm, and Noah speeds into me hard and fast.

But he suddenly feels so soft and warm inside me that I drop my head back, joining Noah in imagining him bare. Each press of his tip against my cervix builds into a full-body pleasure, and the thought of him bursting against my womb's entrance sends me over the edge.

Except Noah's eyes snap open. "Oh, *fuck*—" He grips my hips, gasping over me. "I— I broke—"

Oh shit, he *is* bare inside me.

I cry out, unable to stave off my orgasm as it crashes over me. With a splash of fluid spilling down my ass, I push Noah off me. We both gasp at his rapid exit, but when he sees me squirting a second time, Noah dives back in with his hands. When he rubs his palm hard and fast over the whole base of my pelvis, I squirt against him again, my thighs clamping around his hand. He watches me with ravenous eyes as I curl into a ball beneath him, overcome by his touch.

As I collapse back onto the bed, Noah doesn't look as scared as I expected.

Sure enough, the broken condom is rolled at the base of his shaft. I swallow hard. "Did you—"

"No, I didn't come," he groans, dropping his head. "Thank the Goddess you have some actual sense in your brain. My fucking wolf—"

"Noah," I breathe. He perks up, and I push myself upright on shaky arms. We're nose to nose, so I lower my voice. "Please, don't be mean to my mate. You were just trying to help me feel good. It was just bad timing."

Noah groans, dropping his gaze onto his shaft. "It was worth it then, since it really looks like you did enjoy it. Look at that."

He points me to the long string of ejaculate I've left behind on his shaft. My cheeks flare red, but my groin also aches, wishing he was back inside me.

But that's not my main concern; Noah looks painfully hard, bigger than I might've ever seen him.

With a frustrated growl, Noah's shoulders droop. "Fuck, I don't know, Omega. Maybe I need to take some rut suppressants. I'm worried I won't be able to mate you without breaking every condom we try."

I shrug my open shirt and bra off my shoulders, drawing his focus to my breasts. "Or maybe I can take the edge off in another way so you feel less urgent."

He sighs, giving me the go-ahead with a slight nod.

As I wrap both hands over his bare cock, Noah winces.

My heart flips. "Does it hurt?"

He chews on his lips, closing his eyes. With flushed cheeks, he nods.

"I'm so sorry, love. I'll try to work quickly and give you some relief. Let me know if you want me to stop at any point, okay?"

With Noah's shy nod, I give him a soft kiss.

Using my discarded panties, I wipe the evidence of my pleasure I've left on him, burning my own cheeks. But Noah seems to enjoy my gentle rubbing, his breath heightening.

Scooting back on my knees, I drop my head, using a soft, suckling kiss to taste the drop on his tip. *Is this okay?*

Noah grips my shoulders, his abdomen bumping the top of my head as he doubles over me. "Oh, *fuck*, Omega—"

At first, I'm worried that means I should stop. But Noah's hips twitch, tempted to thrust into my mouth. I pull his tip into my mouth, swirling my tongue around it, and Noah's legs shake.

Is it too sensitive? I ask.

"Aliya, I—" He moans. The sweet sound shoots tingles down my spine, burrowing warmth in the depths of my pussy.

I've got you, gorgeous. Let yourself feel good for me. I bob my head, gently pulling him deeper. Noah moans even louder, placing his hands on my head.

But he's so gentle with me. As I work him faster, Noah holds my head in both hands as softly as I can imagine possible with how heavily he's breathing. He bends over me to kiss the small of my back, giving me light massages on his way. It's so painfully sweet that I whimper over him.

Noah moans again, and I squirm from how good he feels in our bond. He doesn't just feel pleasure, he feels taken care of. He feels loved. I whimper through my watery eyes, and he gasps at the vibration, thrusting into my throat.

Glancing down, Noah catches one of my tears. "F-fuck, sorry—"

Don't be sorry, gorgeous. I love that you're enjoying it.

I swallow his tip against my soft palate, and Noah gives a soft moan, lifting his chin. It shoots my heart up my chest and into the ceiling. I swallow again, applying pressure over the base of his shaft as I stroke him with both hands. Noah's lungs speed faster, this time releasing a higher moan. Goosebumps coat my body, urging me to moan with him.

As I suck him deeper, hollowing my cheeks, Noah whimpers, lifting his hips in time with my bobbing head.

"A-*Aliya*—" Noah gasps. God, I love my name when he says it, each letter carrying the tender affection I see in every breath, touch, and look he's ever given me. As I increase my pace, his moans grow so breathy that my heart pumps hard and fast.

Until his sharp gasp spikes my heart into the ceiling. "Oh, *fuck*. Hold your breath, Omega."

I will, I mindlink.

Loosening my lips wrapped around him, I drag my tongue a little harder down the underside of his shaft. Closing my eyes as I relax my throat, I deepen my swallowing pressure, meeting his light thrusts until he floods my throat. Despite holding my breath, I cough. Noah pulls himself from me with a gasp, coating my lips and nose in his sperm.

"F-fuck," Noah gasps, cupping my cheeks. "Now I really am sorry."

I open my eyes, licking my lips, but Noah already has his shirt in his hands.

"Goddess—" He softly swipes my face clean, but my heart flips when he grabs my chin to press a hard, grateful kiss into my lips. "My sweet, sweet mate," he rasps into my open mouth. "You're so—" He bites his lip, staving off a heavy wave of touched awe in our bond. "Everything about you is so nurturing."

"I love you, Alpha."

Noah growls into my lips, kissing me hard. He hoists me up into his arms, and I latch onto him with all fours. "I wish I could make you a mom today. I know I can't, but I— I want you to hear it out loud while I'm still feeling brave."

I suck in a sharp breath. That wasn't his rut brain talking. I can feel it in our bond; he meant that with his whole soul. As my heart restarts, Noah holds the back of my head, tilting his to kiss me deeper. I melt in his arms.

"I—" My breath catches as my cheeks burn. "I wish I could help make you a dad today too. But I'm happy to wait, as long as I get to keep being by your side."

Noah breaks into a shy smile. He sets me softly onto the edge of the bed, dragging both hands up my torso until he cups my jaw in his big palms. As he gazes deep into my eyes, my heart threatens to explode at his soft, adoring voice.

"You were right. I feel way more relaxed."

I bite back a smile. "Oh, good. Do you want to take a break for water and a snack, or would you like me to lay back down for you, sweet Alpha?"

Noah clears his throat, flushing as his shaft bobs back to life. "That depends. D-do you feel up for more?"

I eagerly nod, and Noah gives me a beautifully soft giggle.

"Then, will you roll onto your stomach for me, my sweet Omega? I want to cuddle you even closer this time."

My belly flutters as he brushes his fingertips over it. When he steps away to grab a condom, I'm left colder than I expect. Sometimes I forget I'm fated to such a warm, adoring Lycan that just the sight of his rolling, regal shoulders gives me butterflies.

I'm aching to return to his body heat, but I do as I'm told, laying back and rolling onto my stomach.

But I've never laid flat on my stomach during sex before. Does that even work with how big my mate is? No, I don't think so. Maybe he meant how he usually mates me when things get wild. I swallow hard, glancing over my shoulder at him. When he looks back at me, I hurriedly prop myself on my hands and knees.

My voice shakes as I stare at my hands. "Did you mean like this?"

Noah doesn't answer. When I peek back at him again, he's already behind me with a huge grin. Noah breaks into a soft chuckle, running his hot palms up my bare back. "Not exactly.

I wanted you to be able to lay down and relax, if you wanted to too."

"Oh. Then, like this?" I drop my chest, smushing my cheek into the blankets with my ass high in the air.

Biting back his smile, Noah drapes himself over me. I suck in a tight breath at his shaft nudging between my legs, shooting pleasure up my torso. His low voice vibrates across my back as he tucks my hair over my shoulder, kissing my cheek. "Have you never tried the position I'm talking about, my sweet Omega? I'm sorry I haven't tried it with you sooner. I think you'll really enjoy it."

I flush. "Can you show me? I'm confused."

With my eyelashes batting at him, Noah's jaw ticks with desire. I let out a mischievous laugh, and Noah breaks into a devious grin. "You're teasing me, aren't you, feisty Omega?"

I laugh. "Maybe. At least until your wolf comes out to play with—"

With one arm around my waist and the other at my knees, Noah effortlessly hoists my lower body into the air. I let out a shriek of a laugh, and Noah chuckles behind me as he settles my stomach flat on the mattress. As he relaxes his wide form over me, I automatically spread my knees and tilt my hips to the ceiling, picturing his big thighs struggling to fit between mine. But when my knees crash against the inside of his, I gasp.

Noah breaks into his sweetest, most genuine laughter, lighting up my insides. "Relax, sweet Omega. I really mean to take it easy and lie flat. Let my horny wolf do the work."

I giggle. "No, but really— How will you be able to reach—"

Carrying my hips, Noah slips a pillow beneath my pelvis. I suck in a sharp breath; his tip automatically prods my pussy from behind in this position.

"Oh. That's how," I whisper.

Noah leans over my shoulder with a sly grin, and I burrow my smile in my folded arms, letting out a shy laugh.

"I'm hoping this adds some nice pressure here," Noah purrs. He skates his fingertips down my ass, all the way to my clit. As he gives it a tender rub, I rock my hips back for more, widening my legs. He's right; I'm already feeling heavier pressure on the front of my pelvis thanks to the pillow stimulating my deepest nerves. Imagining Noah simultaneously rubbing every angle of my insides with his wide girth, I squirm beneath him, letting out a soft purr.

Noah rubs faster, and my pussy gapes for him. It sends my breath into a sprint, and I can't take it anymore. Twisting over my shoulder, I press a deep kiss into Noah's lips. As his fingers slow, I reach between us, stationing his tip to enter me. Noah hums into my mouth, pressing one hot palm into my lower back. Our lips unlock with a smack as he prods me, sucking in a hard inhale as he pushes in.

"*Oh—*" My eyes flutter shut.

Noah pauses, his hot breath pulsing against my cheek. "Is it okay?"

Reaching behind us to grip Noah's ass, I shove my hips back.

"Oh, fuck—" Noah groans. With one slow thrust, he pushes his full length into me, his hips meeting my ass. "Oh, it's— It's not just going to be your new favorite."

I can't laugh. My jaw drops at how rich this angle feels, Noah's tip rubbing directly against my G-spot. I whimper, my feet curling as I grip fistfuls of the sheets. With my head facing forward, Noah drops his forehead between my shoulder blades. His knees compress the comforter beside my wriggling legs, and with how soaked I am for him, Noah can move faster and deeper than my body usually allows us so soon. Within seconds, his hips can smash against my ass so deeply that each thrust ends with a soft clap.

As he presses one hand into the base of my back, pinning me to his heightening thrusts, something primal unlocks. I can't contain my moans, lifting my ass to meet him. Noah thrusts faster, his chest bumping my back as he somehow pushes even deeper. Each slap of his hips against my ass rubs my clit against the pillow, filling my whole abdomen with hot, rising pleasure.

My wolf speaks through me with a moan. "Alpha! More—"

Noah's half-shifted growl sparks a delighted cry from me; he's adding an extra little tilt of his hips at the end of each thrust like he can't mate me hard enough. It's just the right angle to add an intense, billowing pressure against my G-spot. Within seconds, fluid builds in me. I recognize the sensation immediately, breaking into unrestrained moans.

"Noah! It's—" I squeeze the plushy comforter tight in both fists, presenting myself higher for him on instinct.

He growls against my cheek. "What is it, gorgeous? I can tell you like that."

I groan, my toes curling as he repeats the action. "You're— You're about to make me squirt a *lot*—"

Noah's moan shifts into a rumbling growl against my back, his fangs extending. I expect him to mate me faster, but instead, he flops his whole weight over me, shoving his hips as tight as he can against my ass. He was right; I feel like we're cuddling from head to toe, my mate rubbing the deepest massage he can into me with how thick he grows. I drop my jaw, each push of his hips stimulating satiated cries from my lips.

The pressure between my legs only rises. I face forward again, my claws extending beyond my control. They puncture the duvet with little *snap* after *snap* of the threads.

But Noah's hands crash down on mine, just before he breaks into relentless, slapping thrusts. His claws rip through the duvet between my fingers, shredding all the way to my bedsheets. I can hardly breathe as he releases every ounce of building pressure between my legs, a flood of wet heat splashing my thighs.

"Fuck, yes— What a good—" Noah growls, arching up over my back. As he grasps my ass with both hands, he kneads a heftier rush of fluid from my pussy. Drool escapes my lips as my thighs twitch, feeling the start of Noah's knot bulge between my legs. "What a good girl."

My hips raise off the bed as I come, twisting in Noah's hands. He rocks fast and hard into me, pulling every tingle out of my nerves until I'm washed in pleasure. It has nowhere else to escape me except my bleating lips: the heat of his hands, sharp lust in his rutting scent, and his tender focus on my pleasure echoing through me.

Noah stops with a tender press into my core, his tip applying heavy pressure against my cervix as he knots me. A hard lump traps his engorged shaft between my legs, leaving me to gasp through the intense, leftover pleasure.

As Noah collapses against my back, we hold hands so tightly that it almost hurts. I glance over my shoulder to find his forehead coated in sweat, but his eyes are just as bright with passion for me.

Our silence is warm—until Noah groans. "Fuck, I'm so sorry. I'll buy you new bedding."

We break into sleepy, delirious giggles, interrupted by Noah flexing hard into me. Shuffling against each other, we sink into a deeper cuddle with pleased hums.

Our favorite post-knot activity is pillow talk, but we can't stop softly kissing as we stare into each other's eyes. God, I've never loved anyone this deeply. I can't believe this started because we're both craving to become parents together.

Noah's hammering heart against my back is still struggling to recover, but our bond tells me it's not just physically; his emotions overflow with adoration. He's just as in awe of our connection as I am. It's almost scary, my soul winding so tightly with his that I don't know who feels what in our bond; we're just one massive ball of love.

"I love you so much," I whisper.

Noah purrs, pressing another kiss into my cheek. "Goddess, I love you more than anything."

"I can't move, Noah. I'm a wet noodle."

His sleepy chuckle against my lips cradles my heart. "That's okay. I'd lay here with you forever, if I could."

As Noah and I curl up in my bed, turning into sleepy mush in each other's arms, I'm left in turmoil; I don't want to wait.

It's not because I feel rushed to get pregnant, or only because I want to be a mom anymore. It's because by carrying Noah's baby, I'll be providing the world with just a bit more of Noah's love.

I want to extend the existence of his affectionate soul, leaving his mark on the world for generations to come. I want him to look at my pregnant body and know that I chose him to birth a child with, despite it being my most vulnerable life dream. I want to share the love in our bond with everyone we meet, starting with nurturing our child with the knowledge we could change at least their life for the better. But if they're Noah's child, I know it'll extend beyond our family. Any child raised by Noah's kind heart will have the power to change the world with just their warm embrace.

I'm dying to see it unfold, firsthand. To hold his child, and care for them just as deeply as I care for him. To live every second of our child's life with my mate until we die.

With how tender my heart is for Noah's every breath against my cheek, I know I'm ready to be a mom for this man's children. Not soon, but now.

I just don't know how to express it. Is it even okay to express yet? It really is early in our relationship, and these are grand, raw feelings I've never experienced before.

Noah's arms are far too limp for me to bring it up now, so I nestle my back deeper into his chest, allowing his loose, satisfied body to weigh me into a deep sleep.

7

Can you come over? Amy's mindlink throws me out of bed before I can pry one eye open.

Be there in ten, I mindlink.

I expect to feel carpet beneath my feet, but I forgot we switched to sleeping at Noah's place toward the end of our five-day heat and rutting cycle. I remember now, sliding across the wooden flooring on one sock. My forehead narrowly misses Noah's open closet door, forcing Noah to suck in a tight breath behind me. He must've been startled awake by my concern in our bond.

Noah's quiet voice is rough with sleep. "What's wrong?"

My sweatpants are still sprawled over the foot of Noah's bedframe from when he teased them off me last night. I throw them on, letting out an exasperated breath. "I don't know. Amy just mindlinked me to come over, and I'm worried."

Noah is out of bed now too, grabbing yesterday's black T-shirt from his nightstand. "Did she say anything else?"

"No, I just know something's up."

My mate is already reaching for his keys. "I believe you. Let's go."

A soft drizzle on Noah's windshield gives us one last taste of spring on its way out. Clouds block the morning sun, and that's nothing new; half the year, it feels like it's perpetually dusk. But today, it makes my heart feel darker too.

Noah takes my hand, giving it a soft squeeze. "She's okay. Now that I know her a little better, I can feel her."

My eyes widen. "You're that connected to the whole pack? That's *incredible*, Noah."

Noah clears his throat, as expected; my mate never likes to brag about his top Alpha abilities, especially the goddamn incredible ones. I stifle the adoration in my chest, too concerned for Amy to smile.

"What does she feel like, then?" I ask.

Noah winces. "She's... afraid." My heart thumps harder, but Noah's grip on my hand tightens. "It doesn't feel like I should be worried for her safety, though. I just think she must need someone she trusts to be with her."

I swallow hard. "I know. She wouldn't ask for help if it wasn't serious."

The only thing keeping my wolf from ejecting me from the car and chasing after Amy myself is Noah's thumb smoothing over the back of my hand. Now that I think of it, he just decided he'd come with me without question. His dark hair is still damp from his morning perimeter run. He must've snuck back into bed with me to reform our cuddle ball, and I must've been used to his schedule by now to sleep right through it.

But I definitely didn't sleep through Amy's mindlink. It triggered a beast in me I've attempted to bury, but I know burying things doesn't work. My mind flickers through every possibility of what could've happened to her, unable to disprove their likelihood; they *can* happen. No, they did. To me.

"You okay?" Noah's voice sharpens, snapping me out of my head.

I grip my chest, taking a deeper breath. "Yeah. Just a little triggered."

Noah hugs my arm against his chest before pulling our interlocked fingers to his lips. "I can feel it. You're right here with me. No matter what we see, I'm here to protect you both."

I exhale, sinking into the passenger seat as Noah's soft lips grace my knuckles.

But as we pull up to Amy's apartment complex in the heart of Greenfield, my heart kickstarts from a thumping jog into a sprint. Noah is still turning off the car as I jump out.

I rush up Amy's apartment steps, ready to ring the intercom like I always used to for Amy to let me in. But Noah taps his wallet against the digital lock system, and a sharp click tells me it's open. Noah shoves open the heavy door with one hand, leaving space for me to enter first.

I softly smile. "Thanks, Alpha."

He kisses the top of my head as we step through the door, keeping his hand on my lower back to let me know he's following me up the stairs.

I take two steps at a time. *I'm here, A. Almost up the stairs.*

The door's unlocked, Amy mindlinks.

"Should I come in with you?" Noah asks.

I stop in front of Amy's closed door. The second her stressed pheromones hit me from beneath the threshold, I nod. "Please."

Without wasting another second, I turn Amy's doorknob, speed-walking through her living room. I follow her scent down the hall, but I know where she is.

I find my best friend bundled beneath her comforter, her nose redder than ever from crying.

"Oh, *A.*," I whisper.

This, of course, inspires Amy's fresh tears.

I'm relieved she doesn't seem physically hurt. Granted, Amy looks out of sorts. An expanding mass of tissues clutter her lap, each one as rumpled as Amy's sweat-creased pajama shirt, but there's no sign of forced entry into her apartment; her strewn navy, pleated comforter and teetering book stack on her golden-brown, wooden nightstand look the same as always.

I let out a shaky breath. Actually, my whole body is quivering. I take a deep whiff of Amy's scent as I wrap my arms around her.

Noah's voice softens behind us. "You want me to stay or go, Amy?"

Amy shudders through a bout of heavier tears. "Could you maybe stay?"

My heart warps as her eyes cloud over again. I glance at Noah, and his forehead is similarly scrunched in shared pain.

Noah crouches at my side. "Of course I can stay. We're both here."

I tuck Amy's short, vibrant hair behind her ear to nuzzle her cheek. Her straight, red hair is messy from sleep and stress, but it's still so silky that it glides from her ear, falling back into place.

Giving her a soft kiss on her cheek, I rub her shoulder. "Talk to me, A. When you're ready."

She huffs, a strand of hair puffing off her cheek. After a heavy silence, she reaches for our hands. "I need to get us a wolf pile going first."

I flop onto Amy, making her let out a heavy grunt.

Amy sputters into nasally laughter. "Wow, okay! I guess I got what I asked for!"

Noah and I smile, climbing onto Amy and Kira's bed; I pull Amy into my arms as Noah settles into my side. I sigh as I snuggle in, content to be stationed between two of my best friends.

"Where's Kira?" I ask.

Amy sighs, straightening against her headboard with a loud drop of her arms against the comforter in her lap. "She's at work. I told her not to come home for my ridiculous meltdown, especially because we're going to need the funding."

Noah's concern spikes in our bond. "Are you having a hard time making ends meet? Be honest. I want to know, because that shouldn't be happening in Greenfield, so if those Elders—"

Amy shakes her head, looking past me to meet Noah's eyes. "No, no— We're good, Alpha. It's just, we're budgeting for only two people right now, and—"

As if she didn't realize what she was saying until it fell from her lips, Amy's eyes bulge as mine pop open.

"*What?!*" I gasp. "Are you—"

"I'm not pregnant!" Amy squeezes her eyes shut.

My mouth is left hanging as I whir over the remaining possibilities. But the more I come up with, the more my heart hurts. This is huge news, and it usually takes years to even come close to adoption for most prospective parents. Why didn't she tell me any of this?

Amy groans, hiding her face in her hands. "I didn't know how to bring this up with you this week, A. I was going to, but Kira and I *just* started talking about it, literally only on Wednesday, but then last night an opportunity came up out of nowhere, just three days later, and— Fuck, this is all happening way too fast!"

"Hey, hey, let's back up." I grip Amy's arm, pulling at her hand until she allows me to lace our fingers together. "Start from the beginning."

Amy whistles out a slow breath. She bites her nails on her free hand like she always does when she's anxious, glancing between Noah and I before dropping her focus to our clasped fingers. "Remember how you, me, and Kira talked about potentially co-parenting next year?"

I clear my throat, sharing a surprised glance with Noah. My cheeks flush; Noah's puzzled stare tells me he didn't realize how serious I was about having kids so soon before meeting him. "Yes. But that was before I met Noah."

"Exactly. And now that you did meet Noah, Kira and I were talking about having kids of our own too, not just co-parenting with you as your baby's secondary caregivers."

A spike of concern ripples through our bond. I glance at Noah, but his eyes remain trained on Amy's anxious hands.

But Amy's fearful glance pulls my focus back to her. "I hope that's not disappointing, and I didn't want to move ahead without you, but—"

"A.," I rub her shoulder, giving her a soft smile. "Breathe. I'm not mad."

"You're not?"

"I didn't exactly ask your permission when Noah and I started having sex either. We could've already been pregnant. Plus, the three of us only discussed it as a possibility in the near future, but then I said I wanted to go on a few more dates first for a year or two to be sure I wouldn't find my soulmate out there, remember?"

She shrugs, her lips wobbling through fresh tears. "I know, but I didn't want to disappoint you. I just know how much this means to you, and—" She shakes her head, dissolving into full tears.

All I can do is rub her shoulder. I'm a little shocked, staring at my best friend through this severe of upset for what feels like the first time—at least other than the week Amy met Kira and had an epic meltdown the first night they spent apart.

But there has to be something deeper in Amy's tears than just breaking our almost-agreement. I chew on my lip, struggling to figure it out. It's not easy when I also have a whirlwind of emotions blasting through our bond, and I can't figure out what my mate is thinking either.

Until Noah wraps his arm around Amy and I, pulling the three of us into a side hug. His voice is gentler than usual. "It means a lot to you too, doesn't it? Becoming a mom."

Amy's soft cries pause—until they erupt. She breaks into full-blown sobs, nodding her head as Noah and I share a pained glance.

"Yes, I—" Amy's cries choke out her words. "I'm really afraid I'll fuck it all up somehow. What if I'm not cut out for this?"

For the first time since I entered Amy's apartment, my shoulders relax. I smile, running my fingers through her hair. "Guess what, A.?"

Amy groans, "Oh, Aliya, don't—"

"Maybe you *will* fuck something up," I say. Amy glares, but the second we meet eyes, we burst into laughter. "Or..."

"Maybe I won't, I know. I set myself up for that one."

I settle against her side, relishing in my two best friends smiling next to me. "I know I'm not hard to predict, but I'm serious, A. I've always been terrified I'll fuck up everything in the world, but especially motherhood. And I honestly don't think there's a parent out there who hasn't screwed up, at least a little."

Amy shrugs, her forehead warping back into overwhelm.

"That doesn't mean you're not cut out for this," I say.

She huffs. "But I'm not like you, Aliya. I don't have that sweet, nurturing side that kids are drawn to, and I don't have Kira's goofy side that would make them laugh." I glare at her, and Amy laughs. "Don't look at me like that!"

"Don't talk to my best friend like that, then!" I rub my forehead into her shoulder until she falls onto her side of the mattress in a giggling heap. "I don't know where this is coming from after I've spent my whole life laughing beside you, and being comforted by your presence."

Amy is silent for a long while.

My stomach squirms, especially as Noah remains more silent than usual, his swirling emotions in our bond leaving me curious and confused.

But as Amy dissolves into soft sniffles, my heart breaks.

"What's wrong, really?" I ask.

"They sent us a photo," Amy whispers.

My heart skips. "Of a pup?"

Amy reaches for her phone, tapping her passcode wrong twice with shaky fingers. By the time she finally unlocks it, her ribcage tightens in my arms with her held breath.

Amy pulls up a picture of a small Lycan pup, and the air is sucked from my lungs too. The second I see this sweet baby's tight brown curls, round, curious eyes, and pouty bottom lip, I know in my heart she's Amy and Kira's. I cover my gaping mouth, my forehead contorting through fresh tears.

Amy does a double-take over her shoulder. "No, Aliya! Stop it!" She lets out a sharp sob, and we both dissolve into weepy, disastrous laughter. "Dammit! She's just—"

"*Beautiful*," I choke out, my heart pounding into overwhelm. "Oh, my God, she's so little."

"She's only 20 months old," Amy whimpers.

Noah sucks in a sharp breath, leaning over my shoulder to view her with us. As Amy and I continue to melt into a puddle of mush, Noah's eyes rim in red—except he has the biggest smile he can manage.

"I can feel how much you already love her," he mutters.

Amy whimpers, burrowing her face into her pillow. I rub Amy's back, my heart aching as a massive wave of tumultuous emotions pour from her scent. Noah catches my eyes in concern, and I bite my lip.

"A., I can only guess how overwhelming or exciting this must be, but I don't fully understand what's making you smell so sad. I can feel how much you want this, but—"

Amy lifts her head to suck in desperate air. When she speaks, her voice is clouded with congestion. "But that's just it. I want this, but does she? She lost everything already. What if I'm not enough for her? What if I fail her?"

My heart rips. I shut my eyes, breathing through Amy's pained cries.

I snuggle up to her side as tight as I can press. "All you can do is your best. And from all the love you've given me, I know your best can save her life, no matter how imperfect your best might be."

Amy drops her hot forehead into my chest and releases the rest of her tears. With Noah and my hands on her back, it only takes two full minutes of Amy letting it all out for her breath to slow, her eyes falling shut to my gentle scratches against her scalp.

"You're right. She needs us, either way. Her biological parents passed, one after the other, and there are too many other pups to adopt. The orphan rate is higher than ever with all the Rogues seeking asylum and dying from broken mate bonds," Amy mutters.

I glance up at Noah, startled by this.

He nods, but he can't bear to hold eye contact. "A lot of Rogue Omegas are sacrificing their lives, escaping abuse and dying from broken mate bonds in exchange for their pups' safety. But the orphan rate is higher than humans for Lycans in general with how many mates die together, leaving their kids."

My stomach drops. "I never thought through how much higher it'd be."

But now that I am thinking about it, my heart speeds into a sprint. Noah and I are interlocked so deeply, there's no way we won't both die when one of us does. What's going to happen to our future kids? Is it irresponsible of me to want them, just to guarantee them to be left all alone later in life? Maybe even early in life, with how much danger Noah faces daily? I know he doesn't tell me how bad it really is, and the more I've listened to small hints lately, the worse his situation has seemed.

Noah's hand lands on my shoulder, and I jump. He shoots me an apologetic glance, his forehead knitted and eyes scanning my face. *Are you okay?*

I sigh, adjusting my cuddle on Amy until we've mashed into one tangled unit. *Yeah, mostly. That's just a scary thought.*

It is. He drops his stare, analyzing Amy's slackening body in my arms. *But it's life, isn't it? Like you've said to me, everything in life except death is uncertain.*

I swallow hard. He's right, it is life. Now that I know I'm a Lycan, I can't escape this added complication to my own mortality.

Of course no one likes death, but to imagine my dear Noah

leaving this earth? My eyes brim with tears, but my body doesn't stop there. A literal, physical pain hammers on my heart, restarting my breath as I wince. I nuzzle Amy's cheek to soothe myself, and she nuzzles harder back, still half asleep. But before I can torture myself any further, a soft knock at Amy's bedroom doorframe turns all three of our heads.

Kira gives us a sad smile. "Mind if I join you?"

8

With Amy bundled in a blanket burrito on Kira's lap, I snuggle into Noah's side on the royal blue tufted couch we thrifted for Amy and Kira's first apartment back in college.

Amy is much calmer now, a dazed, blissful look glossing her swollen eyes as Kira plants delicate kisses on her forehead.

We've sat in a comfortable silence, Kira and Amy muttering about Kira's leaving work early without telling Amy. But one thing I know about loving an Alpha is that there's no way Kira would leave Amy to feel so small and unsafe all alone in their bed. It was only a matter of time before pure instinct drove Kira back home.

But my mind can't stop whirring. I can't focus long enough to be present for my best friend.

Noah's concerned glances heighten the nerves along my neck. *Come with me for a minute.* He retracts his arm from over my shoulders to stand. "Does anyone need water?"

I stand too. "Or a snack?"

Kira gives us a soft smile. "That'd be nice."

I follow close behind Noah's wide shoulders to Amy and Kira's small kitchen. Boxed in by soft gray cabinets and clean white tile countertops, Noah looks even larger as he turns to me.

What's going through your mind?

I sink into Noah's touch as he rubs my arms, grounding me by the second. *I hadn't thought so clearly about the orphan rate being higher for Lycans before now.*

He nods. *It's really horrific, I know. And I'm so sorry you had to experience it firsthand.*

My heart burns with his words, especially because he understands this pain too. With a deep breath, I whisper what I'm really thinking.

"Since high school, I promised Amy that I'd care for her future kids if anything happened to her, and she'd do the same for me. We agreed we'd be called aunts. But then we talked about co-parenting last year, then I met you, and I don't— I don't know. I hate the thought of losing either of my dearest friends just as much as I hate the thought of our future kids losing us and feeling all alone. I don't feel like it's just the uncertainty, it's also not knowing what to do about it. What will happen to them when we die?"

Noah stares over my shoulder, his brows furrowed. Our hearts ache in tandem in our bond, but Noah's chest puffs. "Well, let's talk about it. Who d-do you want our kids to be left with?"

His breath speeds up in time with my racing heart. I fidget with my jacket sleeve's folds, shuffling on my feet.

"What's wrong?" Noah whispers.

"Is it weird that I feel like it's almost decided for me? I was trusting my best friends to possibly raise a child with me, but you don't know Amy and Kira as well as I do."

Noah shrugs. "I trust your judgment. But from the second I met Amy, she was fiercely defending you from me even though I'm her pack Alpha. That takes some serious fucking guts. Plus, she genuinely loves you, so I trust her too."

My heart pounds into my throat, but a smile bursts across my face. Noah's focus darts between my eyes, his wolf popping up in our bond with a wagging tail.

"Fuck, you're cute," he whispers. "What are you thinking?"

"That you're such a gem, Noah." I giggle as he ducks his head, softly thumping our foreheads together. "And I trust Amy too. But have you ever talked about this with Yasmine or Rainn? Rainn would be an incredible mom."

Noah hums. "I always imagined Rainn to be my number one choice, but both Rainn and Yas seem to want to be childfree. We'd have to ask them. And we'll have to ask Amy and Kira too."

"Okay, yes." I swallow hard. "Wait, like, now?"

Noah lifts his forehead from mine, his feet shuffling between us as an intense wave of shyness crashes through our bond. "Y-yes. I-I mean, especially if we're offering to be future parents for Amy and Kira's baby right now too."

My heart flips. "Oh, my God, I forgot to ask you if you're okay with that. Are you?"

Noah sucks in a soft breath to speak, but my shoulders raise.

"Wait. Don't answer this for me. Really dig in and think about if you'd want to do this for Amy and Kira. Just like you and I agreed on, it will always be our decision to be parents, not our kids' choice to exist. We'll owe that sweet little girl our everything."

A flood of sugary, delighted scent blasts my nose, forcing me to blink rapidly. Noah clears his throat, dropping his hands from me to frantically fix his hair.

"Noah?"

He shakes his head. "You're going to be the best mom, I just—" He places his palm over his heart, taking a deep breath. When he speaks, his soft voice is gentler and sweeter than ever. "I just love every second with you, Aliya. I want to raise Amy and Kira's kids with you just as much as our own. Fuck, I'd be happy if that's all we did, as long as I get to see you be a mom."

When Noah finally meets my eyes, I can hardly stifle my rising breath. Noah's loving gaze traces my features as our collective scent only strengthens.

I throw my arms around his shoulders, smashing our lips together. Noah sucks in a surprised breath, but his hands land on my waist. As soon as he can gather his wits with a purring growl, Noah leans into me until he squishes my ass against the countertops. Our tongues meet, the rising heat between us almost unbearable as it dives straight for my groin. I have to pull away just to breathe.

When I spot an alert stare behind Noah's shoulder, I jump.

Kira smirks. "Getting snacks, are we?"

Noah's wide eyes spur me into uncontrollable giggles. Kira cackles with me as Noah hurriedly turns around, grabbing four cups.

"Got the water," Noah mumbles, rushing out of the kitchen with his head down.

With water and snacks in hand, we return to Amy's side full of laughter.

Amy lifts one eyebrow. "Should I be concerned?"

"We're just lucky I caught them before their raging pheromones sent me into a rut," Kira mutters.

My eyes widen. "Oh, God, what?! I'm nowhere close to being in heat."

Kira and Amy laugh, glancing at one another in a silent conversation I'd never be able to decipher. But after Noah hands us our water glasses, he looks just as nervous as I am, eyeing us three women as he frantically sorts his hair.

Are you going to tell them, or should I? Noah mindlinks.

I swallow hard. *Maybe I should, if you think it's time? I can, right now.*

Maybe we should just focus on their baby first. They might be too stressed to commit to our future kids right now.

I bite my lip. *I don't think so— Amy would be honored. But maybe we should take our time to ask Rainn too. Then we can wait to ask everyone officially once I'm pregnant.*

As the gravity of what I just mindlinked hits us both, Noah's cheeks flush, and my stomach grumbles.

Then I feel eyes on me.

"What's wrong? You have that face," Amy says.

"What face?" I blurt out. My voice squeaks, and Noah bites back a laugh.

Amy's eyebrows flatten. "Girl, just spit it out."

I laugh, plopping to the loveseat cushion beside Noah. "It's not like that, Amy! This is serious."

Amy and Kira's eyebrows furrow in unison.

Then Amy gasps. "Are *you* pregnant?"

"No!" I sputter, rubbing my flushing cheeks. But Noah is faring worse, burying his head in his hands with soft chuckles. Despite his wide palms covering his face, it's doing nothing to hide his bright red ears.

But to my surprise, he sits back with a deep breath. Taking my hand, Noah's low voice silences the rest of us. "We've both talked something over."

"Okay, and that is?" Amy glances between us with tensed eyes.

"We have similar concerns about the future when we start a family. So, we thought—" My stomach tightens, so I look to Noah.

He grips my hand, keeping his eyes on my best friends. "In the horrible circumstances that you're both no longer around someday, we wanted to offer our readiness to raise your child as our own— I-if you'd want that, of course. And if you're o-open to it, we'd trust you to do the same."

"And you don't have to decide this now! We just—" I glance at Noah, softening my shaking voice. "We felt strongly about supporting you in making sure your little one is protected in the future, and hoped that it would provide some peace of mind to know we're willing to be there, no matter what."

I can't help it, I'm death-gripping Noah's hand. He squeezes back just as hard as we stare at Kira and Amy, awaiting their reaction.

But as Kira's lip wobbles, Amy lets out a desperate gasp at her mate's sudden tears. "Oh, my *love*—"

Kira buries her face into Amy's embrace, letting out soft sniffles. "Sorry, it's just— I really was worried about that, so I'm so relieved."

"God, so am I," Amy says. She turns to us, opening her arms to include us too.

We join their cuddle pile, Noah giving all three of us a tight squeeze.

"You really will be her second parents if something happens to us? Just in case?" Amy asks through a weepy smile.

"Absolutely. The second I saw her photo, I knew she was yours, which means I fell in love with her too," I say. "But please, stay here to live an old, weathered life with me. We need you here, and I'm just as ecstatic to be her Auntie for life."

Amy and Kira smile through their tears, their scents exploding with a mix of excitement, fear, and love.

"Shit, we're really doing this," Kira says.

Amy cackles, and my heart soars; she's okay.

As we separate back into two pairs, Amy gazes at me with fresh, wild eyes. "Will you both come with us when we bring her home, then?"

I break into a wide smile, gripping my giddy heart. "We'd *love* to."

After meeting and re-meeting Amy and Kira, Lexi is finally scheduled to go home with my best friends today. Noah and I stand by Amy and Kira's sides, providing moral support for their shaking hands as they sign the final adoption paperwork. Our names are listed beneath theirs in their updated last will, assigning us to their little one, for life.

My heart pounds into my throat. I've never done anything that felt so life-altering before, aside from committing myself to Noah.

Glancing at me with wide eyes, Noah shakes his head in disbelief. *Holy shit. We're signed up to be parents now, Aliya.*

My heart flips. *Oh, my God, we are.* I pull him closer, giving his hand a tight squeeze. *I never thought Amy, Kira, and I would be here so soon either. I feel so lucky to have you by my side to share this moment with.*

Noah softens into a red-eyed, beaming smile, giving me a quick peck on the lips.

But as Amy and Kira share one last sweet, tender kiss pre-parents, I weep through my smile, knowing our lives are all changing for the better.

I can hardly breathe as we wait for Lexi to arrive. I can't imagine how nervous my best friends feel inside, but Kira physically can't keep herself still, and Amy's anxious pheromones blast my nose.

The second a Greenfield social worker guides Lexi out by the hand, allowing her to slowly toddle after her, I cup my hand around my mouth. She's only 21 months old, but she's hyper-aware of us around her, gazing up at what must look like a group of weirdly emotional giants.

But as the social worker points Amy and Kira out to Lexi, I gently pull Noah to the side with a hammering heart. *Let's give them their moment.*

Noah and I cling to each other desperately, helpless to watch as

Lexi hesitates in the doorway. Lexi blinks her wide eyes, glancing between the social worker and my best friends.

But something in Amy's features shift. The room no longer smells of anxiety, instead filling with a sweet, nurturing scent.

Amy gently lowers herself to the ground, softening her voice with a bright, welcoming smile. "Hello, Lexi! It's so nice to see you again!"

When Lexi breaks into the biggest, cheeriest smile to see Amy, my heart melts. But Lexi takes eager, toddling steps. She doesn't stop until she crashes into Amy's outstretched arms, and my best friend's giddy laughter echoes through the lobby.

As Amy and Kira welcome Lexi into their lives, Noah and I dry our wet eyes, watching in equal awe.

I love you, I mindlink.

I love you so much, Noah mindlinks.

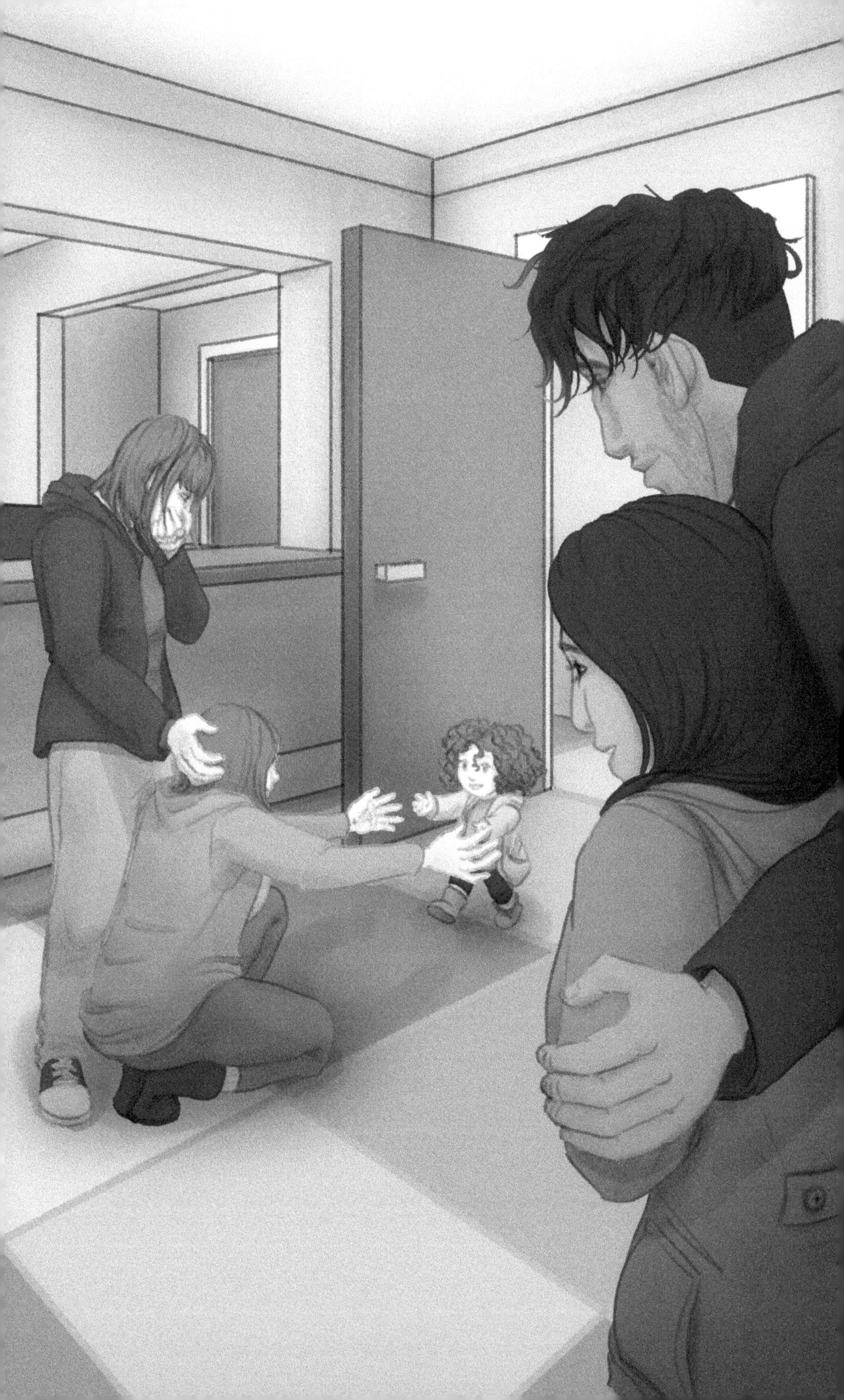

9

Spring has officially left us. Summer heat settles in, evaporating the rainy season and allowing me to wear long, flowing sundresses that catch Noah's eyes when the wind whips through them.

But today, I'm the one tracking Noah's burly, black wolf during his daily sparring practice. I can't stop smiling like a giddy kid. Normally it takes five wolves to challenge Noah, but with Noah's shifting schedule, poor Yasmine is left to face him alone in his free hour. He chases Yasmine's gray wolf like he's playing a casual game of tag, but Yasmine is gassing out. When she shifts into her human form, groaning and flopping into the grass, Noah comes to his classic, screeching halt, his giant paws blasting dirt in every direction.

Yasmine gasps. "You bastard! I'm coated in mud!"

His ears droop. Then he bats Yasmine back into the grass.

Despite her obvious annoyance, Yasmine bursts into laughter. "*Noah!* You big, goofy asshole! What's with you today?!"

He lazily lifts one lip in a weak snarl, and I laugh, knowing how fake it is.

Yasmine meets my eyes, still supercharged with excitement from their practice battle. "Agreed, Aliya. After seeing him chase you around like a puppy, his snarls don't hit as hard." She scoops a fistful of mud off her bare shin, slopping it into the grass with a hard flick. "I'm done sparring with you for today, you obnoxious brute of a wolf. Or maybe I'm done for the next *two* days. It's just not fair."

Noah whines, and I rise to meet him. He shifts before I can

reach him, taking my breath away as his yellow eyes melt into their familiar soft teal.

Well, almost. I expect them to soften into a near-blue, but they're stuck a little green.

"Noah? Are you oka—"

When he pulls me into a kiss, his overheated—and very naked—hips fall flush against me from the start. I let out a surprised hum at the sudden pressure. Encouraged by my pleased reaction, Noah tightens his grip, enveloping me in his desirous scent.

"I'm out of here," Yasmine says at the tree line.

I giggle, breaking our kiss. "Sorry, Yas! Will you still come over for dinner tomorrow?"

She winks before turning her back with a wave. "Anything for you, babe!"

I laugh. But Noah doesn't smile and roll his eyes at Yasmine's incessant flirting like he usually would. He glares at Yasmine's retreating back before tucking his chin over my shoulder, squeezing me as close as he can manage.

"What's going on for you, Alpha?"

"I don't know. I usually miss you so much during the day. It's so nice to see you here."

"I wish I could be here every day too." I pull back, putting on a cheery smile. "But hey, summer break begins soon, so I won't teach during the week. Maybe a year or two after I become Luna, I could stop working at my school to help you with—"

Noah's brows pinch with his irritated huff. "No. Never quit your job for me. If I ever ask you to do that, wolf-divorce me."

I sputter out a laugh. "Noah!? Oh, my God!" He softens into a half-smile, and I draw him back in for a cuddle. "It's just— What if I could help even more kids here?"

"You genuinely love your kids. Just that alone is changing more lives than you know."

I buzz all over, his words hitting deep in my heart. "Thank you. And I do love them, but…"

My throat tightens. I've wanted to ask Noah a favor for weeks, but I wasn't sure if it was fair. I don't want to use his authority for my benefit.

But Noah's story last night about a distraught Rogue mom was the deciding factor. The occasional Rogue is an abuser banished from their pack, but far more Rogues are abuse *survivors*—and their children. It kills me to think there are so many pups suffering without the comfort of a pack community after facing trauma that I know firsthand is lifelong.

What scares me the most are our pack's Alpha-domination men. The newest Rogues have to wait for a full moon to be formally inducted into the pack. Each approaching week before the ceremony feels like a silent threat, awaiting these Alphas' potentially violent acts of dissent. I trust Noah's protection of us. I just don't trust those Alphas—or what they're teaching their kids about their new classmates.

Noah's eyebrows furrow. "What's wrong?"

My voice shakes. "I know we have the Forest School for our pack pups, and that I love my job, but I feel like I see something urgent we might need here, and I feel called to help."

I'm antsy with anticipation as Noah's wolf appears to stare through his piercing eyes, his focus unwavering. "Okay, I'm all ears."

I swallow hard. "I was wondering if it'd still be possible for me to help Rogues adjust to life within the pack somehow, and it got me thinking…" I grip my skirt, taking a deep breath. "What if I helped to start a Rogue daycare here, transitioning them into school with the existing pack pups?"

Noah's eyes widen, and words come spurting out of me.

"It's almost summertime, so I could easily help set it up now, and maybe even work there on weekends, or take the second shift after my half-day preschool classes—"

"Oh. Fuck, *wow*." Noah grips his head, shaking it. I'm so anxious about what he'll think of my request that when his eyes zip back to mine, I flinch. "No, no, it's not bad. I just can't handle— Ugh, fuck, I need to get a grip." Noah bites his lip, his eyes swimming with affection. "That would be *amazing*, sweet Omega."

My heart lifts. "Really?"

"Goddess, yes. I can just picture your presence in their lives being so healing. Not just healing, but exactly what they need, and—" Noah beams, although I sense laced pain hidden in his roaming stare. He adjusts his hold, softening his fingers into gentle sweeps down my arms. "As long as it's something you want, and not just to please me. I'd love to support you."

I chuckle, sorting Noah's frazzled hair. "Okay, there's something else off about you today. You're stuck at 90% wolf brain; I can hear it."

He groans, burying his nose in my neck. When I shiver, he can't seem to help himself. Kissing my neck up and down, Noah reverts to sucking and licking my scent gland, blazing heat through my groin. It spurs my breath into a whimper. My hips grind against his on instinct, and he slides his big hands down my back, stopping on my ass.

I grip his hair, breathing into his heavy grinds as they send pulses of pleasure up my core. "Oh, God. Whatever you're doing, I'm not going to last long. I'm glad I brought condoms with me today."

Noah growls, smashing his lips against mine. His tongue slips into my mouth, and my thighs part for him. He indulges me with a rolling pressure against my clit, his thigh slipping against my flowy skirt.

"Mm!" I tug him to the ground, desperate to feel his weight on top of me.

But as Noah kneels over me on all fours, we jump as someone clears their throat from within the trees.

Noah's yellow eyes bulge. "Oh, fuck— Mom!?"

Lilian scowls with a disapproving shake of her tight, gray bun. "Watch your mouth when speaking to your Luna, Noah Greenfield."

"S-sorry! It's just— We're... busy." His cheeks burn as red as mine feel.

But Lilian doesn't look like she's leaving anytime soon, crossing her arms and settling into one hip.

"W-what's going on?" Noah asks.

"I—" Lilian clears her throat, struggling to meet my eyes. She brushes a leaf off her shirt, busying her focus. "I have a proposition for our future Luna."

My heart flips. I'm still not used to her admitting I'm the next Luna.

She hasn't apologized to Noah for the day I met her, but she's softening up around us. But no matter how nice she can be, I can't trust her yet. Not until she apologizes to Noah—and means it.

Noah helps me to my feet, lacing his arms around me from behind to cover his naked body.

Lilian rolls her eyes. "It's nothing I haven't seen. I raised you, didn't I?"

"That's not the problem, Mom."

My eyes bulge, feeling the very hard "problem" pressed against my back.

I can hardly suppress my laughter, my voice shaking as I smile at Lilian. "I'd love to speak with you, Luna. Please, give us a moment."

I help Noah gather his clothes from his tree hole, keeping his back turned to his mom. Unable to help myself, I giggle at the ridiculousness of the situation. But Noah sighs. He'd normally laugh with me, but he seems extra frustrated today. I have no idea what's going on with him. Has he already had to deal with more of those Alpha-domination jerks today?

Noah meets my worried stare, and his eyebrows soften. "Sorry, sweet Omega. I'm okay, I promise."

He's not, but I trust he'll tell me when he's ready. With a soft kiss goodbye, Noah leaves me to meet Lilian at the clearing's edge.

I roll my shoulders back, stopping in front of her. "Is there something I can do for you, Luna?"

She frowns at my unenthusiastic tone, and my stomach sinks. Shit. I didn't mean to come off like that.

"You're still mad," she says, and it's not a question.

"Well..."

"It's okay. I get it."

My heart flips. "You do?"

She links her arm with mine, guiding me into a narrow path between the trees. Anxiety burns my esophagus.

"Yes, I do. You were right the day we met. I was... cruel," Lilian says.

A hard lump forms in my throat.

Lilian sounds willing to grow and repair things. I have a lot to say, but if I'm not careful, it could damage any progress we've made.

"Thank you for hearing me out. It means a lot that you took my words in, even though I was a bit harsh that day." I glance at her furrowed brows, bracing myself for her reaction. "But I wasn't the only one there. And I'm not the one who needs to hear this apology the most."

She gazes at my feet as we walk, her stoic eyes even more unreadable than usual. "I'll repair this on my own terms. This is not what I wanted to discuss."

"O-okay..."

Just when my hopes fall to the floor, Lilian stops, placing a hand on my shoulder. "You're hoping to become Luna someday soon, I hear."

My stomach flips. She's right; all I have to do is tell Noah I'm ready, and I'll be committed to nurturing Greenfield's safety for life. "If time and circumstances permit, yes. But I want you to have your time to adjust first before we even consider moving forward."

"Oh." Lilian's eyes widen for a fleeting moment before returning to their usual cool. "Well, thank you for that." There's an awkward pause as Lilian prepares to speak, stopping herself a few times between deep breaths. "What do you say if I take my time to teach you what I know? Before handing off my title to you."

I swallow hard, struggling to steady my breath. I can't believe it. She's not only agreeing to hand over her title for the first time since we met, but also wants to be involved in my transition to Luna.

I'm beaming. "Luna, I'd *love* that."

She softens into a smile, dropping her stare.

But she doesn't know I have more to say. My heart leaps with every beat; it's the second time today I'll have to share a vulnerable dream. But Lilian seems open. Hopeful, and maybe even a little timid.

I hope this means she truly wants to repair things. I know if she lets me share my thoughts, it could do wonders for our rocky relationship.

"About the Luna title, I do have another idea for our situation, actually," I say.

Lilian's frown creases her brows, forcing her long forehead scar to ripple. I swallow hard.

When she lets go of me, crossing her arms, I struggle to keep my composure. What if she doesn't understand me again and I make it worse? What if—

Okay, wait— I can do this. I can do hard things.

I face her, clasping my hands before she can see them shaking. "I know I'm not as traditional of a Luna as expected… Which is probably why Noah and I work so well together."

Lilian doesn't chuckle with me. Her mouth hardens into a tight line. "Go on."

I drop my stare. Lilian doesn't like anything about this, I can smell it, but I can't back down. "While I don't want to stray from tradition entirely, I feel like it's wrong to suddenly strip you of your title."

"But that's how it works. Noah even said that to me the day I met you."

I dare to face her scowl. "I know this idea isn't a current tradition, but bear with me for a second, okay? I'm suggesting this because I think your feelings matter too."

Lilian sighs, chewing her bottom lip.

"When I become Luna—" I grip my skirt as her shoulders tense. But Lilian doesn't protest aloud, so I take what progress I can get. "How would you feel about becoming the *Elder* Luna, and continuing your title?"

Her eyebrows shoot all the way up, but she doesn't say a word.

Spurred on by nerves, I just talk.

"I personally don't feel it's right to have all those Elder Alphas and one Elder Beta reigning without at least one Elder Omega's perspective. Omegas represent over half the pack now, so you're more vital to us than ever, Luna. After everything you've done for the pack, why isn't there an Elder Luna title waiting for you? You don't suddenly stop being important to us when you're done birthing pups and raising the next leader. I feel like you should be involved where you want to be. Your work is important, and I want to make sure our pack acknowledges that from now on."

Lilian bites her lip, dropping her chin. My heart aches for her, a nurturing pull gnawing at me from her somber pheromones.

I think she's struggling not to cry. But by how desperately she's determined to keep a stoic, strong face, it shatters me. When was the last time this grieving woman was comforted or acknowledged, rather than only comforting everyone else?

Following my instincts, I pull Lilian into a gentle hug. She lets out a soft gasp.

But as I hold her tighter, extending past the casual-hug range of time, her shoulders soften.

"You're—" She swallows her shaking voice, starting anew with her stoic confidence. "You'll be a good Luna."

My eyebrows warp with emotion, but I'm too afraid to thank her. She could barely whisper that as it was. I don't want to push her too far when things are finally going well.

And I can tell she needs this badly. Her scent emits a potent longing, urging more pheromones from my thudding heart.

I rub her back softly, resting my chin deeper against her shoulder. Her shaky breath gives her tears away, but she pats my back as if she's comforting me.

Until Lilian jerks away, turning her back.

After a tense silence, she treks ahead through the forest so quickly that I have to jog to catch back up.

"Luna? I'm sorry, did I—"

Lilian squares her shoulders as she strides. "Let's go. We have a lot of preparation to do before dinnertime, and Noah tells me you're interested in supporting our Rogues. They'll be pleased to see you."

We trudge deep into the forest, nearing the Community Center, but my heart is still back in that clearing, restless with distress for Lilian. Just like her son, she can't accept being held for once.

This trend needs to end in Noah's and my generation. I want to make sure of it.

We're flooded with wolves the second we arrive at the Community Center. Like everyone has described, it's fuller than I last saw it, growing weekly. There's still room to walk, but remarkably less.

As Lilian introduces me to a few adult Rogues, one little Lycan grips onto my skirt, begging me for a hug with desperate, outstretched arms.

Their grown-up gasps, diving to pull the little wolf back. "Honey, don't interrupt our future Luna!"

"Oh, no, please don't worry about me! I teach preschool for a living, so this is gladly welcome." I pat the little wolf's head, unsure if I should return their hug. But when I look at their grown-up to ask her what's appropriate, I'm shocked by her furrowed brows.

Lilian mindlinks me without a single glance in my direction, nodding along to another Rogue's hushed concerns. *Lycans will misunderstand your "polite" hesitation as disgust if you follow human rules. Especially as a Luna.*

That's right. Noah said he treats all pack members as a cuddly family. No personal boundaries.

Dropping to my knees, I accept the little one's hug. Then every hug that comes flying toward me—and there's plenty. Pups dash in, screeching and laughing. I'm grateful to fall back in my element, letting my laughter calm my nerves as ten little Lycans pounce on me.

Once they overtake my head, climbing up my back, Lilian yanks them off me, one by one.

It's the brightest I've ever seen her smile. "Alright, alright! Our future Luna is busy. Go play chase before I lose my patience."

The little wolves skitter away with squeals of laughter, chasing each other through the courtyard.

The Rogue grown up smiles, a distant look in her eyes as she watches her pup. "Goddess, I gave up everything just to hear that laugh again."

My eyes flush hot with tears. Before I can think, I slip my hand into hers.

Shit, that was my impulsive wolf. Touching her could've startled her after what she has been through—I know from experience—but she must smell my aching heart for her. She turns to me with hopeful, wide eyes.

And I speak my heart despite my shaking voice. "I'd love to support you too. I'm sure it'll be nothing compared to what you've done for your little one, but please, is there anything I can do to make your life easier?"

Her lip wobbles, her stare flitting between my eyes. When she crashes against my chest in a tight hug, all I can do to keep from crying is to hug her back just as hard, squeezing my eyes shut.

"Just being here in Greenfield means a lot," she whispers. "We're doing just fine."

I rub her back, and she purrs. It brings a rush of relief to my heart. "Just fine isn't 'great.' From Omega to Omega, please share anything you'd like with me about your experience here. Even if it's just needing another pair of socks."

She takes a deep breath over my shoulder, huddling into me a little tighter. After a silent minute, she mutters, "We lost everything, Luna. Absolutely *anything* makes a difference."

My heart shatters. How could anyone be so heartless as to act like these Omegas are making up this pain? It's so real, I don't just smell it: I *feel* her agony in my chest.

Maybe Steven forced me to make a choice to leave him, but it wasn't without grueling, torturous questions I weighed for years beforehand. I never knew I was getting myself into an abusive relationship, and I know these refugees didn't either. But with wolves' social pressure to bond with a fated mate right away, tying our souls to someone before we even know them, how confusing must it have been for this woman to need to leave her abusive mate?

She must've held so much hope that her mate was "the one," only to be crushed when they hurt her. Out of countless difficult questions she must've asked herself, every answer had to be horrifying: either fate—her Moon Goddess and source of faith in life—was dead-wrong, fate chose to torture her on purpose, or her mate took advantage of her heart's trust. No matter what, her abusive mate locked her soul into a never-ending pain spiral, and the only way out was to rip their bond apart. I know from experience that leaving meant losing her livelihood, friendships, and status quo on top of already being hurt by her abuser for years prior.

And yet, we both somehow made it here, into each other's embrace.

Following my instincts, I wrap my arms as far as I can around her, holding her close. She grips me like a lifeline. It's not until then that she breaks into tears. My eyes flood with her, just the sound of her broken heart ripping through my chest. But as I whisper my ideas about additional monthly care packages for her and her new Community Center family, she loosens in my arms. A piece of me heals with each of her relieved breaths.

When it's time to say goodbye to the Rogues for today, I follow Lilian through the Community Center Cafeteria, amazed by the details Noah hasn't shared with me. There are Lycan pups and adults everywhere, laughing, playing, and eating lunch amongst each other despite their mixed pack backgrounds.

From what Noah described, cultures are wildly different from pack to pack. Most top Alphas claim mixing them is no easy task, warning potential pack traitors that nothing but struggle awaits them as Rogues.

But as I look around, I have visual proof our top Alpha is right; all I see are relieved, unified smiles as we care for one another. Witnessing this community's healing in action steals my breath.

Is this cafeteria for everyone who lives at the Community Center only? I mindlink Lilian, afraid to break the beautiful vision in front of me.

No, it's for the entire pack. Every night, we offer free dinners for wolves who can't afford it. No questions asked.

That's so wonderful, Luna. And you cook, yourself?

We trade off with any volunteers available. Sometimes we'll make enough to last a few days. She glides through the kitchen doors, and I follow on her heels. "But towards the end of the month, bills are due in the human world. That's always when we need more hands."

I gladly take the apron Lilian hands me. We gather ingredients for five massive pots of stew, lining up an array of meat and vegetables on the steel countertops.

My stomach churns as I dice a large onion, still mulling over my interaction with our refugees. But with one glance at Lilian, my heart aches for her too. I thought I saw some knowing in her eyes as she spoke to the Rogues, but it didn't sink in as to why until now; she knows firsthand how badly it hurts to have her soul ripped apart from her mate.

But she survived too, and now she helps others through similar pain—just like her son.

"I so admire you, Luna," I mutter.

Lilian's rhythmic carrot skinning slows. But as she picks up the pace again, her shoulders soften just enough to warm my heart. I figure she won't have anything to say in response, but as her soft voice wavers, I stop chopping to listen to her every breath.

"Thank you for comforting that Omega," she says.

My heart leaps. I clear my throat from threatened tears, unsure if it's the onion or my wobbling emotions. "Oh, no need to thank me. I'm so relieved I could make a difference for her somehow."

Lilian hums. "I can relate."

I adjust my shaky grip on the knife, recalling what Lilian told me when we first met. "I know you're passionate about supporting those who have lost a mate. And I'm not sure how you feel about this, and maybe it's not the same because my ex wasn't my mate, but I never expected to grieve my relationship with him as much as I did. It didn't matter that he hurt me severely; it was still a huge loss in my life. All those expectations, hopes, and trust in life disappeared along with his abuse, and it didn't hit me how much I lost until he was truly gone from my life." My heart hammers wildly as Lilian pauses to glance at me. "I guess I just mean that I could really relate to the Rogues too, in a way. Since I know you can, in your own way."

After a few silent seconds, Lilian returns her focus to her carrots. She slices them faster than I can comprehend, but her tone remains even. "You're spot on in describing that grieving process. Those Rogues still experienced a loss, even if that loss was in their best interest."

The subject is heavy, but my heart inflates with hope; I feel heard.

I hope she does too.

Lilian gives me a passing smile, stowing the vegetables we've sliced before sliding the next cutting board to me.

As we get to work slicing raw beef into large chunks, I try not to stare too long at Lilian as she bursts into action. Her fingers move quickly but gracefully, every minor movement even-tempered and purposeful. But I know she's watching me in her peripherals too, even before she breaks the silence.

"From Omega to Omega, I thought I should warn you that your Alpha is slipping into a bad, *bad* rut."

I have to stop slicing, too distracted by the sharp sting in my chest to think about anything else. "W-what?! How do you know?"

"Agitation. Intense desire. Nearing a fourth full moon without impregnating his mate." She glances at my flat belly, and I flush to my neck. "I'm surprised he hasn't busted in here yet. He has more self-control than I gave him credit for."

Before I can stop it, my underlying anger simmers into a boil, ruining the sense of safety we established moments prior. "Wait. You think I owe him sex? That it's my *job* to calm his sexual urges?"

"No," she snaps back. "But I think you want to carry his pups. Especially now that you didn't question that major portion of the issue."

I swallow hard.

I never thought I'd be talking about my sex life with Lilian. She's basically my mother-in-law.

Lilian pretends not to notice my scent's stinking embarrassment, slicing the last beef chunks for me before tossing them into each massive pot on the stovetop. I follow her to the sink to wash my hands, hoping she said everything she wanted, but she clears her throat.

"Listen, I— I didn't have my mom around to talk about these things with either."

My heart sinks, threatening tears.

Lilian tosses the towel she used to dry her hands, not daring to meet my eyes as she whisks by. "So if you don't want to look at me as you say it, fine. If you just want me to voice it for you, that's okay too. Goddess knows I'm used to mothering shy, soft hearts. I won't judge you for it."

Her track record doesn't really make me believe that.

But one thing is true: I really miss coming to my mom for support with these things. Mom is missing *everything*. When Noah and I do decide it's time to have a baby, she'll miss me giving birth, let alone our baby's first laugh or smile. My lip wobbles, aching for her more than ever.

"You can hide things from me. But don't hide the truth from Noah," Lilian mutters.

My chest tightens. "I'm not! There's no rush to bring a living, breathing baby into the world. We want to take it slow. Noah suggested it, even."

Lilian puts her hand on her hip, stirring the stew with her back to me.

I grip the countertop behind me, stifling my rapid breath.

Lilian chuckles. "That's what he told you? So you want the baby now, and he says what, exactly?"

My breath quivers as I weigh my response, but Lilian doesn't rush me. She's leaving a surprising amount of room for me to speak, her soothing scent softening my shoulders.

"That's between Noah and me," I say.

"Alright, alright."

"We only met four months ago, and I never grew up expecting to be having a baby with someone right away. Noah wants to respect my cultural background."

She drops the lid onto the fifth pot, turning around to face me. Her stare is surprisingly soft.

"You're welcome to believe what you want. But Noah is like his father. He'd rather let something eat him alive inside than let the people around him get hurt."

I chew on my lip. Noah said the exact same to me—well, in less brutal terms.

"Alphas can't keep track of every birth, death, and major life change in the pack, but they *definitely* hear about the bad ones, whether they want to or not. With the way he looks at you, he's never going to force you to carry that risk inside of you. Quite literally."

My heart pounds as I muster up the courage to squeak out a question I'm dying to ask. "Are you saying Alpha Ritchie did something similar? Not wanting to hurt you by having pups?"

She sighs, picking at her nails to hide her reddening cheeks. "I had to drive him wild to get him to crack. He needed me to."

I can't believe she's telling me this. "And it took you a while?"

She smiles at her shoes, more reminiscent of Noah than ever. "No. I let him mate me in front of everyone the day he welcomed me into the pack."

My gut burns with jealousy, revealing the truth no matter how much it shocks me. I guess I really did want to participate in the mating ceremony after my welcome. I just wasn't ready. Noah hasn't realized I've changed my mind since the first ceremony, but how can he? I haven't told him.

Lilian peeks up at me, and I don't bother hiding my regret.

"Between us, she was my doing—Noah's older sister we lost." Lilian's voice comes out as a whisper, tempting me to lean in closer.

But I'm frozen, awestruck by how much she's opening up.

"Noah was my doing too. I almost didn't survive his older sister's loss—physically, I mean. Although, emotionally, it was difficult to survive as well. Very similar to losing a mate, since I developed a soul bond with her immediately." Lilian's voice remains even, but her words gut me. "On top of being afraid for my health, Ritchie didn't want me to have to suffer through another loss. But I had to tell it to him straight. That was the only way he'd feel safe enough to tell me what he wanted—" She bites her lip, staving off tears. "Even if what he wanted could scar me for life."

If Noah is like his parents, and I'm like my parents, they taught me I needed to stifle my wolf. Hide my truths. Even though it was to protect me, I bet they would regret that too, if they saw me now.

Rules can change.

I imagine it: telling Noah what I want, and when I want it,

straight to his face. Watching him open up. Wanting a baby, right now, as badly as me.

Lilian's expression shifts into concern when my lip quivers over huffing, desperate breaths. She waves me over, quickly wetting a washcloth.

"Come here. Lean over the sink."

I do as I'm told, letting tears slip as a blazing fire pushes its way to my skin's surface. She drapes the cloth over the back of my neck, cool water dripping into the sink below me, but it doesn't quell the burn.

All at once, I remember what it felt like to believe I lost Noah after the first day we met; the furious heat that consumed me is all-too-familiar as it whips my insides. I struggle through every breath with sharp gasps, not wanting to go back there. My whole body shakes as the first cramps hit, my desire so strong that I curl over the sink in overwhelm. Noah has always been there to mate the heat out of me, but now it feels stuck. Maybe it's been worsening this whole time, just like Noah's rutting.

Lilian rubs my back, softening her voice. "You're okay. This is normal."

"It hurts."

"Of course it's going to hurt. You have to stop denying your wolf. They're our inner guides, carrying us toward what our hearts crave most. And your dreams are the whole reason you're alive. If you don't nurture her heart in return, what could be more important?"

"B-but I don't want Noah to feel pressured. It really is early. What if we decide to have the baby, and we suddenly don't love each other anymore?"

"You feel the truth in your heart, don't you? Wolves are all heart, no logic. And your heart is what matters here."

"I want it to be all that matters. But what if it's wrong? What if I'm jumping to conclusions again, and he's not the man I think he is?" I slip into panic, struggling to catch my breath between tears. "I don't want someone to hold my dreams against me again, especially not this one. He can say it's my fault he hurt me again if I ask for it. I don't want to give him a reason to hurt me."

Lilian lays her head on my shoulder, rubbing my back as I

shake the two of us with my tears. I inhale as much as I can of her calming scent—at least enough to allow me to breathe again.

"That was then," Lilian says. "This is now."

I close my eyes, letting out a heavy sob at her words.

She holds me in silence before muttering, "How can you know Noah will do the same, unless you ask what he wants?"

"I did ask. This was his answer."

"You told him very clearly you wanted to have a baby?"

"Yes," I groan. "Someday. And he said he wants to wait until we feel ready."

"Did you tell him you were ready to have one *now?*"

I take the napkin Lilian hands me, quickly hiding my dripping nose. "Well… No…"

When she looks at me knowingly, one eyebrow quirking up, I have to laugh through my tears.

"Okay, you're right. I should tell him the entire truth."

Lilian breaks into a gentle smile. "Come sit."

She sets me up with ice water and a refreshed washcloth at the center island. But before I can fully relax, I'm mindlinked.

Sweet Omega, this is my heads up that I'm already on my way over to help you. No need to dissuade me; I'm never too busy for you.

I groan, and Lilian whips around in surprise.

"Noah's ditching work for me," I say.

She chuckles, readying some premade rolls for the oven. "As he should."

For the first time, she allows herself to show pride for her son around me. It both melts and breaks my heart.

Please, universe, Moon Goddess, *someone*—get Lilian to tell Noah how much she really loves him.

Now that I've made my decision to tell Noah, the heat settles enough to be a quiet, tolerable simmer in my gut. I hop off the stool, gathering spices to add to the stew once it boils. Lilian falls into silent dance with me around the kitchen, handing me more food to prepare with her—as if we hadn't just discussed life-altering decisions that could affect the pack for generations.

When Noah finally bursts through the kitchen doors, I do a double-take.

His teal eyes still edge on green, wild and desperate. Just the sight of him makes me want to soothe his stress.

Then the smell hits.

Alpha musk crowds the room, making my knees weak. My core flexes with desire, heat striking me in the gut.

Oh, God. I want to tell him. Not soon. Not tomorrow. *Now.*

10

Lilian plugs her nose, darting for the door. She whispers as she brushes past me. "Leaving you to it, then."

Our Luna hurriedly slams the door behind herself, leaving me alone with Noah. He swallows hard, taking in the full sight of me in my apron.

But he doesn't seem to want to move.

"W-what's wrong?" I ask.

Noah shifts his weight between his feet, his arms flexing and relaxing beneath his jacket over and over like he can't decide how to exist. "I've never wanted anyone this badly in my life."

His rough, quiet voice makes my heartbeat throb all the way to my groin. But Noah remains locked in place.

"Why aren't you over here, then, Alpha?"

He clenches his jaw. "I don't trust my obnoxious wolf."

My shoulders loosen as his restless, adorable wolf nudges mine for attention. "Noah, nothing has changed there; that big, loving goofball won't hurt me. I trust him."

"Not like that. He won't shut up about getting you pregnant."

My breath catches, tempting me to stifle my desires again.

But my wolf steps in.

"Let me ask you something," I whisper. Noah is listening, his full focus engaged on my eyes. I can hardly see straight as our pheromones erupt, calling out to each other. "How soon do mates normally have pups?"

Noah shakes his head, trying to blink away the haze—and failing. His eyes are a bright green, more electric than the summer grass outside the Community Center kitchen window.

"It doesn't matter," he mutters. "'Normal' doesn't mean anything. You and I will go at our own pace, without any pressure from me about Lycan traditions."

I shake my head. "I know. I trust you. That's not what I mean."

Noah's eyes brighten into gold, his wolf letting me know how deeply this moment is hitting him too. "Then what do you mean?"

"I want to know what the *Lycan* expectation is. Not because I want to follow it, but I think Lycans are all instinct, and I want to know if what I'm feeling is— Is it ridiculous, or senseless, or weird, or—"

Biting my lips, I can't bear to look at Noah's tempting stare any longer.

"It's not *weird*," he rasps.

My eyes widen.

"They mate the second they meet," he mutters. "I-I know you know that, but by mating, I mean… *mating*."

It's difficult for him to admit, fear trickling through our bond, and I know it's because he doesn't want to pressure me.

Noah shuffles his feet. "But we didn't agree on trying so soon, so it doesn't matter. And before you can say it matters because you can feel my obnoxious-ass wolf begging you for it, it still doesn't matter."

I rest one hand on my hip. "Oh, really?"

"R-really."

"I disagree. What you want matters to me immensely. And I think I'm more wolf than either of us knew. And it's not just your wolf. I think waiting is becoming pointless when we both want something *now*."

I'm finding it difficult to breathe, caught between Noah's intoxicating smell, my desperation for him, and the way he's gazing at me like he knows exactly how he wants to fuck me silly.

My breath catches just before I speak. "Maybe…"

Noah's wandering expression suddenly hardens. "Maybe? No, that's not sure enough for me."

"Noah, listen to me before you decide what I need."

He freezes, his breath rapid and shallow.

"This isn't a new desire for me. I've agreed with your wolf this whole time. After doing all this work on fears, I know they're not my friend. Most of the time, I never asked for them. They were placed on me. So if I put them all aside, all that's left is my heart. And in my heart, I'm ready to have a baby. With *you*." I take a deep, shaky breath, overwhelmed by Noah's explosive emotions in our bond. "R-right now."

The flash of desire in Noah's eyes speeds my heart into a gallop.

Okay, it's safe to say this is new information to him, as Lilian predicted. He looks like he's seconds away from losing composure.

I ease my hand down my leg, my heart pounding at the way his eyes track my fingers. As I lift my skirt, ever-so-slowly, I huff in tandem with him. Our bond feels like it could burst with lust.

Rotating my exposed thigh to part my legs, I stare at him straight in the eyes. A wolf's challenge for dominance.

Noah races for me, hot hands sending shockwaves of heat to my groin as they land on my lower back.

Crashing into my lips, Noah nips at them between caressing my breasts, thighs, and stomach. I grasp at his belt, overwhelmed by his hands devouring what feels like every inch of my skin, but he's already up my skirt, his thumb kneading my clit. I gasp for more of him, my knees dipping as pleasure sparks up to my throat.

But Noah wastes no time, his fingers slipping into the base of my panties. I shudder into his mouth as he toys with my soaked core, his growl vibrating through my torso.

"Fuck, you're telling the truth. I can smell how badly you want it."

I flush, overwhelmed by his speeding fingers as it is. But when they slip inside me, I have to grip his jacket at the jolt of pleasure it shoots to my heart.

"N-Noah! Ah!"

I buck as his fingers massage my inner wall, pressing my G-spot over and over again. Between the fire in his eyes and his hot breath all over my neck, the heat within me rushes every drop of my blood to my flexing core.

"O-oh, God, I'm already—"

He huffs as I pant against his lips, my legs squirming as I near the edge. "No, not yet. Come here."

Noah guides my stumbling legs to a dining table across the

kitchen, his eyes a bright wolf-yellow. He effortlessly hoists me onto the table, but even with the table's added height, he has to stoop to reach my lips. Our lips glide in a tender massage, Noah's purr buzzing in my throat as I free his throbbing cock. When I lay back for him, Noah squeezes handfuls of my ass.

His hands slide down my thighs, pushing my skirt over my hips and sending shivers up my spine. When my knees drop open for him, he drags me flush against his exposed cock with a huff.

With nothing between us and no plans to use protection, it all becomes real.

My heart leaps into my throat; Noah's eyes are locked on mine. We're startlingly serious. Waiting for the other to move first.

Tugging my panties to the side, I give him enough of my silent permission to break his freeze. Noah lines himself up to enter me, eyes blazing so bright they're almost glowing. My head is fuzzy with need, whimpering in delight at his warm tip completely bare against my entrance.

But I stop him with my palm flat against his chest. "Wait. Not until you answer my question directly."

He flexes, his tip slipping against my core, and I bite back a moan.

But Noah continues to stare, his hands dragging up and down my abdomen beneath my dress in a tantalizing massage. "Goddess, I just can't process that this is happening yet. Are you really sure about this? About me?"

"What I'm sure about is that I want this with you, and only you. Especially if you want it. You matter to me, Noah." I break into a teasing smile. "I also can't make a baby alone."

Noah's chest heaves, a new rush of his yearning scent fluttering my eyelids. When my hips wriggle on their own, nudging his cock against my entrance, Noah whispers the truth.

"I want to get you pregnant. Even more so now that I know you want it too. Today."

A sharp, panging desire in my gut makes me gasp. As my core floods with wet heat, I urge Noah inside me, guiding his cock between my legs.

My heart slams in my chest as he softly pushes into me. We're really doing this. He doesn't need to fully come for it to be possible; my spine alights as I remember his precum could still contain sperm. With how much he dripped for me, he could already have gotten me pregnant.

I grip his arms hard, gasping as my chest heaves. "*Thank* you—"

"Thank *you*. You don't even know how many little steps of this I'm dying for." Noah works his tip in and out of me, each time dragging just a bit closer to fully gliding in. "I want to see your reaction when you find out it worked."

He grips my hips, soaking in my soft, pleading moans with his full attention as his eyes fuck me.

I snatch fistfuls of his jacket. "Please, *please,* go deeper—"

Noah gives me what I want, dropping his forehead against mine as he locks his arms around my hips. My knees raise to my shoulders as Noah lifts my pelvis to meet him, thrusting in slow and heavy. Pleasure crawls up my body as I drop my head back, my heaving moan filling the kitchen.

"I want to hear your voice light up with need for it, just like that," Noah mutters, his breath hot against my throat.

He eases his thick cock back out of me. The drag of his soft, bare skin makes me flex around him.

"N-Noah! More—"

"Fuck," he hisses. "I want to feel your body urging me for it, just like that."

He growls, his shoulders rippling beneath his jacket as he shudders. Re-entering me, Noah doesn't stop until his tip meets my deepest point. Electricity jolts through my legs in the air.

Noah's bare warmth inside me floods my senses. I grip his back, hardly able to keep my claws from extending.

His pace grows, steady and relentless as my body eggs him on, urging trickles of fluid from my core. I grip the table's edge above my head to keep from clawing him, and his thighs bump the edge until its wooden legs creak with every thrust.

"Fuck, you feel so good…"

I can't answer Noah, my moans heightening with every breath.

Noah responds by dropping his torso, pinning me to the table as his pounding thrusts speed to a breathtaking pace.

"Ah! Ah— Alpha!"

He nips at my exposed neck, the burning sting of his fangs

doubling the pleasure of each deep thrust. Squirming frantically beneath him, my back arches with every bump of him against my cervix. My body's reaction wracks me heavily enough to make Noah protect my head, a searing palm replacing the cold wood.

Bristling every one of my nerves, Noah pumps into my sweet spots with every thrust as he moans with me. I come with heaving, desperate jolts, my arching back squeezing him tighter until his moans shift to pleads.

"O-Omega... Oh, Goddess— I can feel every inch of you reacting to me. Fuck, I'm so nervous," he hisses.

"You're safe. If it's too much pressure, you don't have to come today." I embrace Noah hard, kissing his mark. But as he moans, growing thicker with the safety erupting in our bond, I know he's about to come. My legs wrap tight around his ass, my body begging him to fill me. "Oh, it feels so good, Alpha—"

His moans come out heaving and frantic, the wood crackling beneath my hips. The rising pressure his bulging shaft creates in my core pushes wave after wave of delight into me until I spurt on the edge again, no space left inside me for fluid to reside.

Noah slams his hips into me with one final thrust, billowing heat in my abdomen as he fills me. My muscles clench over him, urging more and more out as I cry out in need. He moans against my neck, emptying himself until I writhe with pleasure with how full he's made me. I shudder, his lips smashing against mine as he finishes pumping every last bit of sensation from me.

A rush of his adoring scent mixes with my lust, his every breath sending a blissful ache to my heart. Tears prick my eyes. I'm comforted by his arms wrapping around my back to hold me as my satiated body loosens.

Noah soothes me with slow, breathy licks on my mark. His rut musk is replaced with his usual sweet scent as his weight sinks onto me. My eyes flutter shut, relishing in our mutual satisfaction and his heavy body over me.

"I love you, Omega. I love making you feel good. I want you to have everything you dream of in life."

"God, Noah, I'd be so happy if I could help make this dream come true for you too." My heart aches with love for him, exploding with joy, anticipation, and newfound connection all at once.

But as I fall slack beneath him onto the table, a loud crack startles me from my reverie. I don't have to look to know why: the table is crying out its last words.

"N-Noah, chair!" I frantically point at the seat beside his hips.

He hoists me off the table, keeping his hips cinched to mine to protect our knotted bodies. Still, the sudden shift in position makes us groan in pain.

Dropping himself into the chair, Noah allows me to straddle him, steadying my hips. But with how wet I still am, his expanded girth pushes even deeper into me than it already prodded. Before I can stop myself, I moan with leftover pleasure, my legs twitching around his thighs. Noah heaves beneath me, his hips automatically bucking, and it only makes it worse: my body jerks until Noah cinches his arms tight around my waist, keeping me pressed to his chest.

We're nose to nose, Noah's breath tickling my lips. "You want more, Omega?"

I flush. "I…"

When I test out a slow rock of my hips, delight heats my cheeks. The doting look in Noah's eyes flips my heart, his palms caressing my back like he's loving every second he's tied to me.

When one hand settles behind my head, the other eases over my thigh. It slips over my thigh's ridge, dipping into the sensitive, smooth skin—just beside where he's knotted in me.

"You're gorgeous," he whispers.

His thumb massages my swollen clit, and I jolt from how sensitive it feels. Skating my fingers into Noah's hair, I ease my mouth against his, indulging in the full weight of his lips.

We kiss slowly and heavily, licking each other's tongues like we're soothing the exhaustion from each other.

But Noah's teasing has grown to heavy, circling strokes, my clit sending shockwaves up my chest until tingles reach my neck. As my legs shake over his thighs, Noah's massage turns into a deep, frantic rub.

"Mm! Ah!" I moan into his mouth, filling his lungs with my indulgence.

His hips nudge his shaft into my core, hitting the deepest spot inside me he can. As if that wasn't torturous enough, he growls his next words.

"Goddess, you're doing such a good job."

My breath turns frantic, urging Noah to kiss me as deep as his heavy bulge in my belly. He rocks my hips over him as my core flutters on the edge, enchanted by his touch all over my body. My hips twitch on their own, kneading my core until my legs shiver beside him, widening to sink him as deep as he can reach.

As I come with breathy, gasping moans, Noah smashes his head against mine, nuzzling into my pleased scent. I collapse against his chest, allowing him to hold my entire body in a tight embrace.

But as he rests back against the chair, a loud crack echoes across the room.

The chair bursts beneath our weight in a crackle of wood chips and dust. We're suddenly on the floor, red-faced and wincing in pain.

Noah grips my hips in panic. "Fuck! Are you hurt?!"

"No…" I gasp, patting Noah all over to check for wood shards. Then I gape at the mess beneath him. "But the chair is. I think you smashed it even harder than me."

Glancing around at the splinters circling our bodies, Noah's stare lands back on mine. We burst into laughter at the same time, nuzzling each other's foreheads in disbelief.

"Good thing this place comes out of my pocket," Noah mutters.

"Noah!? You fund this place yourself?"

"N-not *entirely* by myself, but—"

I laugh even harder, squishing his cute, scruffy cheeks. "Oh, come on! Why don't you ever tell me how amazing you are?!"

He groans, hiding his face into my neck. My toes curl, delighted by his soft nudge against my mark. Noah flexes inside me amongst the wood shards, and I suck in a soft breath.

As Noah glances at our bound hips, his expression shifts, and his wolf spins in excited circles.

I giggle. "What is it, my shy Alpha?"

Skating his fingers to my lower abdomen, Noah's soft, pointed touch flips my heart with emotion. Tears rush to my eyes, my breath shaking as he stares back.

"We really did that," he whispers.

It hits me all at once, a blur of frantic, stimulated emotions that force me to cling to Noah for dear life. He holds me tighter, and it only adds to my excitement pile.

"Holy shit. I could be pregnant right now. With your— Your—" I can't speak through hiccupping tears, smiling and crying just the same.

"Oh, my sweet, sweet Omega," Noah chuckles. He soothes me with his loving scent, his voice delicate as he rests his forehead against mine. "I-I can't believe it either, but yeah. You could be."

He strokes my stomach in gentle circles with the back of his hand, his wolf nuzzling mine in our bond. All at once, my heart snaps, his touch registering as something bigger: a sign of what I've always dreamed of. Noah really does want this too. I can feel it. I drop my head against his chest, breaking into weeping sobs.

"Aliya…" His warm hands soothing my body make me cry harder, my thoughts spilling out of me.

"I never thought I'd have this—" I shake through tears, unable to get any other words out.

Noah kisses my neck, shoulders, and cheek, loving me all over as his deep voice shifts to a whisper. "I know. I've always felt how badly you wanted this. I'm here."

I grip his back, holding him as tight to my body as I can. "Thank you. Thank you so much. Thank you for wanting this with me."

"I should be the one saying that. You'd be the best mom—" Noah chokes up, his quiet voice breaking with tears. I whimper, nuzzling him.

As our lips meet, salty with tears, there's no doubt in my mind about him being the best dad for our future pups.

11

Three days before the next Full Moon Ceremony, my wolf cuddles against Noah's side as we walk. Rainn walks alongside us, her poofy, brown wolf tail wagging every time she looks at us together.

Rainn is painfully cute in all ways. Her puppy energy never fails to make me smile, but especially in her fluffy wolf form, forcing me into happy pants at the sight of those bright green eyes adoring her big brother. I can understand how Noah sees her as his precious baby sister, no matter how old she is. When we become parents someday, I wonder if he'll look at our baby the same way.

He nuzzles Rainn's ear as if he can hear my thoughts, and my heart warms at Rainn's happy whine.

But Noah's fur bristles, freezing us in place. My wolf stiffens, shocked by the sudden seriousness in my mate.

Then I hear it too: a sharp, petrified yelp.

Noah bursts into a sprint, but time slows. Scents vivify, even to my inexperienced nose, and it hurts my head. Angry, bitter Alpha pheromones mix with a nauseating sting of an Omega in danger. It strikes such a primal fear into me that my wolf loses all ability to move.

But Noah is the opposite. He dives straight for the smell's source, racing to the outskirts of our territory. My wolf's nocturnal eyes allow me to see his massive, shadowy form hunker into a deeper sprint in the pitch-black tree line. With his sharp, attacking movement and a roaring snap of his jaws, another large form scampers away.

Satisfied by his chase, Noah turns to sniff something on the ground, which is when Rainn dashes over to help. I'm too terrified to be left alone, so I slink into the leaves and crawl, fighting my fear to follow Noah's little sister.

But what we find horrifies me far further than anything I expected to see today. My mind absorbs everything in simple, quick glances, my PTSD in overdrive: big Alpha just left. Omega is on the ground. Omega is bleeding. Noah and Rainn lick the Omega's wounds. Omega is whimpering like she's scared for her life.

Noah is *mad*.

The pounding of paws against dry leaves approaches rapidly. I don't have time to think before a wolf blasts into Noah's side. A black Alpha.

I yipe in fear, but Rainn tackles me out of the way of Noah's massive form just in time. I scramble back on my paws, shoving myself into a bush, but Rainn is pure focus despite her panicked scent; she drags the injured Omega to my side in the leaves before huddling up with us in a shaking, petrified mass.

My senses burst into overdrive. Noah's fangs flash in the moonlight. He gnashes at the attacker, his fury burning through our bond.

Just by their musky, angry smell, I can tell they're both stubborn Alphas—a sign this won't end quickly. My whines escalate as the wolf bites Noah back, nowhere near giving up.

I don't want my mate to die, Rainn!

But Rainn squishes her side into the stranger Omega and me, keeping a steady barrier between us and the thrashing wolves. *It's okay! Let them work it out. This is necessary.*

No! My mate—

Look at me, future Luna.

Everything in me tells me to either run or fight. But I trust Noah, and therefore I trust Rainn. I gaze into Rainn's emerald eyes, and she whines.

I promise you, he's okay. This happens a lot with Rogues.

My heart flips. *This Alpha is a Rogue?*

No, the Omega is a Rogue, seeking refuge in Greenfield, and the Alpha wants her back. So now this is another dominance challenge—

an extra violent one because Noah is threatening to take this Alpha's mate from him. Judging by what he just did to her, it's no wonder she went Rogue.

This poor Omega, burrowing into my side until her blood seeps into my fur, is the Alpha's mate? I want to vomit, but my whole body shakes hard instead, having to watch my mate get bit just as much as he bites.

I underestimated how disturbing Noah's life must be. How can he find the strength to still fight, day after day of witnessing something this horrific? *I'm* too scared to even help this hurt Omega. My lungs tighten until I can hardly breathe, my frantic whines competing with Noah's angry snarls. All I can do is cover the injured Omega's eyes with my snout, the two of us shaking together like terrified baby birds.

This Alpha smells different than the one who attacked Noah at my Welcoming Ceremony, so I'm not concerned they're connected. I'm not sure that matters; I don't want Alphas to keep showing up to hurt Noah, regardless. I don't want *anyone* to.

But this attack feels different. Fiercer. It's enough to not only terrify my mate, but also to enrage him to a level I've never witnessed before. I'm shocked by the way he treats this Alpha, using his massive body weight to slam them into the ground harder than I think the Alpha could survive. The challenger wolf yelps in pain, no longer snarling back. But Noah isn't done. His anger only rises, forcing me to cower in a shaking heap.

I know this is necessary. The Omega beneath me should never have been treated this way, and we can't allow wolves to get away with abuse on Greenfield territory.

Seeing Noah like this scares me, nonetheless. He tears into the Alpha, not stopping even when it reeks of iron. It's an animalistic justice system, Noah's rapid decision-making giving the Alpha a direct consequence.

When the abusive Alpha curls into a petrified ball beneath my mate, unwilling to move, Noah finally stops. I feel like I could pass out from stress, wobbling on my paws.

Yasmine and Dave finally arrive as backup muscle, but Noah already downed this massive Alpha, alone, in minutes. His Betas tug the black, limp wolf deeper into the forest, and Rainn gets to work licking the Omega's wounds. Noah hasn't looked at me yet. He's pacing in circles, only stopping to shake out his fur. It's only a few more seconds before more Lycans arrive, helping the injured Omega towards safety in the Greenfield territory.

But when Noah approaches me in the dark forest, his eyes are still wild with adrenaline. I can only see the blood in his black fur by how it glistens in the moonlight.

His shadowy form towering above me sets my brain off, an old, familiar horror creeping to the forefront of my mind. Before it's too late, I try to stave it off. To dissociate, or anything else instead. But I can't stop it.

My whines turn into terrified, screeching cries as a memory plays out before me. I try to scramble away from it, but my paws slip in the leaves.

But before I can escape, Noah stands over me on all fours, his eyes tracking mine. *Omega?! What's wrong? He didn't hurt you, did he?!*

Noah whines with me, nudging my cheeks as I live in two places at once, the past consuming most of my focus.

When he nips the back of my neck, jolting me back to the present, I find my claws digging deep into Noah's fur. Fear strikes my heart.

I hurt my mate.

My wolf shrieks again. *S-sorry! I didn't mean to—*

Shh, Omega. It's okay. You're safe. He wraps his wolf body around me, burrowing his nose against my neck as I whine in exhaustion. *You're right here with us. Rainn and I are here to protect you.*

My body still violently trembles as the two wolves cuddle into me, licking away my stress. It takes me ages to feel like I can breathe. When I come up to the surface, soaking in the cool breeze through my fur, I realize what just happened.

I hardly have energy to even mindlink. *I'm sorry, Noah. I haven't had a flashback that bad in so long.*

It's not your fault. I'm sure this was incredibly shocking for you.

I don't know how you can come home to me fine after that. How do you handle all of this?

I don't, I just mask it all. But this is also healing for me. It's so fucking hard, but all I know is that I can't just sit here and let it all happen. I need to do something. His wolf nibbles his mark on my neck with a frantic, affectionate whine. *It's never been this bad, and it's been getting worse. I didn't want to scare you because I wanted to believe I had it under control, but I don't. There are more and more Alphas I've found who believe in total domination, and they hate me for saying their entire belief system is bullshit. I'm so fucking sorry you have to now see the consequences.*

For a moment, I don't know what to say. I feel horrible this is all resting on Noah, especially when there are also Lycans in our pack who disagree with him. How can they look at bleeding Omegas like this one and not see what's wrong here?

I let out an uncontrollable whine. *I still feel safe, just with the fact that you're aware that this is a problem. On top of that, you're actually trying to change it, rather than buddying up to other Alphas just because they're Alphas. I can't even tell you how much your refuge must mean to Omegas like this one. You just risked your life for her. For all Omegas. You're irreplaceable, Noah.*

Noah shuffles his snout deeper into my coat, gratitude seeping through the aching sadness in his scent. It's a long while before he mindlinks again. *I'm protecting Alphas too, they just don't realize they're hurting themselves. I wish I could show them they're enough, just as they are.*

I wish too. But I don't want them to hurt you in the meantime.

I don't want them to hurt you either, which is why I'm not backing down. These fights are worth it to me.

I whimper, knowing this is how the pack lives. And no matter how impossible it feels to get used to witnessing fights, I know I have to eventually.

Why can't I just get over it?

12

Noah holds me for a few hours at my parents' cottage, burrowing into my bed with me in the tightest cuddle ball we can manage.

But when he has to leave to do his nightly perimeter check before he returns to sleep for the night, I try my best not to show my fear as I say goodbye.

Giving him a weak smile, I squeeze his hand. "See you soon, love."

Noah pauses at the front door, his fingertips delicately brushing my hair behind my ears. "I'll be back in less than an hour, okay? Then we'll fall asleep together."

I nod, giving him the best smile I can manage.

After a kiss goodbye, Noah shifts at the forest's edge, disappearing into the darkness.

When I shut the door, I'm faced with a huge problem.

Not this fucking lock.

Twisted all the way open to the left, the front door's brass lock taunts me with my worst fears: *Steven will come back someday, and it'll be all your fault.*

Again.

A rage boils inside me like I've never felt, spouting to the surface in violent, sloshing bubbles. It's so much worse now that I'm alone; no one's here to distract me long enough, or to create enough social pressure to shove my PTSD below the surface. I'm terrified of the agitation stirring in my body, begging me to release it.

What if I lose control and hurt myself this time by accident?

I've never lost control before, but I can recognize whose voice this is. OCD is teaming up with PTSD to trap me even deeper.

But naming it doesn't make a difference tonight. My distress feels too powerful to manage with acknowledgement, my first line of defense, which terrifies me even more. Worse than being alone, I'm being attacked within my own body, unable to stop reliving my worst moments.

How could you let this happen to yourself, Aliya? How could you let Steven do that?

That brutal, doubtful thought stabs a hole in my soul. Was it actually my fault?

No, I've been over this. This was done to me. He was intentionally shocking, horrific, and out of my control.

I'm not sure that's any better. The truth is so ugly, burning acid through my veins with each staggering pump of my heart. How could he do this to me?

Rushing to my couch, I grip the nearest pillow to scream into. My voice ripples through the cotton, escaping from the seams until it fills the room despite my death grip muffling it.

But it just makes me angrier.

I still can't believe that man changed me so severely, and now his actions are affecting Noah. I hate feeling like I'm walking poison, spreading my pain to everyone in my life thanks to Steven. As vivid chunks of his break-in replay, I wish I could go back in time and bite him to shreds.

Guilt gnaws at my stomach for thinking of hurting someone.

See? You're twisted, Aliya. A fucking monster.

But even deeper, I'm more than simply angry at Steven, at myself, and at life. My hands shake, eyes darting back to that door. Waiting for him to come back to hurt me again, just like I've anticipated for years.

I'm still so fucking afraid of him.

"I hate it!" I scream, filling the silent cottage with my rage. I don't want to live like this for the rest of my life.

But I don't have a choice. Steven forced this on me, and now his brutality is superglued to my DNA.

I chuck the pillow across the room as hard as I can. It smashes into one of Mom's candles above the fireplace—a slow-motion rocking that ends in a heavy topple.

I gasp as the candle crashes to the ground, snapping clean in half.

It wasn't anything special. But just like the rest of the decorations covering the entire cabin, it was Mom's.

Aching sadness breaks me out of my panic. The room is eerily silent as I pant, filled with emotions I don't know how to hold.

What the fuck is wrong with me? I need to calm down.

Noah's concern ripples through our bond. *Omega, I was on my way back, but now you seem—*

No, please continue with your work. I'm actually glad you didn't have to witness my ridiculous outburst. I'm going to force myself to lay down now.

By the time I reach my room, my heaviest emotion is embarrassment. I strip my clothes as quickly as I can, begging for this night to end.

Picking up Noah's shirt from last night, I inhale his lusty scent from just before he had sex with me. My core pools with heat—a welcome shift in sensation as pleasurable memories fill my mind.

Slinking into his shirt, I grip the closet shelf like I did last night, reaching between my legs.

As I rub myself over the thin fabric of my panties, I imagine Noah's hands all over me, unable to contain his moans as he slunk into my core from behind, bare.

"Ah..." My breath escapes me as a moan, a rising urge to feel something, *anything* except pain overtaking my mind.

I dig through my closet for a long-lost sex toy, desperate to cling to my desire while I still feel good.

When I see my dildo, I have to laugh. I used to think this was too huge for me, but that was before I had a Lycan mate to lick me silly.

As I close my eyes, sitting myself over it, I imagine it's Noah.

But for some reason, it stings. That hasn't happened for many months.

My heart spikes with fear, amplifying the pain. Yanking it out, I quickly soothe myself with gentle strokes, redirecting my focus to Noah.

My mate. If he were here, he'd start by rubbing me back and forth until I couldn't stand it.

I rub my clit in small circles, pleasure returning to the surface. Inhaling Noah's shirt, I flush hot. Within a few minutes, I'm almost as wet as he makes me.

Oh, duh. I should've been using lube. Digging through my toy bin, I find the bottle with shaking hands. Breathe, Aliya.

I apply a generous amount to the toy before using the rest to thoroughly coat my labia, leaving me breathless. But when I press the toy's tip into me, a sharp pain shoots up my spine just the same.

Panting, I pull it back with a wide, petrified stare. This is just a temporary trauma response, right? No, I don't know that for sure. It might not be temporary at all.

I'm losing the good feelings by the second.

This time, I ditch the toy altogether, settling on using my own hands. These are my fingers, I remind myself. I'm safe, and in control of this moment.

As I slip one finger in, I pause, waiting to feel pain. When it only feels better, my cheeks flush as I remember Noah's desperate breath in my ear last night. I imagine myself backing up over him, shoving him deeper.

"Ah, Noah..." My legs squirm, remembering how hard he came into me, filling me until I overflowed onto the carpet—and leaving us to giggle after as we wiped it up before bed.

Curling my fingers against my favorite spot, my hips arch for more as I replay the memory.

"Noah... Don't stop—"

But the second I come, a heavy, sinking despair re-enters my soul. I deflate against the carpet, my heart still pounding as I stare at my failed attempts to feel better—just another mess to clean up before bed.

After cleaning the toy and myself, I climb into bed, pulling the covers over my head. The second I fall limp, a thought flashes through my mind.

Did you lock the door, though?

"Shut up!" I growl.

I close my eyes, feeling immediately foolish for yelling back at my intrusive thoughts.

Okay, let's try that again. Maybe I locked the door, or maybe I didn't. I don't know. Right now, I'm resting in bed. Waiting for Noah. That's all I have to accomplish at the moment.

Redirecting my thoughts to the present allows any remaining intrusive thoughts to brush past me. After a few minutes, I notice my back and neck aching.

I'm so tired. I forgot how draining trauma can feel.

My eyes zip open. *What if I'm pregnant and all this stress is hurting the baby?*

Fear worms its way back into my mind, stirring my limbs in hot acid. Hugging Noah's pillow against my stomach, I burrow into his scent, allowing it to soothe me.

I've slept with Noah most nights, trading beds and houses every few days since we still haven't moved in together. Now that I think about it, I haven't had a PTSD nightmare since I met Noah, and I don't think it's a coincidence. I feel so safe beside him.

I let my mind seek Noah's wolf in our bond, forgetting everything else for a while. I don't know where he is exactly, but I can feel his paws rushing across the forest floor. As my eyelids droop, I live through his wolf, filled with his determination to return to his mate's side.

But he's not here yet. It's too early to fall asleep.

My eyes jerk back open. *Noah, I'm afraid to fall asleep and have flashback nightmares.*

Our bond ripples in shared pain, pushing a whimper out of me.

Oh, sweet Omega... I'll be there soon. Just rest, and don't be so hard on yourself, okay? Everything will be okay. Maybe not great, but okay. We'll find a way to get through whatever happens, together.

I cling to his words as tight as I hug his pillow, unable to respond from how exhausted I am.

But then I have the dream. Not the good one with Noah, and not the bad one where my parents are dying again. The one about the lock. I know exactly how this dream ends, but every time, it makes me scream.

Because I know it's not just a dream. It really happened.

When I wake up already shrieking, I want to believe I'm still dreaming. There's a shadow of a man in my dark room.

13

My screams shift from grief to panic. I grip my blankets to shield my body from the man's reach. But he approaches anyway, his voice barely registerable beneath my shrieks.

No! I can't let this repeat!

Extending my claws, I slash his outstretched arm as hard as I can.

"Fuck!" Noah backs himself up against the wall beneath my window, gripping his bleeding arm.

Guilt crushes my heart, pushing a sob from me. But as Noah stops the blood with heavy licks, he's only focused on me.

It's just me! I'm not going to hurt you.

I scramble off the bed after him, clinging to him so hard that my fingers hurt. "I'm so sorry! I'm terrible, I—"

"Stop. Please, stop. I'm so sorry for scaring you so badly." Noah's voice shakes in agony, and it guts me. "I should've known better when you're already feeling so—"

My breath catches when I think I hear the front door squeak. "N-no! He's back! He's here—"

Noah releases a heavy waft of his Alpha musk, and before I can register it, my neck falls slack in submission. He licks my mark, heavy and wet strokes sinking me to my knees. He drops to the carpet with me, allowing my limp body to quiver in his embrace.

Noah's gentle voice softens even more for me. "I don't smell anyone else here. It's just you and me, sweet Omega."

"N-no... *Please*, he's going to—"

I wheeze as the memory pushes past Noah's soothing effects

on me, replaying like it's happening now. I squirm away from Noah's tongue, suddenly afraid of being touched.

He raises his empty hands. "Shit— Okay. Let's try something else."

The panic is still so strong that I jerk back, attempting to sit up and away from Steven in my mind's replay. My back hits my mattress hard, smacking the air out of me. I yelp in pain, gripping Noah's chest.

"Oh, fuck, my poor, sweet mate." Noah rubs my aching back, allowing me to cower back into him despite pushing him away seconds ago. As I crawl into his lap, he welcomes me with gentle, measured sweeps over my back. "What's he going to do when he comes back in? Let it out."

My breath sputters as I fight the memory back, trying to shove it down, down, down with angry shakes of my head.

"No, don't do that. Don't bottle it up. It's literally killing your heart to keep it inside; I can feel it." Noah hugs my head against his chest, grounding me. "Talk me through it. Tell me what you see happening."

I grip Noah's shirt until the seams crackle. My entire body shakes in his arms. "H-he's... He'll..."

"Good job. Keep going." Noah says.

"He'll... O-open the front door. I forgot to lock it." I swallow hard, making pathetic, weird cries between breaths. "But he has a key anyway. From when we dated."

Noah's heart sinks with mine, pounding harder against my ear.

"I should've made him give it back. I should've changed the lock, I should've made sure I locked it, I should've—"

"No, you didn't know he'd do this. That was his decision alone."

"Y-yeah..." My voice comes out small and fragile, almost childlike. It's unfamiliar to me, but it's also completely me.

"Then what?" Noah asks.

"Then he'll storm in here, and—" I shake my head, whimpering at the clearest portion of my memory. "I'm scared of him, Noah. He's so scary, standing over me."

"I've got you, Omega. I'm right here with you, and he can't hurt you this time."

I nod, glancing over to the bed. "He's going to climb up onto my bed... From the left side..."

Anger blazes through Noah—just as strong as the rage that broke Mom's candle tonight.

"Fuck," he hisses. "*No*... *This same bed?*"

I whimper, resorting to frantic nodding; I can't manage to speak another word.

Noah whines, rocking me. "Don't you think of it every night, laying in this bed? Did you even move the bed? Get a new mattress?"

"No, because initially... It was my fault. I made him mad."

"Oh, sweet— Fuck, Goddess, no— That's nowhere near true!"

"I know. I know the truth now." I catch my breath, my panic resorting to weeping. "It wasn't my fault. He just told me it was, and I wanted to believe him instead of facing the truth. Because I don't know why someone would hurt me like that, Noah. I didn't even want to hurt him back to stop him. I couldn't."

Noah scoops me from his lap, hunching over me like he's protecting me from the world.

"Tomorrow, we're doing something about that bed. You don't need to be tortured like this." His voice is quiet. Shattered. The gravity of his grief makes my pain feel even more real. "But tonight, we're leaving."

I release a slow exhale, my shaking limbs loosening in Noah's arms. "Please. Get me out of here."

"Can I carry you? Or will that make it worse?"

"No, please, hold me. I want to feel you against me."

Noah hoists me into his care, whisking me from my room. My room's details are swallowed by the dark hall, the childhood my parents gave me nowhere to be seen. Noah is right. All I see is that mattress.

"I'm here," Noah says. "We're going far away from here, okay?"

Noah carries my body through the woods, his emotions dipping and aching with mine.

I feel so shattered inside that I can't speak. I've fallen numb.

I close my eyes, listening to Noah's strained breath. Feeling his hot chest against my cheek. It steels me in reality, allowing me to take one breath after another. Surviving minute to minute.

Until the adrenaline wears off in the thick of the woods, and I feel horrendously sick.

Noah rushes to hold my hair back as I jump out of his arms, seconds before I empty my stomach into the leaves. I cling to Noah's quiet reassurances with every heave of my stomach, hating how weak I feel. But Noah's emotions aren't disgusted, angry, and hot like mine are; he's mourning for me.

When I'm done, I can't even cry. I reach for Noah, and he gingerly lifts me back into his arms.

By the time we reach his den, I'm half asleep and hollow.

Noah sets me down just long enough to shift into his wolf form, his wet nose nudging me into his side. It's easy to curl up into our usual spot together, hiding in his black fur.

The next morning, my heart breaks when I see the wound I gave Noah's arm. He jolts awake as I frantically lick the hot red gash, desperate to heal him and undo what I've done.

But Noah doesn't say a word, stroking my hair. When I realize he's not wincing at all, instead gazing down with worry, I pause to stare back through rush after rush of guilt.

"Sweet Omega, I need to tell you something, okay?" Noah swallows hard.

I grip his hand, giving his arm another soft lick. *Okay.*

"My mom's facial scar wasn't from another wolf. It was from me," Noah says.

My heart skips, tightening my throat. "What do you mean?"

"I didn't realize she was coming to rescue me from the past. And last night, you didn't realize I was coming to rescue you either. It's okay. Really, it is."

It seems like a challenge for Noah to hold eye contact with me, but I'm having the exact opposite reaction.

With how closed off Steven made me, I'm shocked to feel more open than ever after reliving his damage. Gazing deep into Noah's vulnerable stare, my mate makes me feel raw, gaping, and exposed.

But not afraid.

I stroke Noah's cheek. When he kisses my palm, fluttering my heart, I can't resist climbing into his lap.

"When I'm with you, I feel understood," I whisper.

Noah burrows his nose into my neck, his emotions spiking with elation in our bond. As we hold each other, our bond welds tighter than ever.

After the summer sun has risen high enough to heat our den, Noah takes me back to my parents' cabin.

But he stops me on the front porch. "Don't force yourself to come in. I only brought you home to grab your clothes so you can stay with me for a while. And, if you want—" He takes a deep breath. "I can get rid of your mattress."

My heart flips.

He's taking what happened to me so seriously. I never even told him how much that mattress bothered me. He really does understand.

I lace my fingers into his, stroking his big hand with my thumb. "I'd like that, but mattresses are so expensive. That's the other reason why I never changed it."

Noah glances at my cabin, his emotions dampening.

I step closer. "What are you thinking? Tell me honestly."

"I—" He winces, struggling to meet my eyes. "I don't think it's healthy for you to live here. Mattress or no mattress."

My heart sinks, knowing he's right.

"I-I know it's your parents' place, so that's not for me to decide, but—"

"No, that's exactly it," I mutter. "It's my parents' place, not mine. And after what he did, it never fully felt like home again. I didn't even bother changing anything."

As I bite my lip, Noah strokes my shoulders, peeking into my eyes. "D-do you… Want to move somewhere else?"

"Um… I wasn't planning on—"

"Ugh, no. Sorry. That's not what I want to ask." Noah's feet shuffle as he drops his head, suddenly shy again. "Do you want to move in— W-with me?"

Despite everything that's happened, I break into a beaming smile. The bright laugh that spills from me surprises us both.

"I'd *love* to, my shy Alpha."

Noah releases a heavy sigh, his nose brushing mine as we embrace. "Ugh, you're so cute. Don't feel pressured by me, okay? I just thought it would be a good time to ask, since—"

I laugh, squeezing him closer. "Noah, we're hoping to have a baby! Of course I want to move in with you!"

His bright laughter spurs more giggles from me. Noah kisses my forehead, softening his voice. "I guess we did do this a bit out of order. I just didn't want to pressure you to let go of your childhood home, and I knew we'd figure out our living situation when the time came."

I sigh through a laugh. "Me too; it didn't even cross my mind. I guess I just trust us to make anything work."

Our smiles widen by the second.

Noah draws me closer. "But y-you really want to move into my place, for now? You're ready to?"

"God, yes. Please. I want to wake up beside you every day, and hold you every night."

Noah chuckles, kissing my forehead. On the inside, his wolf bounds around mine, making me giggle. "We already do that, my sweet Omega. I can't last a night without you."

"I know, but—" I drag my nose down the side of his, shyness swallowing the strength in my voice. "I also get why it felt like a big step for you to ask. We don't stay in one place we call 'home' together."

Noah's eyes soften as he gazes deep into my stare. "You're right, we don't. I love the sound of that."

"I love it too," I whisper.

As we break into soft smiles for each other, Noah kisses me as gently as he can, leaving my heart aching.

But it's already aching anyway. My trauma still sits beneath the surface, torn back open and bleeding.

I chew on the inside of my cheek. "Before I go back in to pack a few things, are you still okay with helping me do something about that mattress?"

Noah's face dissolves into its stoic default. "Absolutely. Stay here."

I'm shocked at how resolute he sounds, disappearing into my

parents' cottage. Seconds later, he's dragging my mattress out the front door—well, more like chucking it off the front porch.

I jump back, gripping my chest. I hadn't realized how much Noah had been boiling beneath the surface until he hops over my porch railing, claws extended. Noah tugs the mattress through the dirt with one hand, veins rippling down his arms. He looks like he's dragging my ex into the forest by the hair.

As I rush to catch up with him, Noah tosses his clothes off in a sudden frenzy, shifting into his wolf. The sight of him so upset floods me with more emotions than I can process until I can't feel at all, minus the wild, painful pounding of my heart.

After gathering my wits, I help Noah's furious wolf yank the mattress, spraying dry leaves around us as its corner drags through the earth. Triumphing over all other emotions, anger rises in my chest, making it hard to take steady breaths. Noah's thrashing paws charge me, mixed fury and pain zapping through our bond. Noah drops the mattress and meets my eyes.

With the mattress tossed in the small clearing behind my parents' cottage, Noah shifts back to his human form and slips back into boxers. But my heart aches just looking at the mattress.

Noah links his arms around my waist before tucking my head beneath his chin. "I love you."

I grip his bare back, my jaw tense. "I love you too, Noah."

He lowers his head to meet my eyes. One glance at the exhausted bags under his eyes ignites a fire in my heart that I didn't know I was stoking.

I back up from Noah, shaking out my hands.

Worry creases his eyes. "What's wrong?"

"I don't want to hurt you."

"What do you mean? Why would you hurt me?"

"I'm—" My throat tenses around my swallow, clenching harder than my teeth.

"Angry?"

He's right, but I shake my head through threatened tears, not wanting to feel it. Noah misunderstands this as dismissing his guess.

"Then, what? Hurt?"

I seethe, my gaze landing back on that mattress. "No, you were right. I'm so angry that I'm scared. Which makes me even angrier. I'm sick of being scared."

He closes the gap between us, gathering my head in his palms. "Then be fucking angry. This situation is infuriating. He *never* should have done this to you."

The vivid anger in Noah's voice amplifies both my rage and my fear, my breathing rate rapidly rising.

"I-I don't like seeming angry."

"Why? You're too emotional? Too *wild?*"

"Y-yes."

"Who told you that?"

My cheeks flush, tears pricking my eyes. "He did."

"Well, he's fucking *wrong*." Noah's words vibrate through me, making my teeth chatter. "You're a wolf. Get angry. Lose your shit. No one has to know but us."

Just as I'm about to, Noah's emotions dip. His warped expression guts me, pushing fresh tears down my cheeks.

"But please, Aliya, if nothing else, don't hold this in anymore. Don't force yourself to sleep with this nightmare every night, carrying it all alone."

Following Noah's point back to the mattress, it's never been clearer what it represents to me. He's spot on, and that enrages me. My hands ball into fists, my lungs shaking with every exhale.

Noah drops his forehead against mine, his hot breath beating against my lips. "Good. Let it out."

My vision's color warps, my wolf on the verge of showing herself. I growl, gripping Noah's hands still on my cheeks.

"Destroy it. Tear that mattress to fucking shreds." Noah's voice is dark and commanding, rippling bristles through my wolf's fur.

But my heart wavers. My wolf takes a step back with my doubt, the poor girl slumping to the ground in our bond.

"B-but... What if I do something I can't take back?" My voice comes out dry and small.

"Like what?"

"Like... Getting too angry."

"I don't understand. Who would you be hurting by being angry over this?"

I swallow over and over, unable to choke out the words as hot tears sting my eyes. "Him."

"He hurt you, Omega. Fuck him!"

"I *know* it's ridiculous, but I still don't want to hurt him back." I blubber through fresh, shuddering tears.

"Oh, my sweet, sweet…" Noah's shaking touch skates down the back of my head, smoothing my messy hair before he cups my cheeks. "He's not here to get hurt. And even if he was, you have a right to be furious, regardless of how he feels about it. He hurt you, and it's okay for him to face the consequences. To take responsibility for the very *real* damage he caused."

I suck back snot. "T-then… What if I scare you from what I say? Or traumatize you? What if I let my anger get too out-of-control?"

"Go ahead. I *dare* you." Noah's growling anger isn't directed towards me; it's in honor of me.

If this was a few months ago, I'd be amazed that a man's obvious anger doesn't scare me. But I know why it doesn't.

"I trust you, Noah."

"I trust you too. And I trust your anger. It's there for a reason, and I want to see it."

"I-it's ugly."

"I disagree. It protected the love of my life when no one else was willing to."

In a confusing mix of love and rage, my heart boils over.

But as I approach the mattress, it looks larger than ever. I try to imagine punching, kicking, or folding it, but its plushy flexibility has never seemed more indestructible.

"What do I even do with it? Should I shift? My wolf could destroy it in ten seconds." I gaze back at Noah for an answer, but his rigid stare at the mattress tells me what I need to know. "No, you're right. I need to destroy this in the same, human form that he destroyed me in."

But it's not only me Steven destroyed. I watch my words stab my mate, his eyebrows warping and lips reddening before he lets out a desperate gasp. As tears roll down his cheeks, Noah's heavy, insurmountable pain in our bond sparks the fire in me into a roaring beast, exploding in my chest.

Gripping the mattress in both hands, I use my entire weight's momentum to thrust it across the forest floor. Pouncing on it, I dig my claws in, letting out a growl as I rip it open.

The angry yell that escapes me shocks me just as much as the damage I've already done. I freeze, panting through my fears of causing harm. I feel trapped.

But Noah gasps through his crackling voice behind me. "Fuck, yes! Keep going! Don't stop!"

I listen to my Alpha, but I don't need much convincing.

Digging my heels into the dirt, I ram the edge of the mattress with my shoulder. Not just shoving it to coat it in mud—pushing it away from me.

But nothing feels far enough away. I scream, kicking the mattress in frustration. It hardly even budges, and I deflate. "Fuck!"

Noah rushes to my side. "Tell me why you're angry. Let your thoughts out."

My voice gets caught in my chest, my cheeks on fire. All I can do is shake my head; a heavy weight in my ribcage pins my shins to the ground, hardly allowing me to breathe.

Noah hoists the mattress upright, standing it below his chin.

"Fuck it up, Omega. Rip it to shreds."

Using every last ounce of my strength, I pull myself back up on staggering legs. I lunge at the mattress, my growl shifting into a scream.

"I fucking hate him!"

Noah has to brace the mattress in the center as I claw through, foam flying as I grasp massive chunks.

"Why?" He asks.

"Because—"

I choke back tears as I grasp one of the largest shreds of fabric at the top, yanking on it.

"Because he made me so afraid! I'm going to have to live in fear, forever, and it's all his fault!"

Noah has to cling to the mattress with a firmer hold, my fury nearly tearing it from his grasp.

"He ruined sex for me, making it impossible to feel good! He made me think I deserved it!"

I rip into the largest remaining chunk of foam with my teeth, muffling my tears with it. As I spit it out, I grab the mattress for myself, and Noah gladly allows me.

When I see his chest heaving through heavy, face-contorting tears, I only cry harder.

"I hate how he made you have to do this with me!" I throw the mattress down, stomping it into the dirt.

When my foot snags on the rip, Noah is there to catch me before I fall, wrapping his arms around my waist. He sobs into my shoulder harder than I've ever heard him cry, tearing my heart in half. I drop to the mattress on my knees with him, hugging his arms around my waist as he curls over me.

"I wish I was there," he says. "I wanted to be there. I wanted to meet you so badly. I just didn't know who you were. I wish I knew."

No matter how desperate he is to hide his face, I force my body to turn until he allows me to dive for his chest.

Hugging his head to my pounding heart, I take a deep breath. To my surprise, I finally feel like I can breathe.

Dropping my head to the sky, I let out the heaviest exhale I have in years.

Noah rubs my whole back, kissing my collarbone. "You did so well. Thank you."

I don't understand exactly why he's thanking me, but for whatever reason it makes me smile.

Then I laugh, relief flooding my system.

Noah pops up, startled.

"I'm not there anymore, Noah. I made it out." I laugh again, hugging his head. "And now I'm sitting in the middle of the forest. With my mate, who I love to have sex with. Who I feel good with… Surrounded by tiny little pieces of a mattress that we're going to have to clean up."

Noah shakes his head, breaking into a soft chuckle. "I fucking *love* you—"

Smashing my lips against Noah's, I hum into his mouth as his arms squeeze my entire torso from head to hips. His cold, wet cheeks slip against mine, his body flush to mine as I work his tongue.

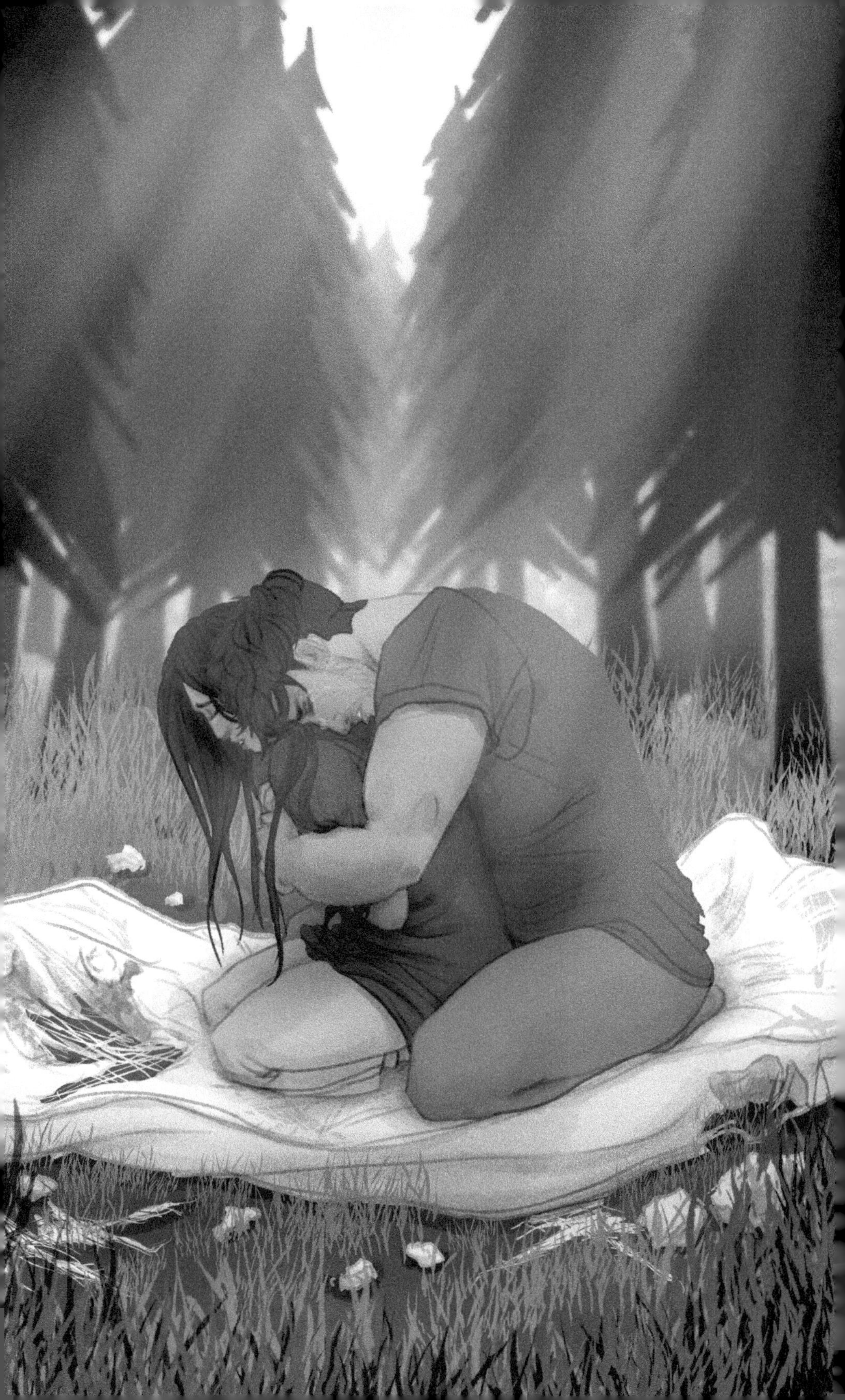

But as I break away to catch my breath, exhausted doesn't begin to describe me.

"Noah, thank you." My voice comes out hoarse and weak.

"You did so well, beautiful." Noah whimpers over me, kissing my cheeks all over.

I'm too tired to keep crying, closing my eyes as I soak in every kiss.

"Good job. Rest now," he mutters against my lips.

After cuddling for a while, Noah helps me mindlessly collect each shred of the mattress, storing it in trash bags. We leave the barren mattress frame to slump against my parents' cottage like a dying flower.

14

Destroying that mattress zapped the energy out of my cells. The rest of the week, I use every ounce of my energy reserve on my job, coming home to Noah's cozy cabin to sleep off mind-numbing exhaustion.

I'm too tired to deal with my parents' cottage, so for now I'm living out of two suitcases. I don't even mind it, as long as I'm living with sweet Noah. But when I come home from work on Friday to Noah's empty cabin, I find my clothes neatly sorted into one half of Noah's bedroom dresser and closet. For some reason, this silent gesture makes me feel more at home than I have in years.

The night of the Full Moon Ceremony, neither of us speak a word. We've traded between kissing and sleeping in each other's arms all afternoon. Noah's bedroom—*our* bedroom—is a blend of our sleepy scent.

An hour after sunset, Noah pries himself from me with a sigh.

I flop my hand out of our warm cocoon to grip his hand. "Don't be sad. I'm coming with you."

"No, sweet Omega. You need to stay in bed and heal."

"I do want to heal." I break into a smile. "Surrounded by the pack."

Noah's raised eyebrow pushes a giggle from me. He sighs, leaning in to kiss my cheek. Then kisses it again. And again.

He's trying so hard to be serious and stubborn about my recovery time, but his goofy, huge wolf spins in our bond, and my giggles overflow into belly laughter.

"Your wolf gives you away every time."

He groans, stripping to his boxers in front of his closet.

I gawk at every rippling muscle in his back, even though I'm too sleepy to do anything but stare.

When he turns back around, he's wearing a button-up white shirt, straining against his arms as he buttons its short collar. I follow his hands to his tightening belt, eyeing the bulge in his pants. He's not aroused, he's just that thick. And Noah knows I'm staring; that heavy bulge twitches to life before me, expanding by the second.

We meet eyes. A desirous flame ignites between us no matter how worn out my body still feels. I bite back a smile, dropping my shoulder to reveal just a bit of extra cleavage for him. Noah flushes, his stare darting over my breasts before he busies himself, picking lint off his embroidered ceremony vest.

But as his yearning scent stings my nose, Noah turns away, ignoring the lust in our bond. He doesn't feel upset, so I don't question it. He's probably just as exhausted as I am and not in the mood.

Noah's fingertips flit through my dresses in the back of his closet, stopping on the whitest one. It's a flowy, white sundress, more casual than I would imagine appropriate for the ceremony tonight. But as I slip it on, warmth encompasses my heart; knowing Noah, he picked it *because* it's far more comfortable than my other dresses, allowing me to relax as much as I can tonight despite my future-Luna duties.

I give Noah a gentle smile. "Thank you," I whisper. He ducks his head, and I giggle. "Come here, my sweet, shy Alpha."

But as Noah approaches me on the bed, he digs into his pocket to reveal a velvet box in his palm.

My eyebrows raise as Noah's wolf paces in our bond. "What's this?"

"It's— It's for you." Noah's voice is so soft and tender that I have to pinch my thigh to keep from squeezing him.

Lifting the box lid, I suck in a sharp breath. Glimmering softly in the moonlight, a crescent moon pendant hangs from a short silver chain. My heart spikes into my throat at how expensive it must be; the stone is so iridescent, even in the dark room, that it has to be a genuine moonstone. The necklace is double-layered,

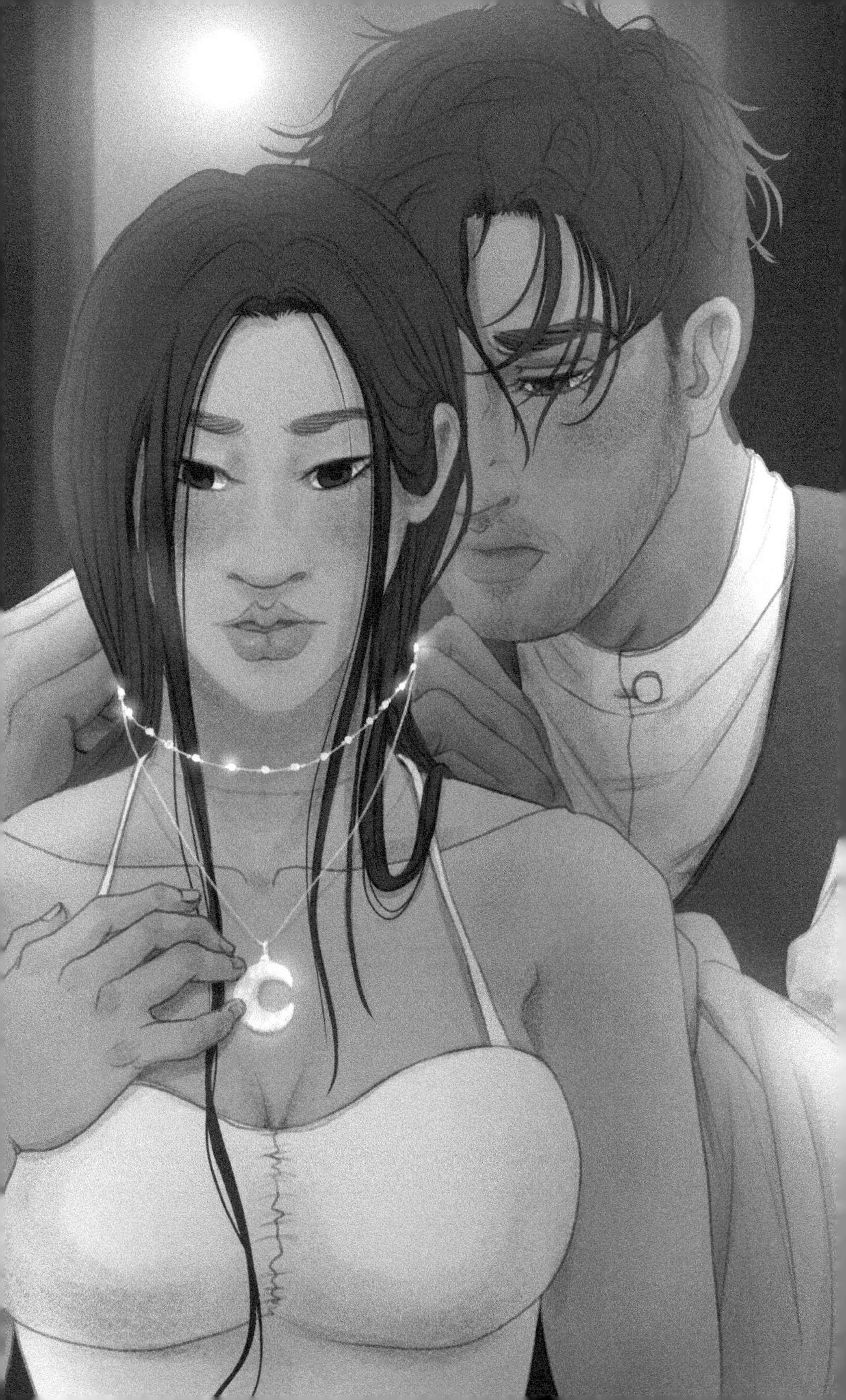

and the second, shorter chain is laced with sparkling crystals, so shimmery that they must dance spectacularly in the daylight.

"*Noah*," I breathe. "Is this really a moonstone?"

He gently lifts the necklace from the box, unlatching it. As he scoots behind me on the bed to hook it around my neck, his deep voice hums through my chest.

"It's the stone of our Moon Goddess. I thought it was fitting for my—" He hesitates at the sight of me in his mirror across the room. After a deep breath, Noah avoids my eyes in the reflection, running his hands down my shoulders. "For my Moon Goddess-sent Omega."

My heart threatens to stop. As I gaze at myself in Noah's mirror, the crescent moon flashes its light with every kiss Noah presses against my shoulder. The necklace elevates my plain dress, giving me an air of absolute importance.

But Noah just told me a white lie. This isn't a necklace for Noah's "Omega." This was a necklace he bought for his *Luna*, and the way Noah still can't bear to meet my eyes tells me we both know it.

"Thank you." My whisper cracks, unable to contain my emotions. The sound draws Noah's eyes straight to mine in the mirror. His nocturnal eyes gleam in the reflection, sending a thrill through my core.

When I stand from the bed to face him directly, Noah eyes me up and down. His fingertips trail my waist, leaving shocks of pleasure in their wake.

I can't take it any longer. Tilting his chin, I draw Noah in for a slow, delicious kiss, dropping myself in his lap. As I caress Noah's wide chest, it rises with desire beneath my palms like it's begging me for more.

But Noah pulls back, breathless. His smoldering stare lingers on my neck, breasts, and lips, but when he leans in for more, all he does is kiss me.

My heart hurts; I have a sinking feeling of what's really happening.

I sit back. "Noah, it's perfectly okay if you're not in the mood, but please don't be afraid to be intimate with me because of what I told you."

He slumps. "I'm not. I'm just tired. Mentally and emotionally. It doesn't stop me from wanting you, but I don't think I have it in me tonight to act on it. I'm sorry."

"Hey," I whisper. I stroke his cheek, kissing it softly until he's willing to look at me again. "That's perfectly okay, my shy Alpha. Please don't be sorry. After everything I shared with you, every moment we're together feels so intimate, with or without sex."

"I feel the same." Noah gathers me closer in his arms, squeezing me slowly but vigorously until I let out a delighted hum. Noah smiles. "There you go, gorgeous. Are you ready for tonight?"

I sigh, my eyelids fluttering through Noah's gentle kisses on my cheek. "Yes, my love. Let's go."

Walking hand in hand, we make our way to the Full Moon Ceremony.

This time, I'm involved in the ceremony process too.

"Welcome to Greenfield, Omega." Noah's soft voice carries across the mossy hill we use as a stage, warming my soul along with the newest pack Omega's smile.

The Omega approaches me after Noah's welcome, already weeping. I embrace them, just like I've done with every Rogue wolf who joins our pack. Then I lick their bleeding palm, healing Noah's pack entrance bite.

I can't believe it. Every single wolf looks so touched. All we had to do was accept them.

I expect to feel exhausted from being around so many strangers, but their joy invigorates me. With every wolf diving into my arms for comfort, the pack bond strengthens. I feel so important. Like I was made by the Moon Goddess, just for this purpose.

Noah can't stop beaming at me, wiping his stray tears when I meet his eyes and smile back.

I was playing around earlier when I told Noah I wanted to heal here tonight, but it's coming true. My heart is so full.

Then the mating ritual begins.

"Come with me, future Luna." Lilian takes me by the hand,

guiding me to a massive field. Noah trails us, his hand on my lower back.

The three of us wait in silence as mates disperse throughout the field, courting each other in their human forms. The pairings are more than just Alpha-Omega mates: Beta-Omega, Alpha-Beta, Alpha-Alpha, and so on, some mated in packs of triple, quadruple, or more mates. While Noah made it sound like they're lacking in progress with wolf sexes, I'm relieved wolves are open to different genders and sexualities. I've witnessed plenty of examples of it since joining Greenfield Pack, but I can't help but weep as open displays of love bloom all around me. Safety burrows a little deeper into my heart.

Regardless of their wolf sexes, all mates here want to be witnessed as they mate. Not just by us; they want to be blessed by the Moon Goddess's gleaming, silver eye.

The pack believes She doubles or triples the chances of pregnancy, particularly for Omegas. But fresh mates can also mark each other for the first time, bonding beneath the Moon Goddess's gaze.

Some mates in the field shift into wolves to privately mate in the forest, but most don't: bare, human bodies grinding until they connect. All of them, however, really get down to business, no matter who's watching.

As various moans echo across the field, the accumulating lusty scent in the wind floods my groin with heat. My cheeks flush in embarrassment, no matter how prepared I was for this.

When the first pair knots, I suck in a sharp breath at its raw power: jaws gaping, bodies cinched tight, and heads nuzzling. Is that what Noah and I look like every time? I swear I just felt their souls merging from here.

Shame strikes my gut for intruding on something so intimate, but Noah strokes my back.

"It's okay. They want us to watch. But if you're not comfortable with it, you're not required."

"I'm okay, just new to it," I whisper. It feels like if I speak too loudly, I'll break the intimate trance around us. But regardless of our whispers, the moans across the field only intensify.

"Do you remember how to bless them?" Lilian's smooth, stoic voice interrupts my thoughts.

I nod, recalling Lilian's instructions from our weekly Luna-training meetings. "Yes."

"Good. We're starting, then."

Lilian hasn't let go of my hand. Which means when she charges toward the first knotted couple, I'm stuck stumbling after her whether I want to or not.

The knotted mates nuzzle, still breathless and moaning. My heartbeat skyrockets, unsure where to look at their nude, vulnerable bodies.

But Lilian softens her stoic frame, lacing the air with her comforting scent in a pheromonal hug. She makes eye contact with the knotted Omega, his eyes glazed with leftover lust. It inspires a genuine smile I've never seen on Lilian, a maternal admiration shining through her grin.

She smooths his short, black hair back into place. "Hello, gorgeous Omega. Where would you like me to bless you?"

"My head, please, Luna." The Omega squeezes Lilian's hand. But then he turns to me, weeping. "And my womb, please, future Luna. We want a pup so badly."

My heart rate spikes, but I put on a gentle smile for him. "Okay, sweet wolf. I'd love to help."

I can't believe he's asking *me* to bless his womb and not Lilian. I hope she's not offended.

But Lilian is solely focused on her Luna duties. She rubs her neck along the Omega's forehead, blessing him with a burst of her nurturing scent.

The Alpha weeps against his mate's cheek, kissing his mark on the Omega's neck over and over again. "I love you, Omega. Soak the blessing in for me, okay?"

"You don't want a blessing today, Alpha?" Lilian asks.

The Alpha hugs his mate a little tighter, his smile growing. "Please give my mate mine for today, Luna."

I'm overcome by the beauty of the pure devotion in front of me, my eyes watering as Lilian dives back in for a second blessing.

I let the mates inspire me as I turn my focus inward, concentrating my emotions into my scent to create my blessing.

I think about my love for every pack member. My hope for this couple's dreams. My joy for every mated pair. My adoration for Noah, allowing me to witness so much beauty I've never seen before. Most importantly, I picture a little pup forming in the Omega's womb, imagining them growing and growing until they're safely burrowed in this couple's loving arms.

Within seconds, I'm oozing a sugary, adoring scent so potent that I can smell myself. Rubbing my scent gland along the Omega's lower abdomen, I'm surprised by the couple's collective sigh. They weep together, murmuring soft love for each other. I brim with tears, amazed by their sincerity.

When I turn to check Noah's expression, his laser-focused eyes are already on me. *I can't believe how deeply I'm in love with you.*

I swallow hard, stifling the pulsing heat in my groin as my heart rate skyrockets.

As Lilian drags me to the next knotted couple, she leans in to whisper. "The mates we just blessed are already pregnant."

I gasp. "What?! How do you know?"

"I could smell it. Honestly, I can smell it all over this field, Aliya." Lilian sighs like I've somehow inconvenienced her, although I can't imagine how.

"What's wrong, Luna? Did I do something weird again?" I ask.

She avoids my eyes, lifting her chin and trudging ahead with a frown. "Thanks to a certain aphrodisiac stew incident in the Community Center, I bet we'll have a lot of pregnancies this month. I'm going to be extra busy pulling pups out of wombs nonstop by the start of next year."

Oh, *that's* how I've inconvenienced her. My heart sprints, and I'm flustered to my core; our baby-making scent infused into the community stew last week.

I gape at Noah trailing behind us. He has to bite back a shy laugh, covering it with his palm.

Lilian wraps her arm around my shoulders. "It's okay. It's a good thing. I'm not sure if you realize this, but you and Noah are sex symbols for the pack."

My feet slow. "What? That sounds a bit degrading for how much hard work it is."

Lilian scoffs, rolling her eyes. "Humans."

Noah growls, and Lilian jumps.

She hurriedly rubs my arm. "Sorry, Aliya. What I'm trying to say is the top Alpha and pack Luna's relationship represents how loving and tight-knit the pack is at its core. Your intimacy inspires the pack to love harder, and sex is a healthy part of wolf culture. It's not shameful, degrading, or frowned upon here. It's an act of bonding and loyalty."

Lilian squeezes my hand, her eyes scanning the field for where to deliver our next blessing.

"It's a crucial honor to be the pack's leading sexual pair. One you already have deep influence in."

As the next mated couple thrusts into each other before my eyes, putting their entire bodies into their lovemaking, I can feel their fierce commitment to each other through their scent. Lilian is telling the truth.

Which means I'm the pack's queen of sex, and Noah is the king.

And to my surprise, especially after all I've been through, there's nothing I want more.

I stop in my tracks. "Wait, Luna—" My hands land on my abdomen, twisting my heart. "Does that mean you can already smell if I'm pregnant?"

Lilian doubles back for me. As she leans in to sniff my neck, my heartbeat throbs into my ears.

"Hmm…" Lilian says nothing more.

My heart sinks, knowing it wasn't an immediate yes. Noah wraps his arm around my waist, and I'm tempted to burrow into him to hide forever.

But his warmth stabilizes me. "You just started ovulating, my sweet Omega. It's too early to tell."

"Oh." My shoulders sink despite Noah rescuing my hope. "I guess I'll keep having to be patient then."

Noah chuckles, kissing me on my cheek over and over again until I break into a smile. Lilian gives me a subtle wink, extending her hand for me to return to work.

From then on, I bless every couple with my full heart, any remaining awkwardness or embarrassment washing away. Considering how my ex made me view sex, the raw power of this moment is hitting me hard. This ritual is beyond healing for my soul. It's transformative.

When I turn to Noah after blessing the last knot, Lilian separates from me quickly, heading for the tree line. It startles me; what's she running from?

"Luna?!" I call after her.

I don't understand why other lingering, knot-free wolves scamper away from us too.

Until my eyes land on Noah's hard bulge, visible even by moonlight.

I swallow hard.

Noah's chest heaves as his stare indulges in every inch of my body. "I changed my mind. I want to make you feel good."

15

Shuddering at Noah's deep voice, I drip into my panties. Squeezing my thighs together, I glance around us at the open field. There's nothing to cover us except a few distant trees.

"Here?" I ask.

"If you want. *Only* if you want." He steps closer, stooping over to kiss my shoulder. Shivers erupt down my spine.

"Noah," I breathe, sinking into him.

His thigh grinds between my legs, and I can feel the eyes on us. My cheeks are hot red, but…

"I do want to," I whisper. "In front of everyone."

We meet eyes, and Noah gapes.

My voice shakes, but resolve fills my tone. "You heard correctly. I want this so badly, I could lay back and drop my legs open for you, right this second."

Noah stares as if he's memorizing me, permanently etching my portrait into his mind. Before I can blink, he draws me in for a fierce kiss, hugging my waist to his hips.

His cock flexes against my belly. I can't resist stroking it through his pants, rubbing more reactions from it until Noah growls.

He pulls back, breathless. "I don't have protection."

"I know," I say. "I still want that baby if you still do."

Noah's eyes gleam brighter in the moonlight, his scent erupting so heavily that my eyes water.

"Of course I do," he purrs. "Relax on your back for me. I want to mate you face-to-face."

My stomach flips, anticipation mixing with the pulsing heartbeat between my legs as I excitedly sit on the damp grass.

But as I lay back for him, the sight of him above me threatens to trigger another flashback.

Noah freezes in a crouch, feeling the shift in our bond. "What's wrong? Talk to me."

"I'm having trouble staying present—" I swallow hard, struggling to explain the worst part. "In this position. I don't want a flashback to stop us."

Noah settles on his knees, opening his hands for me to grasp. "Sit on top of me, instead."

I try to swallow my disappointment as I climb onto his lap, nuzzling into his neck to hide my embarrassment.

Noah nuzzles my head twice as hard. "Just for now. We'll get you there."

He hugs my hips into his lap with one arm, sliding up my skirt with the other. Caressing my ass, his hand slips lower until he strokes my clothed labia through our kiss. I'm so sensitive that I jolt in his lap, tingles whispering down my legs at his delicate touch.

My heart pounds, sensing more and more wolf eyes on us. It only deepens my craving for Noah.

My thighs spread over his lap on their own, a soft moan escaping my lips through our kiss. Every inch of me begs for more, even as nocturnal eyes glint in the distance over Noah's shoulder, so I decide to lean in. I let my hips dip into Noah's touch until his fingers prod my entrance through my soaked panties. As I rub my clit over his stiff shaft, I kiss him as hard as I can, seeking his purring reaction.

When he gives it to me—his growl humming into my throat—I whip open his belt. Its icy metal ornaments sting my overheated fingers as I free his cock.

Noah's breath shudders as I thumb over his wet tip, making him gush a little more precum.

"*Omega*," Noah breathes.

I want to hear more of him.

And I want to hear his lips gasping for air beside my ear as he burrows inside me. Losing the rest of my patience, I slide my panties out of the way, preparing him to enter me.

But the second he prods my entrance, I suck in a pained breath. Noah jolts back, lifting my hips off him. "D-did that hurt?"

It did.

Just like it used to, after what Steven did. It's the same, searing pain I had to train myself out of with Prolonged Exposure therapy, sex toys, and years of horrified, frustrated tears, unable to escape the feeling that Steven broke me.

Every sexual feeling in my body evaporates, replaced by panic.

"No, no, no— this can't be happening!" I gasp, gripping Noah for dear life. "I can't hurt like this again— You finally helped me feel good again—"

Noah squeezes me close, snapping me out of my thoughts before they swallow me. "Breathe. Look at me, and breathe."

I nod, peeking up at him. My bottom lip quivers through the start of tears.

Noah kisses it. "It's okay. It's okay if it hurts right now."

I deflate. "But how? What if it never gets better? What if I leave you frustrated forever, and—"

"All we know is what's happening now." Noah nuzzles his mark on my neck, a shockwave of his pain and love sinking into me.

A full sob escapes my lips. "It might not be just now, Noah. This started happening to me after he broke in, and it took forever for sex to stop hurting again."

Massaging my scalp, Noah's side of our bond aches with heavy concern. After a few more of my sharp sobs, Noah softens his voice.

"Your body probably just needs time after such an awful trigger. But if it never gets better, I still wouldn't blame you for how someone else hurt you." Despite how delicately his words graze over my lips, they ripple gravity-bending emotions through us both. "Please, *please*, Aliya, don't tell yourself it's your job to make sure I'm not sexually frustrated. I never want to hurt you during sex just to get off. That's horrific."

I whimper against his chest. Noah is flaccid beneath me, rooting my fears further in reality.

"But I want you inside of me. I want to have a baby with you, or at least to connect with you closely in all ways, including all types of sex." I choke out tears. "What if we'll never be able to do that again?"

"Let's not think like that. We can't predict the future, yeah?"

"Y-yeah…"

He licks my mark, making my eyelids flutter with a burst of endorphins. "We can teach your body that it's safe now. Right here with me, in my arms."

"Noah, I—" I swallow back a sob threatening to escape. "I still want you tonight. I know I seem like I need to recover, but I'm on the verge of heat. I think you really could get me pregnant."

With a hard swallow, Noah holds me tighter. After a silent moment, his voice comes out soft, but his cock stirs, prodding my core. "Nothing's ruined, sweet Omega. You still have me, and I can still try to get you pregnant beneath the Moon Goddess's eyes."

I can't stop my heart from hammering. "You can? How?"

"I'll show you. Lay down with me."

My eyes remain locked on Noah as he joins me in the tall grass, cuddling against my back. His fingers circle my clit, stirring the heat in my groin back into action.

"It's just us here now. I told the pack to give us space."

My heart sinks, but Noah leans over my side to smash his lips against mine. It relaxes my shoulders, especially as he massages my clit with wide circles of his palm. Wetness drips from me, soaking my panties enough to dampen my thighs, and Noah presses his fingers into it.

"The second you don't want something, even just feeling unsure about wanting it, we'll stop," Noah says.

I nod, panting as I vibrate with love for him. "I trust you."

"Good. Keep looking at me. Tell yourself it's just me."

I can't believe how quickly he's brought me back into my body. Panic convinced me I'd never feel pleasure again, but I was wrong; Noah's gentle breath against my lips sends waves of affection to my heart, reminding me that I'm here now. I already feel pleasure, lying in his arms as the grass sways over our heads.

Cuddling in closer behind me, Noah spoons me in his body

heat from my shoulder blades against his chest to our intertwined legs. But instead of continuing to stroke me, Noah turns his attention on my breasts. He hooks both arms around my torso, rubbing his big, overheated hands over every shivering inch of my body.

Peeling the top of my sundress down, Noah exposes my bare breasts. He quickly cups them in his hands, not allowing the cool air to harden my nipples. What hardens them instead is his gentle, kneading massage, his fingertips flicking over the buds between soft, pulsing squeezes. It drives me into such a sensitive state that every circle of his palms burrows a deeper ache into my groin. Within seconds, my pussy flexes in time with each brush over my nipples. My hips buck back on instinct, pinning his prodding cock with my ass.

Noah's deep, resulting purr sends a jolt down my spine. My breath comes out sharp and choppy as my legs squirm, aching for attention between them.

With Noah's next purr, his deep voice sends tingles down my neck. "Can I touch you lower without anything between us?"

I swallow hard between gasping breaths, unable to stop my eyelids from fluttering as Noah drags both hands over my breasts, abdomen, and hips with heavy pressure.

I let out a soft moan. "Yes. Please."

Noah purrs, dragging his tongue up my mark. A thrill races through my core. Encouraged by my pleased moan, Noah glues me to him, licking harder. I wriggle in pleasure, fisting his hair.

Noah's deep, rolling growl buzzes through my chest as his hands gather my skirt. As he flips it over my hip bones, Noah kisses the edge of my ear. "And you still want me to try to get you pregnant tonight?"

I shudder, running my hand down his side as he presses against my ass. "Yes. I want you so badly." I stop moving, hit with a wave of disappointment. "But I know we can't— We can't do it the same way."

"Hey, it's okay. There are other ways I can try to get you pregnant. Can I slip myself between your legs as I touch you?"

My heart flips, imagining Noah bursting between my inner thighs. I understand his idea now: even if he only comes against the outside of my pussy, it's still possible I'll get pregnant. The thought of his cum glazing my groin sends my heart into a frenzy.

I rub my ass back against his flexing cock. "Yes," I breathe. "I'd love that."

"I'd love that too."

Noah's fingertips trail over my side, whispering over my hip bone before dipping into my panties. I rock my hips into his touch, aching so badly with every flex of my core that it feels like ages before his fingers return to my clit. But instead of toying with my clit, Noah presses his fingertips into the nerve, keeping my clit in place as he gives it a rolling massage.

I exhale hard through the delightful pleasure crawling up my abdomen, my hips twisting into his touch.

Just before I hit a new depth to my pleasure, Noah's fingers glide further. They speed into thorough, wet circles, caressing every nerve down my labia.

My hips buck as I let out a soft moan, chasing his fingertips.

But they slip out of my panties.

I look over my shoulder to find him readying his cock. My heart leaps into my throat when he tugs my panties off my ass, slipping his tip into my waistband; it really looks like he's about to penetrate me from behind with my panties around my thighs.

As I watch him slide between my legs, I gasp through the fresh emotions coursing through our bond. We feel different than how we'd feel if he entered me, but this new blend is intense and wonderful in its own way.

My heartbeat pounds into my ears as I remember the intention behind this moment; Noah wants to father my children as much as I want to carry his pups.

My panties keep him snug against me, each press of his hips dragging his shaft along my core. A soft moan escapes me as Noah indulges in my fluids. My seeping pussy creates slippery, suckling sounds against his shaft, spiking a thrill through my chest.

Noah slows his thrusts, leaning over my shoulder to gauge my comfort.

But I'm suddenly craving so much of him that I can't stand it.

All I have to do is arch my back, aiding his thrust, and Noah slips his hand between my legs to increase the pressure, pressing his shaft tighter against me. Slotting his cock harder between my legs, Noah passes over my clit at the end of each thrust. A luxurious moan escapes my lips.

"Good job, gorgeous Omega. You're doing so well."

I moan at Noah's words, startled by the fire they ignite in me. He flexes his palm against my clit in gentle pulses, and I grip his thigh to steady myself: I'm intensely aware that we're not wearing protection, and Noah's breath beats harder against my cheek like he's getting closer. My body reacts so heavily to him that an intense need to allow him to impregnate me floods the grass around us with my lusty scent.

Noah moans through it, rubbing his forehead against me in bliss, but that only makes it worse.

"Noah—" My legs pulse open as I squirm, aching for him to enter me. I know it'll hurt if he does, so I close my legs, choosing to work him harder instead.

My mate growls as I massage his cock twice between my thighs. He nips my mark, urging a burst of fluid from my core. It douses his shaft, slickening every thrust between my legs with wet, slurping sounds.

I moan, bucking my hips back faster to hear more of it.

Noah groans against my neck. "Fuck, yes. Squeeze my fingers between your thighs for me."

As soon as I do, I release a soft whimper; it amplifies the pressure on both my clit and his cock, my thighs encompassing his thick girth with a squeeze. I can feel how intensely pleasurable it is for Noah in our bond, warmth pooling in my belly. He softly moans against my neck, zapping excitement through my chest until each stroke between my legs sends tingles up my back.

Noah's pumping action pulses pressure up my core, tricking my body into thinking he's thrusting inside me. I clench at the thought, my breath rapid in warning of an incoming climax. But with my wet pussy coating his cock, I think Noah will beat me there; my mate bucks behind me with twice the force, his breath shifting into sedated groans. Not even Noah's rapid, heavy rubbing of my clit can take me faster to the edge, his breath panicked as an intense hunger fills our bond.

"Yes—" I gasp. "Get me pregnant—"

Noah releases a heavy moan, his nose smushed against my neck as his hips press mine closer to the ground. With speeding, shaky breaths, Noah cups his hand tight against my pelvis, intensifying the pressure of his tip thumping against my core.

The tension rippling through Noah just before he comes urges my body to open for him. My core blooms wide as he pulses between my legs.

As my gaping core suckles over his tip, attempting to swallow it, Noah jolts behind me. His hips crash against my ass as his cum spills both into me and across my panties. There's so much of it that it pools, each sharp thrust of his hips squirting his seed between my legs.

I gasp, my heart hammering like a rabbit's as Noah's wet heat coats my groin. I could be pregnant now.

Noah groans, his open lips mashed over my neck as his heavy breath beats over my exposed breasts. As he falls still, continuing to moan behind me, I squirm into his touch, my rampant hormones threatening a full heat.

"Fuck, I— I love seeing you feel good." Noah can hardly breathe as he shudders behind me, panting against my neck. "I don't need to be inside you, Omega. I love every second with you."

"I want to carry your baby," I gasp, on the edge of delirium. "You feel so good between my legs. I was so close—"

Noah growls, sending a thrill up my spine. "Hold still, feisty Omega. I'm not done mating you."

I freeze in place, but I can't stop my rapid breath. My wolf shudders along with me at the thought of our Alpha mating me with his fingers, my core flexing harder as if it's attempting to gather more of his cum.

But before I can process what he's doing, Noah's fingers dip into the pool of his sperm in my panties. I gasp as his doused fingers not only crash across my labia, but circle themselves into my gaping core.

"Does this feel okay?" Noah asks.

But I roll onto my stomach, thrusting my hips into the air out of primal instinct—allowing Noah to mate me.

"There you go. What a good girl," Noah purrs.

I can't bear to respond, struggling to breathe through the flashing, tremendous pleasure blasting up my spine as he sinks two wet fingers into me.

It doesn't hurt. In fact, it feels delicious, billowing pleasure up my spine and into my throat as he breeches my pelvic opening.

All I can do is moan desperately, shoving his fingers deeper. Noah uses his other hand to rub my clit, erasing all discomfort in my body as his soaked fingers bury into my core. He pulls his fingers all the way out, gathers more of his sperm, and dives back in.

"Oh, my— Oh, my *God*—" I moan frantically as I realize what he's doing; he's using his cum as lubricant, coating my insides with its slick heat to make me come.

My jaw drops as he burrows in deep. I jerk back in delight as he circles his cum over my cervix, the mental image of it sending my arousal through the roof. But he's not done with me. Noah curls pulsing, exquisite massages against my inner wall, palpating the nerve just right to send waterfalls of tingles down my spine.

I fumble over Noah's name on my lips as intense pleasure fuzzes out my mind. His deep massage feels so good that I fall limp, completely exposed to him with my cheek smashed in the dirt. Noah has to hook his arm around my waist to keep me upright, holding my ass in the air to pump his fingers into me. He continues to give my nerves such a tender, direct massage that I squirt with every press of his fingertips, splashing the dirt between my legs. The intense heat pulsing through me clashes with the earth's sharp chill against my breasts, my torso writhing into the cool dirt as Noah mates me. Each breath sputters out of me in rapid, choppy bursts, carrying airy moans with it. It only encourages Noah to massage me faster, speeding into a thumping sprint against my inner wall.

As I bare my ass to Noah, my body squeezes every bit of movement out of his touch, electrified by the pleasure racing up my torso and down my legs—until it all comes crashing down. I come hard and loud over his fingers, gripping fistfuls of dirt.

Noah rapidly pats my clit through my orgasm, and my moan escapes as more of a yell with the additional pleasure it introduces.

"Alpha!" I cry into the earth. Each pat on my clit is accompanied by another curl of Noah's fingers, making me feel like he's mating me for the first time in weeks. I can't stop whining, fucking myself over his hand.

"Good girl," Noah growls. "Let yourself come as long as you want."

He's right, I'm still flexing over him, my mind blurred with a flood of hormones stinging my hot cheeks as my orgasm extends. When my legs finally stop jerking through pleasure, Noah's deep prodding in my core slows, allowing my body to slow with it.

"Noah," I whimper, quivering with aftershocks as I flop into the dirt. He tries to pull his drenched hand from me, allowing me to relax, but my body clings on. He gives my G-spot a few gentle, extra rubs instead, shooting waves of leftover pleasure through my abdomen. I slacken in absolute comfort, my toes curling as I enjoy every second of his affection.

But Noah hasn't relaxed. His sudden, breathy moan behind my back lights up every nerve in my spine, making my swollen pussy grip his fingers tighter.

When he groans again, I look over my shoulder to find him on his knees, thrusting through his free hand. Watching me come has Noah on edge again.

Everything in me wants to help him.

But I'm covered in dirt.

There's no way I can get up to clean my hands; I'm still struggling to catch my breath after Noah sent me to the Moon Goddess and back. But my dress is so soiled that I might as well wipe my dirty hands on it.

After using my skirt to vigorously swipe each finger, I pull Noah's hand from my core. The second he's free, he glazes his shaft with a combination of our fluids from his coated fingers. My core flexes, pleased by the sight.

I grip Noah's white sleeves. "Let me help you."

Noah shakes his head. "I-it's okay, you don't have to. It's just—I love how much you trust me to be here for you," he breathes. "I feel so close to you, especially since you trusted me enough to tell me everything."

"Noah, oh, my God... You're the sweetest—"

I cut myself off to knead his lips, slipping my tongue in his mouth, but he can hardly focus on kissing back; I've propped myself up to take over for him, working every angle of his shaft with my free hand. I give extra attention to his tip, running heavy circles over it with my thumb until Noah's breath quivers against my lips.

He suddenly lifts my knee to my chest, exposing my pussy—before he comes all over it.

I gasp.

Then instinct takes over. I waste no time in gathering his cum in my hand, shoving it into myself.

Noah's golden eyes widen. "Holy— Holy fuck…"

As my uterus cramps, dragging his seed deeper, I drop limp onto the dirt to get a good look at my mate above me.

I gape at him in awe, his disheveled hair silhouetted by moonlight. This sweet, shy man above me could've just impregnated me—and in the most unrestrained, vulgar way. I'm grimy with dirt, my soaked panties are lopsidedly stretched over my thighs to the brink of snapping, and bodily fluids coat me, but I never imagined myself feeling so beautiful. Not because Noah tells me I am, but because the pure, unwavering depth to our love makes me feel beautiful to exist. I love us just as much as I love him.

Noah is right. I feel closer to him than I've ever felt.

Especially when I realize his calm, gentle compassion for what I've been through turned our night around, fading my initial panic into pure delight.

I grip my heart through a heavy ache in my ribs. "Noah, I love you with my whole heart. Thank you for accepting me and compromising for me, even if—"

"No," he says. "It's not an 'even if' for me that you've been hurt before." Noah pauses, struggling through his hesitating breath. His words come out soft and shaky. "Just l-like it's not for you."

My heart flips as I gaze into his vulnerable, aching eyes. Tears slip as I process what he just told me: he remembers how I told him I'd never see him differently for his trauma. From what I can see and feel, it meant the world to him that I accepted him too. Believed him.

And now that I let him in, he doesn't see me any differently either.

Noah breathes me in, cradling my head in his palms as he catches my tears. My skin erupts in goosebumps as his lips ghost over my neck.

When his palm covers my hand over my chest, Noah whispers, "Keep holding it for me, but be gentle. You have the most beautiful heart."

No, that's not right. He does see me differently. He loves me more than he ever has.

16

Kelsi giggles in my lap, dabbing a bit of green paint on my cheek with a chunky paintbrush.

I gasp. "Did you do that on purpose?!"

She breaks into rambunctious giggles, her nose scrunching from how wide she smiles. I hug her closer, playfully rocking her back and forth as we laugh together.

But as Kelsi slams her back against me in excitement, I wince, repositioning her to the side. My boobs are swollen and achy today, sending a thrill through my heart despite the pain. I'm supposed to start my period tomorrow, and these PMS symptoms aren't too unusual for me—they just happen to also be early pregnancy signs.

I'm trying so hard not to get my hopes up that I'm pregnant. And failing: I've been secretly prodding my breasts when I use the toilet to check if they're just as sore.

Kelsi's excited cry redirects my attention. I'm relieved she's enjoying herself, especially now that I know a bit more about what she's experiencing at home.

A week ago, Kelsi's aunt wasn't the one to pick Kelsi up; Kelsi's mom stopped by for the first time. She's struggling through the loss of her mate and on the brink of death, so she came to thank me after smelling my comforting scent on her pup.

I had no idea Kelsi was a Lycan pup either, but now I have full permission to cuddle Kelsi from her mom.

It sounds like Kelsi is the only reason her mom is still alive. I really hope she pulls through for this sweet baby.

My heart aches for Kelsi as she pauses her paint strokes.

Whether she can tell I'm worried for her or simply craves more affection, she nuzzles into my shoulder, desperate for a deeper hug. I rub her back, holding her a little tighter. But it's not enough. After checking behind me for any human bystanders, I rub my scent on her head with a reassuring purr.

"What a great job you've done on your painting, Kelsi! What color are you going to add next?"

Kelsi gapes at the paint pots, her grin widening by the second. I giggle, relieved to see her so happy.

But I know it won't be the last time she's distracted by her need for comfort. She needs a lot more physical affection than she's getting, whining and gluing herself to other kids and teachers now that she's growing more comfortable around us. I wish I could help her mom with babysitting after school to help Kelsi feel less alone, but that would extend beyond my boundaries as Kelsi's teacher.

At least she seems content to be painting with me. She's the only one whose grown-up is late to pick her up from school, and I'm trying to keep her focused. It'd break my heart if she realized she's the only one left and felt extra abandoned.

Smashing her hand into her paint pot, Kelsi excitedly splatters bright red paint across the board.

"Oh, my goodness!" I burst into laughter, but Kelsi screams out her excitement, her voice echoing through the empty classroom.

Her sudden, magnificent force whacks paint beyond her mini easel, flicking onto the wall with a wet slap.

Which is right when the principal decides to approach.

"Oh, hello, Mr. Turner! Don't mind our educational mess!" I put on my brightest smile, setting Kelsi down so she can keep painting. But she eyes Mr. Turner warily, gripping my pants leg with her coated fist as her paintbrush clatters to the floor.

This is like a different kid. My stomach sinks at the thought of what else she has seen. Is it just my fears taking hold, or is she extra scared around men?

"Hello, Miss Matsuoka. And how are you, Miss Kelsi?" Mr. Turner bends, his face looming over Kelsi, and she flinches.

I squat beside her with a soothing hand on her back. "We've

been doing some incredible paintings today, Mr. Turner! Kelsi is so creative."

Kelsi tugs on my hands. She guides me back to the easel, pointing for me to show Mr. Turner the rest of the paintings.

"Kelsi, use your words!" Mr. Turner says.

His phrasing churns my stomach, warning sirens alarming in my head.

Many of our students have various disabilities or are neurodivergent. I've worked all year to coax Kelsi out of hiding from what must be educational trauma, and her being nonverbal has never been the problem: it's how clearly traumatized she is by the force and shame placed on her to speak. Mr. Turner should know better by now.

My fears are confirmed when Kelsi immediately tries to stick a painted thumb in her mouth to self-soothe.

I stop her from accidentally eating the paint just in time, then shoot Mr. Turner a pointed stare. "She's communicating clearly, words or not. We can discuss this privately."

He raises an eyebrow as I guide Kelsi to the sink to wash her hands.

Dammit, that just slipped out. I shouldn't have corrected him so harshly in front of a student.

But I can't help it. I feel protective over my little ones, especially now that I'm hoping to carry one.

I do a goofy little dance behind her, rocking us as I scrub her hands beneath the water, and Kelsi erupts into giggles. My heart melts.

Thankfully, Kelsi's aunt arrives just in time to break the tension. We head to the parking lot. The only other occupants are a couple of teachers' sedans, Mr. Turner's empty convertible, and my sweet, patient mate waiting for me in his black SUV. Noah and I give each other a quick smile. It's only as Kelsi's aunt pops Kelsi into her car seat, freeing me of my duties, that I realize Mr. Turner still hasn't left.

My heart drops. It wasn't just me. Something feels off.

Everything okay? Noah asks.

I'm not sure. I'll have to see what my boss wants. Sorry I'm taking so long today.

No worries, sweet Omega. I'm enjoying some quiet time.

My heart stings just as much as I'm relieved. Poor Noah hasn't had a single moment to rest all week.

And I'm getting the feeling I'm about to disrupt his peace if I'm predicting the future correctly. When Mr. Turner follows me back to my classroom in silence, I'm certain I'm right, and he has something else to say. Something important.

And that's almost never a good thing.

I smile, fighting the dread looming in my gut. "Please, come sit."

Mr. Turner obliges, following me to the quiet reading area. We sit on child-sized bean bags with our knees scrunched to our chests—only moderately more comfortable than my toddler chairs.

"Well, I'm afraid there's no easy way to say this, Luna." Mr. Turner produces a letter envelope from his jacket.

It contains a pink slip. My heart drops.

"This will be your last year here at the school. I wanted to warn you a week early, almost as soon as I found out. It's the best I can do."

That completely blindsided me. I'm so shocked that I dig my nails into the beanbag beneath my thighs, clinging on for life. "Did I do something wrong? I thought you were done issuing these."

Mr. Turner sighs, avoiding my eyes by wringing his hands. "The district sprung this on us at the last minute due to a vote on budget cuts. It was a surprise to me too." He clenches his jaw, massaging his thumb joint. "And unfortunately, you're the youngest teacher with the least experience here."

I can't help it; I physically deflate, fighting the rising burn in my chest.

But Mr. Turner isn't done. "Although, I do admit your teaching style is also unconventional. That makes it a hard case to defend with the board."

My shoulders sink, betting Mrs. Jacobs, the kindergarten teacher next door, had something to say about it.

Mr. Turner swallows hard. "I see it as wonderful, of course! I hope you and the Alpha understand."

My abdomen cramps. So he's only fighting for my job because I'm the future Luna? Or is it not even that, and it's just because I'm mated to the top Alpha?

I manage to keep my composure until Mr. Turner leaves. Gritting my teeth, I power walk to the teacher's lounge, darting for the bathroom. Mustering up all the willpower I can find, I smile at another teacher as she exits. The second I'm sure I'm alone, I burst into tears.

Aliya, what's going on? Noah's mindlink appears as I shut the stall door behind me.

My shoulders shake through silent tears. *I got laid off.*

Oh, sweet Omega… Do you need me to come give you a hug?

I cover the seat with sanitary paper, deciding I might as well use the toilet while I'm stuck here, crying. But when I slip my pants down, my heart drops to the floor.

"No," I whimper, choking out a sob.

Oh, shit… What else just happened?

My pained weeping echoes throughout the bathroom, unable to remain stifled. I can't bear to answer Noah.

Omega? I'm already looking for you. Where are you?

Teacher's bathroom.

Between my hint and his nose, Noah rushes in within a minute. But I stay put, hiding my face in my stall.

Noah's sleek black boots stop in front of my door. My heart races into my throat, wondering how much of the truth he can smell.

But his voice comes out soft and pained. "Hey… What's going on?"

"Someone's going to get mad at you for being in here."

"Then let me in."

"No," I whimper.

"Oh. Okay…" Noah's feet point left, then right. "Should I leave, then?"

I sigh, burying my head in my hands. "No. Please, don't go."

My sobs escalate, overturning my stomach in a nauseating threat. I don't want to tell Noah why I'm upset, but I have to. But every time I take a breath to speak, nothing comes out.

Until Noah rests his back on my stall door, his voice softening. "Your period started?"

All that comes out of my mouth is another whimper.

Noah doesn't push me to let him in this time, although I feel how badly he wants to see me in our bond.

My watery voice shakes through every syllable. "With how stressed I made myself, I feel like it's my fault it didn't work. I've felt so sick because of what he did back then, and—" I choke out a heartier sob, its raw sorrow echoing throughout the bathroom. I push through heaving breath after breath, struggling to get out what hurts the most. "I really thought it would work this time, but I let my past get in the way."

I can barely sputter the words through a whisper.

Noah lifts his weight from the door, jostling the hinges. "No, sweet, no. Please don't blame yourself. This is normal. Totally normal. We just started trying, and half the time we couldn't—"

Despite how soft our voices are, we're both aware someone could overhear us outside the public bathroom.

Noah drops his voice lower, whispering through the door gap. "You've been going through so much. *So* much. It's not your fault."

A sob escapes me on its own as I clean myself up, rushing to flush the toilet.

Noah's aching heart only strains mine worse, a fresh flood of my tears spilling as I unlock the door.

When Noah sees me, his expression melts into reflected sorrow. "Oh, Goddess. My poor, sweet—"

I burrow my face into Noah's chest as he cuddles me into his warm embrace.

"It's going to be okay. We have so much time."

I whimper. "Yeah... I'm just disappointed. With everything."

Noah tucks my hair behind my ear. "I don't know what else happened at school, but I could never imagine in my life why anyone would let you go. What else could anyone want in a teacher?" Noah pulls back, licking his thumb to scrub something off my cheek. He breaks into a sad smile. "I mean, look at you. You have paint on your face, love. You're such a sweetheart to these kids."

I sputter out a wet laugh, and Noah chuckles.

"And you wanted to start a daycare program, right? For our refugees? Maybe this is your chance."

I nod, sniffling as I wash my hands.

"No matter what you do or where you go next, you'll be making kids' lives better—achieving your dreams. I have no doubts about that, ever." Noah's massive palms rub my arms and sides, his full focus on me in the mirror.

As I stare at him caressing me in the reflection, I smile, no matter how sad I am. I went from feeling alone and destroyed to aching but hopeful in mere minutes.

"God, I'm so lucky to have you. I love you, Noah."

Noah gives a soft whine, tucking me back into his chest to kiss my head. "I love you so damn much."

We share a soft, salty kiss. I allow Noah's touch on my cheek to soften my tense lungs.

Noah pulls back with an excited hum. "How about you have a movie night with Amy? Weren't you wishing you could go back to doing that together?"

"W-well, yeah, but—" I wince, guilt flooding back into my veins. "I don't want to leave you alone after finding out that I'm not— I'm not…"

Noah shakes his head. "I'm okay. I have complete trust that we'll have our time to be parents. I just want you to take it easy tonight, and I love the way Amy makes you laugh."

I find myself smiling again, my heavy heart lightening bit by bit.

The second I arrive at Amy's door, she shushes me. "I just put Lexi in her crib for the night, and if she hears you—"

Lexi lets out a soft whine down the hall. Amy shuts her eyes with an exasperated sigh. I give Amy a sympathetic smile, rushing to hang my dripping, waterproof jacket and toss off my mud boots.

We scurry to Lexi's bedroom door, peeking in with held breaths.

But there's no point in being quiet; she's standing in her crib, gazing back at us with wide, excited eyes and a head full of springy curls. Within a millisecond of spotting me, she stretches out her arms.

My heart twirls. I can't help myself, dashing for her. "Hello, my little niece!"

She gives me a wide smile, opening and closing her hands. "Annie 'Liya!"

Her small voice is still so young that I groan from how cute she is. I lift her from her crib, planting a big kiss on her cheek. Lexi dives over my shoulder, giving me a tight hug.

Amy crosses her arms, but it doesn't stop her from beaming at the sight of us. "Someone is supposed to be asleep, but she accidentally heard me say Auntie Aliya is coming over. She'd never miss that."

I rub Lexi's back, my heart gushing with love for her happy purring. "Are you kidding? I'd never miss seeing this little lovebug for anything."

Lexi whines, and Amy sighs. "My poor baby. Being so sleepy is no fun, huh? Let's get you back to bed."

My heart drops. "Do I have to put her down already? Can I at least try to rock her to sleep for you?"

Amy laughs, stealing a glimpse at Lexi over my shoulder. "It looks like she's already on her way out thanks to your sweet pheromones, so I guess you'll have to."

We giggle as Amy shuts the door, leaving us with only the soft yellow glow of a little full moon night light in the corner of Lexi's room. Amy rearranges the pillows on her fuzzy rocking chair before I sit, helping me prop up my arms to comfortably nestle Lexi against my chest.

Lexi only fusses for a moment, curling against my chest with her thumb in her mouth. I tuck her curls behind her shoulder, kissing her temple as I rock us. With her sleepy limbs weighing me into the rocking chair, my pheromones explode in adoration.

This was exactly what I needed tonight, I mindlink Amy.

Amy settles on the floor beside us with her back against Lexi's crib. Her touched grin, dimly lit by the nightlight, spurs me into just as wide of a smile.

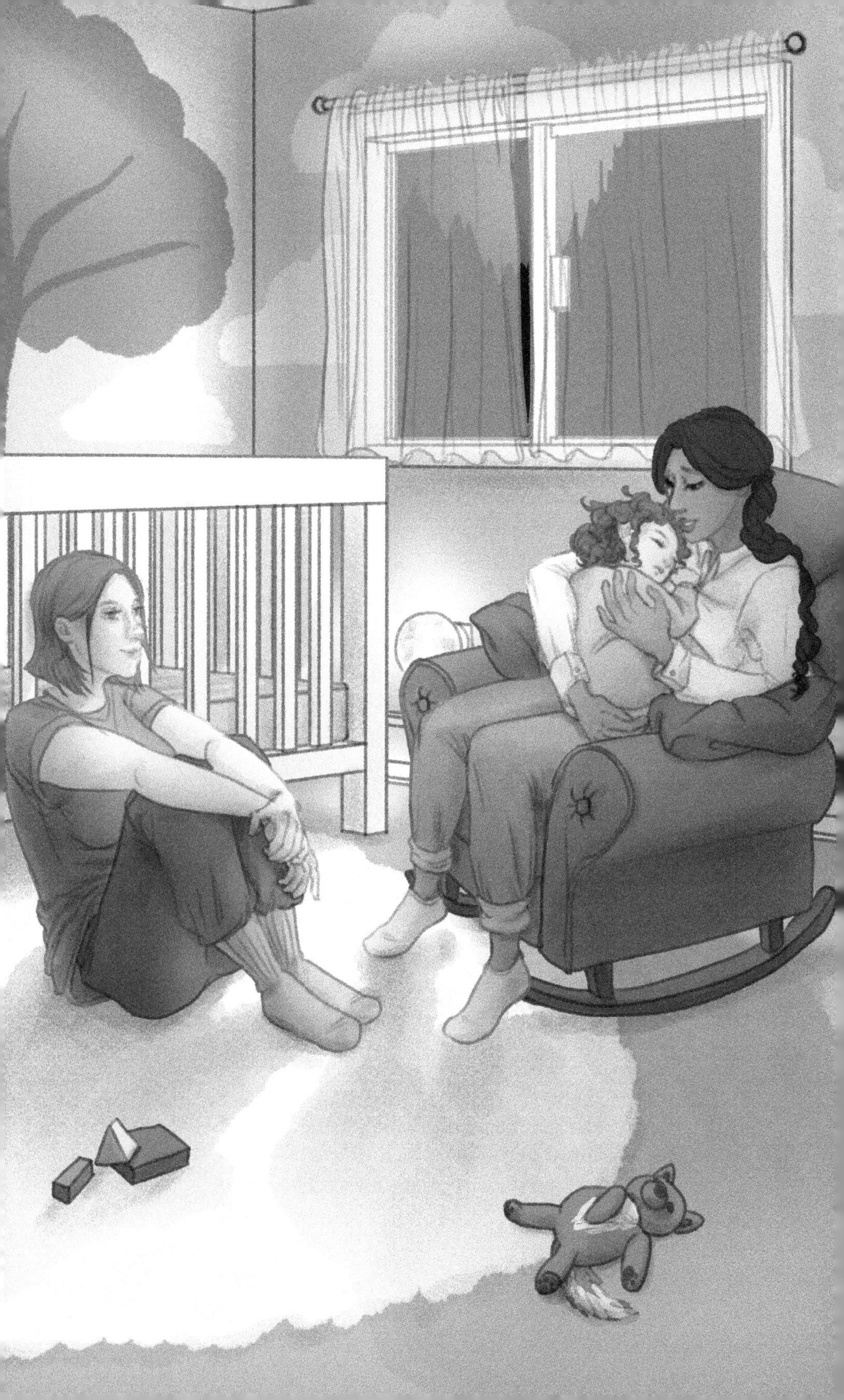

You're a natural, as usual, Amy says.

How has she been doing? I've missed her so much this week.

Amy turns away, fidgeting with a loose string on her tank top. *We've been trying to socialize her more at the Community Center, but she's been having even more trouble adjusting.*

My stomach sinks. *How so?*

She still can't bear to separate from our sides long enough to play with other pups.

Oh, no. I thought she was doing a bit better last week?

She was, but when Kira went back to work, Lexi sobbed her heart out all day, and it broke our souls. That's why I haven't called to ask you and Noah to babysit her alone yet. I don't want her to feel like we're gone too long while she's finally forming a more relaxed attachment to us. Amy stops fidgeting, resorting to biting her nails. *Plus, you seem busy lately.*

My eyebrow lifts. *What do you mean by that? I'd make time for you, any day.*

Amy shrugs, unwilling to meet my eyes. My heart stings.

But with Lexi limp in my arms, Amy stands with me, helping to settle Lexi back into her crib. We tiptoe down the dark hall to Amy and Kira's bedroom, keeping the bedroom lights off until we've safely shut the door behind us.

Amy takes off for her closet without me.

"Hey, what was that supposed to mean? Are you upset with me? Did I do something wrong?" I ask.

"Maybe you did, maybe you didn't." Amy's voice is muffled by her clothes as she sorts through them.

I roll my eyes. "Okay, really though. This isn't a compulsion."

"Really though, if I'm ever upset, I'll tell you when I want to tell you. That's what we both agreed on to fight back against your OCD's crafty mind games, right?"

I sigh. "Right."

She turns to me with a lacy set of black lingerie. "Here it is."

I frown. "What do you mean, 'here it is?' Whose are those?"

"Yours, now. Put them on. They don't fit me, and they're going to look amazing on your ass."

Before I can protest, Amy slaps my ass on the way out of the closet. I burst into laughter, smacking her back. "Excuse me?! I can't walk out wearing lingerie in front of your wife!"

"Just humor me, okay?" Amy shuts the door behind me. "You need a reminder of how badass and sexy you are, I can tell. Put them on, and send a picture to Noah. Then I'll let you borrow that silk nightgown you always used to steal."

I groan, but I'm smiling wide as I strip in Amy's closet. "Fine, fine."

Once I have the lingerie on, I gasp. I've never worn underwear like this before, arching up and over my hip bones to show off the curve of my thighs. Lace frames my breasts, the cups stationed extra low as if they're daring to flash my nipples.

Amy pokes her head in. "Holy *shit*— See?! Okay, you're right, my wife can't see you in this."

I sputter out a laugh. "When should I text this to Noah? Should I wait? What if he comes over and interrupts movie night to mate with me and we ruin your couch?" I giggle harder. "Okay, don't answer that. That was definitely an intrusive thought."

"Wait, no, that would actually be hilarious. Let's prop the girls up to make it come true." Amy's rambunctious giggles make me laugh even harder as she helps me readjust the push-up bra until my breasts look ready to spill from the cups. "And now your hair—" Amy tousles my hair in my face before throwing it back. "Good. Now you look like you started without him."

With my long, black hair messily flipped to over one side, I turn to the side, letting out a loud gasp. "Okay, maybe—" I clear my throat. "Maybe I do have a nice ass."

"Girl, don't even joke. I bet Noah can't get enough of it."

"Amy, stop!" I laugh. "How should I even pose?"

She rotates my hips. "Wait, twist yourself— No, with your ass sticking out— Yes!"

Amy and I erupt into laughter at my awkward pose, showing off both my pushed up breasts and the curve of my ass. She hands me my phone. "Take it, take it! I'll hide."

Diving into the corner of her closet, Amy laughs as hard as I do as I open my phone's camera. My heart thumps into my throat. I haven't taken a sexy picture for anyone in years in fear of blackmail, but I trust where this one's headed. Now that I'm all dressed up, a spicy thrill creeps through my chest.

I stifle my smile as I gaze into the mirror, showing just my eyes over the top of my phone. Amy gasps as I lean into my pose, showing off my body.

Her whisper breaks the silence. "Girl, when he sees that pic, he's going to straight-up come in his pants—"

"*Amy*—" I wheeze, breaking into such heavy, uncontrollable belly laughter that I double over onto her closet floor. Amy steals my phone from me, cackling with her head thrown back. It's such a relief to see her having fun that I cackle with her.

But when she sees the photo, she lets out a sharp, loud gasp. "Oh, my God, yes. Send it!"

Biting my lip with bright red cheeks, I text the photo to Noah, unable to contain my nervous giggles.

> *Me (8:53 PM)*: Amy says this didn't fit her, so you're welcome~~~🖤

Nerves flutter through my stomach, but I don't have to wait long; Noah replies within 30 seconds.

> *Noah (8:53PM)*: ducking hell. almost walked face 1st into a tree

I break into giggles, and Amy peeks over my shoulder. Her resulting laughter makes me laugh even harder, hardly able to text Noah back.

> *Me (8:54PM)*: You wrote it as "duck" again
> *Noah (8:54 PM)*: i guess my phone thinks i like dicks
> *Noah (8:54 PM)*: DUCKS*LOL

Noah (8:54 PM): ok i mean dicks are good too but thats not waht i meant
Noah (8:54 PM): ok sorry no more talking abot dicks
Noah (8:54 PM): jus ignore me
Noah (8:54 PM): u broke my brain omega

I burst into giggles, hugging my phone into my chest as Noah's wolf bursts into a flustered sprint in our bond.

"This is the fastest he has ever texted me—" My voice breaks through laughter, and Amy only laughs more rambunctiously over my shoulder.

Me (8:55 PM): You're absolutely hilarious and adorable. See you in a few hours, my shy Alpha. Miss you already.
Noah (8:56 PM): miss u more, gorgeous.

Noah mindlinks me the rest. *You're so gorgeous any day that I'm surprised I haven't had a heart attack yet, let alone when I just saw you in that. If you were expecting extra passionate sex and an extreme cuddle ball tonight, I've already got it scheduled.*

I laugh. *You cutie. Thank you, I can't wait.*

Amy grips my shoulder, her smile practically leaping off her face. "So?! I know he mindlinked you; Kira would've too. What did he think?"

I groan, hiding my face. "You were right, I feel sexy, and he's super flustered still. I can feel it."

Amy hugs me hard through her bright laugh. "Told you you're fucking hot. Don't let your asshole boss take that confidence away from you, okay?"

I sigh, but I'm smiling. "Okay, A."

"Good. I'll make popcorn while you get dressed. It's in the same drawer."

I laugh as Amy speedwalks to the kitchen, leaving me to steal her silk nightgown from her drawer. Maybe she's not mad at me, after all. I already feel guilty about being too busy to visit her and Lexi this week. On top of that, Amy always sees right through me. I've felt too awful to want to spread my gross, trauma-soaked pheromones onto too many people I love. Amy has enough on her plate without my nonsense.

By the time I'm on Amy's couch in her silk nightgown, she's ready with the popcorn.

But she hasn't sat beside me.

"What's wrong?" I ask.

"Listen, I wouldn't say this to anyone else but you, but—" Amy bites her lip, wincing as she blubbers the truth with a groan. "I like how swollen your nose gets after you cry. It's ridiculously cute!"

I burst out laughing, covering my red nose with both hands. "Amy! Do I have to teach you a preschool lesson about not making comments about people's bodies?!"

"Oh, come on, you know it's true! You're the freaking cutest—I can't stand it!"

She tackles me onto the couch, biting my arm as hard as she can until I laugh-scream.

Kira pokes her head in from the kitchen doorway. "You're lucky our kid can sleep through thunderstorms that sound like bombs going off. Do I have to come in there and separate you two?"

"No! I'll keep my hands to myself from now on!" Amy shouts over my shoulder, covering my ears to protect them.

Kira cackles from the kitchen, and I know she's thinking the same thing as me.

"That'll never happen, Amy," I mutter.

She smushes her entire body into my side, turning the TV on as she hooks her leg over mine. "What? I'm behaving now!"

I giggle, dropping my head against hers as we scroll through an endless selection of streamable movies.

But the longer we cuddle in silence, the more my heart aches beneath the surface. I almost forgot why I came over. Now that Lexi isn't in my arms, the pain of our unsuccessful pregnancy attempts comes flooding back.

A waft of Amy's soothing scent makes my eyes water as she cuddles in closer, wrapping an arm over my cramping stomach.

"Did I ever tell you it took my parents two years to get pregnant with me?" Amy asks.

"Wait, really?"

"Yep. Even as an 'extra fertile' Omega and Alpha couple. Makes you wonder even more if Alphas are all talk, doesn't it?"

"I heard that!" Kira says in the distance.

I giggle with Amy, swiping my tears away. "Thanks, Amy."

She pulls away, nudging my shoulder. "Hey, don't do that."

My eyes widen. She's acting like she's joking, but I know that edgy tone. "What?"

"Don't shut me out. I'm sick of it."

Oh, shit. She's super serious.

I straighten on the couch, facing her glare with a racing heart. "I'm not shutting you out. I don't know what else to say."

"Say what you honestly feel. I'm your best friend, aren't I?"

My heart twinges. "Of course you are! Why would you even say that?"

"Because even though I've seen you recently, you've hardly told me anything going on with you even though I can literally smell the pain on you, Aliya. I don't know what changed, but I've been worried you don't trust me the same anymore now that I have Lexi."

My heart sinks, not just seeing the hurt in Amy's eyes but smelling it. "I'm sor—"

I cut myself off; Amy's jaw flexes at my near-apology. "Just be real with me. That's all I need. Are you jealous, or something?"

"I'm not jealous. I love Lexi to death. And I'll admit, it did change things. But only because I'm ashamed of myself lately, okay? That's what I don't want to admit." I'm surprised by how easy it was to blurt out the truth, but when Amy's eyebrows furrow, my heart races.

"Girl, I love you, but I'm not cool with you acting like your only worth is if you can bear children."

"I know that's not my only worth! That's not what I'm thinking, at all."

I swallow hard in Amy's silence, knowing she wants to hear more from me as my best friend. Needs to. Just like I need her to.

"I'm ashamed that I'm still letting Steven ruin my whole fucking life, Amy." I wrap my arms around my cramping uterus, my eyes stinging. "Noah and I ran into an Omega in a horrible domestic abuse situation. I got re-triggered worse than I have in years, sex started hurting horrifically again, and it's difficult to get pregnant if you can't have penetrative sex, so of course I'm not pregnant. That's why I'm so upset."

Amy slumps. "Girl... Why didn't you tell me?!"

I huff through hot, stinging tears. "Because! How many times do I have to make you listen to me about what Steven did?"

Amy grips my hand hard, gathering my full attention. "As many times as it takes."

My eyes well up. "Oh, A... That's too much to ask, no matter how much of a sweetheart you are."

"I'm serious. You're not a burden on me. Ever. I was there with you through the whole aftermath—"

"Which is why I don't want to keep making you listen to my bullshit—"

"No! That's why I want to keep listening to it. I was there before, after he left that night, and during your entire treatment, and I don't plan on leaving."

My lip quivers, and I shake my head. Amy whimpers, pulling me closer.

"Babe, what your ex did wasn't just painful; it was barbaric. You and I both know Steven waited until you were vulnerable and alone after your parents died. He went and did it anyway, uncaring that it would change you. Hurt you. Most likely for the rest of your life."

My voice comes out airy and weak. "Y-yeah. He did."

"I've never expected an end date for your PTSD. I've supported you, even knowing you might not ever feel 100% again."

"You have. You've been a lifesaver."

"But I just wish you'd let me in enough to help you more. Otherwise, I don't feel like a real best friend."

I sit up, looking her straight in the eyes. "But you *are* my best friend, so stop denying it. I just think it's unfair; you didn't sign up for this."

"Neither did you."

My heart aches at her words, knowing it's true.

"I *did* sign up to be there for you, though," Amy says.

"But it's not your job to help or save me. Technically, it's my job to help you now. To protect you, as your future Luna." I can't bear to keep holding eye contact. "That's why I'm ashamed. I'm claiming to be your future Luna, but I can't even get my shit together."

Amy shoves her hand into mine to shake it vigorously. "Girl, who the hell has all their shit together?!"

I laugh, rubbing her smooth hand in mine. "You know what I mean. You've always been my family when I had none, and I want to make you proud. I— I haven't felt like someone to be proud of lately. Someone Luna-worthy."

"So that's why you've been distant?"

I shrug, dropping my eyes as I warp into ugly tears. "Pretty much."

"Well, that's fucked up too."

"Amy!"

"It's true! Are you kidding me? If surviving absolute hell and still loving someone again isn't Luna-worthy, what is? The person you're painting yourself as isn't who you actually are. You're not a monster, or a burden, or shameful." She pulls her hand from mine, dropping her back against the couch hard with an exasperated huff. "At some point, you have to stop listening to Steven, and start listening to people who actually care about you."

My heart stings with the sudden silence, and Amy shrinks.

She lets out a soft whimper, gripping her head. "God, I'm so sorry, Aliya... That was way too harsh."

I clear my throat. "No, you're right, calling myself those things does sound like him, now that you say that. That makes me sick to my stomach. I'd much rather listen to people I love dearly like you and Noah, and I could never imagine either of you saying those things about me. I'll work on it."

Amy rubs her forehead, hiding her face from me. I don't want her to feel ashamed about her outburst now either. She doesn't always say things in the gentlest ways, but I know where her heart is—and where her intense agitation comes from when it comes to me being hurt.

She also has second-hand trauma from witnessing what Steven did to me. From finding me on my worst day. I didn't know who else to call, and walking through my broken front door to find me changed Amy forever too.

Just like I'm afraid of, my pain hurt her. But like Amy said, she would rather feel this pain than be separated from me. My heart twists so tightly with love for her that it stings.

I tackle Amy onto the couch cushions, startling a small shriek from her.

Laughing, I nuzzle her cheek. "I love you, okay? Thanks for not giving up on me, even when I'm a pain in the ass."

"You're not a pain in the ass!" Amy cackles, rocking me in a tight hug. "You're just too strong for your own good. And I already know you're always thinking about it, beneath the surface. You couldn't even say his name until last year."

"It's true," I mutter. "But now I can. I guess I've made a lot of progress, in some ways."

"Good! Give yourself more credit, babe. I'm so fucking proud of you."

I'm so flustered that I don't know what to say. Instead, I nuzzle Amy's cheek, my heart softening at the giggle it produces from her.

As we settle into each other, I sigh. "We haven't even picked a movie, after all that."

Our heads whip around at the same time at a strange noise, only to find Kira chomping popcorn in the doorway. "You're done fighting, right? I can finally come in?"

Amy gasps. "Kira! Rude!"

Kira smirks, snatching the abandoned remote from Amy's side. "Let's watch that new ridiculous rom-com until Amy pisses herself laughing again."

"Hey, it was one time!"

I burst into laughter, cuddling in as Kira and I trap Amy into an Amy-sandwich. "I guess we really did need an Alpha to come in here and make some decisions for us, Amy. Maybe the stereotypes are true, after all."

Kira snickers. "See, Beta? Omegas are an Alpha's best wingman."

Amy throws her head back with a groan. "Oh, my God, shut up, both of you!"

Kira cackles, kissing Amy square on the lips until she melts into a gushy puddle.

My heart feels looser now that the air has been cleared, allowing me to soften my tense abdominal muscles. I love seeing Amy so happy.

But as the movie begins and I settle back into the cushions, my bond with Noah suddenly shifts into chaos.

Noah's emotions gnaw at my stomach, ripping my insides into shreds as he spirals further into anger, overwhelm, and something too primal to describe.

I'm on my feet in a heartbeat. "Oh, God."

Amy stands with me, her eyes wide with panic. "What is it?"

I grip my chest, panting through Noah's tumbling emotions. "I don't know. Noah feels—"

Kira is with you and Amy, right? Noah mindlinks.

I freeze. *Yes, why?*

I want to make sure you're well-protected.

My stomach drops to the floor. *What happened?! Are you hurt?*

No, I'm not.

Noah pauses, but each second wasted holds too much weight to bear. I grip my arms, scraping every corner of my mind for possibilities of what he's not telling me.

But thankfully, Noah blurts it out. *I found that wolf stalking me again. The one you were worried about.*

I grip my nightgown, gaping at Amy and Kira's wide eyes. Before I can overload Noah with questions, he interrupts my thoughts again.

And I know his name now.

17

My heart throbs in my throat. Noah said he found the wolf that's been stalking us, which should be great news, so what's making Noah so agitated?

The worst possibility comes to mind. I grip the couch arm, struggling to stay upright.

Amy rushes to my side, holding me up by the shoulders. "Aliya?!"

Who is he? I mindlink Noah.

Mason Hart. Do you know him?

Oh. For a second there, I thought he was going to say it was my ex, Steven.

I let out a relieved breath, dropping my forehead against Amy's chest. *No, I don't know a Mason. But it sounds like you do.*

Well, I fucking hate his dad, but Mason? I don't know him beyond kicking his ass. It's just... Something about the way he's acting today is so infuriating that I—

Noah doesn't continue to mindlink me.

Noah?

When he still doesn't reply, I grip my chest, struggling to keep my raging heartbeat under control.

"What did he say?" Amy asks.

I pull away from Amy to walk in a circle, unsure what to do with myself. "He's suddenly not answering. Do you know Mason Hart? Or Mason's dad?"

Kira and Amy glance at each other, then they shrug.

I grip my forehead. "Mason's the one who keeps attacking

Noah. Noah also wants to make sure Kira's here to protect us, and I don't know why. He said something about hating Mason's dad?"

Kira frowns. "Now that you mention it, Alpha Ritchie kicked out a sexist asshole with the same last name: Jack Hart. That had to have been like 20 years ago."

"So maybe they're related?" Amy's eyes widen. "But wouldn't Alpha Ritchie kick out Jack's whole family in that case?"

"I don't know. Alpha Noah and Alpha Ritchie have always taken in Rogues far more than they created them. If Jack's family didn't cause any harm themselves, they could've stayed," Kira says.

"Either way, my mate doesn't sound like himself." I grip my hair, losing control over my breath as it breaks into a sprint. "I need to be with him."

Kira puts a reassuring hand on my back, her protective Alpha musk presenting itself. "Breathe. I'll check around the house, and if it's all clear, one of us can stay with the baby, and the other can travel with you through the woods as our wolves. But do you even know where Noah is?"

My stomach rolls. I hate not knowing the answer to that question now more than ever. *Noah, where are you?*

He still doesn't answer me, but he's alive and alert; his emotions are still blazing.

"He still isn't replying. If I had to guess, he probably doesn't want me to get involved," I say.

Amy's eyes dance between mine. A slow smile spreads across her face. "But you're not going to listen to him, are you?"

I breathe out the acid in my veins. "No. I'm going to see this Mason Hart for myself, and protect my Alpha."

Amy grabs my hand, following after Kira out the door.

We shed our clothes on the porch, shifting into our wolves to better sniff for signs of life nearby.

But after two minutes, all Amy and I find is Kira, her giant wolf head smashed into the crawl space entryway under the porch.

Her tail wags voraciously. *I smell a terrified chipmunk trapped down here, but that's it.*

Leave it, Kira! This isn't the time! Amy says.

Kira's tail droops, her giant ears popping out of the crawl space in her retreat. *Yeah, yeah.*

Amy's ears flatten. *Wait, now that our house is clear, who's going with our best friend, and who's staying to protect our baby?*

Kira's ears twitch. *Shit, I don't know. Can you two stay in the shadows if I let you go alone?*

Yes, I mindlink through my wolf's growl. *And if anyone spots us, I'd never let anyone hurt Amy.*

Kira gazes into my eyes for longer than usual, studying me with one ear rotating to the side. Then she lets out a sharp huff. *I believe you. But stay hidden so it doesn't need to come to that.*

We will, my love. Amy nudges my side with her nose. *Come on, let's go.*

With my nose dusting the forest floor, I seek my mate's scent.

My wolf growls through her frustration. *There's no trace of him anywhere near here.*

Amy bounds beside me, agile paws beating in time with mine as we run. *I'm here with you. We'll find him in no time, I know it.*

Comforted by Amy's fur rubbing against my side, I scatter the leaves beneath me with a huff from my snout. I can do this. Reaching within, I seek out the most familiar soul I know.

The second I call on Noah's presence, his pulsing emotions erupt in my chest as if they're my own.

A growl forces its way from my throat, releasing a bit of Noah's emotions before they explode within me. *Shit, we need to hurry. I can sense he's closer.*

Amy's wolf hunkers into a prowl. *Where? I'll keep watch while you lead the way.*

I sprint through the trees, my sole focus on the magnetic pull in my chest guiding me to my furious mate. Sinking into a sprint, my chest brushes against loose leaves as I fly low to the ground. My paws meld with the earth no matter the terrain, finding themselves in just the right pockets to keep me moving.

Where'd my klutzy best friend go? You're freaking fast, and graceful as hell! No wonder Noah won't stop talking about how beautiful your wolf is. Amy's compliments tug at my heartstrings.

He does always say that, doesn't he? God, I love my sweetheart of a mate. But my moment of adoration doesn't last long with his despair pummeling my core. *I need to be with my Alpha.*

I know. You're almost there.

The wind scratches the skin beneath my fur, urging me to pick up speed. With it, a hint of Noah's sour, angry scent enters my nose.

He's nearby!

Amy catches up to my side, her huffing snout locking onto Noah's scent with me. *I've got your back, but keep your ears alert. There are a lot of wolves nearby.*

One ear rotates at her suggestion, helping me focus in on distant rustling. The wind carrying their scent tells me it's multiple Greenfield wolves with Noah, back near the rock where we met.

Mate! I mindlink Noah.

Oh, Goddess, Omega. You're here?! Noah's wolf bristles in our bond. *Don't come near—*

No, I'm coming to protect you!

I expect to feel relieved when I spot Noah pinning Mason to the ground, surrounded by familiar, safe wolves—Rainn, Yasmine, and Dave at his flanks with an army of Greenfield allies—but a sickening growl bubbles up my throat at the sight of Noah wrapped up with Mason.

Noah is so agitated that his fur is fluffed all the way out, making him appear twice as large. Even worse, Mason is gloating at the reaction he's creating in Noah, baring his teeth with an irritated tail wag.

What's going on here? I mindlink our closest allies, dashing for Noah.

But multiple wolves swoop in, forcing Amy and me to a scrambling halt.

Dave's hulking wolf blocks our view in particular. His stocky, brown-and-black striped wolf pants like he's been sprinting as hard as us. *No, Luna. It's not safe.*

Yasmine rushes to my side, herding away other wolves except Amy, Dave, and Rainn. *Your Alpha has lost his shit. I've never seen Noah this angry, but whatever Mason mindlinked, it locked Noah's jaws.*

My throat tightens. *Mason is still taunting his pack Alpha, even after losing this badly?*

I'm assuming, but I'm not fully sure. Yasmine growls, including Noah in our mindlink. *Your Alpha is just as stubborn. We can't separate them to talk it out.*

And we won't *separate if this asshole won't shift back to show me his human face. It's suspicious as fuck.* Noah only seems to grow larger, his fur rippling with each growling breath.

Mason's mindlink makes me shiver with the anger coursing through its force, each word shoving its way into my mind. *I guess you don't know what it's like to have a deadly animal pinning you down, Alpha. How can I shift if I feel unsafe?*

That was completely insincere. Mason obviously feels safe enough to keep baiting Noah.

When Mason glares at me, his scent reveals utter distaste, blaming everyone else for the mess he put himself in. My muscles spasm on instinct, jerking me backwards.

Noah snarls loud enough to make me quiver. His jaw tightens until saliva leaks onto Mason's neck, and Mason yipes in pain.

But when Noah pauses, Mason still chooses to glare at me. With my ears slicked back and body curled, my paws sneak back a few steps.

Until I get a good whiff of Mason's scent.

Oh. He's just scared, deep down, Noah.

He should be. Especially if he tries anything else around you.

Around me?

Yes. The day you and I found each other, I beat the shit out of him for trying to keep me away from you. But now he's upset I went "beyond necessary measures" to protect my mate, and says he has it out for vengeance.

My heart pounds hard enough to make my wolf pant. *Wait, Noah, this is freaking me out. I knew he found us that day, but you think he was being possessive over me? Why didn't you tell me this before?*

It's not like that. My dad always warned me about the day I'd find my mate. You and I were omitting a mating call scent, and it's the best time to challenge an Alpha. Noah's growling heightens, raising the fur on Yasmine's back. *If he kills the pack's top Alpha before I* mate with my Luna, he ends my lineage, replacing it with his. His ears flick back, irritation and dismay tensing every fiber of his shoulder muscles. *So once again, you're just caught in my mess.*

Noah, it's not your fault. I whine, my tail tucking harder. *But what if he's not actually Mason? What if he's someone else you know, plotting to hurt you? Shoot you?*

Trust me, this is Mason. His dad was one of the only Rogues my dad ever created, and Jack's obsessed with Alpha domination, just like this asshole. But Mason hasn't done enough to justify kicking him out. With how much other packs hate Rogues, it's basically like issuing a death sentence.

Oh, God... So you really do think this was just a dominance thing?

I want to think that, but now that he's going with that story too, it's hard to fully believe it. Noah's snout curls into a tense snarl. *I think he's hiding something else he did. But the way he's challenging me pisses me off. No one should use you to get to me.*

I think back on the night I met Noah. Mason attacked Noah in front of me that night, just like Mason attacked Noah at my first Welcoming Ceremony. Both times, Noah was vulnerable. The only times I can remember Noah letting himself have an opening is when I've been upset.

Guilt and anger burns my lungs, forcing my wolf to let out a heavy huff. *It's a clever tactic, Noah.*

What? His deep snarl makes Mason flinch between Noah's teeth.

It worked, twice. He saw an opening to dominate you while your sole focus was on me, and he took it. His motivations make perfect sense. But now he's distracting you from the real problem: why isn't he shifting back?

Noah stops growling, his eyes tightening into a disgusted squint.

Which means he's using the same tactic a third time, mentioning me to make you vulnerable and upset, I mindlink.

Shit, you're right. God, he's so fucking obnoxious.

He is, and I think it's on purpose. He knows he's at a loss, and this is his last-ditch effort: he's hiding something serious enough to keep pushing back, even when he's cornered. My tail curls over my ankles as I sit on my haunches. *But he doesn't stand a chance against my gorgeous, powerhouse Alpha, does he?*

Noah's growl is cut off by my compliment, his chest puffing with pride. *Mate...*

I can't help but wag my tail. *There's my big, goofy Alpha.*

As Noah releases a delighted purr, it finally feels safe to approach. Rubbing myself along Noah's side, I soak him in my adoring scent. *I love you. We're okay. I love you.*

Noah's ears soften. But then he sneezes in annoyance. *I'm not going to drop him.*

You're at a standstill if you keep him pinned, my adorable Alpha. Something has to change to resolve this. There's no way Mason will give us any information if we don't play into his cards a little.

Noah's wolf gives me a wavering grumble despite flashing his puppy dog stare. *Sweet Omega, I don't like the sound of that...*

At this point, he's only gathering tactics to piss you off more. Let's try our hand at his game. Let him go to trap him further.

Ugh... Only because I love you, and you're a damn genius. Noah's eyes squint into irritated slits, rapid flicks of his left ear telling me he hates everything about this. *But you should be the one to order us to play nice. It'll piss him off the most.*

I can hardly resist wagging my tail, but I force myself to regain my composure. It's time to mindlink everyone present at once. Play the game.

Enough of this. Let's have a rational, adult discussion, I say. *Please drop him, Alpha.*

Yeah, Alpha, drop me.

Mason's grating response charges me from nose to tail with rage, making me lose sight of our game just as it started.

Noah growls at Mason, but I snarl so viciously that both of them flinch.

Don't forget what I look like when you attack my mate. If you try anything, I'm even more prepared for you this time.

Mason's ears flatten, his breath rapid. He can't bear to look into my eyes. After a few silent seconds, Mason growls. *Fine. I'll stay and talk.*

Noah puffs his chest even higher as he beams at me. *My feisty Omega.*

Releasing Mason, Noah makes every other wolf pace with his vigilant stance. We circle Mason, but the beaten down Alpha shakes his coat clean of dirt and slobber.

Is this a dictatorship now, Alpha? No one can challenge you?

Noah rotates one ear back as if Mason is speaking gibberish. *You made this personal, Hart. No Alpha would let this slide, especially not when you keep involving my mate.*

When did I ever involve her? I've only gone after you. Or are you admitting all Omegas are weak and biologically dependent on us, after all?

Noah bristles, and I rub against his shoulder.

Giving into his manipulation is a waste of energy. He knows exactly what he's doing.

Noah stares deep into Mason's eyes. A tense, extensive silence falls over the forest. I'm tempted to shiver.

Low, dark rumbling erupts from Noah's chest. *I'm going to ask you this one more time only, Hart. Are you going to shift into your human form? Or are you going to make a social enemy of yourself in the eyes of the pack?*

Mason's tail wags, but it's not a happy wag. It's a cornered, agitated wag.

Warning signals alarm in my head. Varying scents clash around me in dissonant chords as every wolf bristles.

This is authoritarianism, Alpha, and I think more wolves are going to agree with me than you'd care to admit. Mason glares.

That's when I see the other eyes in the forest, glinting over Mason's shoulders in the moonlight. Unfamiliar wolves stalk closer.

I press closer to Noah, my tail tucking. Noah leans closer in response, his counterpressure acting as a wolf-hug.

Come on, man. You're suspicious as fuck, and you won't cooperate after presenting yourself as a threat. I don't like that you're unwilling to show your face, Hart. That's not normal.

One of your Betas recognizes my wolf. Or did you not listen to him either?

Noah paws at the dirt with a grunt. *Dude, cut the dramatics. You have something to hide, and you're doing a shit job of hiding it.*

Mason growls, and my heart leaps into my throat. I can't

believe he's still challenging Noah this heavily. He's completely outnumbered.

I have something to hide, huh? Mason drops his chin, gazing at us with a flash of the whites of his eyes. *Maybe I do, maybe I don't.*

For the first time, my body runs cold at the familiar phrase Jenny and I say in Exposure and Response Prevention therapy. Only Amy, Noah, and Jenny know I have OCD, but the way Mason said that makes me feel sick. Like it's not a coincidence.

Mason turns his back, padding through the forest.

Noah's breath hitches, his lips curling to show his enraged grin. *That's how you're going to play this, huh?*

What? I'm showing you my back, Alpha. Completely vulnerable to you. You're gonna go after me when I'm already hurt?

Mason isn't just cocky. He's dangerously entitled.

I want to humble him. I'm afraid if I don't do it now, he'll only tighten his hold on the situation.

I stalk after Mason, circling in front of him to look him in the eyes. He tenses, tracking my every step with raging, frantic eyes.

Omega!? What are you doing?! Noah bristles in the corner of my eye, sneaking closer.

Don't threaten him, Alpha. I just want to talk, I mindlink.

Mason stands straighter, his tail rising in a proud taunt. *That's hilarious, did she tell you to stop? She doesn't need protection, anyway. Right, Alpha? Omegas don't need our strength.*

Ignoring his taunts, I sit on my haunches, staring him straight in the eyes. Let's hope this dominance challenge doesn't get me into deep shit.

But Mason hasn't moved. As I glare, a momentous rage wells up in my core.

Instead of letting it consume me, I exhale it through my snout like dragonfire.

Mason Hart.

He loses any and all remaining confidence when I mindlink his name, his wolf going rigid.

There'd be no conflict between us if you hadn't created it, yourself. You know that, right?

Mason sneers, but he's unable to hold my stare. My fur bristles, craving deeper dominance over him.

Maybe you're not used to anyone seeing through your cries for victimhood. But from an actual victim to a clear manipulator— My lips lift on their own, flashing my fangs. *I recognize you for who you really are. You can't hide from me.*

Mason's tail tucks, his breath short and rapid. He backs away quickly, pressing lower and lower to the floor.

But it's not enough for me. My dominant scent extends on its own, making every wolf shrink—except for Noah and his alert, tilted head.

Omega, you smell like... Noah's awe trickles through our bond, but I have to keep focused. Glare at Mason until he realizes I'm serious. Serious enough to end his life if he threatens to take ours again.

When I lower into the deepest growl I can manage, baring my full fangs, Mason scampers away, his tail tucked as tight as possible in submission.

In Mason's absence, there's dead silence. I spin around, confused.

All eyes are glued to me. Everyone awaits my next move. Like they usually do for Noah.

18

I shrink into myself whether I'd like to or not, worried I did something wrong. *What? Why are you all looking at me like that?*

Noah's upright ears soften. He approaches me first, ducking his head to let me know he's safe to be around.

Our noses touch, cold and wet as they drag across each other's snouts. With Noah against me, I finally take a deep breath.

He sheepishly wags his tail, keeping himself low. *Mate. I can't stand how much I love my beautiful, powerful mate.*

I whine, my tail thumping against the forest floor at Noah's puppyhood coming back to him.

You did so well. I adore you, I— Noah growls as his wolf playfully tackles me to the ground, lick-attacking me before I can defend myself.

Alpha? I whine, gripping his head with my paws as he grooms my face.

I don't want anything to happen to you. Ever. You're too precious.

Then don't maul me!

Noah groans, nuzzling my chest until my tail slaps the ground even faster.

But then Noah starts sniffing me all over. Hard.

My fur stands on end as he buries his nose deep into my neck, inhaling as much of my scent gland as he can. The surrounding wolves lean in, awaiting Noah's assessment. My ears fall flat in embarrassment.

Noah whines. He stops sniffing to give my neck soft, careful licks.

But he doesn't say anything.

Noah, are you sure I didn't do anything wrong? Why are you sniffing me like that? What's everyone thinking?

He purrs, licking me harder. *Fuck, I love you. I love you more than ever.*

Answer me.

I'm... working on it.

What's that supposed to mean?

I just don't understand yet. You're still my mate, and you're still my sweet Omega— His wolf silences his breath, golden eyes tracing mine. *But you also smell like an Alpha.*

My heart flips. Glancing at Amy, my confusion shifts into panic when the best friend I've known my entire life shies away from my stare on instinct—in submission.

W-what?!

Noah's head tilts. *Okay, now you smell like pure Omega.*

I whine, burying my head into Noah's chest fluff in an attempt to disappear.

Don't be scared, my love. It's okay. Noah's paws tighten around me as I shrink beneath him, shielding myself with my fluffy mate.

Is there something wrong with me, Noah?

No. Don't ever let anyone make you think that.

Noah turns away from me to snap at everyone in company with a deep growl. They scatter into the woods in flashes of fur amidst dark thickets.

The second I'm alone with him, his ears perk back up. He gazes down with pure excitement over my existence. My heart melts. Even with everything that just happened, he's so happy to be with me. I'm itching to feel the same, nuzzling into his comfort.

Are you saying I'm an Alpha... My Alpha?

Noah's ears slick back as he beams at me. *Not exactly... I don't really have a word for it, but you've got an interesting mixture of scents.*

I can't stop whining. *Do I smell weird? Do you still like me the same? Are you attracted to me the same?*

Don't even ask that. I want to eat you, I love you so much.

Before I can whine in response, Noah captures my entire head into his mouth.

I yipe. *Noah?! You big goofball!*

His high-pitched, excited growl echoes through the trees.

When I squirm, Noah releases my face to flop on his side. As he bats at me, my tail thumps at his silly panting face; his entire tongue is flopped out the side of his mouth.

Noah gives me a soft "roo." *You're the most beautiful wolf I'll ever meet in my life. No one could ever come close. I love that I got to see this side of you so clearly for the first time. Please don't think I'll do anything else except love you more and more for the rest of my life.*

Ugh, I love him. I want to eat him up too.

Releasing a playful growl, I clamber over Noah, licking him until he shivers from head to tail.

Opening my mouth as wide as I can, I glomp my jaws over Noah's snout. His ears perk all the way up. But it's not enough. Nipping at Noah's neck, I rapid-fire bite until he pants hard.

Noah's shrill yipe excites me to my core. He grips me, his claws applying tingly pressure into my back.

He bites me back, and we lapse into a mini biting war, each nip dousing me with more and more excitement.

But as we wrestle, I end up pinning Noah to the ground.

An urge wells up inside me.

I bite his neck, and he freezes.

But then he doesn't just freeze; he *fawns*.

Whimpering for me, Noah's scent dissolves into something I don't recognize.

And my scent screams Alpha.

O-oh God! I'm so sorry! I release him, scrambling off his body and diving behind the nearest tree.

Omega, wait!

I scramble into a bush, desperate to bury myself in embarrassment, but Noah's stark growl stops me in place.

Wait. Please.

Alpha, I'm so sorry...

His big nose nudges me out of the bush, but I can't bear to lift my head to meet his gorgeous black wolf's golden eyes.

Look at me. I don't care if it turns into a dominance challenge against me. I just want to see you, face-to-face.

Peeking up at him, my core ignites with warmth as our eyes lock.

Noah's ears twist as he stares, attempting to figure out my every breath.

I lower myself, tempted to roll over for him in apology. *I'm sorry, I don't know what's wrong with me—*

Noah's deep growl makes me flinch, but more in the fear I've stepped out of line.

His ears droop. *Please... Just be yourself. You're wonderful.*

I drop his stare after all, smushing my forehead into his chest. *I just want to go home now.*

Sweet Omega, we will. But listen to me. He nuzzles into my neck, nipping at the mark he left until I melt onto my back.

As he licks me, pleasure heats my core to dangerous levels. Noah's resulting purr makes it even worse.

I mean it, Aliya, I love you more than ever.

I love you more than ever too. That's why I'm afraid I'm ruining this by suddenly... changing.

Nothing has changed between us in a bad way, and I'm not sure you've actually changed, at all. I think you're more comfortable now, so we're just seeing parts of you that you haven't felt safe enough to let out yet.

Our bond does feel safe. So safe. I whimper, cuddling in deeper.

I think this is us getting to know you, at your core, Noah continues. *And if it turns out you're more Alpha than Omega, or vice versa, I'm honored to witness your wolf coming out of her shell. I love every beautiful second of it.*

I whine at his heartfelt words, absolving into ferocious lust. *I love you too much, Alpha. Shift back and mate with me—*

Noah quickly de-mounts me, his breath rapid and heavy. I whine, rolling around on my back as heat pounds my core. Noah's flustered wolf locks onto my every move.

Okay, fuck. We really should go home before my wolf loses all blood to his head.

Before I can disagree, Noah trots off into the forest, forcing my horny wolf to scramble after him.

Rubbing along his sides and chest, my wolf courts Noah the entire way home—I can't help myself.

But about a quarter mile to his cabin, Noah's mood plummets. My ears droop with his, hating to see my mate sad. I don't know what he's thinking.

I gaze up at Noah, letting him know I'm listening. Noah's ears switch from flattened sadness to slinked-back adoration.

I smash my head into his cheek until we do a full circle, and Noah's delighted tail springs into action, gazing at me with his classic puppy eyes.

I'm here, Noah. I want to listen, no matter what you're feeling. I accompany my words with a soft cheek boop, and Noah shivers.

Ugh, cute. So cute. You're so damn sweet to me.

Stopping at the trees in front of his cabin, Noah shifts back into his human form. I quickly follow. He tackles me with a hug as soon as I'm standing at my usual foot below his human height.

I close my eyes, breathing him in. His bare skin warms me despite the cool summer wind brushing my exposed back. I cuddle in deeper, forgetting we're not in our wolf forms anymore and seeking out his face with my nose.

Noah chuckles, cupping my cheeks as he gazes down at me. *My love, I'm sorry I haven't been able to protect you from him either. From Mason.*

My stomach flips. *Noah, it's—*

"No, it's *not* okay." His deep voice rasps, strangled with emotion. My lungs pick up the pace as his serious but calm scent cuts through the air.

This is how a true Alpha feels. I'm nothing like this.

But Noah's mind remains on Mason, his jaw tensing. "I'm doing something about it in the morning. Will you join our Pack Safety meeting?"

I blink a few times, struggling to grasp the full scope of his words. Only Elders and Noah's direct advisors hold Pack Safety meetings.

"Oh. Of course. If you want me there." My heart pounds as Noah continues to stare. His feet shuffle between us. "What is it?"

"Will you... join a-*all* of my meetings? Forever?"

I suck in a heavy breath, my eyes flicking between Noah's for signs of uncertainty or pressure to please me. But it's true. He's keeping his promise to not require it of me before I tell him I'm ready, but he wants me to be his Luna. It's not just a tradition to him.

I can't stop the smile from reaching my eyes. "Yes, Noah. A thousand times, yes."

Burying his fingers into my hair, Noah's eyes close even before he kisses me, trusting I'll meet his lips. As he holds me, naked in the middle of the dark woods, I've never felt more secure.

19

I drag Noah inside by the hand, taking him straight to bed.

I hardly allow him to wipe his forest-y feet before urging him under the covers with me.

"Feisty Omega." His soft giggle warms my heart as he climbs into bed.

I clamp around him with my whole body the second he lays down.

But I make sure to hold his head to my chest, both arms wrapped around him as even my head hugs his. Our cuddle ball shifts as my doting scent reverts back to lust, craving more of his touch. Noah lifts his chin to kiss me, but the soft, loving pecks he gives aren't enough.

He seems to agree, tugging me lower by the hips so he can smash every inch of his lips into mine. Each kiss loosens my muscles, parting my lips. Noah's tongue glides into my mouth, meeting mine in a slow, erotic dance.

As I buck my hips down for his cock on instinct, his tip dips into my entrance. We jolt in surprise.

Noah's sudden seriousness flushes my cheeks as he pulls back to look at me.

I'm unraveled and aching with need for him, but most of all…

"I feel so safe with you," I whisper.

He huffs out a heavy breath, his fingertips sliding into the roots of my hair behind my head. My heart pounds as his eyes glide across every part of my body; he's absorbing every second of my breath as if he's reminding himself I exist.

"I feel safe with you too. No one protects me like you do, Aliya."

I kiss him harder than I have all night, whining through the love coursing through our bond. Reaching below me to position his cock at my entrance, I attempt to bind our bodies even further.

But then I remember something. "Dammit, I'm on my period."

Noah releases a heavy breath, his eyes wide. "T-*that's* what you're worried about? You almost just put me inside you, and it seriously hurt you last time."

"I know, but I— We have to practice if we want it to hurt less, right? And I'm feeling extra turned on, so—"

Noah's wide-eyed stare softens into steady desire. I hardly have time to take it in before he presses his lips to mine, his Alpha musk rushing straight to my groin. I respond by widening my legs.

Let me at least help you warm up first. Noah is too busy making out with me to speak aloud, each of his heavy kisses stirring pleasure through my chest. He rolls into the opening I left him between my thighs with a growl, easing a hand down my abdomen until he brushes my clit. I whine through rapid, uncontrollable breaths, my back arching with every completed circle of his fingertips. He massages each wave of pleasure so deep into the sensitive nerve that my legs squirm at his sides.

Noah absorbs my moans with each kiss as his fingers travel even lower. His slow, gentle tug on the string between my legs slips my tampon out with ease. My heart squeezes as hard as my inner core, delighted by what it means: I'm now empty for him to enter.

"Holy— I've never had a tampon be something sexy in my whole life," I giggle.

Noah chuckles, but we're far too eager to fully laugh, gazing deep into each other's eyes.

When he reaches for his pillow, I know it's to support my back during penetrative sex.

He's agreeing to try.

I swallow hard. "I'm going to get your pillow messy with blood."

"I don't care. You like this angle." He peeks at me from the corner of his eyes, his irises enveloped in a soft yellow sheen against the moonlight. "I want to make you feel loved from the inside out."

Noah lifts my hips to slide the pillow beneath me. This simple act ignites our bond with anticipatory desire.

My mate breaks into a playful grin. "Plus, I got that waterproof mattress protector for a reason."

I groan, hiding my face in my palms. "God, I'm sorry—"

"No, no, no—" Noah pulls my hands off my face. "Trust me, it's a huge compliment to need one. Seriously, it makes my fucking day, every time."

"I-I actually—" I swallow hard, flushing to my chest. "I actually didn't used to squirt like that. I haven't with anyone else—except for one or two times, by myself."

Noah freezes. "What? Really?"

My heart pounds. "Really. That's why I've been a little extra embarrassed that I keep messing up the bed."

As his wolf's chest puffs in our bond, I sputter out a shy laugh. But Noah's expression dissolves into a serious, touched silence. With a kiss on my burning cheeks, Noah softens his voice. "Fuck, Aliya. It actually means a lot that you trust me enough for your body to feel so relaxed and safe with me. I thought it was a treat before, but now it's even more beautiful."

A rising, uncontainable whimper comes out of me. "I want you *so* badly, Noah." I'm surprised by how desperate I sound, but Noah shudders, slow blinks soaking in every bit of my lusty scent.

As he positions himself in front of me, one hand on my thigh, he looks straight into my eyes.

"I'm right here. Do you want me to use my hands first, or my mouth?"

I bite my lip with a giggle, stifling my rising breath. "I-I'd—I'd like you to touch me."

Noah's voice settles into a deep purr. "I'd love to, gorgeous."

His fingertips swirl across my core, but my eager body opens wide, swallowing one of them. I shudder, gripping his wrist for more as Noah eases his finger deeper. He's so gentle that I'm surprised by how easy it feels—as if I've had no problem with penetration lately.

"Does it hurt at all?" He murmurs against my lips.

"No, I—" My jaw drops. "I love it."

The slow, penetrating drag of his finger tugs directly on my heart muscles, overpowering my senses. But when my body quickly gapes for him, Noah adds a second finger. Tingles ricochet throughout my chest.

"Ah... *Yes*—" I breathe out every word.

"You're so warm and soft, gorgeous."

My pussy clenches around his fingers at his words, intensifying the pleasure of his touch. He prods me faster, curling against my G-spot with lush, massaging motions.

"Oh, God, Noah—" My knees drop open, lifting my entrance for him as my hips rock over the pillow.

"Fuck," he whispers, his eyes roaming over me like he can't capture enough of this moment before it slips away from him.

I tilt my hips, shoving him deeper as I clamp down on his fingers. Noah's cock twitches every few breaths, but it jolts as I squirt across it with a cry.

"Ah! I'm about to come, Noah—"

"I know, gorgeous. I'll work you back up again. Enjoy yourself." His deep purr sinks deep into my heart.

I drop my head to the side, and Noah takes his chance to lick my mark. Each lick builds pressure in my groin. As he plunges his fingers deeper, nudging my cervix, my nipples harden at the pleasure shooting up my chest.

"Ah! Mmm—"

My moaning orgasm is stolen with a kiss, Noah's breath heaving as he rapid-taps my favorite spot. Wetness seeps into the pillow below me, and my legs shake with leftover pleasure.

"Good job, beautiful. You did so well." Noah kisses me through my soft moans, his thumb stroking my cheek in gentle admiration.

"Noah," I breathe. His shaft flexes at the sound of his name, and I bite my lip. "You're so hard."

"Fuck... Yeah, I guess so."

Noah eases back into motion, slipping his fingers in and out— testing out how I'd feel if I was penetrated.

"Oh, God," I breathe. "Oh, it's still good. I want it, Noah." I whine as his big fingers slip from me, leaving my core flexing for more. "Try it. Try entering me. Please."

His warm hand on my belly urges me to release a slow breath. "That's my sweet Omega. Breathe deep for me."

He grips his cock, circling it around my entrance until my back arches.

"Oh! Please—"

"Relax, gorgeous. Please, relax."

I nod, my lips parted with pleasure as I gaze into his heavy-lidded stare. As he nudges my core with his bulging tip, I instantly wince—followed by intense, luxurious pleasure at how thick he is. The introduction of his warm, soft skin feels so strong that it's like he's touching all of me.

I breathe out a delighted sigh, my eyelashes fluttering.

But all Noah notices is the wince. He slips back out of me, not even an inch inside in the first place.

"Wait, it felt so good!"

"Aliya, it hurt you—"

"Alpha, I swear it felt good after the first part. Let's just see what happens if you go further in."

"I-I want to… But I don't want to hurt you." Noah bites his lips. "You said it was bad before, right? What helped make it better? Or was it still this bad before we met?"

"Well, it got a lot better. Mainly because I— Well…" My cheeks flush. "It's a trauma response, so I graduated myself from toy to toy until it all felt good."

Noah's wound shoulders soften. "Okay, so maybe we can try something in-between first?" Noah's eyebrows raise as I deflate in disappointment. He chuckles. "Or maybe you just need some encouragement."

My heart flips. "What do you mean?"

His incisors gleam in the moonlight, sending a thrill up my spine. "I mean that you've been taking it so well for me lately, gorgeous. I'm so proud of you."

I'm speechless, buried beneath a flash of shyness too powerful to silence. In fact, it only grows louder as Noah returns his fingers to me with a thorough massage, fluttering my eyelids.

"Fuck, what a good, sweet girl," he murmurs.

Every inch of my face flushes hot, so I'm almost relieved we're in the dark. Except Noah can absolutely feel my shy, supercharged excitement in our bond from his dirty words, and he's grinning like he knows exactly what he's doing to me.

With a deep growl, Noah rubs his tip between my legs, arching my back. "There you go."

I expect him to try to enter me again, but Noah sticks to swirling himself through my fluids. I'm a squirming, panting mess beneath him, lifting my hips in desperation to meet him. "Noah, I want it so badly—"

"Hey, I've got you, remember? Let's make sure you're feeling okay first."

I groan, stopping him with a hand on his chest. "I don't know if it'll feel 100% okay, Noah. It might still hurt me a bit, but that's the only way I can get myself used to it again."

Noah traces my eyes "Then how about this: you're in charge. Pull me in as much as you want me, and I'll walk you through it."

"Okay," I whisper.

Nerves strike my core. I reach between my legs, stroking his shaft. It's dripping with every eager flex, just as desperate for attention despite Noah's obvious concern.

"Just don't hurt yourself, please. I love you too much." He drops to his elbows beside my shoulders, nudging my nose with the tip of his.

Our bodies fall flush from head to toe. It softens the remaining worry between us, Noah's every shift and squirm sliding against my bare skin.

Hands drag across each other's backs, fingernails in each other's hair. Our hands lace with a tight squeeze as we ease into long, deep kisses. Our hips rub against each other, daring to connect. Noah feels so good against me that my heart clenches, physically aching from how much I love him.

"I adore you. I love being this close to you," I whisper.

He purrs into my mouth, dragging his tongue across mine. His hand behind my head deepens every kiss, his hips rocking in motion with my heavy breaths.

As I prepare him to enter me, I allow the natural flow of our grinding hips to guide him in, bit by bit. My breath hitches in pain as his massive cock stretches my pussy, but when Noah stiffens in worry, I grip his ass. "Deeper. *Please*—"

"Okay, sweet Omega. You've got this. You've done such a good job, getting so wet for me—"

I gasp as he pushes past my sore entrance, suddenly slipping into my swollen core. He's more immersed inside me than he has been all month. The bliss is so heavy, it aches, and I gush onto the pillow.

Noah's eyes stare deep into mine, living every millisecond of sensation with me with heaving pants. My legs clamp around his hips, dragging him further, further, further.

"Oh, fuck," Noah growls. "You're such a good girl, I can't stand it."

Dropping my head back with a heavy inhale, I moan as he brushes the deepest point in me. "Ah— More—"

Noah's heavy moan cuts me off as his eyelids flutter, carefully dragging his cock back just to plunge deeper again. "Fuck, you feel so fucking good, and I'm so weak to it. I'm sorry, I'm— I'm already—"

His intense pleasure hits me deep, making my hips squirm. My nails dig into his ass, urging him to meld with me.

"More, Noah! Please!"

He pulses into me gently but steadily, careful not to slip too far out. Our lips mash together, and we grip each other's hair as we trade moans back and forth.

Goddess, look at you. I can't believe how well you're doing. Noah's breath speeds against my cheek, his hips twitching with impatience. When he releases my lips to kiss me with tongue, I moan into his mouth at how good it feels to have him inside me in more than one way. But the extra emphasis on his inward stroke makes me cry in delight, each brush of my cervix fluttering my heart.

I break our kiss with a panting heave. "*Noah*, you're about to make me—"

"Ah, fuck—" Noah buries his cock into me as deep as he can, filling me with burst after burst of thick fluid. My head drops back as I claw into his shoulders, taken by the heavy warmth his cum spreads throughout my core. His knot consumes all remaining room at my entrance, his tip compressing my cervix with massaging pressure until I yell with every moan.

"Noah! Ah! Ah—"

"I've got you—" He kneads my clit with his wide thumbpad, and my hips writhe with gratification. "Fuck, you're doing so, *so* well—"

As I come hard over his knotted cock, Noah's frenzied gasps against my lips wrack my heart. He cradles my head as my eyes roll back, immersed in the blooming pleasure in our bond as it steals my vision. Noah whimpers over me, kissing my jawline until I can finally see again enough to kiss him back.

"Noah—" I breathe. "Oh, my— My *God*, I—" I want to tell him how hard his loving comfort just made me orgasm, hitting every nerve in my body with bliss, but his soft, exhausted kisses tell me he understands.

"Good job, gorgeous. You did such a good job," he whispers.

God, I still don't know how to respond to his genuine, sultry praise. All I can force myself to whisper is a shy, "T-thank you— F-for your help."

I'm too pleasure-limp to open my eyes, nuzzling Noah's cheeks as I urge more and more kisses from him. The purring cuddle between us morphs from lust aftershocks to indulgence, huddling into each other's cozy embrace.

I'm tempted to doze off with my face squished against Noah's and our limbs tangled, but every time I open my eyes to gaze at my mate, I'm reminded of how much I'm loved.

Noah is still looking at me with heavy-lidded eyes. He hasn't spoken a word, but I feel his thoughts in his hands cradling me to him, the sharp, heart-clenching breaths he takes when we meet eyes, and each uptick of his love in our bond when another purr escapes my lips.

Eventually, he answers my curious gaze with his mindlink. *I couldn't imagine living the rest of my years with anyone but you. Thank you for trusting me to hold you through your pain.*

I huff out the tender, loving ache that strikes my heart. Crashing into a cuddly, deep kiss, I breathe in every second of Noah's satisfied scent. *Thank you for being here on this planet with me.*

Noah's warm, spreading smile soothes my heart.

20

After an intimate night wrapped in Noah's arms, I wake up energized and content. The sound of Noah's sleepy feet sliding across the kitchen floor charms a giggle out of me. I better get up so I can love on him and still get to school on time.

I stop outside the shower, turning to the side to glance at my period-bloated abdomen.

The sight of my fingers caressing my swollen, empty uterus no longer breaks my heart. This time, I can imagine Noah's arms around me, holding our growing baby with me from behind. I can imagine him nurturing me through labor, all the way up until we hold our newborn together.

Glancing at my red eyes in the mirror, I burst out laughing at my gushing tears.

I want to have a baby with Noah, worse than ever. But like he said, I know we'll have our chance to be parents. I just don't know when.

And that's okay.

The clanking of plates outside the bathroom door brings me back to Earth. Noah is probably starting breakfast. I should get dressed so I can hurry and help him.

It's only as I grab my clothes that I realize this school day is unlike any other I've experienced so far. My movements slow as my heart deflates; I almost forgot I got laid off. Instead of counting down the days until the school year ends, I'm counting down until I'm no longer a preschool teacher. The thought burns my stomach. I guess I'll just have to focus on making it a good day for the kids.

As I dress, I mentally review today's agenda, including hearing about Noah's plans for Mason after I come home from work.

I just don't get why it's normalized to have top Alphas under constant attack. Was it like this for Alpha Ritchie too?

Then a thought hits me in the gut. One I've staved off since I met Noah.

What if I was right, and our dads were actually *murdered?*

Not just by a hunter's accidental shot, like the cops told Mom and me originally, but an intentional, premeditated shooting. What if I wasn't paranoid for thinking that in the first place, and they were killed on *purpose?*

I swallow hard, swiping my tears as they come. No, I can't think like this again. That got me nowhere in the past except ostracized.

I try to regain the smile Noah left me with this morning, but my heart aches as I enter the living room. There's a sharp metal *ting* of Noah setting down a fork or spoon, followed by the wooden floor's creaking as his feet rapidly approach.

When I see him, he's wearing a pressed black button-up beneath a casual black blazer, dressed extra nicely for the meeting tonight. The sight of him all put together strains my heart even worse.

It's not just the thought of our dads' potential murders that hurts. It's the thought that my sweet, gorgeous mate could be killed just the same.

I whimper, choking through fresh tears. "H-hi, handsome—"

Noah's eyebrows contort with mine. He rushes for me, pulling me into his arms. "Oh, my *love*. What's wrong?"

I bite my lips, shaking my head to will away my tears. He holds my cheek to his chest, and I take a deep breath of him. Vanilla wafts from his clothes. I can't tell if it's his nurturing scent or what he's cooking.

I laugh off my upset. "Thank you. I'm sorry for getting all emotional this early."

"What are you thinking about?"

"I'm just sad. I'm going to miss being there for my students." My heart throbs, knowing I'm not admitting the full truth yet, but it's still honest; I'm gutted about losing my job.

Noah hums in understanding, bending to kiss my forehead. "Don't worry, sweet Omega. You're going to help so many pups here, just by being yourself."

I break into a sad smile. "Thank you, my sweet Alpha."

Thankfully, Noah doesn't press further. He takes my hand, guiding me to the vanilla aroma I keep smelling on his skin.

I gasp at the glorious breakfast display he set out for us: pancakes, fruit, bacon, and yogurt in a line—and a chocolate donut.

Noah fidgets with his blazer button, unable to look me in the eyes. "I-it's the first time you've had your period since we moved in together, a-and I figured period food cravings were similar to heat food cravings, so—"

I throw my arms around his neck, giving him the hardest kiss I can.

Noah chuckles into my mouth, hoisting me into his arms. *Ah, so I was right.*

I giggle through a nod, unwilling to release his lips. *Very right. Thank you, gorgeous.*

He sits on a barstool with me still in his arms, allowing me to straddle his lap with my back to the food. His giddy smile intensifies the pride rising in our bond—despite his flushed cheeks burning even darker.

I can't stop a laugh from breaking our kiss. "Are we not going to eat your beautiful breakfast?"

Noah tilts his head, considering my joke as if it was a serious option.

I laugh. "Noah!"

He stabs a strawberry slice with his fork, placing it in front of my lips. "There. Now we technically—" He gapes when I kiss the strawberry. "Um…"

My lips part. Noah's full focus sticks to my tongue dragging beneath the fork. I stare into Noah's eyes as I pull back to suck the strawberry off the end, giving him a soft, pleased hum. Twitching to life beneath me, Noah's cock urges me to inhale a heavy gasp as I chew.

The sweet vanilla air mixes with my sudden lust. All I can

think about is Noah's warm palms resting on my hips, and how hard he came into me last night.

"O-Omega…"

Noah's voice is so rough that I can't help myself; I slide my fingers into his hair, giving it a gentle tug as I kiss him, hard.

Growling into my lips, Noah squeezes my hips. I hug his waist with my thighs, aching for his touch.

Suddenly, I'm on the kitchen island.

"Noah, the food!" I laugh.

He rotates me slightly to the left, avoiding a majority of the plates.

"That's hardly better, you adorable—"

Eager lips catch my laughter. Clinging to Noah's rocking hips with my legs, I pin him over me.

By the time we've worked ourselves up and stripped our bottom halves, I'm dying to try what we did last night. Noah lifts my hips as I lay back on the island. He gazes into my eyes as he lines up to enter me, hungry for my reaction.

But it's not what either of us expect.

"Agh—" My voice catches with sharp, horrific pain, shooting all the way up my core into my heart. Tears prick my eyes before I even realize what happened.

But Noah's mood does a complete reversal. He exits me as quickly as possible, and his side of our bond warps into fear.

I burst into tears.

He whimpers, patting me all over like he doesn't know where it's okay to touch me anymore. "O-oh, Goddess. Oh, fuck. I hurt you."

I try to shake my head no, but I can't speak through the tears—heavy, wracking breaths shaking my chest.

Noah's pained expression guts me, only making me cry harder.

"I-I'm sorry—" I finally choke out.

"Shh, my love. Shh, no…" Noah tugs my panties back on, his breath trembling as he pulls me into his lap.

Noah squeezes me hard, like I could fall apart if he let go. I grip his shirt, shaking my head in disbelief.

I choke out my words. "I-it felt so nice last night. I'm sorr—"

"No. *Please*, no more sorries. Just breathe, my love. I'm the one who's sorry."

Noah strokes between my legs, attempting to rub it better. I kiss his cheeks, but there's no reversing the situation.

"It's not your fault, Noah. You didn't do anything wrong."

He's silent for a long time.

Eventually, his whisper comes out like it's scraping the back of his throat. "Are you sure?"

"Yes. I'm really sure it was nothing you did. I just—" My lips wobble, choking me out. I can't stop my voice from shaking no matter how hard I try; despair hits me full force. "I was so excited to move forward with you. All my hopes came crashing down when I saw how upset you looked."

"Oh, sweet—" Noah blinks hard and fast, his eyes rimmed in red. "I'm so fucking sorry."

"Steven really fucked my life up. I'm so sick of it."

Noah nods, hugging me closer. "I'd *never* hurt you like that on purpose."

"I know. I trust you still, Noah. It wasn't your fault, I swear."

He doesn't respond, stroking my head until my tears slow. I'm grateful for his doting touch as he helps me eat my breakfast, still holding me close as I chew.

My heart remains shattered throughout the school day, hating how much poor Noah hurts alongside me. Lycan toddlers in particular notice my reeking sadness, my heartbroken scent clinging to the air around me like a needy parasite.

I hate that this is one of my last days with my students. I'm smiling, but I can't bring myself to fully fake it. Kids can always tell.

At snacktime, Andy tugs on my shirt. "Miss Matsuoka?"

"Yes, Andy?"

He keeps tugging on my shirt, so I bend closer. His little hand cups around my ear, preparing for his sloppy whisper. "You're supposed to say, 'I need attention.'"

A smile spreads across my face, taking the place of tears. But even deeper, my chest burns with guilt. It's not his responsibility to worry about me. I'm a terrible teacher today.

I squat to his level, opening my arms for a hug. "Wow! You're doing such an amazing job at knowing how to ask for what you need, Andy!"

He hugs me as hard as he can, spurring a giggle from me.

"Don't worry about me, okay? It's not your job to help me; it's my job to help you."

Andy puffs his chest, pulling back to face me with a frown. "But I'm an Alpha! I have to protect my Luna!"

"Andy." I lower to a whisper, hoping he copies my energy before humans take notice. He falls silent, leaning in to listen. "You're right; you're an Alpha. But I'm also your teacher. At school, it's your job to be a student and have fun while you learn, okay? Not to take care of me."

He drops my stare, his brows furrowing.

"I mean it, buddy. I'm so proud of you and all you've learned this year." I hold his shoulders. "I just want you to know it's never a kid's job to take care of the adults."

Then he peeks up at me, asking the same question I used to when I was young. "Why not?"

I wait for him to fully look at me, making sure he knows I'm serious. "Sometimes adults have big emotions, just like kids do, but adults have had many, many years to learn how to take care of themselves. Do you know how old I am?"

"Ten?" He mutters.

I smile. "Twenty-nine."

Andy's eyes bulge. "Are you an old lady?"

I bust out laughing. "Maybe! I'm very old compared to four, right?"

"Yeah." Andy squares his shoulders. "But I can do things all by myself too."

"You're right, you're so good at learning how to do so many things lately! And it's okay to still be learning. Kids haven't had a chance to learn all of the same things as adults have just yet." With Andy's nod, I smile. "That's why it's our job as adults to teach you. It's not fair for adults to ask you to take care of them. We need to go to other adults for that help."

"Okay…" He frowns. "But when my friends are sad, I want to help."

The way he stares into my soul with worry wracks my heart. I inhale, and whether it's intentional or not, he takes a deep breath with me. I smile, giving his shoulders a soft squeeze.

"It sounds like you're such a great friend. I also want to help my friends when they're sad too. But I'm not a student in preschool, right?"

"Right. You are my teacher." He leans in to loudly whisper. "And my Luna."

I laugh. "Exactly! I'm one of your grown-ups. My job as your teacher is to be someone who helps you learn. It's my job as your Luna to keep you safe, even if you're a smart, independent Alpha pup. Even if you can sense I'm upset, it's okay for me to work on it, myself, or with another adult."

He hums, thinking over my words. Eventually, he nods. "Okay. I'm going to go on the playground now."

I stifle a laugh, blinking a few times to zip forward in time with his ever-present wolf brain. "Oh, how fun! Did you finish your snack so you can go play?"

"Yep! I'm going to play tag with Cory."

He darts onto the playground. I smile at my screeching, playful students before falling back into my thoughts.

Do all Alphas take over-responsibility like this on instinct, or is it a social expectation placed on them? I can feel how gutted Noah is every second today too. I wish he didn't blame himself for my pain, but I don't know what else to say to convince him he's not at fault.

By the time Noah picks me up after school, I can't stop picking at my nails in the car. Noah places his hand over mine, stopping my nail-picking with his eyebrows drawn.

"I'm so sorry. I hate making you anxious."

I hug his hand to my chest. "You're not the one making me anxious." I drop my head against my chair's headrest with a sigh. "And you didn't intentionally hurt me, this morning."

"So, basically, I'm not taking in what you're saying about

accidentally hurting you, and therefore, I'm making you anxious." Noah bites back his smile, peeking at me for a split second as he continues to drive.

I burst out laughing. "God, you're such a cutie! What am I going to do with you?"

"I love you with my whole heart, sweet Omega." Noah's smile falters. "That's why I'm so crushed about accidentally hurting you. I can't stop replaying it, wondering what I could've done differently to prevent it."

I suck in a breath to debate him, but Noah squeezes my hand.

"But that's not your problem to solve. I need to work through this on my own, okay?"

My heart pounds as I gape at him.

Oh. I'm taking over-responsibility too.

Noah clears his throat, parking in our cabin's driveway. "Did I say something weird?"

"No! Sorry, was I staring?"

"Y-yeah." He chews on his lips, unable to stop a slow smile from growing. "But I guess that's sort of normal now."

I giggle, throwing off my seatbelt. Noah's grin is such a relief to see that my heart squeezes as I wrap my arms around my mate. "I'm just amazed by you. You've taught me so much about myself and about life already."

"I feel the same, sweet Omega."

Noah tilts my chin with a delicate finger. His eyes trace my stare before he leans in with a slow, thorough kiss. Each millimeter of his lips sends tingles down my spine, urging me to hold his cheeks for more.

Noah purrs, nuzzling my nose as he shuts his eyes. *Something else is on your mind.*

My mind darkens, racing back to our fathers' deaths. It feels too irrational to talk about aloud, but with the concern behind Noah's stare, I blurt out the truth before I can overthink it.

"A few things are on my mind, actually. Things that I want to talk to you about before the meeting. Privately."

Thankfully, Noah gives me a soft smile. "Okay. I'll make us some tea."

21

We're still holding hands as we face each other on Noah's kitchen barstools. Two mugs steam on the counter, piping out a delicate blend of freshly ground herbs from Greenfield Forest. Otherwise, the kitchen island is now free of Noah's thoughtful breakfast plates, wiped perfectly clean.

But my mind doesn't feel clean at all, scattered with too many thoughts to hold on my own. I release my tense grip on Noah's hand to wipe my sweaty palms on my jeans. All I can think about is how my dad's body must've looked, bleeding out on the forest floor. I don't know if I can stomach talking about every gritty detail of his death with poor Noah. How much of his father's gruesome death replays in his head too?

Noah rubs my arm, leaning in. "What's on your mind?"

God, this is a painful question to ask Noah. I don't know if it's okay. If it's too insensitive, or if it'll bring back too much trauma for him. But this question is killing me, eroding at my insides like leaking battery acid.

"Aliya, what is it? You seem really serious."

"Sorry. I've been thinking a lot about the way our dads died."

Noah's worry shifts into pain, and I wince. Fuck, I don't want him to think I blame him at all.

My breath picks up. "I've been wondering— If their deaths were planned. Like—" I hesitate, unsure if a particular word is okay to say.

This word burrows into my chest, almost too heavy to speak.

But the harder I hold it in, the sicker I feel. Its weight crushes down on my heart like a hydraulic press, threatening to end me.

I squeeze my eyes shut, wincing. When Noah's heart aches with me, I know I can't do this to him any longer.

I open my eyes to find his anxious stare. The word spills out of me, exposing one of my deepest secrets. "A homicide," I breathe. "It's not the first time I've wondered, either. Every time I shove the thought down, it comes back twice as hard."

Noah sits rigid, but he hasn't stopped staring. I have no idea what he's thinking.

So I just talk. "I-I mean, I used to wonder why *that* day? Especially since he'd normally go out to eat with me at that time. But then I thought murder was silly of me to even consider. Hunting accidents happen all the time. But that sounds like a really easy cover-up for a murder. Especially here, where no one does much about these people."

Noah's eyebrows flinch. "W-what do you mean? No one does much about who?"

"Like… No one does anything about dangerous men. Like with Steven, what I told you about not being able to file a restraining order, even though he left… *evidence*—" I shake my head, my throat catching with nausea. "That's another conversation I can't stomach right now. My point is, I don't think they'd be caught if it was on purpose, either. Especially if the hunters claimed they thought they shot two wolves." I glance at my mate, unable to read his flickering emotions. My teeth chatter with nerves. "I mean, what do you think really happened that day?"

Noah blinks hard, like he forgot to this whole time. His stare roams around the kitchen. "W-well, they were shot by hunters, and—"

"No, I mean, not the story we've been told. How do you think it *actually* played out?"

Noah clears his throat, dropping my stare. The tense silence gives me goosebumps, crawling up my skin and begging me to act.

I can't back down now, no matter how horrible this is to talk about. I need someone to hear my thoughts. To understand.

"I know this is awful to say, but are you sure it was really an accident?" My voice comes out small. It makes me feel pathetic. Like an insensitive, whiny—

To my surprise, Noah's furrowed brows soften.

This minuscule shift cuts off every thought I have. Our bond shifts in preparation for something. Something big.

"Between us—"

Noah clears his throat. His voice is so soft that I feel like I have to lean in, but I wouldn't dare move. The intensity of our rumbling emotions pins me in place, daring me to not even breathe.

When Noah speaks, his usually smooth, deep voice comes out strained. "I've always wondered the same thing."

My heart leaps, forcing me to swallow it back down.

But Noah's breath heightens. "N-no, that's not right—it was more than 'wondering.' I tried to prove it." He grips his hair. "Until everyone started asking if they should dethrone me for erratic behavior."

"Oh, *Noah*... I can't imagine being thrown into a leadership position like that, right after losing so much." I grip his hand. Noah squeezes tight, nodding despite his bowed head. "Everyone thought I was irrational too. They said I asked questions that didn't need to be asked."

Noah's exhale comes out hot. "Oh, they need to be fucking asked. Something in my heart knows it."

When he looks me in the eyes, I can feel it too. The same angry, confused pain at the injustice of it all.

"You carry it everywhere, don't you?"

Noah rubs his forehead, hiding his eyes. Eventually, he nods. "But I've never found enough evidence to prove it. It's nearly impossible since the cops didn't even know my dad died. We had to say he was our pet, and we were wildlife conservationists. He was just a giant, dead wolf."

My heart flip-flops as I lock onto Noah's every move, grief stinging my eyes.

But then it hits me.

"I never thought about that before. My dad was in his human form when he died! He had to be!"

Noah's smile is riddled with pain. "Your dad saved us so much grief and confusion. If he didn't shift back before he passed, we wouldn't know nearly as much about how they died. The hunters wouldn't have run after discovering a human body beside my dad's big wolf. They would've taken their kills like it was nothing."

My cheeks flush with the rage in Noah's core, blazing through our bond until my lungs quiver.

"Noah, I have an awful feeling about the whole thing. Beyond the obvious reasons why this is endlessly painful."

Noah shakes his head, frantically rubbing my hand with his thumb despite his slouched torso. "I can't believe you have to feel this too. I hate it."

"But now we're not alone in it anymore."

He peeks into my eyes for the first time in minutes. My heart aches at his sudden exhaustion, aging him years.

"Were you able to find any evidence at all?" I gasp. "Oh! Were you able to track their scents?"

Noah is silent for a long time. It looks like he can hardly swallow, his jaw flexing as his Adam's apple crawls down his throat. "The hunters were wearing wolf hides to mask their scent. We're almost certain they were Lycan hides."

I cup my mouth, horror shredding my stomach. "They killed others?"

Noah rubs my shoulders, rage switching to worry. "I-I'm so sorry. I know, it's fucked up. But it's not proof. We tried to figure out who else they killed, but the hides weren't from our pack. We have no clue."

I rub my temples, groaning away the thought. "The more I'm hearing, the more this doesn't add up."

"What do you mean?"

I clear my throat, my heart beating hard enough to thump through my ears. What if I'm just in over my head with speculative nonsense again?

Noah sees right through me. "You're smart as hell, Omega. I trust you."

"I trust you too. That's why I wanted to talk to you about this. Only you."

"Good. I'm not like all those other people who'll dismiss you on the spot. Right now, it's just you and me. I don't care if we sound like conspiratorial freaks. Share your honest thoughts with me. I want to hear them."

His words inspire me to breathe deeper, building on a confidence I've never had around this subject.

Finally, someone's listening to me without calling me crazy.

Or rather, he doesn't care if I am.

But so many things feel off to me. Where do I even start?

With Mason on the mind this week, one topic seems like the most rational guess. "These Alpha challenges happen so often, and they seem extremely calculated. What if this was another one?"

Noah tenses. "W-what? Why would they do something like that for a dominance challenge? It's supposed to be wolf-to-wolf combat in order to properly forfeit the top Alpha title."

"Do they seem like the type to take the noble option and fight face-to-face? Why else would they want to kill specifically those two high-ranking wolves?"

Noah bites his nails, shaking his head. "Those are great points, but something big is still missing there. I don't think any ego-boosted Alpha would resort to something so easy. They'd be giving up a chance to steal my dad's title and win dominance over our massive pack."

I deflate. "Oh. I guess you're right."

Noah gives me a sad smile. "I know. It's frustrating as hell."

"It is…" I bite my lip.

"But what?"

"But I still feel like it's too important to rule out just yet. I just feel it in my gut, like you said. It feels like someone chose them, specifically, and it's too much of a weird coincidence that they happened to be two hugely important members of the pack. Especially if those weren't just wolf hides, and were actually Lycan. I don't even feel like we should discount the hunters being other Lycans."

Noah's eyes flicker between mine. "Okay. I won't discount it either, then."

My shoulders soften. "Thank you."

We reach across the countertop, giving each other's hands a soft squeeze.

But as Noah's stare burns into the wooden countertop, a sick, dark hum rumbles in our bond. "That's the other thing, though:

they aimed at your dad first, so I didn't think it was to steal my dad's title. But when they shot my dad, he died instantly. It took us way too fucking long to find them both, so—" Noah rubs his head. "I couldn't track them without feeling them in our bond anymore. I'm so fucking sorry, Aliya. I still feel like I should've gotten there sooner to— To help them—"

"Noah." I pull him closer, blinking away hot tears. "You know I don't blame you, right? You couldn't have done *anything* to change what these hunters decided to do to them. To all of us."

My mate can't look at me.

I watch the oven's digital clock, and for a full three minutes, we sit in pure silence—minus my soft sniffling.

Until Noah mutters, "What else do you think feels off?"

I sigh. "Well, I think it's weird: if they masked their scents with wolf hides, they expected wolves to smell them."

"So no matter what, you think they were hunting wolves?"

"Right, which is very illegal."

Noah's jaw flexes. "And also explains their bullet choices."

"Oh, you're right. I used to always wonder why my human dad was shot with bear-sized bullets, when all I used to see in the forest is deer."

"Yeah, and the bears and mountain lions steer clear of our pack, so even the humans know they rarely show up here. Which means…"

Our bond flickers into a newfound darkness, shoving my breath out in sharp bursts.

"Fuck. Yeah, they were hunting our pack, in particular," Noah hisses.

Noah stands so rapidly that I have to catch his stool from falling. He doesn't even notice, running his fingers through his hair over and over again as he paces across the kitchen.

Noah suddenly stares deep into my eyes, yellow irises glinting back. His agitated wolf paces with him.

I grip my barstool. "N-Noah—"

He gasps out his words. "It's still my fault. Especially if it was a dominance challenge."

"What?! No—"

"I should've sniffed them out," he growls. "I should've still gone on the perimeter run. I should've—"

"Stop, right there." I grip his hands, halting his frantic pacing. "I didn't share my main point yet."

Noah freezes in place, his breath rapid and shaky.

"It's even less of your fault if this is all true. With how massive, terrifyingly strong, and menacing you are in your wolf form, I'm willing to bet they specifically looked for a day that *you*, Noah Greenfield, weren't there to stop them."

Noah's breath comes out in short bursts like he's unwilling to breathe, pleading for reality to shift into something else. Anything else. It guts me.

He winces, his eyelashes suddenly darkening with the wetness pooling around them. "So— So m-maybe— I could've—"

"No. If you went that day, they'd just find another chance, and another... Until they got what they wanted."

"S-so... There was nothing I could do?"

I shake my head, afraid of how he might take this information, now that it's finally landing.

But after a focused silence, Noah's shoulders relax. His head drops back as he closes his eyes. My heart pangs as a tear slides down his temple. He quickly tries to hide it with a hard rub over his eyes.

"Y-you really think there was nothing? Please, be honest. Pretend I'm not here, and speak the full truth." His voice is so fragile that my heart rips.

"T-the truth is—" I pick at my nails, rocking on my feet as I stare at him. "No, my love, I don't think you could've done anything to stop it. I know it's so hard to hear, and I'm so sorry to say it, but I think it was completely out of your power."

Noah lets out a slow, extended breath.

When he drops his chin to face me again, his eyes are their familiar deep teal. But they're also lined with an inflamed pink. He holds my face in his palms, gazing deep into my eyes.

"What are you thinking? I'm worried about you." I say.

Kissing my forehead, Noah stays there for a while, still catching his breath. "I'm thinking—" He clears the searing emotions from his throat. "If I hadn't met you, I would've willingly walked through life carrying that until I died." His words drop a weight in my heart, sending it to my knees. "I'm thinking you keep saving my life, every single day."

I grip his hands, biting back tears. "And if you went back in time to stop it like you want to, they'd probably shoot you too, Noah. And I was waiting for you, even before I knew I was part Lycan. I would've kept waiting and waiting, not knowing you'd never arrive."

Noah whimpers, glomping onto me with his whole body. "No, you're right. I'm so fucking happy I'm here with you."

"Me too, Noah. Thank you for skipping your perimeter run that day."

"Thank you for surviving so much grief to make it to me."

With my face smushed into his chest, I close my eyes, breathing through our conversation.

Noah doesn't say anything more, sniffling for minutes on minutes until neither of us feels like crying anymore. His full-fingered grip on my back tells me he doesn't want to stop holding me, and I'm content to stay put.

But when I glance back at the time on the oven clock, I gasp. "Noah, it's almost time for the Pack Safety meeting!"

He groans, burying his nose into my shoulder.

"Should we cancel it?" I ask. "You've been through way too much emotional stress today."

"So have you. But if we don't come up with a solution about Mason tonight, I won't be able to sleep. Then I'll *really* be stressed."

I groan. "Okay, then we're going. But let's try to be gentle on ourselves tonight, okay?"

"Good. I like that thought, when it comes to you."

After sharing a heavy, cuddling kiss, Noah releases me so I can prepare for the meeting. I toss off the sticky preschool clothes, jumping into something worthy of a Pack Safety meeting.

Staring at myself in the mirror, I freeze, startled by my own expression. I look exhausted, as expected, but there's something else there. A clarity in my eyes I've never noticed.

Our conversation freed yet another piece of me, loosening my shoulders and softening the tense corners of my eyes. This novel image of myself burns into my brain, even as we leave the house.

On our drive there, I squeeze Noah's arm, breaking the thought-ridden silence. "Thank you for believing me."

"Always, my sweet Omega. I'm right there with you." But Noah sighs. "I don't want to be a downer, but there's something else I'm thinking about all this, now that I'm calmer."

My heart drops. "Oh, no. What?"

"If they had no idea our dads were important, they really could've just thought they found a big kill," he mutters. "Or maybe some humans thought they found 'mythical werewolves,' and wanted to prove it by memorizing our run schedule."

My stomach churns and my eyes sting hot. "So you don't actually feel the same way? You don't think it was premeditated?"

"No, my love. That's not what I'm saying." He squeezes my hand, grounding my racing heart. "I think if we told anyone what we're thinking right now, that'll be their counterargument. We need to find definite proof the hunt wasn't only intentional, but also that they knew exactly *who* they were killing."

After a deep, calming breath, I nod, squeezing Noah's arm again. "Okay. I have no idea how, but I'm sure we'll think of something. We have to."

The silence we share isn't silent at all in our bond. Our aching hearts tangle, meeting each other where we're both at until we find a new, sorrowful equilibrium. We're gutted, but we're okay.

Noah parks outside the Community Center, turning to stroke my hair. "I'm so fucking glad I'm not alone in this anymore, Omega."

"So am I, Alpha." I grip his jacket collar, urging him to my lips.

Our kiss is laced with a blurry mixture of relief, hope, and fuming, torrid grief.

22

As I give thorough hello hugs to every touch-heavy wolf I know, Noah lazes back into his chair beside me. I can't stop gazing at his sharp profile, softened by his plump lips. They're pinker than usual after crying earlier. The second he catches me staring, Noah melts into a gentle smile.

God, my heart. Just that smile makes me feel like everything will be okay.

I lean against his side, and he wraps an arm around me, stabilizing me against him. I hum contentedly.

But when the Elders finally arrive and the meeting hasn't started, I look around to see who's still missing.

I turn to Noah. "Where's your Luna?"

Noah looks me up and down with furrowed brows, then scans the room. Then he softens. "O-oh, I guess you're right. My mom isn't here yet."

My stomach flips. Did he just look to me first like I'm already his Luna?

Noah suddenly won't look me in the eyes, turning away to fiddle with his chipped chair seat. Our bond gives him away; giddy embarrassment races through his frantic wolf.

I break into giggles, no matter how serious the atmosphere. Noah's smile bursts across his face, his head still bowed. Our shared laughter lifts my heart ten feet.

"I love you, my shy Alpha."

"I love you too, my sweet Omega."

Once Lilian arrives, our warm, knitted hands are the only thing stabilizing us through an otherwise stressful meeting.

Noah debriefs Lilian and the Elders about last night's Mason incident. Everyone's faces sink lower the more Noah describes, the atmosphere plummeting with them.

Finally, Noah announces his conclusion on the situation's consequences. "After this latest stunt, I want to send out an order to hold 24/7 surveillance on Mason Hart."

The collective scent shifts to unease, and my stomach groans in response.

Okay, that wasn't just a groan. More like a screech. Everyone turns to look, and I flush in embarrassment as I give the Elders an awkward smile. "Sorry. Please, continue."

Noah's tense posture softens into threatened laughter, his eyes closing and lips bitten. *God, I fucking love you.*

I love you too. Sorry for interrupting your meeting.

Trust me, I needed that. Thank you—and your adorable stomach. Noah has to scrub his jaw, containing his grin as the Elders charge ahead in the discussion.

But I allow myself a smile. After how upset Noah was this afternoon, his relaxed shoulders are a welcome relief.

Unfortunately, the Elders aren't on the same page.

"How the hell are you going to justify 24/7 surveillance?" Elder Alpha Frank growls. "Are you sure he doesn't have a point about acting like a dictator? What are you going to do, put up surveillance on every wolf who challenges you?"

Noah allows the board to voice their fears, but they trail off when he shakes his head. "I have reason to believe Hart is stalking our future Luna too. If he has any intention of hurting Aliya, I need to know."

My stomach gurgles even louder this time, but it's not funny to me. Noah drapes his hand on the back of my neck.

Fuck, I'm sorry, that came out completely insensitive. Are you feeling okay with this conversation, sweet Omega?

When he strokes my mark with his calming, protective scent, I do everything in my power not to sigh in bliss. *Yes, I'm okay. As long as I'm with you.*

Noah takes a deep, soothing breath at my words, and my heart aches with love for him. This is stressful as hell, but being together makes anything manageable. This last month has proven that.

"I believe you, Alpha." Yasmine steps in with the mediation she does best, her clear, elegant voice sending a burst of Noah's relief through our bond. "And I also know the Elders have a point. We don't want any reason for mutiny on our hands. Do you have solid proof he's stalking her? For the official side of things?"

Noah shifts on his feet, dropping his head. "I haven't seen what he's doing outside of when I've seen him challenge me. So nothing I can prove is separate from dominance challenges towards me just yet." His expression hardens, his scowl burning a hole into the floor. "I just don't like that he was trying to stop me from meeting my mate at first. And the way he looks at her feels off, I—"

"You sound like a loving Alpha, protecting his mate. Which is wonderful to see, truly," Elder Beta Terrence chuckles. "But you need more proof than that."

Yasmine crosses her arms. "I agree with our Alpha, though; Mason is super suspicious. Especially with his unwillingness to show his human face."

Elder Terrence nods. "Yes, that is odd. Surely someone here must've seen his human form in the past?"

Elder Frank grumbles. "His adult human form, you mean. Most of us saw his kid form."

The room steeps in silence. Noah tenses, and Yasmine steals a glance at him. They must be referring to when Alpha Ritchie banished Mason's dad, Jack Hart, from Greenfield.

But Dave raises his hand in the corner. "I've seen Mason Hart's adult form. But I don't have a picture of him, or anything. Like most wolves, he doesn't have any social media I can find, either."

"So there's nothing that stood out about his human form? Nothing either identifying or that he might find embarrassing about his appearance?" Elder Terrence asks.

Dave shrugs. "He's just another white, blonde dude, a bit bigger than me but no tattoos or scars I can remember, or anything."

"Then why would he hide it?" Elder Aaron frowns.

Yasmine releases one hand from her tightly crossed arms to rub her temple. "When I got there last night, he was refusing specifically to show *Noah* his human face. And being pretty offensive about it."

Elder Aaron hums. "That's extremely strange, and annoying, sure, but being a nuisance isn't enough to be put on surveillance."

Rainn chimes in with a protective hand gripping her brother's arm. "But he's clearly hiding something, Elder! Don't you think that's suspicious?"

"I agree, the refusal to shift is the most suspicious out of everything here. We could use that as a reason, Alpha... If you have any idea of what he's hiding."

We all turn to Noah, hoping he has something.

Noah's eyes flicker between every one of us, his brows knitted and chest puffed. But he sighs, dropping my gaze to scrub his forehead.

"I don't know. I've been trying to think of one of the hundreds of unsolved crimes it could be. But also where I'd recognize him, on the spot—since why else would he hide his face from me? I just can't think of *anything*. If this was the case of an unsolved offense already on my mind, I would've sniffed him out immediately."

Elder Frank scowls. "Then, what? You're truly doing this for no reason? Going on a feeling?"

"Are we going to ignore the elephant in the room?" Lilian mutters in the corner.

Noah erupts with defensive, panicked emotions, sending icy anxiety through my veins. I grip my chair, struggling to grasp what Lilian could be talking about.

"He's *not* Jack," Noah snaps.

No one speaks. Hell, no one moves.

"And I can't arrest Mason for being related to him," Noah growls.

My heart ticks into my throat, tempted to cower from Noah. I've never seen my mate like this.

Yasmine's clicking, irritated tongue is the first to snap everyone out of our frozen state. "Well, we all know Mason's asshole father, and even though we have to treat them as different people, Mason does sound like just as much of an Alpha-domination cultist."

Elder Terrence sighs. "But Alpha Noah is right: we have a duty to be fair to every pack member, and Mason hasn't physically acted on his beliefs. Not enough to banish him, like Jack."

"And I don't plan on letting it go that far," Noah hisses.

The air thins with Noah's rampaging pheromones, bringing on a heavy silence.

Eventually, Elder Aaron mutters out his thoughts. "I understand your bias against these Alpha men, but they're still your constituents—"

"I don't give a fuck," Noah booms. "I don't want to hear a single other Omega was hurt by these domination fuckers in my own pack. I'm not waiting until something happens again to act!"

Noah's voice has an edge to it I've never heard before. The tension in the room rises, everyone avoiding Noah's eyes. I'm physically shaking, unsure how to process my mate's behavior. But everything he's saying sounds perfectly logical; we *should* be upset about wolves abusing other wolves.

So why is everyone acting so weird? What am I missing here?

It sounds like someone here didn't act quickly enough on Jack. With the horrors I know Noah witnesses, often daily, what did he have to witness to make him react like this? I'm positive Jack abused Mason's mom, but why wouldn't Alpha Ritchie listen to her? Or was it that he did, and *these* wolves around me didn't believe her, just like no authority believed me?

Acid crawls up my throat as my shoulders rise. My heart pounds so rapidly that I'm tempted to hide.

But the more I overthink, the more Noah's anxiety skyrockets. I jump to my feet, afraid he's about to have an anxiety attack.

Noah backs away from us quickly, holding out a halting palm. "I'm fine, I'm fine. Give me a second."

Turning around, Noah takes a few deep breaths with rapid strokes of his hair. All I can see is immense stress threaded throughout his shoulders, winding them so tight that it looks like Noah has to fight to expand his taut ribcage.

He's right; Mason is causing immense, unnecessary stress for all of us. With how volatile Mason has been, his actions could catch up with his words before we're prepared to stop him. When he confronted us last, there were far more than the ten to fifteen Alpha-domination cultists Noah mentioned he had his eye on, a horde of wolves ready to back Mason up. And if Mason's at the top of their miniature hierarchy, we need to figure out how to handle him as soon as possible.

My stomach rolls, millions of possibilities crossing my mind of what Mason could be hiding. But I can't get something out of my head. That phrase Mason used as he walked away: *maybe I do, maybe I don't.*

I'm almost certain he stalked me enough to find out I have OCD.

Oh, fuck. This might be our missing key.

But can I trust these wolves to share something so intimate about me, right after I learned they might not be as safe as they seem?

As I let out a shaky gasp for air, Noah rushes back to my side with a sorrowful ache in his eyes. He leans in to nuzzle my cheek, softening the harsh tone he left hanging in this eerily silent room. "It's going to be okay. I have every intention to keep you safe."

I swallow hard, softening to a whisper. "It's not just that. I think I have some evidence."

No matter how quiet my voice is compared to the room's agitated hum, I hold more weight here than I ever have.

All eyes are on me, listening intently.

Damn wolf hearing. I should've mindlinked Noah instead. I don't know if I want to tell the whole world I have OCD.

What if they no longer believe I'm able to be Luna? If they have deep-rooted biases, I won't be able to defend myself; I've seen OCD wildly misunderstood and miscategorized too many times to believe they would understand me. They might even play it off as acting nice in the moment, but believe I'm "crazy" once I leave the room. Hell, they could even lock me up.

I swallow hard, struggling to parse my thoughts. I'm already triggered enough to have no idea what's intrusive and what's a valid concern.

Or maybe they're valid concerns, regardless, and they don't need to be parsed. Maybe the real problem is that I'm only looking at one half of my "what ifs" again.

What if this is a group who *will* finally listen to me? What if I'm making too many assumptions about what happened in the past, and these Lycans could be more understanding than most humans?

Now that I think through it slowly, they're only asking Noah difficult questions to help him find a way to achieve what he wants: stopping Mason. They don't want someone like Jack to succeed in their harm again, either.

Maybe they didn't act quickly enough in the past, but maybe they've learned. They're acting now.

It doesn't excuse the past, but it does help me feel safer.

My shoulders loosen, although my heart still races. I've never shared my OCD diagnosis with a room full of adults. I'm not sure I'll have to, but I've seen many people react to needing a therapist the same way—questioning if I'm stable enough to run my own life, let alone others' fates. In reality, I might even have more tools to manage life stressors than they do thanks to therapy.

But Lilian grabs my hand, scooting closer. "Allow us to protect you. Share your thoughts."

Yasmine doubles down, reaching over the table to rub my arm.

With Noah behind me, bending to kiss my cheek as he releases wave after wave of his protective scent, my shoulders turn into mush. I drop my neck for him, presenting my mark.

His breath brushes my neck. Goosebumps climb my arms with my body's muscle memory of his affections there.

Just before he bends to lick the hell out of my mark—his wolf hungrily courting mine in our bond with hard nips—Lilian clears her throat.

"Noah. Pay attention."

"S-sorry. My wolf is—" Noah's anxious wolf slinks against mine in our bond, attempting to calm himself. "Share only what you want to, sweet Omega. We're all here to support you however we can."

Looking around the room, I have to stifle tears. He's right. I really feel like I have a huge family now. Maybe I don't have to hold this alone, either.

And maybe I don't have to share *everything*, just like Noah said. Maybe I can trust them just enough to help us all feel safer.

"I-I go to therapy every week," I mutter, testing the waters. When no one seems to bat an eye, I speak up. "And it's a very specific type of therapy. One that uses the phrase 'maybe, maybe not,' to accept uncertainty in life. Especially 'maybe I will, maybe I won't.'"

Yasmine's eyes widen. "Oh, *fuck*. And Mason said, 'Maybe I do, maybe I don't,' when Noah accused him of having something to hide."

I swallow hard. The absolute silence grates my nerves.

When it doesn't change after 30 seconds, my voice comes out choppy and weak. "I-I could be wrong, but it felt directed towards me. It was just so specific. So pointed. And it was the only time he ever spoke to me, saying something only I'd feel uncomfortable from."

As Noah jerks away from us, a burst of his raging scent doubles my breathing rate.

"Fuck. I don't like that at all. Not at all."

Everyone jumps up with him, chairs tossed aside in alarm.

Elder Terrence manages to keep some of his cool, holding out a steadying hand. "Wait, Alpha. Let's go through this carefully to cover all our bases."

But Noah isn't the only stressed wolf. I'm suddenly crowded by protective-yet-stressed scents, twisting my stomach.

Rainn loops around Noah to join my side, cuddling against me. "Oh, Goddess, are you okay? I believe you, proof or not."

"Let's all take a deep breath. I believe we can find enough proof with this," Elder Terrence says. He turns to me, softening his voice. "Future Luna, how do you know he isn't just reading about your treatment somewhere on social media?"

"I don't post anymore. And I haven't told anyone except Noah and my best friend about where I go for therapy and why. Not even my ex knows I have this diagnosis, or my parents before they passed. There's no other way for Mason to find out because—" Dammit. If I remind Noah that Steven was the one who made me so cautious, he's really going to flip. "I-I'm a very private person."

Growling, Noah paces behind me. "No, I don't like this."

Elder Aaron takes a step towards us. "Alpha—"

Noah's incisors gleam as he snaps. "This isn't just a protective Alpha thing! This is serious. She goes there the same time and day every single week. It's too easy to track." He struggles to catch his breath, letting out a pained whine. "If he hurts her while she's alone there, or kills her, I-I'll lose—"

"He hasn't even touched her before. How do you know he'd go so far as to kill her?"

"We're hoping to have a baby, and he wants to end my lineage. He already tried to intercept us when we met. What if he kills her when she's eventually pregnant?"

Oh, God. That's a disturbing thought—like Noah just blurted out my intrusive thoughts out loud.

Oh. Oh, *shit.* He's having a PTSD episode.

I spin to track him, awkwardly holding out my hands as worried wolves scurrying between us separate me from my mate. I'm so frazzled by the chaos surrounding Noah that I don't know what to do or say. How to help. The pained, rippling ache on Noah's features make me want to sob; I know how awful it feels. How much it feels like you might lose your life, you're so scared, and I hate that I might have to just let him suffer through it.

Noah slips into panicked whimpers. "I-I think I'd *die* if he kills her, I'd *want* to—"

Before I can rush to Noah's side, he's swarmed with wolves gripping him from all angles.

"Alpha, slow down. We can have someone with our future Luna at all times for her safety." Elder Terrence grabs Noah's arm, but Noah shrugs everyone off, backing off with rapid steps.

"No! Why should she lose all her autonomy because of someone else's behavior? Hart needs to face actual consequences." Noah grips his head as everyone else gapes at his rising meltdown.

Anger bubbles in my core, threatening to burst.

Then it hits me: I've been reining my wolf back, but she's been clawing to be let out this whole time.

Noah taught me something huge about her through the mattress. Her anger isn't irrational. It's to protect us.

As I set her free, my voice comes out sharp. "Excuse me. I have something to say."

I'm already standing, but I gather the room's attention with their collective flinch.

Shit. My Alpha-weirdness must be showing.

But I'm too upset to care what they'll think of me, fists clenched at my sides. "This whole conversation is pointless. Why aren't we talking about *Noah's* health in all this? He's already being stalked!"

The Elders gape at me.

But Yasmine, Dave, and Rainn nod their heads along with me, meeting each other's eyes.

"I don't care if he's supposed to be the strongest wolf here, no one should have to be okay with being stalked. We're all sitting here, acting like it's totally acceptable, just because some random guy is power-hungry. But Noah has already beaten Mason multiple times. There's no reason Noah should have to tolerate this."

Noah's breath restarts a few times, shaking as he sputters out, "I-I'm okay, I—"

Yasmine scowls. "No you're not. Our future Luna is right, this is barbaric."

Then a voice speaks up that I've hardly heard from this meeting.

Lilian's monotone, quiet voice stills the room. "Alphas deserve protection too. We all do. And Noah provides that protection for us. The least we could do is provide it back."

My eyes bulge. Lilian just defended Noah.

It's about time.

But my heart tears into shreds as Noah's breaks. "I-I'm fine. I don't need reminding that you think I'm w-*weak*, Mom."

Her stoic stare dissolves into disgust. "Are you serious? Now you're mad at me for having your back? After all those times you've been upset with me for—"

Noah points at the door, his breath rapid and shaky.

Lilian rises to leave without another word.

I shrink where I stand, guilt crushing my breath for bringing this all up. With one look at my cowering stance, Noah dissolves into guilt.

"I-I'm sorry," he rasps.

"It's—"

"No. It's not okay. And..." Noah shakes his head. "I'm sorry for more than that. That everyone here didn't have a proper goodbye to your last Alpha, and you all just got stuck with my bullshit. I wanted to work on it more before I took charge—go back to an outpatient thing to never act like this again—but I ran out of time. I ran o-out of time. I couldn't even give Dad a retirement to enjoy before he was fucking *shot*, and now—"

My favorite Elder, Beta Terrence, comes to the rescue with a comforting hand on Noah's shoulder. "Alpha Noah, no one here blames you for what happened to Alpha Ritchie—"

"It's fine!" Noah shouts. He winces, lowering his voice to where we can barely hear him, as if he's trying to cancel it out. "You can. I'm fine."

No one takes a breath as Noah struggles not to crumble before the most important people in his pack.

"You're not fine," I say. "And that's okay."

Panic overwhelms Noah's eyes, blocking him from accepting my words. In my heart, I know he desperately wants to. I could feel it the second I spoke.

I steady my voice. "If no one can accept you have actual emotions, they shouldn't expect you to care the way you do. You have an incredible heart, Alpha. It's sensitive in the most beautiful way because that's how it protects us. And even if no one else here wants to protect it back, I still will. I will *always* protect you."

It wasn't what I intended, but Noah's wall breaks at my words. My heart snaps as he buries his eyes into his palms, his shoulders shaking through the start of heavy, gut-shuddering tears.

"Oh, *Noah*—" I hold my breath as every wolf in the room rises at once, circling my mate.

Noah's emotions ripple into fear, and I gasp.

Oh, God, what's going to happen? Is someone going to take advantage of his vulnerability? Challenge him right here?

My heart sprints and my claws extend, ready to defend him.

But then, one by one, each wolf nuzzles against Noah. Rubbing their comfort along his sides, stomach, arms, and back, they soothe my mate.

I cover my lips, but my tears slip on their own. The whole room smells like love. Adoration. Gratitude.

Noah's silent tears escalate into soft weeping.

I wiggle my way in, pressing myself against his overheated body until he frantically squeezes me to his chest. As he hides his face into my neck, I brush soft kisses onto his mark, each kiss laced with a nurturing scent I can't contain. Everyone's hands are on him, their scents rising with mine until the comforting smell softens every muscle I own.

"We love you, Alpha. Take it in, my love," I whisper.

He shakes his head. "I need to protect you. All of you."

"You already are. But you're not a god, and we shouldn't expect you to be. It's okay to be protected and loved too. Really, it is."

Noah squeezes me with his arms wrapped as tight as they can be, letting out a soft sob against my shoulder.

Elder Terrence smiles. "You two are really something special. This reminds me of the days Takahiro was here."

Elder Aaron chuckles. "You're right. He'd always melt Ritchie into a puddle when Ritch was convinced he was too invincible to have needs."

My heart aches with Noah's at this news, but I crave so much more.

"Really? My dad would do that?" I ask.

"Yes. And Ritchie would let him." Elder Aaron chuckles. "Takahiro used to laugh at how much Ritchie secretly loved it when we all swarmed him with affection like this. We just didn't think Noah felt comfortable enough to let us in just yet."

I kiss Noah's panic away, unable to resist slipping my tongue against his mark.

Noah shudders, finally revealing his swollen face to meet my eyes. "You're right, I wasn't comfortable enough yet. My mate has helped me beyond words." His voice is raw and soft, but it stirs avalanches of love for him in my heart. "I can't let anything happen to her."

The pain in his voice breaks me.

But the hands surrounding us lift my heart back up, steadying Noah's soul on its feet with it.

"We won't. We have both of your backs," Elder Frank says.

"And I think it's safe to say we're in agreement about surveillance," Elder Terrence says.

With a collective hum of approval from the Elders, Noah lets out a tremendous sigh against my neck.

When we get home, Noah is too exhausted to eat. He stumbles to bed while I reheat leftovers, keeping the lights dim.

Within 15 minutes, I shovel my food into my mouth and join Noah in bed. He stirs in his sleep, just for me—pulling me to his chest and draping himself over me until we're intermeshed.

Neither of us have spoken much since we left the Pack Safety meeting. We don't need to. I can feel how much he's still processing today, but I can also see it on his face. Even in his sleep, there's a faint, agonized strain to his eyelids.

I trace his bare back with long, sweeping motions, mesmerized by the way my gentle touch loosens his every muscle. As his breaths slow back into sleep, I hold his head to my heart, hoping he can feel how much I love him.

I love sleeping cuddled up with him. Instead of getting old, it just gets better every single day. He feels like home.

23

After the second-to-last day of school, I'm cuddled up with Noah for a much-needed movie night.

But Noah can't stop staring at me instead of the screen.

I giggle. "What is it, cutie?"

He drops his head with a smile, only able to peek at me in short bursts. "Nothing. I just love you. And you look adorable drowning in my shirt."

I laugh, tugging the base of his giant black T-shirt lower over my thighs as a makeshift dress. Noah's smile is so bright that I can't help but nuzzle his cheek, kissing it over and over again until his lips get jealous and steal the last one.

Laughter sputters from me. "Hey!"

Noah chuckles, cuddling me closer. "Sweet Omega, it made me so happy to see you light up when the Elders talked about Takahiro the other day. And I know I told you I'd tell you more about him. I'm sorry I haven't been in a place to do that yet."

My stomach flips. "Please, don't worry about that. It's a hard subject for both of us.

"I know, but—" He sighs. His thoughts whirl a snowstorm of emotions through our bond. "Maybe, if it h-helps you to talk about it, it'll help me too."

I smile, amazed by how much he's been opening up since the pack showed him it was safe to show his emotions. "Okay, I'd love that."

Noah straightens with a rising smile. He shuffles on the couch cushions until he's facing me. "Is there anything about his involvement in the pack that you're more curious about? I can do my best to answer."

My heart aches with both love and pain, but I can't stop smiling. "There's a lot, actually. I guess one of my main questions is how well you even knew my dad?"

Noah hums, tracing my arm with his warm fingertips. "Our dads had been best friends forever, as you know, so I knew him for as long as I can remember. Takahiro felt like my uncle."

My heart lifts. "Yeah? That's how Ritchie felt to me too. I'd get not one but two dad hugs when I'd come home from school on a day Ritchie was over."

Noah's hand freezes, a slow smile breaking across his face. "That makes me *so* fucking happy."

I giggle. "They were good dads, weren't they?"

"They were, and they were good pack-dads too. They prepared almost their whole lives to do what Yas and I were thrown into. Mediating, problem-solving, refugee support—" Noah's smile fades. "I really regret not being able to give them a break. They were involved in pack work since they were teens, and I'm not sure they ever had much of a life outside of it. Takahiro was the natural choice for top Beta when my grandmother died."

I sit up. "I still can't believe she led the pack back then. Weren't the Alphas twice as hard on her?"

"Yep. But she didn't give a fuck."

I laugh. "God, I love her. She sounds like you."

Noah chuckles, dropping his stare. "That's a high compliment. My mom loves to pretend I'm the first Alpha to break traditions, but my grandma nipped countless gender roles in the bud. We've never been the same pack since."

Neither of us can stop smiling. Noah lightly tugs on my hand until I come closer, and I gladly sit in his lap.

He cuddles into me, wrapping his arms around my waist and nose into my collarbone.

"I'm probably the way I am because of her in more ways than that though."

My heart spikes along with Noah's rising emotions, unsure where they're coming from. "How so?"

"It's– It's about the wolf pheromone thing." He swallows

hard, dropping his forehead against me to hide his eyes. "I trust you, but I don't tell a lot of people about it. Especially since so many Lycans can't even accept the most basic thing of all of us deserving equality."

I don't want him to feel pressured, so I stroke his hair, giving him a soft hum so he knows I'm listening. But the longer we sit in silence, the bigger his incoming confession feels. When he draws in a breath to speak, my stomach flips with his rising nerves.

"Maybe she saw something in me that I didn't when I was a kid. I was really shy then too and only got worse later on, but when she was alive, she had a huge part in raising me. But she didn't see wolf sexes the same way as everyone else, and between us—" He takes a sharp breath before softening his voice even further. "She let me in on a huge secret about how Lycans actually work. She'd let a lot of Omega pheromones out when it was just us, even though she was an Alpha. I didn't really understand it at first; our sexes seemed so set in stone. But then I realized my Alpha grandma could control her pheromones as easily as she could control her smile, letting out certain vulnerable scents only around the people she trusted. She was an Alpha around everyone else, but an Omega around me. It made me realize that—"

My heart pounds. I'm not sure where this is going next, but Noah's hesitation amplifies my nerves.

"That I was controlling my pheromone output too. And it wasn't just me altering how I presented: every wolf I knew would change themselves when other people were around, acting a little different and putting on airs depending on the company. It made me realize we're not as straightforward as we all want to seem. But like I said, most Lycans aren't ready to take that in."

The more he explains, the more ridiculous it feels that Alphas hold so much social dominance over everyone else. And now that Noah's trying to change that, they're clinging to their final semblance of power. It makes me wonder if deep down, they know they're wrong, attacking my mate who speaks too much truth for their comfort.

I don't realize I'm gripping Noah's shirt until he sits up. Stroking my hair, Noah traces my eyes in search of my thoughts. For some reason, my heart aches enough to stiffen my voice.

"Is that why you were okay with my—" I flush hot. I didn't realize how much shame I carried around this subject until it floods my throat. "My Alpha weirdness?"

Noah's eyebrows soften. He gives me a gentle smile. "No. It's why I think having some Alpha in you isn't all that weird in the first place."

A hidden tightness in my chest loosens on its own. Noah's smile relaxes into a full grin. The longer we gaze at each other, the freer I feel. He really loves me for who I am, just like I love him.

I dive for his chest, hugging him as tightly as I can. "Then I guess Grandma Greenfield raised you into the most beautiful man I've ever met." Noah's wolf melts into a giddy puddle in our bond, spurring me into adoring laughter. "I wish I could've seen you two together."

Noah's human side chuckles with me, kissing my cheek. "Me too. I really felt her loss when she passed, especially since my parents had to jump into action to take her place. Your dad was my hero when my parents were too busy, Omega."

The unspoken ache in Noah's words guts me.

"Oh, love…" I take his hand, breathing through the past with him. "You were alone a lot as a kid?"

"Yeah. But Takahiro tried to keep Rainn and I company whenever we hadn't seen my dad for a while. He was—" Noah scratches the back of his head, his choppy hair blocking his eyes from my view. "Well, whenever I think of the type of dad I want to be, I think of your dad."

There's no way I can keep from crying now. But I'm beaming from ear to ear at Noah's shy stare. "What type of dad was he to you?"

He clears his throat. "Someone w-who made time for what he cared about. Someone thoughtful about the earth, the pack, his loved ones…" Noah fiddles with my fingers, his soft and rapid breath the only clue as to how excited his wolf is internally. "No matter how busy I am, I want to make time for us. A-and eventually, for our family."

I rub his chest until he flashes me a soft smile, still too flustered to meet my eyes.

"I love my dad, but he couldn't time-manage for the life of him," Noah mutters.

My hand slows, only my thumb tracing the center of his chest. I wish it could soothe the ache in my heart, knowing it must feel ten times worse in Noah's.

Noah continues. "I know he felt bad about that, and jealous of Takahiro at times... But I know he loved Takahiro for it just the same. Your dad would take me through the forest, teaching me all about the plants and insects—" Noah scrunches his nose. "Especially the weird bugs. Rainn loved that part more than me, honestly."

I help him wipe away my tears as I laugh, and Noah seals it with a kiss.

"God, that sounds *just* like him," I breathe. "He did that with me too. I feel like it made me much more sensitive to the world around me, and my impact on it. Our forest walks are some of my best memories." I sit up with a gasp. "Wait, did you ever smell me there?"

"No. Whenever I was really curious about your scent on their clothes as a kid, Takahiro made it extremely clear I was *never* to speak to or witness his daughter in my lifetime." Noah bites his lip. "Looks like I sort of broke my promise."

Noah gives me a sheepish look, and I bust out laughing.

"You're not sorry at all, you sly wolf!"

His bright laugh sends flurries of sparks throughout my chest.

"No, I'm not sorry. And I think he was right to be fiercely protective of you. You're so fucking incredible, I could eat you alive in my lap." Noah's eyes suddenly widen. "Oh, Goddess, I would've been a mushy, rutting mess if we knew each other when we were teenagers. We'd probably have ten pups." He grips his forehead with a groan. "Okay, no, I don't 'think' he was right, I 'know.' I would've made a mess of our lives."

I can't stop giggling between kissing Noah softly. "Still. I would've loved that mess."

"Me too, sweet Omega." Noah's voice softens as we draw closer on instinct. "But what we have now is more beautiful than I ever imagined."

I gaze into Noah's eyes, soaking in his love until my heart

overflows. His lips are tender when I kiss him, alighting my every vertebrae. "You're right. I wouldn't trade what we have now for anything."

Noah's hand skates up my thigh as our kisses grow heavy. Between his heavy touch and hot tongue, I squeeze my thighs together, desperate for his sexual attention.

But Noah pauses, tracing my eyes. "I sense some sadness in you, sweet Omega. Different from grief."

I drop my stare, my cheeks reddening. "I know we've managed to try having sex like we used to a few times, but it hasn't been fully the same, and—" I bite my thumb, desperate to quiet my hammering heart. "Deep down, I'm really embarrassed about the trouble I'm still having, feeling pain during sex."

"Oh, my sweet—" Noah's fingertips skate into the roots of my hair, holding my head in place as he plants a firm kiss on my forehead. "Our intimacy doesn't revolve around one type of sex. I love what we've been doing. Don't you?"

"Yes, but—" My forehead warps. "It's my fault we haven't been able to keep trying for a baby."

Noah kisses my tears away, shushing me gently. "It's okay. It really is. It's only been a month since we took a break. We'll get there."

"Still, I— I miss the deeper connection I feel with you when you're inside me."

Noah swallows hard. His breath heightens against my cheek. "T-the other day, I had an idea of something that might help with your pain."

I pull back to meet his eyes. They roam to my lips, then to his hand rubbing my hip, then to my mark as my head tilts in primal submission. When his Alpha musk flourishes into desire, my thighs squeeze together. This time, Noah's eyes fall straight to my aching groin.

His voice is quiet, but rough with want. "You know how Lycans lick our wounds, and we heal ten times faster?"

My heart flips. I squeeze my thighs tighter, unsure if he's implying what I think he is.

"I thought... Maybe I could give you some extra attention there. With my mouth." Noah drags in a deep lungful of my eager scent, his grip tightening on my hip to give me a soft squeeze. "Maybe it'd help."

I flush to my neck, my hips squirming at the thought.

Noah's stare ignites, hanging on my next move. His thumb rests tantalizingly close to my inner thigh. When my thighs part for him, he huffs.

"You want to try?"

"Yes," I whisper.

Noah kisses me, long and deep before hoisting me into his arms.

I let out a surprised giggle through our kiss, but his eager hands on my ass urge my tongue into his mouth. When he drops me on the couch's long sectional, climbing over me, he pauses, realizing his mistake.

"Shit. W-was that triggering?"

My eyes are wide, but more because I hadn't remembered this was a problem. I gape at Noah's wide form towering over me, amazed. "Actually, no. That was fine. I'm doing better much faster than I usually would, thanks to how patient you've been. I really do trust you, Noah."

He breaks into a proud smile, and my heart soars. But as he strips my bottom half bare, softly parting my legs, my heart pounds into my ears.

Why am I so nervous? It's not like we've never done this before.

Kneeling at the sectional's end, Noah peeks up at me as he gives my clit a soft kiss. I suck in a sharp breath, my thighs twitching.

"I want to do this with the intention of healing your wounds," Noah says.

I swallow hard, biting my lip. "T-thank you, Noah."

Noah draws back, his hands sliding down my calves as he relaxes on his heels. "Is that actually okay with you? You seem uncertain."

I sigh, rapidly tucking my hair behind my ears. "No one has done anything like this before for me. I don't know how to take it in."

I'm surprised by my tears, especially as Noah's curious expression melts into sadness with me.

"I just know what it's like. Trauma hurts like a physical wound," Noah says.

I nod, combing through his soft hair.

"That's why I wanted to see if I could help, somehow. I know it sounds crazy, but maybe it really is a physical wound too. Our body definitely remembers, even if we can't see it anymore with our eyes."

His words strike my core.

Noah's thoughts about PTSD resonate deeper than what anyone else has said to me about the disorder. I hate to think of why he understands so well. Whatever happened to him, it's still buried too deep for me to ask.

Noah continues, "So, if it's okay with you, I'm going to think about what you've told me. If I know the wound, it helps me know how to heal it."

There's an extended silence, my chest rapidly rising and falling. "You want to think about the spots he hurt me the most... On purpose?"

Noah nods, his puppy-dog stare tearing at my heartstrings. "I-I can't promise it'll work, but Prolonged Exposure, and all—" He shrugs, giving me an earnest stare. "Maybe it's worth a try to sit with it for a bit."

He's right. That's what I had to do with Jenny to get as far as I have with my trauma healing. His idea of acknowledging my pain directly is better than just waiting it out, especially because I know PE works incredibly well on me. Which means I really do want to tell Noah where it usually hurts.

I'm just afraid to say it out loud. Afraid to make Noah think about it. To allow someone else to carry the sharp, vomit-inducing fear I store in my core—the source of this pain.

But Noah couldn't be clearer about what he's comfortable with. He's staring me deep in the eyes, fingertips brushing over my groin until I flex.

Noah's eyes widen as I point out an invisible scar to him.

"H-here. This part hurts if I'm not warmed up enough, ever since—" I swallow my pounding heart before it leaps from my throat. "Since then."

Noah's emotions rattle and warp through me, hitting me like an icy wave.

But as he slips his hands beneath my hips, tilting me to face him, he gives that spot a gentle, slow lick.

I gasp through it, afraid of what I might feel.

To my surprise, it's the best thing I've felt in a while. The soft pad of his tongue glides over my sensitive skin, loosening a bit more of the tension in my belly with its radiating warmth.

"Where else?" Noah's breathy whisper sinks into my core, and I squirm.

With shaking hands, I open myself up to him to point out another, deeper spot.

I can't believe we're doing this. Noah looks so serious. With no hesitation, Noah sticks his finger into his mouth, coating it in spit. My heart leaps as he holds eye contact, gliding his finger deep into his throat. My wolf goes wild. But Noah is so focused, he doesn't seem fazed by what he's doing.

When he slips his wet finger into me, he rubs the portion that keeps stinging lately.

But it doesn't sting today. His gentle touch flutters my eyelids. In combination with soft kisses across my clit, Noah's sweeping prodding sends a drip of fluid onto the couch cushions.

"I'll come back to that spot." He removes his finger with a nod, noting the heaviness of my breath as he stares at my gaping lips.

I'm turned on by how soaked his hand is as it scoops beneath my ass, angling me against his tongue. When he licks the entire base of me, I let out a shuddering gasp at how potent it feels. My knees pop open on their own, begging for deeper attention between them.

Noah's eyes flick up at me, absorbing my heaving reaction as my gasps shift into moaning pleasure.

His next lick is slower. Harder. Extending all the way up one side of my labia. My hips tilt into his tongue as it sinks pressure into me, nudging my nerves into action.

But he doesn't give me time to recover before licking me there again. And again.

By the time I'm squirming, he switches to the other side.

"Ahn— Noah—" My head drops back with a heaving breath,

and Noah softly purrs against my clit. It makes my hips twist in his hands, so Noah grips them harder, squeezing entire handfuls of my ass.

A sudden rush of fluid slips out at his tongue's massage, coating Noah's chin. I gasp.

"S-sor—"

Noah growls, lifting my hips into his face for better access as he straightens up taller.

His tongue slathers the entire base of me in rapid circles, urging my body to open itself up to him like we're about to mate.

"N-Noah— Ah!"

He purrs at my soft cries for him, closing his eyes as I tug at his hair.

There's a possessiveness in his scent, but it doesn't feel like a dominance over my body. It feels like he's reclaiming my body from abuse, and giving it back to me.

As his tongue naturally dips into me, I moan louder, my voice echoing across the living room ceiling.

"Oh, my— Oh, my God—" My words come out like whispered breaths, shocked as Noah adds deeper pressure. He licks heavier and heavier until I feel like I'm being penetrated without his tongue actually entering me.

When he stops to gently suck my clit, my back arches, tilting my hips into his mouth.

"Oh, you're so— You're so good!"

I'm just listening to what you want, Omega. I'll only do what you want.

He widens my thighs with his thumbs until my knees drop as far open as they can stretch. My hips beg for more, bucking into the air without any sense of rhythm.

Noah's growl buries itself into my core as my body welcomes his tongue inside.

I've never had the urge for his tongue to penetrate me, but when he hits just an inch past my entrance, I melt. "Oh! Ah!"

My shaking legs urge him to tongue-fuck me until I'm lightheaded. Pleasure scales my belly, breasts, and throat. Dropping my head back, I cry out as he switches between endless stimulation—sucking my clit, penetrating me, and licking every inch of my labia—until I gush onto his face.

Noah's growls shift into moans, his hips grinding into the edge of the couch beneath me. As my head fuzzes in bliss, I grip the cushion above my head, my hips slipping over his face. My knees raise on their own, baring my body to him as Noah licks pleasure into every little corner—until he focuses right on the spot that usually hurts. He trades between coating the invisible wound and dragging his tongue deeper, each cycle of his tongue building on itself until my whole chest fills with pleasure.

I pant hard, struggling to breathe through how good it feels as my knees squirm beyond my control. Noah rocks my hips over his mouth as I come, my thighs slamming shut against his cheeks.

As I catch my breath, wave after wave of relief hits my system. I can't stop moaning.

Not just because it felt good. But because it felt good with *Noah*, and his primary motive was helping me to re-discover my pleasure.

I'm still buzzing, forced to resort to mindlinking. *Oh, my God— I feel like you really did heal me.*

Noah huffs between my legs, his breath tightening my core with leftover pleasure. His erection is throbbing and huge, stretching his pants as he separates his hips from the couch.

"Come here, gorgeous Alpha." With loose muscles and a heaving breath, I urge his hips between my legs.

As I free his shaft, Noah shivers over me, his hips jolting at my touch. Grinding my soaked pussy on the bottom side of his shaft, I caress the top side, keeping him slotted between my legs. Noah still hasn't said a word, panting and moaning as he works his cock over me.

He grips the couch above my head, his shaft expanding against my palm with every stroke.

"I... I can't stop thinking about how good you just felt through our bond—" Noah comes all over my stomach, gushing enough to spill past my sides and onto the couch. "Fuck—"

With Noah's raspy breath above me, I'm stunned. He was that turned on by making me feel good, and his whole reasoning behind it was to help me heal. I never thought someone would love me this much.

Noah collapses against my chest, and I hold him as hard as I can, squeezing my eyes shut. Getting re-triggered terrified me that things would never be the same, and I was right; they're not. My heart is opening to Noah past anything I've ever felt.

Noah props himself over me, swiping leftover wetness from his cheeks. His focus drops to my legs, spread open to him. I stay exactly as I am, staring back at him. I'm laid out and bare, and he's meeting me there.

As I hook my arms around his neck to kiss him, his relaxed lips signal he's fully satisfied.

I'm so stunned by my love for him that my heart flutters. I retrace how we got here, trying to process it all.

But as my head clears, I'm hit with another realization altogether.

Noah's words before he pleasured me repeat in my mind: *I just know what it's like,* he said.

"It" could've been referring to PTSD, yes. But I know my mate. Was that "it" loaded heavier than it seemed?

I won't confirm my assumptions until Noah tells me the full truth, but I feel it in my gut. I think Noah has sexual trauma too.

I cup Noah's cheeks, unsure of what to do with the heartache in my chest as I'm blasted with pain for him at my revelation. If it's true, that makes Noah's willingness to trust me sexually just as major as my trust in him. Just as challenging, just as painful.

Which makes his pleasure even more of a miracle to witness. How many times has he allowed me to see him so vulnerable? I knew it was a gift to witness, but it feels even larger than a mere gift now. It feels like I'm healing his soul just as much as he's healing mine.

Noah's expression warps as I verge on heavy tears. My lip shudders with my hard, skipping breath and contorting expression.

"*Fuck*—" He gasps, his grip firm on my shoulders. "Oh, shit. Was it not okay? Did I trigger you somehow?"

I shake my head. "It's not that, it's—"

My lip quivers as I run my hands all over him, unsure how someone so kind exists.

How heartless could someone be to hurt him?

"I'm just *so* grateful for you," I rasp.

As I lose myself to heavy tears, Noah soothes me with slow, sweet kisses and reminders that he's right here. I'm not sure he realizes I'm crying for his silenced heart.

24

I can't believe my kids are graduating preschool today. I hope they'll feel special at their mini graduation ceremony after their final recess with me. To look the part, I'm wearing a vibrant, color-splashed button up shirt tucked into my black slacks, and desperately trying not to let my adoring, yet grieving emotions heighten too far.

My students still don't know I won't be teaching at this school next year.

Seated at the snack tables outside, I'm surrounded by my preschoolers and their loving grown-ups. The Lycan grown-ups invited their "Uncle" Noah to the graduation. He stands behind all the grown-ups, taller than everyone here.

Even though I'm constantly aware it's my last day as a teacher here, I can't stop smiling. My kids are happy, their grown-ups are excited, and my mate beams every time I meet his eyes.

I bite my lip, stifling the giddy, teenagerish laughter in my chest as Noah winks. But with one glance at my watch, I gasp.

I cup my hands around my mouth to amplify my voice. "Alright, class! Let's line up for your graduation ceremony!"

With some help from the grown-ups, we manage to shuffle the kids into a formation somewhat resembling a line. They lean past each other to look at me as I address their grown-ups.

"Welcome, grown-ups! Thank you for joining our class for a very special day today: Class 34's Preschool Graduation!"

The kids all scream louder than I expect, and I burst into laughter with most of the grown-ups.

"One, two, three, eyes on me!"

They're all silent in a second, and I allow myself a bright giggle.

"Okay, Class 34. When I call your name, come get your certificate!"

I call Cory's name first. His shy smile grips my heart as he makes his way over to me. Cory waves to his mom, and his pride in his accomplishment is apparent in every step when she claps for him extra loudly.

"Great job, baby!"

I bite the inside of my cheek. The way they just looked at each other was so sweet—like they're each other's favorite people in the universe. Just thinking of Noah and I sharing the same bond with our future kids makes my eyes hot.

No, I'm refusing to cry. Which means I definitely can't look at Noah.

His wolf has the zoomies in our bond, nudging my wolf over and over again between spinning in circles. Despite trying my hardest, I can't help myself, sneaking a glance at Noah just before I hand Cory a certificate.

Noah's smile is covered by his fist, so all I can see is his doting stare. It flips my heart.

He shakes his head. *My sweet Omega... You're absolutely beautiful with these kids. I'm having a total moment.*

I bite my lip, my heart pounding. He's picturing us watching our future kids graduate preschool, isn't he? Just like I am.

Cory takes his certificate with a tooth-gap grin, turning to show his mom.

I squat beside him for a photo—his mom ready with her phone—but Cory turns to me, giving me a massive hug. My heart melts as he squeezes me hard, squealing in excitement beside my ear.

Oh, God. I can't take this, Noah.

I verge between crying and laughing, my hands shaking as I rub Cory's back. "I'm so proud of you, buddy! Congratulations, kindergartner!"

"Kindergartner!?" He squeals.

Cory's mom laughs. "What do you say, Cory?"

"Thank you, Miss Matsuoka!" He dives in for a second hug, and the crowd of grown-ups burst into doting laughter.

But now I'm really struggling not to cry. Noah's wolf courts mine in our bond, steadying my heart.

And I need it; by the time I get to Kelsi, every single kid has wanted a hug, and I'm an internal wreck.

"Come get your certificate, Kelsi!" I smile.

She's distracted, searching for her grown-ups in the crowd.

Fuck, her mom couldn't make it to the ceremony.

Just before my heart snaps, Kelsi's aunt stands, her small figure emerging from the crowd. Kelsi's aunt turns her phone screen, showing Kelsi her mom watching the graduation on a video call.

Kelsi lets out a squealing giggle, running over to me to get her certificate.

I burst into laughter, relief flooding my chest. "Oh, my goodness! Congratulations, Kelsi!"

When she leaps into my arms for a hug, my heart aches. I'm going to miss her. Thankfully, she's in our pack, but I won't see her every day anymore. I squeeze her tight as the grown-ups laugh, unaware I'm about to sob if this little one doesn't let me go when I set her back down.

Thankfully, Kelsi releases me, darting into the crowd to show her aunt and mom her certificate up close. Once the last student has their certificate, it takes at least 20 adults to herd the excited toddlers for a final picture. My heart burns as I look at their sweet, smiling faces, most of them already losing focus and wanting to go play. I should've gotten a group photo with them all too. Everyone is already dispersing.

My shoulders sink as the grown-ups reach for their kids, but Andy's mom steps forward.

"Wait, we need one with Miss Matsuoka!"

The kids meander back to their spots, and I know better than to miss out when toddlers are cooperating. I rush behind the class for a photo, and the preschoolers giggle at my frantic run.

I sputter out a laugh. "You think that's funny, huh?" I exaggerate my panicked movements, giggling with them. My laugh is genuine, screaming "cheese" with the kids for the camera.

The grown-ups lean in to snap another picture—or ten. Noah is behind them, taking one for me to keep.

I meet his eyes and laugh at his huge grin. If I could imagine how his inner wolf looks when he's at his happiest, these eyes squinting with joy would be exactly it.

My heart might explode any second; I don't think it can take much more cuteness today.

But all eyes are on me, expecting me to close out the ceremony before it erupts into chaos.

My stomach knots. I really hate saying goodbye on a normal year, but they don't know it's my last year teaching here, yet.

Swallowing hard, I smooth my clothes and put my smile back on. "I won't keep you kindergartners long so you can go play, but I just wanted to say—" I glance at Noah, taking a deep breath. Then another. "I had so much fun with you, Class 34! I'm going to miss seeing your bright smiles every day next year, especially since it's my last year teaching here."

I'm too afraid to look at anyone's reactions, judging by the sudden movement I can see out of the corner of my eyes. My focus remains locked on Noah, allowing him to ground me.

"I'm so proud of every single one of you for how much you've learned about sharing, friendship, and the world. I know you'll do such an amazing job in kindergarten. Congratulations, learners! Give yourselves a big hug for me!"

As I take a step into the grass to join the crowd, I'm stopped by multiple concerned grown-ups.

"Miss Matsuoka, did you say it was your last year?"

"Wait, so she *did* say that?" Cory's mom clutches her shirt. "I wanted my daughter to be in her class next year."

Andy's mom gapes, her forehead knotted. "Is it true, Miss Matsuoka?"

All eyes are on me, worry replacing the smiles from just moments before. The Omega in me wants to crawl into a hole and disappear. This is supposed to be their day, not mine. What do I say now?

Before the voices stepping forward overwhelm me, my eyes catch on my mate.

Noah gives me a sad smile. *Look at the impact you've had. They're ready to fight for you for a reason. You probably have no idea of the depth you're actually helping their kids.*

I bite my lips, dropping my head as tears flood my eyes. I turn around, quickly brushing them away.

"Oh, Miss Matsuoka…" Andy's mom mutters.

But a smile bursts across my face as I turn back to address my students and their grown-ups. "I really wish I could return to teach, but with the budget cuts, I won't be returning next year."

The grown-ups deflate, muttering to each other.

Cory's mom shakes her head. "I'm so sorry to hear that. So many of us have younger kids we wanted to be in your class. But you'll keep teaching, won't you?"

The desperate hope in everyone's eyes crushes me.

"Well, I'll be moving on to create something new in Greenfield—" I eye Noah for permission to share, and he nods. "Maybe a cross between a daycare and organized homeschooling for kids that need behavioral support in that town."

Andy's mom in particular brightens up—a weight lifting from her eyes as she practically hops in excitement. "Oh, that's *wonderful!*"

This relaxes the atmosphere just enough for groups to start breaking off, guiding their kids to the playground.

Okay, I got through it. Thanks to my sweet Alpha.

As I return to my mate's side, his soft touch on my back allows me to stand straighter and swipe away my remaining tears. Wolves pour in from all over the field, desperate for a chance to talk to us—well, particularly for a rare chance to talk to Noah.

But Andy's mom seems to want to stick around after talking to him, eyeing me nervously. I wave her aside with a smile, settling beside her on a playground bench.

"Andy made such incredible leaps this year! I'm so proud of him," I say.

She hugs me out of nowhere, squeezing me tight. My heart crawls into my throat, flooded by her grateful, yet sad scent.

Her voice is soft and shaky. "I don't know how to thank you. After how awful school was for him last year, I feel like I got my happy kid back."

I release a soothing scent on instinct, and Andy's mom sighs, releasing me.

"I love him no matter what, of course. But with Andy having

to repeat preschool, and all his anger issues that came up—" Her lip wobbles, tearing at my heart. "I just hated seeing him so sad. So I can't thank you enough for helping him feel like it's okay to be who he is. He's a positive, energetic kid again."

My heart throbs with every word she says. "Oh, it's my absolute pleasure. He took in everything I said and implemented it on his own. It's his accomplishment." Then I chuckle. "And I think it helped that he wants to be an Alpha protecting his pack Luna."

Andy's mom gives a hearty laugh, drying her eyes. "It's not just that, Luna. And it's not just about his resiliency, either—although, my kid *is* incredibly resilient."

She leans in, her eyebrows furrowing. With how deep the pain on her face sets into the soft wrinkles at the corner of her eyes, I can tell this pain existed long before Andy was born.

"No other teacher knows how to work with wolves around here. We all love Teacher Rainn, of course, but I and many other Lycan parents want our pups to grow up suited to blend in with human society, not confining them to our hometown so they can lead any life they want to. Andy's older brother, Jason, struggled the same way in human school. But Jason didn't have a teacher like you. I really think it changed him, no matter what I could say or do to try to help." She shakes her head, quickly swiping away fresh tears. "You've always met your students where they're at, and it changed Andy's life. He was so stifled and shamed last year that he hated school. At three years old!"

My heart snaps. "Oh, Andy… I didn't know. He was my most enthusiastic student most days, and got the whole class excited in whatever we were doing."

She smiles. "Well, I saw improvements in Andy's mood from the very start of the school year. He'd come home, telling me everything he learned. And I know I only heard half of what havoc he must've been creating, but I know how patient you've been with him." She winces. "Like with the biting incident."

She hangs her head, but I grab her hand.

"And I really believe patience and emotional processing is all he needed that day. I'm just so grateful he took it in. Andy even came up to me this week, applying what he learned that day to a new situation. I was so impressed!"

Andy's mom closes her eyes, her palm pressed to her heart with a heavy exhale. "Did he? Oh, my goodness, you have no idea what it's like to hear that."

"Considering what you're sharing, Andy has given it his all, no matter what happened in the past. He's an incredible kid."

She rubs my arm, releasing some of her doting scent until my heart pounds ten times faster. "You're such a sweetheart. I know you're not going to take credit over my son, but just know, you've always been the greatest Luna-like figure for our little community here, even before you came to Greenfield. Thank you, Luna. Thank you."

A part of me feels like bawling as Andy's mom rejoins her family's side. Her vibrant laughter tells me she's in love with Andy's happy screech more than ever, but she has no idea a fire has been lit under me too. One I didn't expect.

My wolf whispers to me. *Luna... I'm ready to be Luna.*

I'm shocked; I've never had such a clear awareness of my desires, other than when I met Noah.

Uncertainty floods my mind without giving me a single heartbeat to recover. How do I know I'm good enough for the job? Can I ever know? But my wolf stands her ground, puffing her chest high above the flower field in our bond's inner world.

Noah notices the shift in her, turning to meet my eyes despite the wolves surrounding him. They continue speaking to him, but his eyes are glued to me.

I stare back, my cheeks flushing with desire.

No, I need *to be Luna. His Luna. As soon as possible.*

Noah's shoulders rise as he tears his eyes away from me, unable to contain his wolf bounding through our bond.

That's not the main problem. I can't control my wolf at all, and she's rubbing her horny scent all over his wolf to rile him up. The more I try to restrain her, the worse she behaves, baring her backside to tempt Noah's wolf. I slap my forehead and look at the sky, trying to drown out the image with thoughts of clouds and birds.

But only 30 seconds later, Noah turns back around in his human form. His breath is heavy, and his scent carries itself on the wind. I'm hit with a rush of sexual pheromones so strong, my wolf begs to be let out as wetness seeps from my core.

Yes, my wolf says, dragging her body across her Alpha. *I want to make my mate feel good.*

As heat clouds my head, I can't stop her.

Wolves across the field cover their noses, their eyes glued to me and Noah. Humans adjust their collars and fan their faces, likely blaming their sudden arousal on the summer heat.

The last of my wits has my head whipping over both shoulders, seeking an exit. *Noah, we can't do this here!*

He doesn't answer. When I look back at him again, his expression only darkens. *Omega, your wolf... She's all over me.*

I know it's *my* wolf ravenously courting Noah's in the first place, but she genuinely won't stop. And unfortunately, it's having just as strong of an effect on Noah. His teal eyes are already morphing to yellow.

Sorry, you're right—I started it. I can't contain her, I mindlink.

W-well, I don't know why it's hitting me so hard, but whether it's the start of your heat or not, I'm about to slip into a serious rut, so...

My heart flips. Noah's wolf pants in our bond, warning me he's further gone than he looks in his human form.

OCD harm fears grant me a breath of clarity: what if we lose control, mating on the playground and disturbing everyone around us?

That intrusive thought sounds ridiculous, and it's also horrifying enough that I trust that we won't act on it; Noah wouldn't do anything I don't want.

Except we're not the only Lycans I'm worried about. Itching, jumpy wolves are peppered across the playground, sweat creasing brows as Lycans fan themselves. What if our scent influences other wolves, just like the stew incident? I can't promise the other Lycans understand human culture around sex. Not with their enthusiastic, culturally-expected exhibitionism that most humans do *not* share.

Right on cue, two separate Alphas grab their kids, heading for the car with shifted eyes. When I spot one mate stealing a sneaky grip on their mate's ass, I gasp. My eyes land back on my mate.

He hasn't stopped staring.

My heart flips. *Noah?! What's going through your mind?*

He chews on his lip, eyeing me up and down.

All he mindlinks is, *Mate.*

Oh, God. We have to get out of here before we cause a major scene.

Meet me in the teacher's bathroom. I take off for the bathroom first, but I can feel Noah's wolf stalking close behind. *Tell those wolves that you and I need to talk in private.*

I glance over my shoulder to find Noah not even bothering to excuse himself, setting his sights on me. His prowling stare only encourages my wolf. My lungs tighten as the distance closes between us. A deep instinct within me begs to make him chase me, and I automatically pick up the pace. I breathe harder as he strides faster, an electrifying craving striking our bond.

The second the building shields us from the playground's view, Noah deepens his chase. Excitement pumps through my veins, encouraging me to race faster. But Noah's long legs easily close the gap. When he reaches out to capture me, I gasp at how intense it feels, even though all Noah does is hug me against his side.

I grip his shirt, tugging him closer. But that was a mistake; with burning eyes, Noah's hyper wolf shines through. He scoops me up by the hips, throwing me over his shoulder.

I sputter out a laugh, and Noah fast-walks us into the empty teacher's lounge, straight to the bathroom. Within seconds, I'm locking a bathroom stall door behind Noah's back, cramped into a single stall with my massive mate.

I get to work unlatching Noah's belt.

But with a gasp, Noah backs up. "Fuck, wait. I just got back into my rational head a little." He rubs his eyes hard with the base of his palms before shaking his head clear. When he looks at me again, his eyes have settled to green. "I don't know what you have in mind, but I haven't prepared you enough to mate the way your wolf's begging me for."

My heart flips, imagining Noah pounding into me for the first time in ages—in a bathroom of my ex-workplace, of all places. With how spontaneous and risky this moment is, I actually feel more prepared than usual; my panties are thoroughly soaked just from Noah chasing me.

Actually, I might be too prepared. Fire burns my core—a silent, incoming threat. With Noah's yearning scent stinging my eyes, it's only mere minutes before I slip into a full heat.

"That's perfectly fine, Alpha," my wolf purrs through me. I drop to my knees, unbuttoning my shirt until he has a full view of my cleavage. "I'll just take the edge off for you down here first. Then you can knot me from behind."

Noah blinks a few times until his yellow eyes shift back to green. "W-wait, *what?*"

I freeze. "Sorry. Is this okay?" I gaze up at him, already salivating.

"You sound—" His eyebrows furrow as he grips the wall for stability, taking a deep whiff of my scent. "Oh, fuck, did I put you in an early heat? God, it's fucking *strong*."

I purr, licking his cock even harder over his thin boxers until it flexes against my tongue.

Noah gasps. "H-holy fuck— I think we're screwed. We can't leave the bathroom like this."

His eyes blaze yellow as I tug his boxers to his thighs, nuzzling against his shaft as it bobs free.

I purr. "I want to please my mate."

"O-oh, Goddess— You're 100% wolf brain, aren't you?" His chest heaves. "Because I'm about to be too."

"Then, do you still want me to use my mouth on you, Alpha? If you're worried about hurting my mouth too, I'll make you come over my breasts at the end instead."

"Oh, *my*— I—" He grips the top of the stall. The metal creaks as he writhes against my tongue. "I'd love that, but I mainly want to try to get you pregnant. That's what your wolf is begging me for, and my wolf is dying to give it to her."

My core clenches as my vision reverts into shades of gray, yellow, and blue, my wolf surfacing.

She must be showing herself on my face somehow; Noah purrs, stroking my hair back with mesmerizing sweeps over my scalp. "Oh, my gorgeous mate. You like that idea, don't you? Looks like I'm not going to be able to get you home until we try."

"But I—" My hand travels to my groin at the thought, and

Noah breathes even heavier. "I want you to do it by knotting me, Alpha."

Noah's cheeks flush as even his wolf is rendered speechless. With a delighted hum at my fingers circling between my legs, I lick the drop seeping from Noah's tip. Noah flexes against my touch, but when my tongue roams to his thigh, I can't resist giving the dense muscle a little nip.

Noah steps back with a hiss, grabbing my chin. His sharp, serious stare sends an icy thrill through my veins.

Sorry, Alpha. I got a little too excited by you. I lick the drop of blood my fangs left on his thigh, peeking up at him guiltily.

My mate furrows his brows. "Fuck, Omega. We've had so much mating sex, I forgot how horny your wolf was in heat. But today, I don't get it. It's almost like she wants me to play-fight with her."

I nod.

But that feels so odd to me that a bit of my usual, human vision slips through, pink hues seeping back into our skin tones.

One of Noah's eyebrows raises as mine furrow; I'm struggling to push past my wolf's judgment to see reality. Why are we so riled up today? I've never liked conflict, so why do I feel like pestering my mate on purpose? Enticing a genuine growl out of him?

Noah studies me. "What is it that you need, feisty Omega? Your wolf is rolling at my feet again. Does she want me to roughhouse with her?"

I hum, staring at Noah's tempting thigh. When I open my mouth to nip him again, Noah growls. I shrink, but with a burst of my elation in our bond.

Noah breaks into a sly grin. "Oh, I see. She wants me to put her in submission?"

Excitement floods my veins. I stare back into his eyes, challenging him directly.

"Try," I whisper.

I can't stop myself. I rush in to bite his thigh again, but Noah growls—earnestly growls, glaring down and everything.

Just like I wanted.

"*Feisty* Omega. You're naughty today."

I gasp at the rush of heat his words burrow into me. Noah freezes.

Then he frowns. "Wanting to play-fight is one thing. But if I didn't know you better, I'd think your kink suddenly reversed itself."

"My kink?" I blink a few times. "What kink?"

He tilts his head, a slow smile creeping over his face. "You don't know?"

I glare at him. "Don't laugh at me."

We both freeze; Noah's chest puffs in response to my gaze.

Oh, shit. I just challenged his wolf somehow.

Unintentionally challenging my Alpha sends such a hearty thrill through my chest that I tear my eyes away, tensing like I've been jumpscared. With it comes a rush of heat to my pussy so indulgent, I'm forced to swallow a shuddering moan.

Even after a stabilizing breath, my wolf's voice comes out shaky. "I don't know what you're talking about. If anything, my kink is just mating with you."

Noah chuckles. "Okay, okay. Either way, you're confusing me today, Omega. Almost like you're in a different headspace than you've ever shown me before."

I clean his thigh with an irritated growl, but Noah places a hand on my head with a gasp.

"Oh, fuck, wait. Look at me again."

I obey, but when I see his curious, adorable head tilt, I whip my head away on purpose with a smile, forcing him to move me himself if he wants to look at me again.

He's gentle with me, but he does guide my face back to him, urging me to look at him with a stable grip on my chin as he looms over me.

When we meet eyes, Noah's grin widens. "Oh, I think I nailed it by accident." He turns my head side to side, analyzing my eyes. "This isn't my sweet Omega. This is my sweet Alpha, isn't it?"

My lungs pulse faster with every second that my powerful Alpha's eyes challenge me head-on. I don't want to look away, no matter how many times it flips my heart. Eventually, I can't bear the rush of it, dropping my stare to Noah's knees as I gasp for air.

He's heightening my heat. Every inch of me burns,

concentrating my pleasure in my core. It almost feels like his eyes have already been mating me silly, my pussy pulsing with an aching, wet fire.

"You want more, don't you?" Noah purrs. "Which part is it that you like? Do you feel that buzzing in your chest when I look at you? Challenge you? Does it feel good?"

Shivering at his words, I peek up at him, *desperate* to feel it again. His stare hits ten times as hard; Noah's wolf smiles through him, showing his full incisors. He's smiling, but his stare remains sharp, heated beyond what I can withstand. As my eyes dart away, Noah hums. "*That's* what she wants. She wants to be bossed around today. She wants to be challenged. Am I right?"

All traces of Noah's rational side have left his body, and my wolf loves it. I spread my scent against his legs, rubbing my head, neck, and breasts all over him.

"Yes," I mutter into his knees. "I feel that thrill each time I challenge you, just like you said—"

I freeze; Noah's grip tightens on my hair. It's gentle enough that it doesn't hurt, but hard enough to give my scalp a blissful massage. With my humming pleasure, Noah purrs.

"Stand up." His voice rumbles against the stall walls, chilling my spine.

I do as I'm told, but my wobbly legs threaten to give. Noah catches me, hugging me to his chest.

He nips my ear, his voice rough even as it lowers. "Turn around, little Alpha."

I stand straighter, even though it makes my heart pound wildly. "I'm not little."

Who am I kidding, Noah towers over me. As my mate stands even straighter too, his fangs extend with his grin, shooting excitement down my spine. "Yes, you are. And that's exactly why you're deadly as fuck."

I drop my head. "You're making fun of me."

Noah chuckles, cupping my cheeks until I meet his stare again. As his eyes roam over my face, I only grow hotter, hardly able to withstand the strength behind his burning scent. "You don't realize the power in what you're doing right now, do you?" Noah's eyebrows raise as mine furrow. "I'm not actually joking

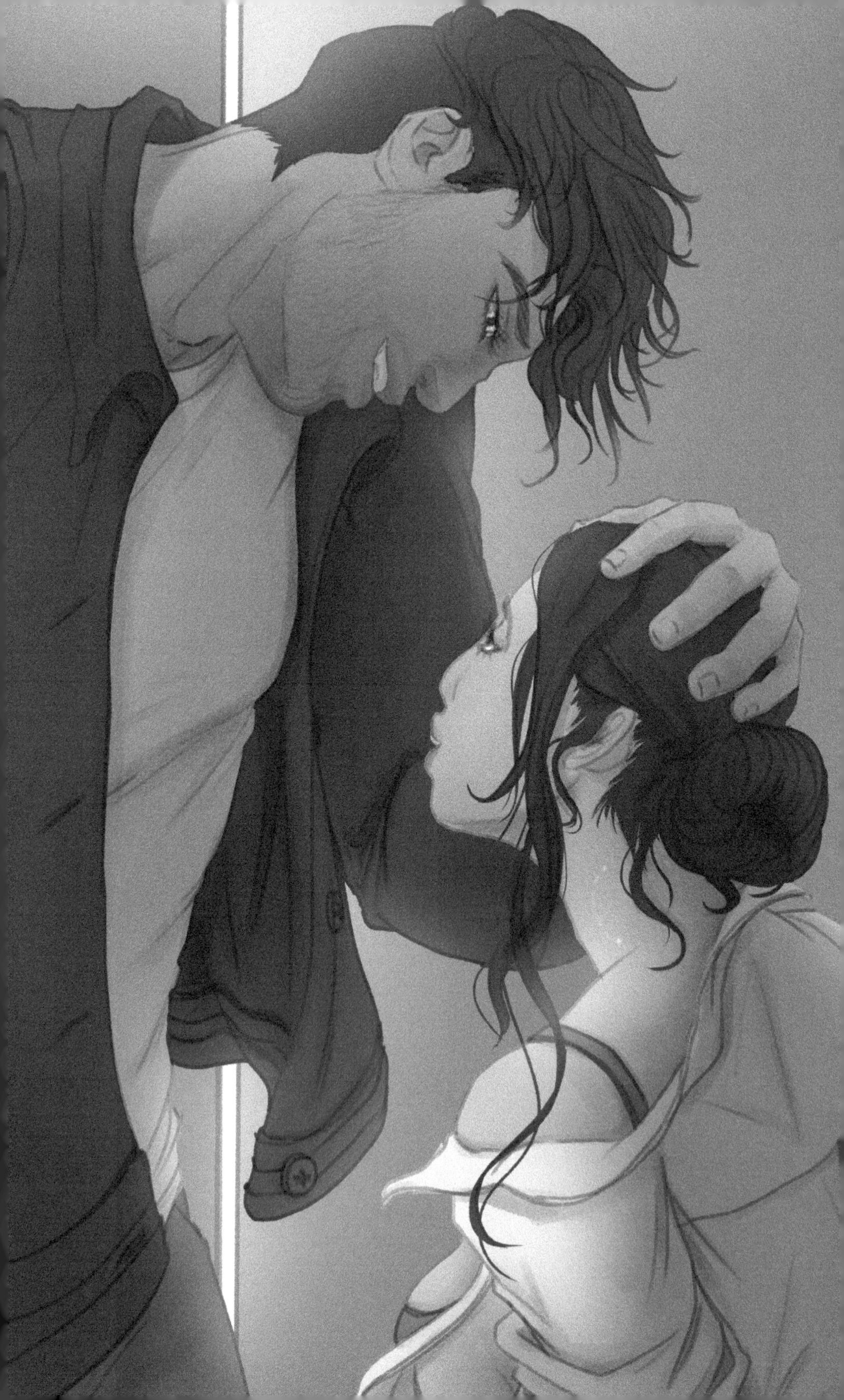

at all, Aliya. But I'm glad you don't understand what I mean. It means I've done my job well in keeping you feeling safe here. Now turn around, Alpha. Palms flat on the wall."

My heart rate spikes at how serious he sounds. I'm desperate for him to roughhouse with me, so before turning around, I dive for his mark, giving him a quick bite. Noah gasps, but I don't give him time to retaliate; I whip myself around, dropping my palms flat on the wall, as requested.

With a fiery growl, Noah reaches around my waist to undo my pants button. His body heat emanates across my back, and his heavy breath fans against my neck until I fawn for him. Noah gives my mark a sharper bite than I expect, and I jump in his arms.

But I'm not letting him be the only one driving me wild. In order to keep my palms flat on the wall, I have to stretch above the toilet, doubled over with my ass out. I take my chance to rub myself on Noah's erection, hoping it riles him up even worse. And there's no denying its effect in our bond, his urgency stealing my breath. Noah's purr shifts into a deeper growl. His hands roam down my back, stifling the rising desperation in his wolf with a few gentle humps against me.

Before I can whine about him taking his sweet time, Noah yanks my pants to my thighs, trapping my knees closed. I gasp, freezing in place.

Bent over the toilet, I'm fully exposed to him as he runs his fingers down my entrance from behind. His touch spreads tingles down my legs so strong that my knees squirm.

"Fuck, you're drenched, little Alpha."

My body welcomes his big fingers into me, slotting them deep in one slow thrust as I push my hips back.

A heavy moan escapes my lips. It echoes beyond the stall, bouncing across the tile walls.

"Shh... We're in public." With his free hand, Noah slips his fingers into my mouth, and my inner muscles flex over him in surprise. "Oh, fuck. You really want me in your mouth today, huh?"

I gladly bob my head over his fingers, hoping it urges him to do what I *really* want.

He's thorough with his fingers, widening them to massage

my G-spot until I'm letting out desperate little cries over his knuckles. As pleasure wells in my core, my hips squirm on the verge of orgasm from being fucked from both ends.

But I'm not satisfied with this. I yank Noah's fingers from between my legs with a low growl, turning to glare at him as I continue to suckle his hand.

No, Alpha. Not your fingers down there.

Noah's breath hitches as I reach for his cock, swallowing his fingers deeper before saliva spills from my lips.

"O-oh, *shit*. No, wait—" Noah's voice is clearer than it has been since we locked ourselves in the stall.

His fear snaps me out of my focus. I freeze, his fingers still in my throat.

What? Did I do something wrong?

"No. I just don't want to hurt you during sex. Are you thinking it through enough to understand that, or are you running on pure impulse?"

I turn over my shoulder, hoping he sees the resolve in my eyes. *Neither. I'm paying attention to how my body feels, and I'm so ready that I'm literally dripping for you. Set your wolf free with me. Mate me any way you want to.*

After staring for a few agonizing seconds, Noah huffs through the rising desire in our bond. "Okay... Okay."

He removes his fingers from my mouth, urging me to kiss him. My lips are soaked and kisses sloppy, but Noah's grasp is firm on my hips, his tip fitting into my entrance. Just its soft prodding breaks our kiss with my rapid, anticipatory gasps.

Moaning, I grip Noah's hands as they tighten around my hip bones. "It— It feels nice, Alpha. I want you so badly—"

Noah growls against my back, hugging me around my abdomen. With a heated kiss, he presses into me. My moan shudders against his lips just as heavily as my thighs quiver. As he sinks in, my core has no room to escape his internal massage. A sugary spike of lust pounds through my aching heart muscles.

H-how is it? Noah asks.

I sputter out thick, uncontainable gasps against his lips, grateful we're using mindlink. *Good! So good—*

He hugs me closer and closer, using our embrace to penetrate me—allowing my body to welcome him at its own pace.

After he pulls back, I shiver at how easily his soft skin glides back in. My knees dip in delight.

But when he bumps my cervix, my spine ignites like tingling fireworks. "Mmm!"

Noah releases my lips with a heated smack. His nose brushes my throat, taking a deep whiff of my pleased scent.

"You're all Omega now," he purrs, dragging his palms over my belly and hips.

When his hands sweep up my breasts, giving them a circular rub, it feels so good that I shove my ass back into him, burying him to the hilt. I'm so deliciously full that I can't squeeze his swollen shaft. With every soft pulse of Noah's hips, my whole body rolls through the tingling warmth he stimulates.

My arching back steals Noah's breath, squeezing him inside me. He breaks from my lips, groaning. By how hard he's growing, I'm positive he's already on the edge. "Oh, *Omega*— Oh, Goddess, I think our timing was off this whole time."

I can hardly grasp his words as he pulls almost all the way out, dragging pressure along every nerve inside me. When he stops moving, I can only blubber out a single word. "What?"

Noah groans against my scent gland, urging burst after burst of my lusty scent with dense licks. With each caress of his tongue, my thighs strain harder against my waistband, thrusting me back over his cock until he's fully inside me again.

Noah shudders, pressing my neck to his open lips as he pants. "I'm about to get you pregnant. I can smell it—"

I suck in a surprised gasp, just as Noah pulls back to rebury himself in a slow, tender roll of his hips. Moans burst from me, unaccustomed to his size after we've taken a break lately. The pressure is intense, but after giving me a chance to accommodate him, Noah purrs against my neck in delight at my body's quick, urgent squeezes. The sound of his soft, satiated hum softens my muscles, my body begging him to sink deeper and enjoy all of me.

As he rocks into me like I'm delicate, frustration rises in both of us, but Noah continues to work me gently. No matter how careful he is, I gasp for air at how thick he swells, stretching me to my limits every time I think I can handle him.

But it doesn't hurt.

Sweat slips down Noah's cheek, warning of his approaching knot, and my wolf finally snaps.

She growls in her Alpha's face. "Stop holding back!"

When Noah's eyes flick to mine, they're back to their brightest. "Is that a challenge, Alpha?"

I can't respond; my breasts are now smushed against the icy bathroom wall.

Crying out against the tile with every massaging press of Noah's tip against my cervix, my jaw drops. "Ah! *Yes*—"

Noah steals my words with his tongue, licking my mark as his claws prick entire handfuls of my ass cheeks. With his hips picking up the pace, echoing wet slaps across the bathroom, I'm ready to burst. Noah's approaching knot expands with every growl, taking up so much room at my entrance that I can hardly breathe.

"A-Alpha! Ah!" I drop my head back.

But Noah's fangs prick my neck. The sting shoots to my groin as heat clouds my eyes. Rippling pleasure scours my body as he kneads the deepest part of me.

"My—" Breathy and desperate, Noah's half-shifted voice makes me cry out in want. My moans urge him to grip me harder, keeping himself stationed deep into me with small, rapid pulses until I'm drooling from my gaping jaw.

"Oh, my sweet—" He cuts himself off again, unable to speak through a moan that threatens to send me over the edge. With that aching, sultry growl, I want him to call me his Omega, his Alpha, his anything.

But what comes out of Noah's mouth is something I didn't expect.

"My— My sweet Luna—" His words set off a cascade in my body, leaving me no room to escape the pleasure.

I fawn for him as I come. Noah takes his opening to sink his fangs into my mark, telling me his wolf meant every word.

I explode from the inside out, moaning to the ceiling like I'm praying to the Moon Goddess. Noah covers my mouth as

I come louder than I ever have, every cry squeezing more and more sensation out of his thrusts. He groans against my neck, and Noah's thick burst of fluid in my core extends my orgasm with his every spurt.

I didn't know our bond would change if Noah marked me twice, but now that he has, our bond crackles into a million shards. My breath catches in panic, but as our bond reforms, I fall limp into his arms, unable to stand on my own from the emotional waterfall overcoming me. But Noah clings to me like his life depends on it, his desperate breaths against my neck telling me it's hitting him just as heavily.

Our bond knits ten times as strong, weaving deeper than I knew possible. The inner world we've created washes over with our affection, everything we've felt for each other since meeting flashing before my eyes.

Noah doesn't just love me, he loves being alive alongside me, just like I love being alive alongside him.

As his knot stations itself hard between my legs, I burst into tears, relishing in how close I feel to him. Each flex of my core urges more seed from him, pulling it towards my womb. I can't catch my breath between sobs, panting like I just ran a marathon in his arms. Noah licks the blood from my neck until it stops, and he whines as he holds me against him. It ricochets such a conflicting mix of emotions through me that I whine with him.

I love every second of it.

But as Noah whimpers against my cheek, his emotions dissolve into panic. "Shit, was I too rough? Goddess, you're so upset— I-I'm so sorry, I didn't mean to hurt you—"

"Noah— Noah, listen—" I grip his arms, struggling to soothe his panic.

Whether it's leftover from his rut, my heat, or our fresh bond, our emotions are in full blast, and Noah hasn't lost the clouded quality to his voice. He breathes hard and fast, and I know he needs me to ground him, but my wolf won't stop whining with him long enough to calm him. I just love him so much.

I take deep, steady breaths, moaning through the hard, satiating prodding from Noah's shaft against my cervix. Once I can manage a slower inhale, I sharpen my voice on instinct.

"Hey, listen."

My strange, Alpha-like scent slips from me again, freezing Noah in place. With a hammering heart, I shove that piece of me back down, softening my voice.

"Sorry, it's just— You didn't hurt me. I'm so in love with you that I can't stop crying, especially because I can't stop thinking I might be pregnant with your baby now."

"Goddess— Oh, Goddess, I can't even process that yet." Noah shudders, kissing my cheek over and over. As he sheds a few tears with me, Noah's lip quivers. "Fuck, Aliya, why am I such a wreck?"

I nuzzle him back, desperate to soothe his tears. But his hands don't stay on my waist. I gasp, my eyelids fluttering as his hot palms instinctively protect my filled abdomen. He caresses my belly like I'm already pregnant, thrusting my heart into a rollercoaster of emotions.

Until Noah stops with a groan. "Shit, no, I also f-fucked up just now. My blurry rut head isn't an excuse. I didn't mean to pressure you with those words about the— The future. About being Luna so soon. I don't expect—"

My heart drops. "Noah, stop. Please, don't continue that sentence."

I swallow my disappointment. A selfish part of me wishes he'd beg me to be his Luna now, no matter how unhealthy it'd be. But Noah is right; it should be my call to say I feel ready. Not only will we be performing the equivalent of a marriage ceremony in front of the entire pack, but part of my lifelong commitment will be dedicating the rest of my life to everyone in Greenfield. Claiming I'm ready impacts far more wolves than just us.

He whimpers. "Fuck, please don't be sad. I said that wrong—"

I hug his arms around me, giving him a tender squeeze. "I'm okay. But I did miss doing this with you. I love you so much that my heart aches."

Noah's shoulders droop, cocooning him around me. "Oh, my sweet—" Noah huffs, dropping to a shy whisper. "Fuck. S-sorry—"

My heart leaps. Did he almost call me his Luna again?

Noah smashes his lips against mine, his chest heaving against my back. He caresses my body, but I stop his palm on my stomach, loving how it feels.

Furrowing his brows, Noah strokes my abdomen with his thumb. "You okay?"

"I really like that," I whisper.

This slows Noah's worries to a stop. He breaks into a weary grin. "My sweet wolf with baby fever is still in control too, isn't she?" He circles his fingertips around my abdomen, making me shiver. He purrs, softening his voice between gentle cheek kisses. "Okay, I hear you. I've got you, Omega. You're okay. We're both okay."

I whimper, nuzzling into his lips for more. "I want to carry a baby for you so badly."

He blinks through our kiss, some of the stark yellow fading from his vision with it. With a deep breath, Noah loosens his voice into its usual, gentle hum. "I know how much it means to you. I can smell, feel, and see it. Just don't put so much pressure on yourself that you don't enjoy it, okay? I'm okay to wait, as long as we're here together."

"But it means just as much to you too. I could see it today, on the field, and feel it right now, in your wolf."

Noah kisses me slowly, nodding along to my words. "Y-you're right. Maybe that's why my wolf just freaked the fuck out, smelling you in heat. I want this with you so badly too."

My heart leaps, my wolf whining in delight.

"But we won't have to wait much longer, okay? We're going to figure this out soon, one way or another. I know it." His words turn my body to jelly, but Noah keeps me pressed against him in a full-body hug. "There you go. Relax, gorgeous."

I lean into him, allowing him to hold my weight.

"Good girl. I've got you."

My heart squeezes. "Noah…"

We nuzzle each other's heads, stroking each other's bodies everywhere we can reach. Noah kisses my sweaty temple, brushing my hair back into order.

But I'm lost in his every breath, dropping my head back against his shoulder as he holds me. A stupid grin remains plastered to my face no matter how hard I bite it back. I just can't stop staring at him. I feel all mushy.

Noah breaks into a heavy-lidded grin. "Is this still my wolf mate looking back at me? Or my human mate?"

"It's both of us. We're thinking the same thing."

He chuckles, his lips barely grazing my cheeks. My blinks slow, relishing in every second of his affection.

Noah smiles. "And what are you both thinking?"

"That you're beautiful."

His shyness takes hold as expected, fluttering my heart. But to my surprise, he holds my stare. Braving the discomfort for me.

"You're the most beautiful wolf on the planet," he whispers.

Our lips meet on instinct, and our prodding tongues flex Noah into my cervix. I give Noah a soft, pleased moan.

Which is when Mrs. Jacobs enters the bathroom.

"Miss Matsuoka? Are you alright in here?"

25

Noah's eyes are wider than ever, but I grip his arm, clinging to him for dear life.

"Y-yeah! I'm good!" My voice cracks, exhausted from how heavily Noah just pleasured me. Noah shuts his eyes, breathing away his amusement at the shocked look I just gave him at my own voice. *This is so bad! Do you think she saw your feet, Noah?*

Shit, I don't know how she couldn't have. They're hard to miss. He hobbles forward as quietly as he can. *At least my jacket is covering my giant, bare ass, but—*

Mrs. Jacobs gasps. Noah and I freeze.

"Oh, goodness. Are you sure you're okay?" Mrs. Jacobs asks. "I saw you run off to the teacher's lounge, but you've been in here a while, and you sound stressed."

I flush, gripping my forehead. "I-I'm fine, thanks. I'll see you back out there."

There's an uncomfortable silence. Mrs. Jacobs seems to rock on her feet, her heels tapping the linoleum. "W-well, just before I go, I wanted to say—"

Oh, my God, is she serious, Noah? What if I was taking a shit?!

Noah rushes to bite his knuckle, barely stifling a laugh. *Oh, Goddess, Omega, stop. You're fucking killing me—* He flexes into me with the laughter tensing his abdomen. I have to clench my jaw to withstand how good it feels. *Maybe she really hasn't noticed me?*

"It's sad to see you go. I hope you know I value your efforts for our students here—" Mrs. Jacobs clears her throat. "Although, I know I might not have shown it in the past."

Irritation flares in my chest. I drop my head against Noah's shoulder as I mindlink him. *Nope, she's clueless. Of course she finally decides to care about me right when my mate is buried inside me!*

Noah bites his lips, squeezing his eyes shut to keep from exploding. *Aliya, stop making me laugh! I'm going to—*

I take a deep breath, trying not to giggle with him. But Noah's silent laughter shakes me anyway, his knot pushing deeper as his tip bumps against my cervix, over and over.

I let out an uncontainable whimper.

And Mrs. Jacobs takes another step closer. "Goodness, are you okay?"

My nails dig into Noah's arm. "N-no! Don't come closer."

"No, you're not okay?"

"I-I'm *fine!* I'm just—" I look at the toilet beneath my arched torso and blurt out the first thing I can think of. "I'm just puking a little."

"Oh, goodness," Mrs. Jacobs says. "Are you sick?"

"I-I don't know. I'm—" I glance at Noah behind me, wincing at what I'm about to say. "I've been trying to get pregnant with my fiancé, so…"

Noah slams his hand over his mouth, forcing back a laugh. *Oh, Goddess, Omega… Good thing that's out of context and she doesn't know we're literally trying in here—*

Stop! It's the truth! I bite my lips, staring at the ceiling before I burst into giggles with him.

But his shaft won't stop prodding me, building enough pressure to make my knees dip for more. When I squish my ass as tight as I can against his hips, Noah's silent laugh is interrupted by a soft gasp.

Then Mrs. Jacobs is silent for a long time. Too long.

Oh, my God, Noah! She's getting closer!

Sorry!

It's not your fault; why isn't this lady leaving?!

Mrs. Jacob's voice quivers, scandalization emanating through every syllable. "I-is your fiancé in there with you? I heard a man."

"Mrs. Jacobs, please, leave us. He's— He's helping me hold my hair back, so you don't have to worry about me."

Then Noah clears his throat, placing his hand back over my

abdomen. "You feel nauseous again, don't you? It's going to be okay, love. Just let it out."

My eyes widen, realizing he's doing his best to save the situation.

But my heart nearly bursts at the way he's holding my belly, considering the context; not only did we just have unprotected sex, but he filled me up so much that I feel super pregnant. Especially when he holds my stomach like that.

My breath doubles in speed, my hand skating over my abdomen with him. Emotions erupt in our bond until my heart leaps into my throat, Noah's wolf nipping my wolf's neck.

But Noah's human form hugs me tighter, refocusing me.

Omega, you're going to have to scare her off. For a species that's all about privacy, humans made ridiculous bathroom stalls with big-ass gaps.

The heat in his stare tells me he knows exactly what I'm thinking, but he's right; Mrs. Jacobs needs to leave.

I make the best fake gagging sound I can manage, interrupted by a laugh I can only disguise with a heaving cough.

"Good girl. Let it out," Noah says.

"O-oh, goodness! Excuse me—" Mrs. Jacobs leaves as quickly as she can, the heavy door slamming shut behind her.

As soon as Noah's wolf ears signal it's all clear, we break into laughter, moaning and gripping each other.

"Why wouldn't she just leave?" Noah says.

"I don't know! She usually hates me!"

Noah laughs, groaning against my shoulder. "Well, she helped with our knot situation."

My eyes widen. "Noah, wait—"

But he's already pulling out of me. I gasp, my knees giving out in both exhaustion and fear that I'll drip. Noah squeezes me tight to his chest, cupping my swollen entrance before his sperm spills across my clothes. My cheeks have never been redder as he reaches for a tissue to clean me up.

Noah does a double take. He erupts into giggles. "After everything we just did, why is this making you so shy?"

"B-because! You're completely taking care of this for me, and—"

He chuckles, dropping to his knees to finish licking me clean. I gasp, covering my mouth.

His wolf is still in full force as he stares back shamelessly. *And? I made this mess of you, didn't I?*

"O-oh, my God! Noah Greenfield!"

"What? You better get used to it, sweet Omega. Especially now that I just got you pregnant." He plants one last kiss on my lower abdomen, right above my uterus.

I'm left gaping and speechless. Noah laughs with his full chest, his sly grin telling me he knows he just tortured my ovaries.

I have to laugh with him. "N-Noah! What am I going to do with you?"

"That's what I think when I see you every single day. I just love you too much."

"I love you too, so much." I sigh, my smile growing. "Are you happy, my love? You look happy."

Noah bites back his grin, nodding as he helps me hobble from the bathroom stall. "My wolf is losing his shit over everything that happened today. And so am I."

"Good. I love seeing you both happy."

By the time we can exit the bathroom towards the car, I'm pleasure-soaked and ready for bed, even if it's only noon. I can't unlatch myself from Noah's side. He has to keep nuzzling my neck, reassuring my wolf that he's still there.

"Omega, are you going to be able to make it through therapy without your Alpha?"

"Yes? I think…"

Noah sputters into laughter, cuddling me closer against the side of his SUV. He presses my back flat against the car, butterflies consuming my belly as he kisses me, long and slow.

Despite how heavily we just mated, my wolf won't shut up. *Luna… I'm ready to be his Luna.*

So when I'm sitting in my therapist's office, Jenny allows me to sit in silence for a good minute before finally speaking up. "Would you like to share what's on your mind?"

"S-sorry! I—" I bite my lip, returning to my thoughts.

It's harder and harder to explain everything about the pack to Jenny in human terms. But in human terms, I want to marry

Noah after only dating a few months. That's going to sound impulsive as hell.

Jenny is waiting, regardless.

"I'm worried what you'll think of something I've put a lot of thought into," I say. "And even though it's what I want, you might think I'm totally irrational for it."

Jenny rests her chin on her palm, leaning on her chair's armrest. "Maybe I will."

We laugh. Silence chases after it, my worries catching back up with me. Jenny folds her hands, allowing me to take my time.

I glance at the diamond on her left hand. "When you married your husband, did you just look at him one day, and know he was your future husband?"

Jenny breaks into a warm smile. "I knew the day I met him. Which I think you can relate to, judging by that smile."

"The *second* I met Noah, I knew I wanted to marry him." I brush my mark, passing it off as fumbling with my moonstone necklace. I haven't wanted to take it off lately. "I've been thinking about how I don't want to wait around any longer in my life to enjoy the good things. I want to marry Noah soon."

My heart leaps as I admit it aloud.

But I can't stop myself. "Like, eloping-during-this-month's-cultural-ceremony-if-he-agrees-to-it type of soon. I've never felt more certain about anything in my life."

Jenny stares back for a long time, shifting in her seat.

"W-what are you thinking?" I ask.

Jenny smiles, and I can't help but laugh, knowing she's about to deflect my reassurance-seeking compulsion.

"If you're more certain about this than anything, does it matter what I think?"

"No. But I want to know from an outside perspective if I sound irrational."

Jenny straightens, matching my serious energy. "Okay, then let's walk through this. If your past self saw you right now, what would she say?"

I break into a smile as I think of all that's changed. But most of all, how I've found what my past self always dreamed of.

"She'd be crying," I say.

Jenny's eyebrows raise in alarm. "What do you mean?"

"She'd be crying because—" I clear my throat, feeling my eyes heat with emotion. "She'd know all that grief and pain would be worth it to live through over and over again, just to get to where I am now."

Jenny stares for a long moment as I grab a tissue, smiling through joyous tears. Soon after, Jenny has to grab her own tissue, and we both laugh.

"You've come so far just to be able to say that at all, honey. That's incredible."

"Thank you."

"If I'm being honest, the first thing I thought when you told me you wanted to marry him was—" She shuffles in her seat, tracing my eyes for a moment. "Is this the same woman who was shaking in my office a couple years ago, apologizing ten times for breaking my pencil lead?"

My cheeks flush. I forgot my harm OCD was that severe.

"And you know what? This *is* the same woman," Jenny says. "The same woman who dragged herself through hell, knowing that she can do hard things, as long as she follows her heart."

I let out a sob, wiping my eyes even though the tears keep coming. Jenny crosses the room to sit beside me, and I lean against her, allowing her to hug me.

"I think you should keep following your heart, whatever that means to you."

My heart pounds, begging to leap closer to Noah.

"What are your fears about it? That you'll get divorced quickly? Regret it all? Get hurt again?" Jenny asks.

I think about it, long and hard. "I don't have fears about Noah. I only have fears about myself. What if I let us down somehow, and ruin the relationship? What if I change somehow, and I'm not the same person one day? What if I lose all my progress in therapy, and become the scared, trapped person I don't recognize again?"

They're just thoughts, but my heartbeat gallops, begging me to jump up in overwhelm. But this is something I often experience in Jenny's office, pushing my limits to build my uncertainty muscles.

"Well, what if? We could work on that fear, whether you're married or not."

I smile, my shoulders already relaxing as I break from our hug. "You know, that's a good point. Whenever I wonder these things, I don't stop to think that I could get through them, eventually—just with some work."

"So in the moment, they feel all-consuming. Endless."

"Yes, exactly," I say. "But whenever I let Noah in, everything feels survivable. Like I have someone who's by my side for good, whether I do something incredible or pointless, or do nothing at all. I want to be that person for him too—I love to be. And after being so afraid to be seen or heard, I also love taking up space in his life. Letting him see me."

Jenny shakes her head in awe. "I'm so proud of you."

My heart jumps into my throat as my smile widens.

Jenny grins. "You know what? I'll give you one little bit of an answer: from an outside perspective, you sound like someone who knows exactly what she wants, and she's finally asking for it."

I can't stop thinking about my conversation with Jenny, long after Noah falls asleep. His chest rises beneath my arms, his lungs humming against my chest as I keep him snug against me.

But then my heart starts to pound.

Luna... I want to be—

Noah stirs, his eyes still closed as he shifts himself higher.

Before I know what's happening, our cuddle ball morphs into him blanketing me to the bed. He presses sleepy kisses into my mouth, melting my worries away as we squeeze each other in our cuddle ball.

Noah pulls back, prying one eye open. "I can feel you thinking in my sleep."

I groan, stroking back his messy hair with gentle scratches over his scalp. "I'm sorry. Go back to sleep, please."

He grins. "No. I want to know what my mate is thinking. You've been thinking hard all day."

Noah latches himself around my waist, hugging me with all fours. I laugh-cough as he crushes me. Noah lightens up, rolling off of my chest, but I don't want to stop holding him. I throw my leg over his hips, and Noah laughs, scooting me against his side with a firm hand on my ass.

"Come on, Omega. You're freaking me out."

I swallow hard, propping myself on one elbow to look him in the eyes. "Okay, I wanted it to be special, but I can't wait any longer, either."

He tucks my hair behind my ear, keeping his hand there to stroke my cheek. I drop back down to my side, his warm chest automatically rotating to face me.

But he's serious as we stare into each other's eyes, waiting for me to speak.

I take a deep breath, bracing myself to feel scared. But the second it comes out of my mouth, I'm not scared.

"Noah Greenfield, my Alpha, I'm ready to be your Luna."

Noah doesn't seem to breathe, gaping at me. I rub his chest, nudging him into taking a breath. When he sucks in an inhale, it's sharp, igniting an excitement I've never seen in his eyes.

"W-when—? You—? I—" Noah swallows hard, and I know he's stifling his wolf; the big beast rapid-taps his front paws in our bond.

The Alpha tackles my wolf in our bond anyway, and I break into a smile.

"What, Noah? What are you thinking?"

"D-do you mean, like... for this upcoming Full Moon Ceremony? In two weeks?"

I bite back a smile at his precious stare, hope shining through every green and blue speckle of his eyes. "Is that too early?"

Noah huffs out an offended breath, sputtering through nonsense syllables I can't make out.

I burst into laughter. "Noah, what—"

Before I can finish my thought, Noah tackles me even harder than his wolf, kissing me into the pillows.

I squeal against his lips as his excitement pours throughout every muscle in my body. Noah kisses me over and over again, growing frantic.

I pull back, burying my face into his chest just so I can breathe. "Noah! Talk to me—is it too early?"

"No, it's not! Hell, no!"

I sputter out a laugh at Noah's exasperated tone, tracing my nails across his back to settle his charged energy.

"Oh, *Goddess*," he breathes. "I just can't believe my favorite wolf in the world wants to be my Luna."

I lift my chin, gazing at him hovering over me. "What?! Of *course* I do. I did when we first met, and now I love you more than ever!"

"I-I know, but it's different, now that it's finally happening after waiting my whole life for it. This is a million times better than what I dreamed of as a kid. Because it's *you*." He shakes his head in disbelief, unable to contain his massive smile. "Fuck, maybe I'm still asleep. *You're* going to be my *Luna*."

I had no idea it was this important to him. He tried so hard to protect me from feeling pressured that he stored all this hope inside himself. I don't want him to do that with me anymore.

I cup Noah's face between firm palms, making sure he's looking straight at me. "Listen to me, okay?"

He nods, hyper, nocturnal irises glinting in the darkness as they flick across my face.

"I already know you're going to protect me, so this is my way of signifying my commitment to you and your pack. Let me be your protector and nurturer, for life." My heart is racing, but I've never felt so certain.

Noah melts above me, his shoulders crumbling as he droops against my chest. As his lips crash against mine, his shaking breath tugs at my heart.

"T-thank you." His voice comes out as a broken whisper. Noah's tears drip onto my cheeks, startling a gasp from me.

I lean in twice as hard, desperate to share the love overflowing in my heart. Skating my fingers into the back of his hair, I urge him to my lips over and over again.

I've got you too, sweet Alpha. Always.

He whimpers, caressing my back as our kissing turns into a full-body makeout. Noah rolls his hips into me, kneading my clit in a slow, tender dance. I moan into his mouth as his hands worship every inch of me, my knees opening to welcome him between my legs.

As we gaze deep into each other's eyes, mating face-to-face, I know my life has been upended today. I'm no longer a school teacher, I'm committing myself to Noah for life, and I'm asking for exactly what I need.

And I couldn't be happier.

26

The start of summer vacation is no longer a "vacation" anymore without a job to return to, so I don't know what to do with myself. I could think up some more ideas on the Rogue daycare we'll open in the fall, but I promised Rainn we'd do that together next week. I could plan more for my upcoming Luna ceremony, but other than mentally preparing for my induction and our mating ritual, there's nothing I can prepare for alone.

With the added pressure of being the ceremony's front-and-center, I'm just as anxious to perform the ceremony steps correctly as I am excited. Maybe I'll get it all wrong and ruin the ceremony, or maybe it'll be the best day of our lives thus far even if I make minor mistakes. My stomach flutters just thinking about it, but every uncertainty is worth becoming Noah's Luna.

I can't stop smiling as I fetch the new scrapbook I purchased yesterday. Gathering my old, cut-up magazines and decorative cardstock, I sit down with one image in mind: creating a visual representation of my bond with Noah. I want to surprise him with the first spread before my Luna Ceremony, keeping the following pages blank for us to add to over the years.

Although, I'm not sure if he's as sentimental as I am. There aren't many pictures lining his cabin walls. Instead, fuzzy rugs and blankets coat every floor and couch, allowing me to curl up in Noah's residual scent.

Familiar comforts have been necessary the last few days. I'm not sure if I'm coming down with something, or if it's just my usual crash after a stressful school year. All I know is I'm *exhausted*.

My heart flips; I could also be pregnant. Noah and I did mate without protection on the last day of school, and again every night since, but it hasn't even been a week since the first attempt—a bit too early for a pregnancy test. I'm trying so hard not to get my hopes up that my stomach rumbles in complaint.

After an hour of scrapbooking, I'm happy with my progress. Hiding the scrapbook beneath my side of the bed, I fetch my laptop and head out the door.

Yasmine waits in her old convertible with a fanged grin. She puts her arm around my seat just before I get in, giving me a nod. "Hey, Luna. Nice necklace."

I bite my lip, clutching the moonstone Noah gave me. "I know it's a little too fancy for coffee, but I just thought—"

Yasmine waves me off. "I'm giving you a hard time. That thing is gorgeous on you, but it's also really special, you know? Only Lunas wear moonstones."

My heart flips over itself as Yasmine shifts into drive, throwing my hair back in the wind. By the time we're racing down the country roads, my mind finally catches up with Yasmine's words. "*Only* Lunas?"

Yasmine does a double take at my gaping eyes before bursting into laughter. "He didn't tell you, did he? As Luna, you're basically our pack's figurehead of protection, nurturing, fertility, and emotional safety, so the moonstone is supposed to provide it all back to you from the Moon Goddess." Yasmine cackles as my stomach somersaults. "My best friend is such a sneaky bastard. The dude's mad in love with you, if you couldn't tell."

I let out a bright laugh, shuffling in my seat. "God, I don't know how to thank him enough, Yas. For everything he's done for me, but especially for accepting me as his Luna. Even with our bond, I'm having trouble scoping out what he might like as a gift for the Luna Ceremony. What I have so far doesn't feel big enough."

"Just you being there is what he wants. He's more of a sentimental sap than a physical gift lover. Actually, the last time I gave him a physical birthday gift, he turned bright red for two whole minutes. I timed it."

We burst into laughter, slowing to a halt at the first red light we've come across in Greenfield. Once we cross the bridge over the river, we'll be back in Westfield. It's where I've worked daily for years, but now that I lost my job, it registers in my mind as "where my old apartment with Steven used to be."

My stomach gurgles, and I shift in my seat in discomfort.

"You okay?" Yasmine asks.

I sigh, closing my eyes. "Yes. I'm just a ball of nerves, lately. It's all approaching so quickly. And, to be honest, I have an idea of something sappy Noah might like at the Luna Ceremony. It'll make me anxious as hell to do, but in the best way."

Yasmine grins. "Besides fucking him in front of thousands of Lycans?"

I cup my forehead, letting out a nervous giggle. "U-um, yes. Besides that."

"Oh, spill it, *please*. I want to know something the Alpha doesn't."

I laugh, fidgeting with my purse strap. "From what you've all described, the Luna Ceremony sounds a lot like Noah and I are getting married in front of the whole pack. So I was thinking, at a human wedding, I'd vow myself to Noah in front of everyone I love, letting them hear me pour my heart out about how much I love and devote myself to Noah. I'm not sure if that's standard for Lycans, but— But I think it'd be special for us, at least."

For the first time since I've met her, Yasmine is speechless.

I laugh, tugging on her arm. "What?! Yas, you have to tell me—is that a bad idea?"

"Dude, you *have* to! Please, do it! Oh, he's gonna cry."

I let out a bright laugh as we turn into a parking spot outside the tiny coffee shop. The Cozy Roast is cuter than I remembered it, crumbled brick accents and low lighting giving it an aged, sheltering atmosphere. We order lunch and drinks, settling at a corner table with our laptops.

Yasmine stretches her neck with a quick shoulder roll. "Alright, Luna, let's get to work."

I exhale, struggling to calm my racing heart. "Good luck!"

Hopefully Yasmine won't notice I'm shaking. I didn't want to tell her anything I didn't have to, but Noah and I haven't been able to think of anything to prove our dad's deaths weren't accidental. Yasmine thinks I'm planning for future Luna responsibilities, which isn't a total lie. I'll be working to protect us all this way, but I won't be carrying out this investigation publicly.

Tapping the search bar on a fresh browser tab, I type in the first thing I can think of:

signs someone might be a murderer

It feels a bit silly, but I don't know where else to start. But when I press search, my stomach plummets.

Article after article shares lists of "signs," but they're all online forums or gossip magazines. Just reading article titles and excerpts, my heart thumps faster. Not because of the content, but because my father's potential murder never felt more like a joke to society.

I click on the most familiar source, hoping it's less gimmicky, but no: it's a linked summary to an "Ask Me Anything" question on one of the popular forum sites…

The forum Steven used to use, just before his behavior escalated.

I grip my head, unable to calm my racing heart. I'm not triggered as much as I am furious, scrolling through "real" accounts of people who claim they distantly knew murderers before they killed victims. Steven used to show me forums like these, laughing about twisted real-life issues he'd claim were proven to be true by moderators. This article has a similar air of mystique and excitement, as if killers are enticing, fantastical phenomena, not violent thieves playing God.

The general public might not put the pieces together, but with how intimately I'm haunted by the brutal aspects of Dad's sudden death, there's no way victims' families wouldn't know the crimes mentioned in these detailed comments were referring to their loved ones being brutalized. How must they feel, knowing their family members died an early, violent death, only for society to have some sick fascination with it? Wait, my dad might've been murdered alongside Noah's too. How do *I* feel about this?

Wincing, I grip my grumbling stomach. It's not just rocking with anxiety, it's gurgling with intense nausea.

Yasmine's eyebrows are furrowed. It isn't until then that I realize she hasn't been typing for at least 30 seconds, watching me from across the table. "You good?"

I sigh, closing the tab. "Yes, sorry. I just saw something messed up online."

Yasmine's lip curls in disgust. *Plenty of humans are twisted as fuck, so that makes sense.*

I'm part human. Am I twisted too? What if this is human nature, and I'm secretly a murderer?

Wait, I can't answer that; that's just OCD talking.

Nibbling my lip, I pull up a fresh tab. Yasmine just gave me an idea.

scientific studies on killer psychology

These results are much better—well, as in, these articles at least take the horrific situation seriously. Otherwise, the subject matter is just as revolting.

But something sticks out to me as important in our search: serial killers often prey on strangers, but most homicides are committed against victims the killer knows. "Homicide" yields more specific search results; perpetrator motives, profiles, and killing methods vary from serial killing.

I don't feel good about any of it, but I'm relieved I'm making progress, settling into a numb focus.

After 30 minutes of my face remaining neutral, Yasmine stretches her arms. "I'm gonna use the bathroom. Be back in a minute."

"Okay," I mutter, already buried in a new search.

The more I read about singular killings, the more familiar the perpetrators sound: a lack of guilt for victims, seeing victims as objects, a need to assert power, an inability to see right from wrong, and seeing themselves as exempt from certain social or moral rules. Most often, perpetrators target significant others.

There's no way Mom or Lilian killed our dads. Lilian may be heartless toward Noah now, but she sounded warmer before Ritchie's death. Mom refused to ever touch a gun, let alone shoot the man whose loss killed her from pure heartbreak. I'm well-aware of what domestic violence looks like, and Noah seems well-versed too. Unless our parents hid aspects of their relationships from us, I haven't seen signs in either couple.

That doesn't rule out our closest friends and family of past and present: Yasmine, Dave, the Elders, Amy, Kira, or Steven.

My gut curdles at the last one. I'm tempted to rationalize the thought away; although Steven was abusive in multiple ways, he never seemed capable of murder.

But he didn't seem capable of breaking in and assaulting me, either.

I shuffle in my seat. It's nowhere near the first time I've thought about how Steven had the physical power to kill me the day he broke in. He didn't kill me, of course, but he could've. He still could. Present-tense. Jenny and I have discussed how this uncertainty might remain extra uncomfortable for life.

But he didn't do *this*, right?

As I scroll back through my notes on killer psychology, chunks of Noah's list about Steven appear in my mind.

- lack of morals around how to treat others: highly objectifying.
    - manipulative, word-twister
    - demands power, control, and dominance, especially over women ✱✱✱
    - doesn't like to face problems head on
        ↳ could use to our advantage when confronting him

*** *fixated on beliefs to the point of violence*
↳ *proof of potential to hurt others*

Oh, God. No, Steven couldn't have. Could he? Is this just an intrusive thought?

He was into hunting like my dad. The way Noah phrased our dads' shooting makes me sick; their unusually massive wolf forms would be a high-value kill. A hunter like Steven would never pass up the chance to brag about it.

But is he vicious enough to discover he shot my dad, ditch his body, then come back home to reassure me through my worst grief?

With how Steven treated me shortly afterwards, I don't feel confident that the answer is "no."

"Oh, God," I say out loud this time. Gripping the table, I can't stop myself from shaking in fear.

But it's worse than that. I can't stop my stomach from lurching.

As my eyes bulge, I cup my hand around my mouth. Am I going to throw up? Scents heighten by the second, adding a nauseating chill down my spine with how powerful everyone's food and drinks smell—stinging mustard, sharp meat, and roasted coffee colliding. My stomach lurches again, this time leaving me mere seconds to act. Oh, God. I *am* about to throw up.

My eyes land on the bathroom, the lock's OCCUPIED sign shining hot red. The trash can has a rocking lid that I'd dirty, and the door is too far to run for. I won't make it in time no matter what, and this cute little coffee shop is packed—stuffed with people having a nice, pleasant drink or sandwich.

I'm going to soil it all.

With my surge of rampant OCD harm fears, it happens. I open my bag frantically, dumping my wallet, keys, and makeup onto the booth cushion, just in time to lift the empty bag to my mouth and spill the contents of my stomach. Stifling any noise the best I can, I shake in my seat, quietly doubling over. It's only a flash second, but as I come up for a deep breath, it feels like I've been subjecting the whole coffee shop to a disgusting, warped version of reality for an hour. I'm mortified, glancing around the room.

Everyone's eyes are glued to their laptops or friends, laughing, chatting, or typing away with their headphones in.

No one noticed.

But I'm still left with the most disgusting purse I've ever owned, tempting me to vomit again. Smacking my bag shut, I gag again.

Jumping from my seat, I set my sights on the door. *Yasmine, I'm really sick. I don't know what's happening, but I have to leave our stuff to run outside in case I throw up again.*

Holy shit, okay. I'm coming.

Yasmine opens the bathroom door, gaping at me as I sprint across the small shop. Now people are noticing me. God, I really hope they can't see anything wrong with my bag, or that I didn't miss anything that splashed onto my clothes.

Threatened tears burn my eyes. How could this happen? Trauma triggers sometimes make me puke from all the stress stewing in my gut, but that's usually after my initial panic. I've never been sick uncontrollably like this before.

With the fresh air blowing in my face, I'm smell-free. My stomach relaxes, but I burst into tears.

Carrying my laptop, Yasmine throws open The Cozy Roast's door. When she sees my ugly crying face, she grabs my shoulder with petrified eyes. "What happened?"

"I threw up, but it's— It's okay. I'm fine." My voice hitches through sobs.

Yasmine bites back a smile. "Um— I mean, clearly you're not okay, emotionally."

I groan, gripping my rocking stomach as my anxiety returns. "No, I'm not. I probably grossed everyone out."

"Oh, really? I thought you mindlinked you threw up inside, but I didn't see anything at our table. Some lady asked if you were okay because you looked scared when you ran out, but she didn't mention anything about you puking."

With a whimper, I drop my head. Yasmine sits at one of the outdoor tables, plopping our belongings in front of her. She's staring, awaiting my explanation. Now that I know Amy is another Beta, I can see why they're so effective at mediation; Noah's best friend also has truth-serum eyes.

I can't bear to look at Yasmine as I hold my bag out, pinching the corner like it's infected. "That's because I— I threw up in here quietly and ruined my purse."

Yasmine gives me a sad laugh, returning to my side to rub my back. "Poor Luna. Your sad face is gutting me. No wonder Noah says he's regularly totaled by you. Here, let me help you with that."

Before I can argue with her, Yasmine takes the bag from me, striding to one of the big public trash cans at the street corner. I try to sputter out words as she opens my purse, but a sharp, revolting pain strikes my gut. All that comes out is, "Oh, *no*—"

Yasmine does a double-take. "Are you going to throw up again?"

I lurch a little, clasping both hands on my mouth. *Yes, if you touch that! What are you doing?!*

Emptying it for you. Just close your eyes.

I can't close my eyes. I'm too horrified by the thought of someone taking care of my disgusting mess for me. With my body shaking like it's in active trauma, this is way beyond the normal exposure-safe anxiety limit. I make a mental note to bring this up to Jenny as I cry out beneath my hands, fighting an aching compulsion to keep Yasmine contamination-free. Although, I think I'll pass out if I have to handle that bag myself.

Or, maybe I will now. My vision reverts to spotted, starry lights, blocking out big chunks of Yasmine's face.

"Whoa, hey—"

I can't see her, but I hear the clatter of my bag on the concrete as Yasmine catches my stumbling body.

"Dude, you're not okay at all. I'm taking you to the Pack Doctor— Well, after I take you to the—" Yasmine steers me to the trash can, gripping my hair behind my head just before I throw up again. "To the trash can," she mutters. "Dude, you've gotta actually let yourself puke. That was hardly anything, so no wonder you're still gagging."

I don't want to make you watch. I shudder over the can, catching my breath as my vision returns.

"Well, too bad, because you're looking like you're going to pass out if I don't hold you up. If you hold it in like that, you'll only make yourself feel worse. Your body's doing its job to protect you from something, and I'm here to help, so don't strain against it. Let your poor stomach do its job."

Her soft rubbing on my back somehow makes me even more nauseated. I'm terrified to do it, but closing my eyes, I relax as much as I can through the next wave of sickness.

Every second is disgusting and scary. A wet sound escapes me, but I survive it. By the time it's over, I actually feel worlds better.

As promised, Yasmine carries most of my weight for my wobbling legs, helping me into the car. She shifts into reverse, and I relax into her passenger's seat.

My tears resurface. This time they're hot and sad, ripping apart my heart.

Maybe it's OCD talking, but I feel so guilty. This was all my fault for triggering myself too badly, just like Noah warned me about. How will I handle becoming Luna when I can't even stomach my intrusive thoughts? Thoughts are just thoughts, and I should know that already.

God, that sounds like an intrusive thought too. I'm officially in meta-obsession territory.

"Hey, you okay?" Yasmine softly says, rubbing my forearm as she drives.

I can't bear to answer, my lip wobbling as I suck in a shaking, sad breath.

"Your mate is meeting us at the doctor, okay? You'll be alright. I promise."

"That's not it," I whisper through tears. "I'm so disappointed in myself."

Yasmine frowns. "For puking? Last time I checked, no one's a better or worse person for puking or holding it in."

Burying my head in my palms, I let out a small laugh. "It does sound silly when you put it like that. But I think I triggered myself too far, and that's what caused this."

Yasmine is silent, but I can hear her thinking in her puzzled scent.

"What?" I ask.

"Aren't you trying to get pregnant, though? It could be that too."

My heart flips. But I grip my seatbelt, turning away. "I know Noah is convinced I am, and I told him he could share his excitement with you, but we just tried for the first time in a while a few days ago. It's way too early."

"Oh," she mutters.

Even deeper disappointment rattles my heart. Maybe I don't want to go to the Pack Doctor and find out if I'm pregnant or not. If it's another no, I don't know if I can handle it. Today was hard enough realizing my ex could've murdered my dad.

Stabbing, sharp pain sinks into my gut as my fear comes flooding back. I grip the paper bag Yasmine gave me, just in case. But as I let out another tense sob, I retrace the triggering research session.

Was that all just one big intrusive thought? Maybe I got ahead of myself and made too many assumptions by landing on Steven as the perpetrator. I thought of everyone I've met, but there's a key difference in Steven's behavior that I didn't consider: unlike the hunters who killed our dads, Steven was always willing to be found by me. *I'm* the one who pushed him away with my failed restraining order, and blocking him everywhere I've found him online.

Except, now he's hard to find again. He's since changed his social media accounts, address, and who knows what else. Steven was always cautious about his address, so without a scent to track, he's been hard for Noah to find without access to human police records.

So maybe I can't discount Steven, but I forgot an important detail: someone else in our lives also refuses to be tracked. Someone I'm guessing I've never met, so I didn't think of them initially.

Noah's abuser has always refused to be found. Like the hunters, his abuser has somehow escaped my mate, the most powerful Alpha in the Pacific Northwest, and they have a deep, harrowing past with Noah. Whatever happened between the two, it feels violent. Dangerous.

What if his abuser was one of the hunters who shot our dads?

What if they decided they didn't elicit enough power over Noah, stripping him of Ritchie, his ultimate protector?

This thought doesn't feel like an OCD or PTSD nightmare. It sinks into me, rattling my core like a numb, rational truth.

I hate it. I don't know how I'll safely bring these thoughts up to Noah, but I have to find a way.

But will it trigger him too drastically?

As we pull up to the Pack Doctor, I shut my eyes, breathing through what's to come. Noah will be here any second, and I can't ask him now. Not here.

27

Yasmine helps my shaky legs out of the car, but when I look up, I find Noah's SUV racing into a parking spot a few spots beside us. He barely takes the time to put the car in park before leaping out to run to me with wild, bulging eyes.

I laugh out of both anxiety and guilt, hating to make my mate so stressed. But as he pulls me into his arms, I suck in a horrified breath; Noah has two long gashes across his chest. Blood darkens his black t-shirt, and the end of one gash stretches up his chest to his collarbone.

I lift my hands off his chest as quickly as I can, afraid I've hurt him worse. "You're bleeding!?"

Noah cups my face in his hands. "I'm fine. Just some asshole Alphas teaming up on me."

As I stare into Noah's eyes, I know exactly who distracted him. Whose foolish panic could've gotten her mate killed. My heart drops to the floor. I teeter in Noah's hands along with it, and he gasps.

"Shit, okay. We're getting you inside. Yas, can you spot me?"

"On it," Yasmine says behind us.

Noah scoops me into his arms. "Fuck, you're so pale, Aliya. What's going on?"

"I-I don't know." My voice wobbles.

But as I drop my head against Noah's bleeding chest, a deeper whiff of his blood stings my nose. For some reason, I breathe more of it in. A sharp, iron-stained scent pierces my nostrils, burying itself into my lungs. I expect it to make me nauseous, but I can't stop sniffing as my wolf takes over.

I scramble higher on Noah's chest to lick his wounds. Noah grips me tighter, leaning back in shock. "What are you— Oh. Uh— W-what's going on?"

Making quick work of lapping up his blood, I purr as my gushing drool heals him twice as quickly as usual. When my licks deepen further, leaning hard into the deepest gash, Noah scoops his hand around my shoulder, tugging me off him by the chin like I'm a puppy stealing cake.

Noah stands frozen outside the Pack Doctor's office doorway, gaping down at me in his arms with a mix of surprise and confusion in our bond.

Embarrassment flickers through my core. What the hell has gotten into me? I'm horrified to admit it to myself, but Noah's blood tasted really good. As Noah continues to stare in shock, I lick the blood off my lips as my cheeks flame hot.

"Sorry. Hi," I rasp.

Noah lifts one eyebrow, breaking into an amused grin. "Hey. You wolfing out, sweet Omega?"

"A little…"

"Your little fangs popped out and everything." Noah chuckles. But when he nods to Yasmine to hold the Pack Doctor's door open for us, he frowns. "Am I not cooking you enough meat? Maybe you need iron."

It's a good theory, but now my stomach kills from swallowing blood. I groan, leaning into Noah's damp chest.

Except we're not alone anymore. The Pack Doctor's office overflows with Lycans waiting to be seen. There's nowhere for us to sit, and hardly enough space to stand. Noah once mentioned they don't have as many Lycans in the world who understand our biology enough to provide diagnostic care, but I didn't realize it was this bad.

A nurse rushes out from the back to meet us. "Hi, Alpha. Right this way."

She opens the door to guide us to a private room, but I stiffen in Noah's arms. "Wait, it's not our turn."

Noah opens his mouth to speak, but the nurse laughs.

"Luna, it *is* your turn. You're very unwell, so you're high on the priority list."

My chest burns. "No, I'm okay enough. Everyone else was waiting here first, and it's not an emergency. I don't want special treatment."

I look to Noah, awaiting his backup, but his concerned frown melts into a touched smile. Within seconds, Noah and I are surrounded by a horde of concerned Lycans.

"Who's next on the list to be seen after our future Luna?" An older Alpha woman asks.

"My question exactly," a young Beta mom nods. "I've been waiting 20 minutes, so I might as well wait a few more."

The nurse flips through her chart. "Actually, it was our top Alpha, for deep wound cleaning. But I don't see any gashes on you anymore, Alpha Noah."

"Oh, I—" Noah bites back a laugh. "My mate took care of that for me."

The older Alpha scoffs. "Then she's already made our wait easier for us! Please, Luna, you smell so uncomfortable. We all want you to be okay."

My heart twists as I gaze at the concerned eyes around us. I know the pack takes care of one other, but I didn't think about how much they'd take care of *me*.

Just as I brim in tears, the nurse rubs my shoulder. "I'll just start you off with some bloodwork and vitals, then leave you to wait in a room for a while, anyway. I'll call in whoever's next as soon as I'm done. No need to worry, Luna."

"Okay," I mutter.

Noah gives the nurse a polite smile, carrying me through the open door. He sets me into a chair in the hallway, and the nurse hops into action, taking my vitals and preparing to draw blood.

"Natalia already ordered this based on your symptoms, but I also know you've been feeling a bit queasy and dizzy. Let me know if you feel faint, okay?" The nurse says.

"Okay," I say.

But Noah isn't okay. His eyes flick between the nurse and me. As the nurse pricks a vein on my inner arm, Noah tenses his chest, drawing even closer until his wide form blocks the overhead lights.

The nurse laughs. "Alpha, please just let me do my job without hovering."

Noah flushes, taking a step back. "Sorry, I'm just— I don't know. My hormones are a little raised after everything today."

God, now I really don't feel like I can tell him what triggered me.

Right on cue, Noah's eyes flicker to mine. *Are you still feeling nauseous? Yas mentioned you had a trauma trigger that caused you to feel sick?*

Unfortunately, yes... And those Alphas you mentioned, were they...?

I don't even need to finish asking if they were Alpha-domination cultists. Noah suddenly can't meet my eyes.

He's never come home with an injury from them before. Does he hide his wounds from me, or are things getting even worse?

"You're all set, Luna! Here's your room, right in front of us." The nurse waits for Noah to help me through the door across the hall. When I'm nestled safely on the examination bed beneath a blanket, the nurse gives us a bright smile. "Natalia might need some time, so please make yourselves comfortable."

With the door shut behind the nurse, Noah presses a soft kiss into my cheek. "Are you still feeling triggered?"

"A little."

Noah raises one eyebrow. "You smell like you're hiding something."

I sputter out a laugh, burying my head in my hands. "I'm not intentionally hiding something, but you're right. I didn't want to admit that I got myself way too worked up trying to solve our dads' potential murders on my own, ultimately triggering myself instead."

Biting my lip, I glance at Noah for his reaction. Thankfully, his tense eyebrows soften. "Oh, my sweet Omega. Let's put that aside until you feel better, and then we can work on it together when we're both feeling ready. You don't have to go through that torture alone anymore, okay? I'm on your side."

I sigh. "God, you're right, thank you. I'm on your side too."

"How triggering was it, exactly?"

I groan. "Well, it was more of a momentary thing. Now I

mainly feel really exhausted and sick—and dizzy after I puked my guts out in the cafe, then in front of Yas. It was so embarrassing, Noah."

He whines in sympathy, hugging my head to his chest.

His leftover damp blood on his shirt hits my nose again, and I hum. "Maybe you're right and I am anemic."

"I think that's possible, but I'd also want to know why. You really think it was just stress, and not—" Noah clears his throat. "I still think you're pregnant."

Biting my lip, I groan as my racing heart aggravates my nausea. "I don't know. Didn't you say I smelled like I just started ovulating yesterday? But I was too tired to have sex beyond ten minutes, so I mainly just laid there like a boring lump."

Noah sputters out a laugh, backing away from my bedside to plop into the room's additional chair. "I mean, I enjoyed it. If you weren't pregnant already like I thought, you probably are now."

I laugh with him despite my cheeks flushing hot. But my focus wavers, landing back on the blood staining his shirt. Now that he's a few feet away from me, the browning coats more of his chest than I thought, curling my guts.

Noah's smile fades. "I'm not going to let them hurt you, okay?"

"But they hurt you."

Dropping his head, Noah scrubs his forehead. A low, stinging hum strikes our bond. I've never felt dread like this, but it has my heart racing in seconds. I shuffle on the bed, struggling to stave off my nausea.

"Talk to me," I say.

Noah puts his head in his hands. He takes a deep breath. Then another. "I'm starting to really panic, Aliya. I don't know if I can handle this Alpha-dom situation alone. It's growing bigger than I expected, and I really hate admitting that, especially if you're pregnant. These assholes have the worst timing possible, every time."

My stomach flip-flops over itself, but something in Noah's words sticks out. "You don't have any allies you could talk to about this? Maybe some other top Alphas out there who could back you up?"

He leans into his elbows on his knees, clasping his hands

beneath his chin. "You're right. I do have some across the world, so maybe I could move our meeting sooner. We're scheduled to talk soon about this huge event. Fuck, I need to tell you about that bullshit too."

"What bullshit?"

Noah groans, dropping his eyes into his palms and pressing hard. "The fucking Alpha Summit. So, patriarchal bullshit."

I have no idea what he's talking about, but stress vibrates through his tense shoulders. I hop off the bed, plopping my butt in his lap. Noah breaks into low chuckles, scooting me closer by the hips until we're huddled up tight.

Gazing into his worn, worried eyes, I give him a soft smile. "No matter what, I'm going through every second of it with you. You don't have to handle this alone without me, either. Even if—" I bite my lip as Noah breaks into a smile. "Even if you're right and I'm carrying your baby."

Noah's shoulders loosen. His hand slides off my hip, swooping over my abdomen. But he keeps his palm there, warming my belly.

We're not smiling now; nerves crash through our bond. But the longer we stare, the fresher Noah's gaze grows. I break into soft, shy giggles. Noah giggles with me, diving for my lips.

A woman tears open the door with a booming "Hello!" I jump off Noah's lap, spurring him into more giggles. This woman has just as loud of a smile, her incisors gleaming white as she throws her arms out in excitement. "Alpha Noah! I've been waiting for you to introduce me to our future Luna! And she shouldn't be on her feet."

My heart flips as Noah ducks his head with a smile. This must be Natalia, the Pack Doctor.

"Agreed, Doc." Noah helps me hop back onto the bed, settling the blanket over my knees.

Natalia drops into her rolling chair, whizzing across the room. "I only have a minute, but I wanted to stop in and say hello. It's so nice to meet you, Aliya! My future Luna!"

"It's nice to meet you too! Thank you for working so hard for us," I say.

"Oh, I'm happy to, Luna!" She leans in without warning,

sniffing my neck. I fawn, and she pats my arm. "Oops, sorry. And I'm also sorry for the wait. Alpha Noah mentioned you're attempting to conceive?"

My stomach swirls. I grip my shirt, struggling to come to terms with the fact that I'm finally here, talking about this with a doctor. "Yes, I— *We* are."

Noah chuckles. "Or we *have*. At least, I think it worked."

I choke out a laugh. "*Noah*—"

Natalia breaks into booming laughter. My stunned stare meets Noah's, and we burst into giggles.

Flipping my wrist, Natalia pokes at my veins. "Oh, Alpha Noah, I think so too! Symptom-wise at least."

I gape at her. With a skyrocketing heart rate, I replay what Natalia just said. Did I hear her correctly?

But as Natalia looks into my eyes, her smile softens. "However, I happen to know you're a hybrid."

My heart sinks to the floor.

Before she even says anything else, my eyes sting hot with tears. Natalia's hand lands on mine. "Oh, sweetheart. Don't you worry, okay? I'm here to help you."

Noah stands. "Natalia, what do you mean? I've never heard anything about hybrids having trouble conceiving. No more than other Lycans."

"Not with conceiving, but carrying to term. In order to shapeshift into such large forms, Lycans are denser and require different nutrients than humans. If a hybrid's DNA contains more human than Lycan traits, it may strain the hybrid carrier, and all the usual pregnancy risks are higher."

Noah's wide eyes hit me the hardest. I try to cover my mouth, but as Noah meets my eyes, the pain in our bond triples, and I break into sharp sobs.

He rushes to my side, hugging my head to his chest. "No, I've never heard of this being a thing. How do we know this? Has it been properly studied? And either way, her wolf is a powerhouse. She's got a lot of Lycan in her, and I really do think she's already pregnant. Isn't there a way I could give her what she needs? Someone in the world I could take her to that specializes in this?"

Natalia opens my file, pulling out a dense packet of pages.

She hands them to me, and I take it with shaking fingers. "Oh, our poor Luna and top Alpha, I'm not meaning to make you so concerned. It's my duty to clearly explain the risks to you both, but I want you to know that I've researched this heavily in my own time since the day I heard Alpha Noah found his mate—and that you were a hybrid. I'm already prepared to support you both through this."

I suck in a sharp gasp. "So there's— There's some hope?"

"Absolutely, Luna. I said the risks are higher, but it doesn't mean you need to necessarily have them. I just want to be straightforward with you from the beginning so you both know what to expect in case those risks arrive."

Natalia rubs my arm, but it doesn't soothe Noah's poor heart throbbing against my ear. I shut my eyes, breathing through the heavy ache in my gut. I know I can't change or choose my DNA, but I feel guilty that Noah hurts over this too.

But as he kisses my head, running his hand over my back, he lets out a sharp huff. "Thank you so much for looking into this, Natalia. Please, let me know how we can help her. I'll do whatever I can."

Oh. I can't choose my DNA, but I did choose Noah to bind my DNA with to have a child. And he chose me.

Noah perks up. "The blood from my wounds. She seemed— Uh, really into its smell, earlier. Anemia is a pregnancy risk, right?"

"Absolutely, and with just one look at you, Luna, I'd suspect that too. Luckily, this one is easy for us to take care of, and common with Lycan pregnancies if the carrier isn't eating enough meat."

Natalia launches into an explanation on how to better boost my diet to carry a Lycan pup. I try to smile and nod along, but as Noah asks questions and Natalia excitedly answers, my mind fuzzes out their voices. All I can feel is Noah's desperate touch on my back, and my quivering palm on my abdomen.

For days, I've been denying Noah's prediction that I'm already pregnant, but now that I know I could lose this possible-baby, I'm heartbroken beyond anything I've ever felt before. My body has numbed into full silence. I hardly even notice we left the office to go to the car until Noah opens the passenger door for me, and I feel his eyes on me.

When I meet his terrified gaze, my heart drops. I can't lose Noah's baby. I don't think I could survive it.

Just before I crumble into guttural tears, Noah grasps me, pulling me to his chest.

"Look at me," he rasps. His eyes are just as red as his swelling lips, warning of heavy tears. I melt into whimpering sobs, but Noah shakes his head. "I'm not giving up on you, or that pup. I know you don't believe me yet, but I feel it in my gut, Aliya. I think you're pregnant, and I don't think we have to worry. We're going to make it through. Even if I'm wrong, and we'll have to try again, I'm right here. I'll always be here, baby or no baby. You just have to promise me one thing, okay? And I'm so sorry, but it might be one thing I can't give you a choice on."

My heart spikes hard enough to freeze my tears. That was so unlike him. "What do you mean?"

He opens his mouth to speak, but his breath hitches. Noah shakes his head, looking up to blink away his tears. When his stare returns to mine, my lungs ache from his pain in my heart. "Aliya, no matter what happens, you have to survive this, first and foremost, okay? I need you. I'm so sorry, and I know it's selfish of me, but—" He bites back sharp, heaving tears. "Please, don't leave me here alone."

Noah's desperate, shattered stare breaks through my dissociative state in a way I didn't expect. Numbness evaporates from my limbs, leaving me with a stinging, raw wound in my heart.

But I love it. This pain means I already love Noah's baby, whether they make it long enough to exist here with us or not. If all Noah needs at the end of the day is for me to exist, and all I need is for him to exist, then we're okay. We'll be okay.

I break into a weeping smile, straining on my toes to reach his lips. Noah hiccups against my lips, tugging at my heartstrings. I pull from his salty lips with a pop, wiping his nose with my sleeve.

"My poor, sweet Alpha," I whisper. Noah shuts his eyes, indulging in my slow, gentle scalp scratches. "There you go, gorgeous. I'm right here. We're in this together, and I couldn't have chosen a better mate to do this with. Even if it ends in heartbreak, all I need is you to exist beside me too. I'm here. We're both here."

Noah glomps onto me hard, leaning us against his SUV. We cling to each other in silence for a while, breathing through our tears.

On the drive home, our hands are knitted tight over the center console. My heart feels an odd lightness to it. I can't stop staring at Noah's profile as he drives. As my eyes roam over his scruff, the extra sloppiness of his dark hair, and the soft sniffles from his ridged nose, my stomach flutters for a very different reason.

I squeeze his hand. "Noah, did it sink in for you yet?"

He furrows his brows. "Which part? There's so much to think about that my head's spinning."

When I break into nervous giggles, Noah's lips twitch like he's tempted to smile despite his heavy heart.

But I can't stop giggling, so Noah chuckles with me. "What is it, sweet Omega? Goddess, you're so fucking cute."

My heart hammers wildly, stunting my laughter. Noah nibbles his lip in the silence, only aiding my nerves as I tug on his hand. Noah allows me to move our locked fingers freely. I unfurl his clasped palm. Placing his open hand over my lower abdomen, I force myself to remember to breathe as a crashing boom of excitement hits our bond.

I can't stop my whisper from shaking. "She said we might be— That I could be—"

My mate's face shifts from one extreme emotion to the next, wide eyes giving way to a beaming smile and ending in an explosive laugh. I burst into laughter with him, squirming in my seat at the panic, joy, and fear racing through my chest.

"So you finally believe me?!" Noah's supercharged eyes are neon yellow.

I sputter out a laugh, knowing I'm talking directly to the massive black wolf with zoomies in our bond. "I didn't say I fully believed it yet. Just that someone else is on your side—the Pack Doctor, at that."

Noah groans through his smile. "How many days is it again until you miss your period and start believing me, then?"

As I break into heavier laughter with my mate, he keeps his

hand on me, rubbing my flat stomach with his thumb. It might be too early, but I'm tempted to let myself enjoy it. Deep in my heart, I know that as long as I can continue to witness Noah's bright, beaming smile, everything will be okay.

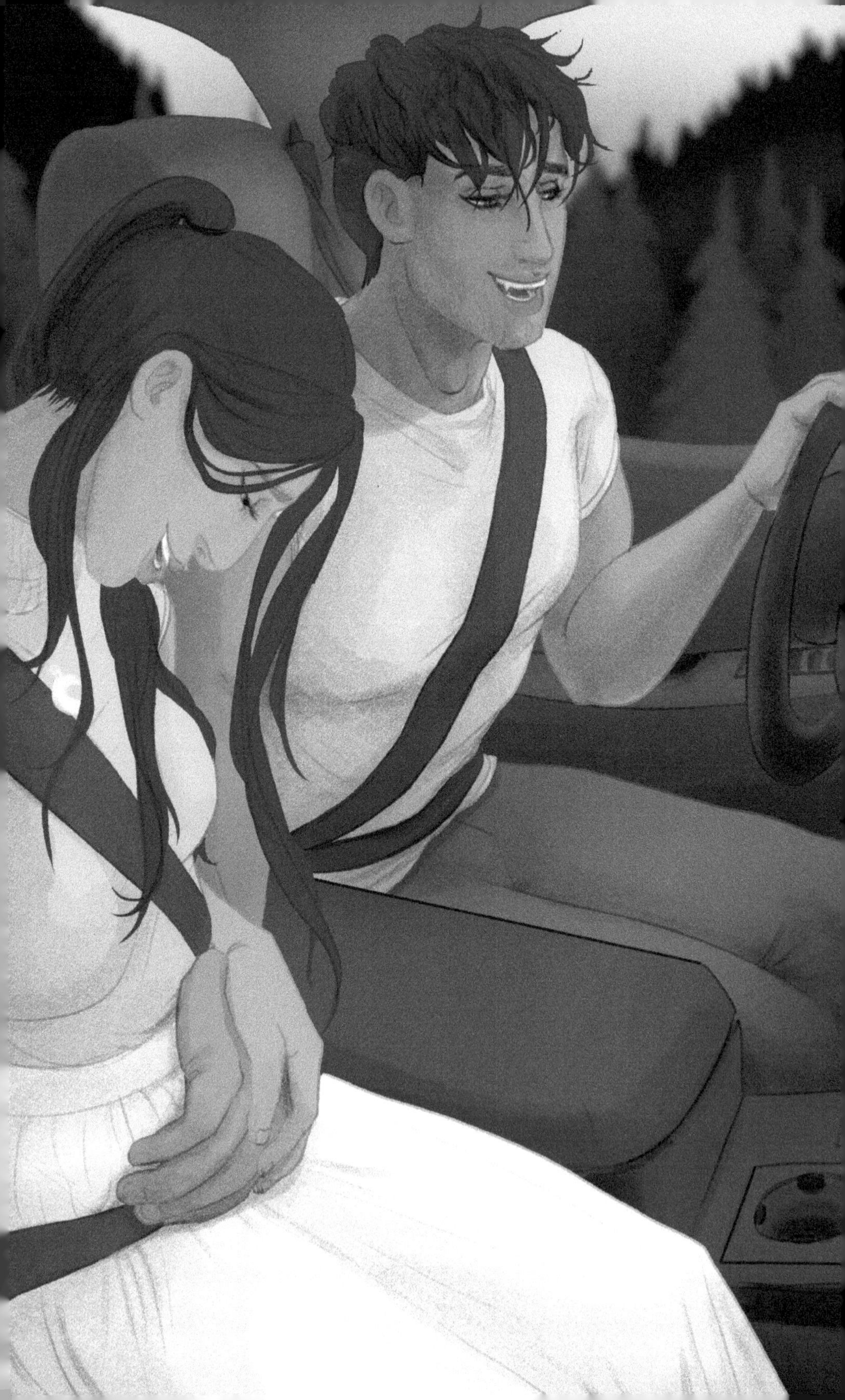

28

I've eaten more meat in the past three days than I have in two months. Natalia was right: I stopped feeling nauseated with a hefty, iron-rich meat intake, eating small portions every two hours. Even though it has helped, the sight of fibrous, tender meat still makes me a little queasy. As Noah drops another plate of steak in front of me in his cozy office, I sigh.

He breaks into a smile. "Sniff it before you judge it, at least."

I frown, leaning in to sniff the meat sitting on Noah's rich-brown wooden desk. As soon as I catch a whiff of the sharp, iron-filled beef, my mouth gushes with drool. I swallow hard, desperately grabbing my fork and knife. As I shovel three bites into my mouth, I turn to find Noah pressing his fist hard into his lips, doing nothing to hide his shaking shoulders as he silently laughs.

I cover my stuffed mouth so that I can safely laugh without flashing my half-chewed meat. "Don't make fun of me!"

"I'm not, I'm not!" Noah raises his open palms, rotating away from me in his black, cushy rolling chair. He whips open his laptop, clearing his throat. When he speaks, it's barely above a whisper. "You're just so pregnant, that's all."

Shaking my head, I pretend like Noah hasn't spiked my heart into my throat for the millionth time this week at the thought of carrying his baby. I'm leaning towards agreeing with Noah, but with our rising stress from the potential risks involved, it hasn't been the celebratory time period I've imagined. My heart shreds at the thought of it being a chemical pregnancy and losing Noah's daily smile over my symptoms.

But as Noah fetches a link for our vital video call, he grows silent. It's been three days since Noah was injured on patrol and we met with Natalia at the Pack Doctor's Office. Since then, Noah has had worse and worse disagreements with the Alpha-domination cultists. I haven't had a single second to mention my theory on our fathers' murders, especially when Noah comes home to me dog-tired every night.

Thankfully, Noah's closest global allies agreed to meet online to discuss the rising issue. Even though Noah vowed to include me in his important meetings from now on, I've been both surprised and nervous to join him for this one—with the world's top Alpha of top Alphas, the King Alpha, in attendance. I don't know what to expect. Is it even normal for Lunas to be in attendance?

I only have two minutes until I'll find out; it's 11:58 PM here, 8:58 PM the next day in New Zealand, and 8:58 AM in Sweden, the only time we could find where we'd all be ready and awake.

I shovel the rest of my midnight "snack" into my mouth, chewing ferociously. Hot, salty liquid floods my tongue, curling my toes in bliss. With my delighted hum, Noah loses some of the tension in his shoulders, breaking into breathy giggles. The steak reinvigorates me, sending bright, fluffy gratification throughout my core for my mate's warm meals. I huddle into Noah's side, and he wraps one big hand around my thigh, pulling me closer in my rolling chair.

With my cheek squished against Noah's bicep, I beam at him. "Thank you. That really did hit the spot."

Noah breaks into the sweetest smile. "Yeah? Good. I know it's hard to force yourself to eat while you feel sick, but you're doing such a good job taking care of yourself. I'm so damn proud of you."

Kissing my forehead, Noah leaves me a flustered mess. His devilish grin inspires fresh laughter from me, even as we pull up the video call.

But as Noah gives me another kiss, he sucks in a sharp breath, jutting back. "Fuck, I've been so busy, I forgot to explain the Alpha Summit!"

I glance at the clock. "Well, you have one minute left."

Noah laughs through an anxious groan. But as he drops his

stare, my heart springs into action. What is this Alpha Summit, really? If ever-stoic Alpha Noah looks this worried, that's a bad sign. A terrible one, in fact.

I lose control of my thoughts before I can manage them. Is Noah going to be safe? Will I be safe? What if I really am pregnant, and the three of us die together at the event?

Noah's eyes return to mine, sensing my rising anxiety.

I swallow hard. "Give me something, at least—before we talk to the people we'll meet there. I think I have the wrong idea that it's just a conference for top Alphas."

"Fuck, I— Well—" Noah huffs, scratching the back of his head. "It's not a conference. It's an annual event where Top Alphas across the world meet once a year, but the main event is that we compete in friendly... ish ways."

I blink a few times, struggling to find what I'm still missing here. "Um... That sounds... nice?"

Noah bites his bottom lip, struggling not to look at me. No matter how worried I am, I melt at the sight of my shy, goofy Alpha.

I let out a loving sigh. "Noah Greenfield..."

He bites back a smile, peeking at me with his best puppy-dog stare. "Y-yeah?"

I laugh, drawing in closer. "You're a terrible liar." Noah sputters into giggles with me, flipping my heart. "What type of competitions are these, exactly? 'Friendly-ish' doesn't sound the most friendly, to be honest."

Noah chuckles, rubbing his forehead. "Uh, yeah, well... We kind of... Go at it fighting in our wolf forms until someone comes out on top. For sport."

I close my eyes. "Okay, let me get this straight." When I open my eyes, Noah is wide-eyed and horribly guilty. "We're going to be hosting a modern-day gladiator contest?"

Noah bursts out laughing, his cheeks burning red. "Listen, I-I'm— I'm sorry. But yes. That's *exactly* what it is."

"Oh, my *love*." I shake my head with a groan, tempted to laugh no matter how irritated I am. "I need you to be safe, Noah. Especially now."

He softens, rubbing my knuckles with a quick glance to my belly. It sends my stomach into fizzy knots.

"It *is* safe. We're all allies, so we don't fight to the death. Just... close."

I sputter out a laugh. "Oh, my God. That's not exactly reassuring!"

We laugh together, but Noah draws closer. Mischief is laced into his smile. "And we won't be hosting it, so there's no extra stress on us to plan. We'll be flying to Sweden, where you'll get to meet every other top Luna in the world. Plus, I'll finally get more alone time with you."

I perk up. "So, sort of like a reunion and honeymoon, combined?"

"If we ignore the fighting part, yes. We love to spoil the hell out of our Lunas, too." He grins, kissing my forehead. "I-I've never had a Luna I've been mated to before, so I've been excited to introduce you."

Dammit, he's too cute. "Okay. Then, as long as you think you'll be okay, I trust you."

Noah chuckles. "Thankfully, it's always planned during the new moon. We wouldn't dare put a shit-ton of Alphas together during the *full* moon. Then I'd actually have to warn you about it."

He giggles as my eyes bulge wider by the second. Eventually, I just have to laugh with him.

"*Alpha!*" A voice booms through the speakers, and I squeak in surprise.

Noah laughs, stroking my hair to soothe me. *Poor Omega. It's not the first time Tāne's scared the shit out of someone with his happy yells.*

I sit straighter, my heart hammering into my throat as I take in the golden-brown skinned, curly-haired Alpha on the screen. He's so bulky that he can hardly fit into his webcam, his luxurious black hair eating up all the extra room around his head.

This must be the New Zealand Alpha. I thought his name would be spelled "Tani" by how Noah pronounced it, but the name at the bottom of his screen says, "Tāne."

Noah rapid-taps his volume button down, breaking into a relaxed smile. "Kia ora."

"Kia ora," I echo with a wave.

The burly Alpha on the screen beams even wider, returning his own, "Kia ora!" Tāne grins, scooting even closer to his webcam. "Looks like I've missed some big news here, bro. Go on, then, introduce us."

As I watch Noah glance at me through our webcam's preview, his doting grin flips my heart. "Tāne, this is Aliya, my m-mate… A-and in a week and a half, my Luna."

Tāne breaks into heavy, booming laughter, crackling Noah's laptop speakers. Noah ducks his head, and I giggle, wrapping my arm around his back.

"We've got too much to celebrate! Dammit, I should've brought my little Omega. She's finally getting some rest, though, so it's for the best, ay," Tāne says.

"How's the baby?" Noah asks.

"Good, good! Already almost one. Lemme grab a pic."

As Tāne whips out his phone, another person enters the call. Everyone snaps to attention as his name appears: Viktor Abrammson.

The King Alpha. My heart leaps into my throat.

But he's not turning his video on.

Noah leans his full weight back in his office chair, prompting a pitiful squeak out of it. With a wavering chuckle, Noah's gentle voice raises in volume. "Vik, the mic's on the bottom left. Video too." With no response from Viktor, Noah breaks into hearty giggles, popping up in his chair. He sends a push notification to Viktor about turning on his audio and video—with no luck. Tāne breaks into laughter with Noah, and I press my fingertips to my lips, not wanting to make a bad impression on the King Alpha who can absolutely see us laughing at him.

By the time Viktor finally pops up on screen, it's only thanks to his mate, Annika. The strawberry blonde Omega leans over him in an unzipped hoodie, one hand on the computer mouse and the other on her baby's back as she breastfeeds. Annika's messy bun bounces as she bolts out of the room, but Viktor turns around, calling after her in Swedish. All I can pick out is, "Greenfield Luna."

Annika gasps in the doorway. "Aliya is there?! Vik, you should've told me sooner! I'm not dressed!"

Viktor winces. "I'm sorry! I forgot we'd all be able to see each other." Turning back to the screen, Viktor squints at us. "Are you guys still there?"

Noah and Tāne break into harder laughter.

"Kia ora, bro. We can see and hear you now," Tāne says.

"Huh?" Viktor shouts. "What'd you say? Where's the volume on this thing?"

Noah drops his head into his hands, his shoulders shaking through heartier chuckles. I can't stop myself from laughing anymore, leaning against Noah as Viktor laughs along with us.

I guess the King Alpha isn't as scary as I made him out to be. He is stunning, though; dark brown skin glimmers beneath his desk lamp, only adding to the warmth of his sharp, sultry smile. My wolf is scared to meet his hunting eyes, even through video chat.

But once Viktor pulls himself together, the Alphas launch straight into a serious discussion. Viktor and Tāne's stark scowls deepen as Noah tells them all about the Alpha-domination cultists, including Mason.

"I wanted to share this with Aliya today too, but something one of them said to me this afternoon confirmed it for me: I think Mason Hart is the one leading this. Not just leading, but actively recruiting and convincing other Alphas in the pack to join him."

"You said 'Hart?'" It's the quietest I've heard Tāne's voice.

Noah's nod silences the whole group. The tension pushes my shoulders to my ears.

With a harsh sigh, Viktor puts his head into one hand, scrubbing over his short fade. "You're not going to like this, man."

Noah's sharp spike of anxiety in our bond churns my stomach. "Just say it."

Viktor continues to scrub his head for a while. The longer we wait, the more I notice Tāne also tensing his jaw.

"It's not just Greenfield," the King Alpha says.

My stomach clenches, but Noah doesn't move. He grips his chair, stifling his breath. "I'm not sure I'm following."

"Bloody hate to say it, bro, but it's true. I've got a few Alpha-dom cultists popping up here too. They're organized. I don't know if it's global or not, but now that you've had issues too, I'm starting to wonder."

I feel like I've been slapped. Both arms wrap around my abdomen in a protective fear.

But my mate's heart settles in our bond. He lets out a low growl, dropping back into his seat. "Alright, then we're moving the Summit up. We'll remind them what they're up against. If that doesn't work, we'll deal with them together, right there."

Viktor and Tāne hum in agreement, affirming they're mindlinking their allies and Elders of the change in plans to move the Summit a whole month sooner.

I'm shocked. Why isn't the King Alpha the one deciding this? With a single sentence, Noah just altered the schedule of the entire set of global Lycan leaders.

The Alphas don't seem as shocked as I am. They brainstorm with Noah, planning a number of spying and damage control tactics to carry out in the meantime.

But the horror of what Viktor and Tāne disclosed about the Alpha-domination cultists wins over my confusion. What if this is a global, widespread uprising of Alphas? Alphas have been provided better fighting and defense tactics for centuries due to strict Lycan gender norms. If these Alphas feel enabled enough to band together, aren't we sending ourselves into a death trap at the Alpha Summit?

As the men shift into simple pleasantries toward the end of the call, I realize there's no choice in this, for any of us. Whether the Alpha-domination cultists have organized or not, it's our job to protect our packs.

And pregnant or not, I'm about to be included as another leader responsible for thousands of lives. I grip Noah's arm, fear pounding through my heart.

Noah tenses. "Hey guys, I've gotta hop off. Thanks for meeting up on such short notice."

Viktor deflates. "Aww, man, Annika wants to meet you, Aliya. At the Summit, then? We'll have a proper hello."

"Yes, absolutely! I can't wait to meet you all!" I smile the best I can.

But once we say our goodbyes, Noah turns to me with taut shoulders and puppy-dog eyes. "Aliya, I— I'm so sorry—"

Noah drops his head into his hands. With his head by his knees, Noah's breath speeds into a heaving sprint. It's not until then that I realize he's shaking.

I swivel in my chair to face him, tugging on his shoulders. "Noah? Noah, what are you thinking?"

My stomach drops as he breaks into sharp, quiet tears. The sound shreds through me, flooding my tear ducts with shared sorrow.

His voice comes out choppy. "I'm so sorry, Aliya." He reaches for my waist. Placing his forehead against my stomach, a pulse of his panic shoots through my heart. My mate's usual deep voice is replaced by an agonized, small whimper. "I'm so sorry for doing this to you—"

Noah can't bear to speak another word, his voice stolen by another harsh sob. I close my eyes, holding his head through our shared pain. I thought I was afraid, but Noah is petrified. I don't know what I'm missing about the Alpha Summit and Noah's status in the Lycan world, but if I'm right, he's the one holding the whole world together.

And I know what I want to do about it.

I rise from my chair, dropping to my knees beneath Noah. Softly pulling at his hands, I reveal his contorted, agonized frown. It rips through my chest.

But I close my eyes, pressing my lips into his quivering mouth. *Noah, I'm choosing to be your Luna. To me, that means I want to be by your side, no matter what life throws at us. I'm right here, and I'm staying.*

He sucks in a sharp breath. I open my eyes, holding his wet cheeks in my palms. Noah stares back, his reddened eyes shining a vivid blue.

"But what if I'm right? What if you're—" He shakes his head, choking through a sob.

Noah rubs his hand over my back as guilt throbs through our bond. His emotions are so powerful that I can feel the reasoning behind them; he wishes he could take this all away, and let us start our family in peace.

I catch his tears with my thumbs. "I know. But if you don't make it through this, our possible-baby won't anyway, and neither will I. So no matter what it takes to support you and the other packs, I'll be right here, protecting you too."

Noah drops his forehead against mine. "Fuck… Thank you, sweet Omega."

The air burns between us, ignited by stress and worry. But deep in my heart, my wolf settles us both. Like Noah's wolf affirmed for us outside the Pack Doctor, she thinks we'll be okay, and I want to trust her. Especially if Noah is right about this possible-baby.

29

My favorite women surround me outside Noah's cabin, organizing themselves as we prepare to hop into Amy's car. Kira wrestles Lexi's car seat into place, my niece is safely tucked into Amy's arms, Yasmine and Rainn giggle quietly about something as Lilian raises a skeptical eyebrow, and I pull up my phone's map, inputting the address Noah gave me for today's outing. In a few minutes, we'll be off to find my Luna Ceremony dress.

I have no idea what this Lycan ceremonial dress shop is like, but when I asked Noah what would be best to wear, he suggested something on the fancy side. It's over 90 degrees here, so the best I could do was a thin white button-up tank with lace framing my chest and collar. The shirt tucks well enough into my black pencil skirt, but it won't fit for long if I really am pregnant; I'm already a bit too bloated for it.

Kira pops up behind me, resting her head on my shoulder. "So what is this human tradition, exactly?"

I smile at her puppyish head tilt. "Usually the human bride's best friends and family shop together for a wedding dress. You've all been so welcoming to me in your traditions, so I thought it'd be fun to find a Luna Ceremony dress together."

Rainn hops on her toes with rapid little claps. "I love that! I'm so excited!"

Amy puts her chin on my other shoulder, prompting us into a giggle fit.

As we break apart, Amy picks off a stray hair from my cheek, tucking it behind my ear. "I'm curious why we had to look extra nice, though. Did you say Noah gave you an address?"

"Yes. Noah said it was a pack dressmaker living on the territory outskirts, and it's not *too* far of a drive, thankfully. But still a couple hours."

Yasmine straightens her back at this, breaking into a sly grin. "All the more time to talk about Noah behind his back."

I sputter out a laugh. "Yas! That's not exactly the point—"

Lilian looks over my shoulder at our destination's address on my phone screen, refocusing the group with her stoic stare. We await her reaction in a frozen silence, even little Lexi gaping at Lilian.

The current Luna hums in approval when I show her the shop Noah recommended, but she doesn't comment further.

We pile into Amy's new minivan with three rows of seating. Yasmine and Kira smush in on either side of me in the third row, making me feel even smaller. Cuddling in like the wolves they are, they look at my phone screen without permission.

Kira grips my arm. "Girl, what the fuck?!"

My eyes bulge. "What?!"

"Language!" Amy plops into the front seat with a scowl.

But Yasmine's eyes are just as wide as Kira's. "Holy ship, though! *That's* where we're going?"

Lexi breaks into giggles. "Holy ship!"

"Wait, where am I taking us? What do I need to know?" Amy whips around to face us, waiting to start the car.

Her mate shakes her head, still gaping. "Noah's sending her to the heckin' *Celestial Couture Shop*."

Amy's jaw drops, gripping her car's center console until she can turn around far enough to look me in the eyes.

My shoulders raise. "What? Is it weird? I mean, I'll admit I thought 'Couture' sounded a bit excessive."

Lilian groans in the passenger's seat, dropping her head back. "She's a *Greenfield* Luna. What do you all take her for?"

Rainn gapes at her mom from the second row despite Lexi death-gripping a strand of Rainn's wavy hair. "Mom, come on! Who does the Celestial lady ever take as a client?"

"Who else would she take except the Greenfield Luna, you mean?" Lilian meets my eyes, giving me a soft smile. "Almost no one."

I'm already self-conscious about the eyes that'll be on me today, so my heart rate skyrockets.

Yasmine gapes. "Dang, Luna. So you went to Celestia for your Luna dress too?"

Lilian smooths a hand over her silver bun. "Of course I did."

Rainn gasps. "Mom! Why don't you ever tell me these things?! Does that mean she'd take me as a client too?"

"Of course, Rainn." Lilian melts into a smile I recognize: the one I only see when she thinks of Alpha Ritchie. With everyone falling into an awed hush at her expression, she softens her voice. "Your father spoiled me to death, taking me to the best dressmaker in the Pacific Northwest. He'd want the same for you."

I swallow hard, reaching between the seats to rub Rainn's arm as a bittersweet excitement rushes through her watery smile.

In the following silence, anxiety bubbles throughout my core until my stomach loudly growls. I clear my throat. "But I thought we'd be going somewhere similar to a wedding dress shop?"

Amy uses the back of her seat to yank her body as far around as she can manage beneath the steering wheel. "No, girl, this is in the middle of the flipping woods—"

Kira grips my arm. "On a bleeping mountain—"

"And she makes mating ceremony dresses, yeah, but she doesn't alter them for most wolves. Mainly only Lunas."

"Bleeping mountain!" Lexi laughs.

I laugh with her, reaching over the seats to squish her little shoe. "That was so silly, wasn't it?"

"Yes!" Lexi steals my hand, placing her toy car onto it. I'm not sure if it's on purpose, but she successfully softens my tense shoulders.

Yasmine crosses her arms as she drops back into her seat, spreading her knees despite her tight skirt. "Huh. Yeah, that all checks out, actually. Especially for our top Alpha's Luna."

With that, Amy starts the car.

By the time we reverse onto the winding forest road, the ever-present wolves have already moved on like Noah always does. Everyone settles into their seats, accepting this conclusion only a minute after making a huge fuss.

But I haven't settled. Something strikes me as off. Of course

Noah is the top Alpha of the Greenfield pack, otherwise I wouldn't be the Luna.

Between this uncertainty and my nerves about becoming Luna next week, I groan at the heavy rolling in my abdomen.

"You okay?" Kira asks.

"Yeah." My voice comes out shakier than I expect. "I just feel a little sick."

Only Amy, Kira, and Yasmine know it's because I might be pregnant. Thankfully, Kira rubs my back, releasing her protective Alpha scent before anyone has further questions. "Let's pull over, Amy. We've gotta eat something before there's no restaurants in sight, anyway."

I'm grateful to stretch my legs, especially when I'm welcomed by Rainn's warm hug.

Affection wells in me whenever I smell her sweet, familiar-but-not scent; a touch of her scent overlaps with Noah's. I bet it's similar to how Noah's children will smell when I finally get to hold them.

That thought only heightens my nerves, too much excitement flooding my wiry stomach. I grip it, taking deep breaths as we enter the restaurant.

Rainn slips her soft hand into mine. "Hey, do you want me to get you something for your stomach? I bet they have some crackers."

"Thanks, Rainn. I actually feel better now that we're holding still."

She nuzzles against me, and my heart leaps. My surprise must show in my scent; Rainn instantly pulls back.

"Oh, sorry. Did I startle you?"

I soften into a nearly inaudible whisper, knowing Rainn's expert ears can still pick it up. "Aren't we in a human restaurant? I didn't think we wanted to do— um— *wolfy* things in front of them."

The wolves sniff the air in unison. I have to bite the inside of my cheek to keep from laughing.

Kira smirks. "Nah, I don't smell any human. Except *you*."

Lilian's chin juts. "You mean Lycan-human hybrid. She's not

just one or the other, and we shouldn't shame her for her human side."

As the group's Alpha shrinks apologetically, Lilian's correction gives me goosebumps. She really is defending both Noah and me now.

I wish she didn't hurt Noah so badly before coming around. He can't trust any progress she makes, and I don't blame him.

As I sit surrounded by my favorite girls, I feel a thousand times better. I kiss Lexi's head of curls, huddling in to chat with her about funny animals as she scribbles all over her menu. My closest friends laugh together in a rapid-fire chat with ever-changing topics. It's been so long that I've had an outing with a group of women that my heart feels a little fuller, even if I don't join in on the conversation too much.

Although, I am a little uncomfortable with how the adults keep glancing at me with intense curiosity—a universal language no matter our shared species.

Yasmine props her head on her chin with a sultry grin, and I can guess what's coming. "Alright, future Luna. I'm ready to hear how you *really* feel about the mating ceremony. Between us."

I bite my lip, but it doesn't stop my smile. "About the ceremony in general, or...?"

"Nah, the fun stuff. What do you think of the whole public sex thing?"

I clear my throat, playing with my napkin to settle my nerves. Of course I knew that's what Yasmine was asking, but with everyone's eyes on me, it's sinking in how I've never talked about sex with an entire group of people before. At most, Kira and Amy gushed about their sex life in college while I sat back, full of red-faced giggles.

But I've always wanted to feel connected enough with my friends and family to talk about how I really feel, and it's coming true. Maybe I can share more than I usually would.

"To be honest, I'm—" I cut myself off.

They probably expect me to say "excited" or "nervous." While that's true, there's an even deeper truth I haven't dared to share.

"I'm craving it," I mutter.

With my announcement, Amy's eyebrows raise, but she rubs my arm the second I duck my head in embarrassment.

"Heck yeah, girl, spill it! We're so excited to hear all the juicy details. It's all going over someone's head, anyway."

We glance at Lexi, who remains absorbed in her scribbling with quiet, rambling humming.

Yasmine's hushed voice is laced with heavy excitement. "Which part are you craving? Is it Noah? My shy best friend is probably a secret exhibitionist, isn't he?"

I glance at Noah's sister and mom, my neck flushing hot. But Lilian sips tea with a smile, as if the thought that her children have sex is as normal as knowing they eat lunch.

I guess it *is* normal to Lycans, but it's still new to me.

A thrill rushes through me as I decide to keep sharing anyway.

"Yes, a lot of it is because I'm craving that moment with Noah. He— um… He seems *really* excited by it, and I—" I clear my throat. "I want to let myself go enough to show everyone how deeply we love each other."

Amy giggles, Yasmine and Kira tease me with winks, and Lilian nods in understanding.

But Rainn beams, her eyes rimmed in red. "I'm so happy for you and my brother. Whenever I see you together, I can tell you're bonded deeper at this stage than most mates I've known." She swipes her eyes, softening into a warm smile. "The pack will be so honored you're letting them celebrate your bond alongside you. And I know they'll benefit from witnessing the pure love you two share, inspiring everyone to be more loving mates."

Tears prick my eyes at Rainn's wholesome view of the ceremony. "I guess it is a celebration of our bond, isn't it? I'm really curious how it'll feel in the moment. With everyone watching us, and being so bare and vulnerable on top of it, I'm imagining I won't even know how nerve-wracking it'll really be until we're there."

My cheeks flush as I admit the truth, but their patient, attentive eyes spur me into blurting out more.

"It's so nice to be able to talk about sex this freely. It was seen as so shameful, growing up around humans. And that's why the dress is important. I honestly want to look really good while mating with Noah."

Amy grins. "It'll be a surprise for Noah, right? The dress?"

I laugh. "Yeah. Noah was cute. He was so bummed he couldn't come with us today until I explained it was specifically to surprise him. Then he was all for the idea."

Yasmine's eyebrows raise as she chuckles. "He's a big, smitten puppy dog of a wolf. Never seen a man so taken in my life."

I giggle, ducking my head. "I love him."

Amy rubs my back, giggling with me. "You're not trying to get all dressed up *just* for him, right?! Or am I going to have to give my best friend a reality check on how incredible she is?"

I can't bear to look at the kind faces around me a second more, the lid on my emotions threatening to burst. "No, it's not solely to surprise him. It's mainly to boost my confidence when we mate. I want to look like I'm confident enough to know what I want and how I want it, even when I choose to be beneath my Alpha."

My heart is on fire with how raw this confession feels, but everyone's collective scent only rises to meet me, wide-eyed and focused on my every word.

"Heck yeah—sweet, sexy, and cool! I can picture it!" Yasmine says.

"That pretty much describes you, girl. The world needs more Omegas in power like you," Amy says.

My chest tightens, afraid of what Noah's mom might think. But Lilian's smile is brighter than ever. Her doting scent wafting over the gentle candlelight tells me it's genuine.

Piling back into the car to drive up the mountain, I sit in Amy's passenger seat to keep from feeling carsick. But I can't help but turn and look at my favorite women every few minutes, loving the giddy energy surrounding me.

"Thank you all so much for coming with me today."

The wolves all straighten in attention, widening my smile.

"This means so much to me. Before meeting Noah, I never thought I'd have any bridesmaids, other than Kira and Amy."

Rainn's brows furrow. "Wait, I just realized why that human phrase sounds so weird. Is it supposed to be like we're your maids?"

Kira's smile warps, her jaw dropping like Rainn just slapped her. "Girl, what? Is that true, Aliya? You call your female best friends *maids?* Humans are so sexist!"

"No, no, no, not a *maid!* A *brides*maid! It's one word for all of the bride's favorite people featured in the wedding." My eyes widen. "Although, wait— That is kind of weird, now that I think about it. What if it really is supposed to be like the bride's maidens-in-waiting?"

Everyone except Lilian groans.

I have to laugh. Amy sputters out a laugh with me, and our attention whips to her. She grants me a sarcastic smile before returning her eyes to the road. "You're enjoying the idea of us waiting on you that much, huh?"

I laugh, grabbing her shoulder. "Amy, no! It's dark, but... Okay, maybe it's a *little* funny because of how mad Kira is about it."

Amy cackles as Kira rolls her eyes. She sighs through the end of her laugh, sparking warmth through my heart with the smile I've always known. "I'm messing with you, girl. We've all got our own traditions that are a little twisted if you look closely."

But Kira growls beneath her breath in the backseat. "Nah, I'm not being a stinkin' handmaiden. We need a pack name for our new mini—"

Kira cuts herself off with a gasp, and Amy laughs even harder—assumedly feeling the panic in Kira's eyes through their bond.

"Oh, *no,*" Kira hisses. "Don't tell Noah I suggested breaking into a smaller pack or he'll kick my Alpha butt for treason!"

I bust out laughing. "What? He wouldn't!"

"She's kidding! ...Kind of," Amy says. "But I agree, babe. I think we should call ourselves something about sexifying our Luna."

Yasmine snaps her fingers. "Oh, yes! How about the Sexy Luna Taskforce?"

"Dang, I like that," Kira says.

"Oh, fudge yes, Kira!"

They high-five over Rainn's head, forcing her to duck, and

when Lexi squeals, her little arms poking above her car seat to high-five herself, the whole minivan bursts into laughter. Lilian shakes her head in the far back seat, but her giggly energy radiates from here.

I'm so happy. I allow myself a soft touch on my belly despite how premature it feels to celebrate the possible-baby growing inside me. But the longer I keep my hand there, the more my heart aches at the deep, nurturing love blooming in my heart. I hope Mom can join in our fun with us, wherever she is.

30

After a long, dizzying mountain drive, I wobble on my feet outside of Celestial Couture.

I'm clammy with nerves. I hope I look nice enough.

But once we're inside, the grandiosity doesn't hit me the way the women described the shop. It's beautiful, but it looks a lot like other wedding dress stores I've seen. Maybe Lycans aren't used to how elaborate human weddings are.

Rainn takes my hand, running me to the nearest dress rack. "What do you think? Do you prefer something minimal? Maximal? Big and flowy, or tight and lacy?"

I grip the back of my neck, struggling to not hide my bloated stomach as nerves settle in. "Well, what do Luna Ceremony dresses usually look like? I know they're white—"

Kira drops five blaring-white dresses on the floor across the room with a loud clatter. Yasmine backs up with Lexi in her arms, accidentally stepping on the de-racked dresses as she allows Lexi to yank another off the rack.

My stomach sinks. "Oh— Oh, my God—"

Amy rushes over to whisper-scold them, but the minute I turn back to respond to Rainn, she's face-deep in the wedding dresses, giving them deep sniffs.

With that, I speed-walk to Amy's side, better equipped at wrangling toddlers than a group of stubborn, hyper Lycans.

Amy nearly drops the dresses she's cleaning up when she takes one look at me. "Oh, God, what's wrong? You look pale."

Everything is chaos, and we just got here!

Amy bites her lip, failing to keep from laughing at me with a

Celestial Couture

snort. *I don't know what to tell you with a pack of excited wolves, girl. Impulse control flies out the window.* She stands, linking her arm in mine. *But hey, they're behaving better now, aren't they?*

I look back to find Kira and Yasmine doing their best to fix the dresses, singing a clean-up song with Lexi, and at least Rainn is only sniffing them.

But then Lilian disappears behind the staff-only door at the back of the store.

My heart flips. "Um, is she supposed to go back there? It looks closed off."

Amy shrugs. "This is a Lycan store, and Lilian is the Greenfield Luna. I doubt Celestia minds."

Why is everyone suddenly acting like we're snobby royalty who can do anything we want? I know Noah gives off regal vibes, but that's just him. Lilian is too approachable with her pack members to expect the royal treatment, and Noah doesn't even accept an extra pay cut from the Elders unless he can donate it all back to the pack.

Before I can contemplate further, my friends call out from the store's every corner, holding up dresses.

Kira beams. "You have to try these on! We're making a pile of the hot ones!"

"Oh, um—"

"At least try one!" Rainn says.

Two breaths later, I'm bombarded with a dress pile-on from all angles.

Amy can't stop laughing. "Now that you can't see a thing, let me guide you into the dressing room."

With Amy steering me by the shoulders, I tuck myself into a small dressing room with two sloppy armfuls of white fabric. The second I look in the mirror at my aghast, windblown expression, I laugh. I really do look like I've been wrestling with a pack of wolves.

I didn't preview any of these, but my friends are so excited that I better try on the one that I like best to show them.

Flipping through them, I do find a favorite. Its bodice slopes against my ribs, framing my breasts in a lacy heart shape and making them look fuller. Actually, are they bigger? My heart flips.

They certainly look it—far more so than when I mistook PMS for pregnancy.

I hoist up the dress to analyze them, but my brows furrow in the mirror at my flat expression. Every dress is gorgeous and expensive, and I love how this one looks.

But they're wedding dresses. And I'm not getting married, I'm becoming the pack's Luna. Noah's Luna.

My shoulders deflate in the reflection, and my hopes fall with it. I don't know what I'm imagining myself to look like, but when I imagine myself mating with Noah in this, it's not quite there.

But I don't want to have to go out there and sound like a spoiled brat for not feeling this one. I'm *not* royalty.

Amy pops her head in, and I yelp in surprise.

When she jerks her head back, offended, I have to laugh. "Hey! What if I was naked?"

"Are you serious?" She breaks into a devilish grin. "There's not a single portion of your body I haven't seen after your first heat—"

I slap my palms over my eyes. "Oh, my God, stop, stop! Don't remind me! My wolf had zero filter for everything I said and did that day."

We laugh, but my smile quickly fades as I catch a glimpse of us in the mirror. I can't bear to look at Amy's sobering expression.

She softly strokes my back. "Hey, you okay?"

I try to smile, forcing back the water clouding my vision. "Sorry, I'm overwhelmed."

Amy draws me in for a tight embrace. I sigh in her arms, laying my head on her shoulder. She whispers, ensuring no one else can hear us, but it feels like we're 13 again and having a sleepover. "Are you still having a lot of pregnancy symptoms?"

"Yes. I really need to pee again."

Amy giggles. "Then let's go. They can all wait a few extra minutes."

Wriggling ourselves out the dressing room door in an epic battle against this fluffy skirt, Amy and I dissolve into giggles. She has to hold my dress for me as I pee, and I groan.

"I don't think this one's going to work for a mating ritual."

Amy's grin darkens, and I know I'm in trouble. "Yeah, how's Noah going to find your clit in this mountain of fabric?"

I gasp. "*Amy!*"

We erupt into laughter, howling loud enough for Kira to knock on the door. "You two sound like you're up to something in there. Everything okay?"

"We'll be out in a minute!" Amy laughs. Then she sniffs the air. "Hey, this might be kind of weird, but my wolf smells something different on you today, A. Especially since you just peed."

"Ew, stop! What do you—" I check behind myself to wipe, and my heart stops. I cry out, forcing Amy to suck in a panicked breath.

"What's wrong?!"

I'm in tears within seconds, hardly able to breathe. "Amy, *no*— There's pink— It's blood—"

Amy gasps. "Aliya, wait! Wait, look at me—"

I shake my head, choking out desperate sobs. I thought I wasn't getting my hopes up that our pregnancy attempts worked this time, but now I feel my world crumbling, spinning on its head just before it falls. The first thing I imagine is Noah's crushed expression when I tell him tonight.

Right on cue, Noah mindlinks. *Are you okay?!*

But Amy steadies me on the toilet seat, gripping my shoulders hard. "Listen to me before you freak out: it's not what you think!"

"What?" I grip my aching heart. If Amy gives me false hope, I'm afraid it'll destroy me.

But she squeezes my shoulders again. "Right before you saw that, I was about to tell you something huge, okay? Take a big, deep breath."

I try to suck in a shaky inhale, but it ends in a harsh cough. "I can't. My heart hurts so badly, Amy—"

"You're pregnant, A.! It's implantation bleeding. I can smell it."

My tears stop instantly. Amy breaks into a wide smile, but my brain still hasn't caught up.

"How do you know what you're smelling? What if it's just my period, and it's all just been chemical?" My voice quivers like it's ready to shatter.

"Remember when my friend Evelyn got pregnant in college?

And she thought her light spotting was a period, but I tried to convince her otherwise and she didn't listen to me?"

My heart flips. "God, I forgot about that. You were so concerned for *weeks* that I finally convinced her to stop drinking at parties, just in case."

"Yes! My wolf knew right away, but of course I couldn't tell either of you why I was so sure. And when Ev missed it the next month, turns out she was pregnant the whole time." Amy pokes the tip of her nose. "She should've believed my wolf nose, since she was absolutely, super pregnant after that. Just like you are now, babe."

I swallow my racing heart, too terrified to trust Amy's confirmation. "But why are you so sure about me?"

"Because your pheromones started smelling super, super sweet this morning, and it's only getting stronger. And that tiny speck of pink isn't how your period usually starts, is it?"

She's right. I grip Amy's arms, unable to stop my rising smile. As nausea wracks my core, I choke out a giddy sob. "Oh, my God, I think you're right. My symptoms are extra strong today too. I could puke from how bad this bathroom smells, if I wanted to."

Amy erupts into laughter. "Oh, shit. Hurry, hurry— Let's go back to the dressing room."

I hobble to the sink on shaky knees, still processing.

Aliya? You feel okay now, but I thought something horrible happened, Noah mindlinks.

My heart flips. I forgot he mindlinked me. I can't tell Noah yet, not until we're face-to-face. Plus, I'm having a hard time believing it yet. And a dark reminder is glued to the back of my mind: I still haven't missed a period, so it's still possible I won't carry to term like Natalia warned. *Sorry, my love. False alarm. I'll tell you later.*

Amy quickly dabs off my running mascara, but she freezes when she takes a full look at my face in the mirror reflection.

Her grin spreads. "Are you going to be okay?"

I laugh. "I'm just— I'm *stunned*, Amy. Do you really think—"

Which is when someone knocks on the door. Amy opens it to reveal Lilian with an unfamiliar, lavishly dressed woman in tow. I quickly blink away my fresh tears, gripping Amy as this stranger sputters like we've done something atrocious.

"Oh, Goddess! Oh, Luna Lilian, no, no, no! Are these your Greenfield wolves?! Where is my soon-to-be Luna?" The woman holds her palm against her forehead, her sharp, black nails fanning high in the air.

I step out from the dressing room, my heart pounding into my ears. "Um, hi."

The Sexy Luna Taskforce swoops in, surrounding me with their supportive scent.

"Here she is!" Rainn says.

Kira leans in, utmost seriousness deepening her voice. "We need her to look sexy as hell."

"Sexy," Lexi whispers for the first time.

Amy's eyes bulge in horror, and I bite my lips, tempted to laugh.

But Celestia waves her hands, every gesture sweeping over the air like she's smoothing fabric folds. "That's precisely what I'm saying: you're in the *wrong* section!"

Amy and I give each other an amused look as we follow Celestia into the back of the store, behind the staff door. Passing through a dim hallway, the light at the end of it richens into a golden, airy hue, hitting the beaded fabric at the doorway at just the right angle to make it glitter like snowflakes. As we step into a room with high ceilings and carved wooden walls, we find the most lavish, intricate, expensive-looking clothing I've ever seen in my life.

I stop mid-walk, gaping at the dresses around us.

No, these aren't dresses. They're ornamented *lingerie*.

Good thing I wore nice underwear today.

Amy meets my wide eyes and barely contains a laugh. *Are you surviving?*

Amy, did you ever imagine me getting married in lingerie?

Her eyes sweep my body. *Girl, I don't think anyone will complain.*

I flush—right as Celestia looks me in the eyes.

"Much better, yes? Take your time to look around. I'd be happy to alter anything you'd like, no extra charge."

"Oh, wow. Even with the rush charge?"

"Absolutely, Luna! I've been awaiting your ceremony since you both met!"

My heart flips. She's the second professional now to say so—another reminder of the eyes that will be on us, not just at the ritual, but the rest of our lives.

I smile. "That's so incredibly generous of you. Thank you so, so much!"

The women gape in excitement, shock, and anticipation, hanging on Celestia's every word.

But I don't know what to do or say. This is a lot more attention than I'm used to—well, outside of Noah's attention.

Celestia smiles, striding to the most glamorous dress rack. "I recommend these more intricate mating dresses for you, of course. But you're welcome to try on anything here."

"Wow, this is…" I run my fingers along the nearest lacy dress, large slits on either hip and airy, sheer fabric from bust to toe. Noah could just slip his hands up my thighs, parting the fabric in one swift movement, and—

I cover my mark with my palm, hoping it hides the sudden burst of lust in my scent.

Now that I've had a moment to recover from my panic in the lobby and near-meltdown in the dressing room, it's clear my emotions and reactions are heightened beyond control today. Are these mood swings?

Celestia absolutely notices my scent, her grin widening. "You like this one, don't you?"

"I—" Swallowing hard, my eyes land on the whopping price tag. It far exceeds what Noah and I agreed on, nearly tripling the amount I'm comfortable with; while I want to dress fancier than I ever have for the ceremony, I'd much rather put a big chunk of our money down on a new house than on a dress I'll wear once.

Celestia flips the tag over. "Oh, pup, don't look at that. I owe your mate a favor much larger than that."

My stomach drops, and Celestia only smiles wider.

But I grip my arm. "What? No, that's not right. I'm not taking anything here for free."

"Oh, it is right. From one Omega to another, there's no more survivable pack out there for us than your Alpha's."

I stiffen. "Thank you for supporting my mate, but I'm my own woman, and—"

Celestia covers her mouth with a gasp. "Oh, goodness! I'm so sorry, that's not what I meant. You're my Luna too. Of course I want you to feel like your best self for your mating ceremony. It's my honor!"

"Oh, sorry, I—" I cut myself off, studying Celestia's confusion. Maybe I'm the one fumbling cultural norms by missing something huge, as usual.

Okay. No more apologies. I'm just going to focus on the important part of this issue: maybe Celestia would be honored to gift her work to me, but I'd like to respect her value as an artist and working Omega.

My stomach burns the second I return my attention to the stunning dresses at my fingertips. "Are you sure you want to give anything here away? This is your gorgeous handiwork. Gorgeous, *gorgeous* handiwork…"

"Let's just say… I wouldn't be here without Greenfield. This is nothing." Celestia's sudden sincerity doesn't help my raging heartbeat. But her words still strike me the wrong way.

"*Nothing?* This is better than anything I imagined."

Celestia laughs. "But? You're not jumping to try them on."

"But… Nothing. There's not a single thing I don't like about the dress. Any of these dresses."

"You're worried you can't pull it off, aren't you?"

My telling silence lends to Celestia's smirk.

"Most Omegas feel the same." She leans in. Her cool hand on my shoulder sends a shiver down my arm. "But a good Alpha knows the timid ones come with the hottest surprises."

My heart spikes with excitement—and fear.

She whispers into my ear. "Don't let a label tame you, pup. I can smell the dominance within you, waiting to be unleashed. Let the dress carry you there. Indulge."

Celestia pulls away with a wink despite me flushing down to my neck. When I realize she's not leaving anytime soon and likely plans to help me try on dresses, I grasp Amy's hand.

Like the best friend she is, Amy jumps in without hesitation.

"Trust me, Celestia, we're not letting her go home with anything less than she deserves."

Celestia beams. "You have a good set of friends here, I see. Well, good. I'll be chatting with our current Luna when you need me."

I give her a forced smile. "Thank you for your generosity, Celestia. Truly."

The Sexy Luna Taskforce swoops in—minus Lilian as she keeps Celestia occupied.

My friends lower their voices, but that isn't saying much.

Kira lowers into a hiss, but only after putting her palms over Lexi's ears. "Are you fucking kidding me?! She's giving you the goddamn dress for free?!"

Amy grips Kira's arm. "Shh, Kira!"

"For reals, though! What the hell did Alpha Noah do?!"

"I don't know either, but I'm not comfortable with taking the dress without paying her for *something*," I say.

My best friend is a sneaky philanthropist, though. Yasmine checks over her shoulder, deciding it'd be safer to mindlink. *I can only guess she was a Rogue at some point. There are plenty of anonymous Omegas that Noah and Ritchie saved from abuse in other packs. And Noah has a terrible habit of forgetting to tell us when he encounters some seriously horrible shit. Maybe he really did save her life and kept it private for her, especially if it made her feel extra vulnerable.*

Everyone's excitement dulls into an aching sadness. I'm sure Celestia can smell it, but her eyes remain glued to Lilian.

Amy puts her arms around Kira and Yasmine, leaning in. "Alright, regroup. We're the Sexy Luna Taskforce, and we have a job to do."

Rainn's classic smile returns. "You're right, Amy. What style do you like most here, future Luna? Let's try to narrow it down somehow."

I try to stay centered, but my voice shakes through my fading smile. "I don't even know where to begin."

Amy frowns, grabbing my hand. "Give us a second, ladies."

She pulls me to the back of the store, stirring my frozen legs into action.

Plopping us down on a tufted bench, Amy grabs my hand. "Talk to me. What are you thinking?"

"I'm not a goddess, let alone royalty. Everyone's acting like it, but I'm really not special. I just want to buy a dress. What if I'm in over my head?"

"With Noah?" Amy's eyes widen.

My wolf growls through me. "No! I'd *never* say that!"

Amy sputters out a laugh. "Damn, okay! Just checking!"

I grasp my temples. "God, sorry, I'm so weird today. But I love Noah with my whole soul, Amy. This is so important to me."

"Aww, babe. Then what's wrong? I mean, maybe I'm overstepping here, but are you having trouble letting yourself be taken care of again?"

I swallow hard, looking down to my feet. "Not like I used to. I want to mate Noah in front of everyone... And I *do* want to wear something like this while we mate."

"That's incredible in itself! You were nowhere near a place to do this before. Just your *interest* amazes me." Amy squeezes my arm. "But if you're trying to force yourself into it, that's not okay. I don't care what anyone might think, not even Alpha Noah. If you're not into any of this, we can call it off. I'll have your back, all the way."

My head snaps up, staring directly at Amy. "I love you, Amy. But please, don't worry. I'm not forcing myself. I want this."

We're both stunned at the conviction in my tone. But then my cheeks flare with embarrassment.

Amy slumps. "Oh, *babe*... Seriously, what's wrong?"

I shudder back tears, trying not to hiccup as they come pouring out of me. "I want to be the pack's sex symbol, so badly. But I don't know if I'm ever going to feel okay enough to do what I want. What if we go through the whole ceremony, and after all this special treatment, I panic in front of everyone?"

I hold my rocky stomach, hoping it doesn't overturn.

But Amy squeezes my shoulders, sincerity wiping out her worry from moments before. "You know what? That's possible."

My heart throbs, worsening my tears.

"But everyone will have to accept whatever happens. Whether you do it or not, you're their Luna, and you deserve respect."

"But why does that mean I deserve respect? Just because I love Noah?" I groan. "Everyone's acting like I'm supposed to be some spoiled princess. If I'm only important because they see me as his pet, it's demeaning."

"This isn't about Noah, but I hear you. I think you need to talk to him about his opinion on Lunas to clear that up. And I also don't think you know how much you've already helped this community, even though you just got here. You weren't born into being their Luna, and you were given a choice. You *chose* to carry this weight for the pack. That means something huge to these wolves. More than you'll probably ever know."

My heart throbs into my ears. "I have an idea of what it means to them, at least. That's why I care so much about being good enough for them."

"But that's the thing. You'd still deserve their respect, even if you don't do a goddamn thing. And I think you should own it. I can see you want to."

I grasp Amy's hands, pulling her in closer. "A., I do want to be looked at with respect— And maybe even admiration. Even if it's selfish to want and that selfishness makes me a bad person."

A grin erupts across Amy's face, and I'm stunned. She looks inspired.

I've never thought it could help others to be selfish, yet it's real, and it's happening. Maybe I *can* be a symbol of hope for our pack by taking up space. Maybe I can nurture them even better this way.

I flick my tears off, chasing the desire in my heart. "I need to mate with Noah in front of everyone, acting as the pack's leading sex symbols. I don't just want to, I *need* to. And I know that sounds weird when I say it out loud since I'm not the usual personality type to be a sex icon, but—"

"Really? Because I think you are. Just because you want this. I love sex, but *I* wouldn't want this."

My breath heightens, stoking the fire my wolf won't let go.

Luna… I want to be Luna.

Amy cups my cheeks, staring me straight in the eyes. "There she is. You know what I see?"

"Um—" I wince at how foolish I'm about to sound. "A sex symbol?"

"No. You're not just a symbol. I see a sex *matriarch*. And we're going to make sure you look like one."

Amy drags me across the room back to the most expensive dresses, grasping the one I had my eyes on.

She thrusts it into my hands. "Try this, and *at least* two others you love. Fuck what everyone else thinks. Trust your wolf."

Facing the dresses with fresh eyes, they don't look like lingerie anymore. They look like how I want Noah to envision me for the rest of my life.

I want him to desire me. Not just my body and heart, but my confidence. I want him to witness the security in myself it takes to wear this after all I've been through.

With shaking hands, I grab not three, but four of my favorite dresses—without imagining anyone else's input.

Shit, this was easier than I thought. Is it supposed to be decided this quickly?

But Amy beams, her voice shaking as she rubs my shoulders. "So?! What do you think?"

"I... I absolutely love these. I can picture enjoying myself in at least one of them."

"Fuck, yes! I love you so much."

"I love you too, Amy."

"Now go try these on while we pick out the sexiest lingerie for you to enjoy after the fact."

"What?!"

Amy cackles. "You wanted to pay for something, right? Don't let Celestia pressure our soon-to-be Luna out of getting what she needs today."

I nearly drop my armful of dresses as I tackle Amy with a hug. "I really do love you."

"I really do love you too, girl. Always have, always will. Even when you piss me off."

I sigh. "Just be nice to me when I inevitably have about 20 nip slips in the next hour."

Amy bursts out laughing before calling the rest of the Sexy

Luna Taskforce over. "With what she picked out, you'll all want to see this!"

Yasmine beams, her fangs on full display. "Our future Luna is trying something on?"

Rainn smirks in a way only a sibling can. "Noah's going to be so jealous we saw it first!"

Lilian and Celeste follow behind them as our mini pack streams in, all eyes on me.

I keep my shoulders from slumping, breathing into my wolf's determination to be Luna. "I think I already know which one I love, but I'm trying them all on first—" I bite back a smile. "To give you a show."

My friends cheer and whistle, and I escape into the dressing room with the biggest smile I've had all day. Amy follows close behind, helping me sort the dresses and slip into the complicated getups.

"You've got this, girl. I'm so fucking proud of you," Amy whispers.

I blow out a shaky breath, gazing at myself in the mirror as I strip to my underwear. Most of them don't feel as exciting as I hoped. My heart sinks when I try the final dress on, and the lace scratches against my skin. I already know it'll irritate my neurodivergent brain all night.

"What's wrong?" Amy asks.

But I'm no longer looking at Amy in the mirror; something catches my eye over her shoulder, glittering in the corner.

"Aliya?"

"Oh, my God, Amy... What is that?"

She spins around. Amy falls into a hush as we approach the stray dress. "Whoa. It looks like it's never been released before. We'd have to ask Celestia."

I bite my nails. "Do you think that's rude?"

"Oh, hell no. I think she'll fucking love it."

My heart pounds as I look into Amy's eyes. If I want that dress, I'll have to be selfish and request it. My feet shuffle. "Amy, I love all of these, but *that* one..."

I nibble my lip, staring back at the dress with Amy. It consumes the silence in the room, filling it with gentle shimmers under the store lights.

"Let's ask her," I whisper.

Amy bolts out the door the second I say the word. Within a minute, Celestia rushes to remove the gown she's been working on, helping me into it with a beaming grin.

This is by far the most incredible, expensive dress I've ever worn. It feels so luxurious that I'm afraid to touch it.

But as I step into my soon-to-be Luna dress, I'm overcome with anxiety, excitement, and an intense, unavoidable hunger. I can feel her rising to the surface, more than ever: the Luna I want to be.

When I look into my own eyes in the mirror, she's already there, staring back.

My breath short-circuits as my eyes roam across every visible scar, flaw, and oddity beneath the sheer fabric. A faint outline of my nipples peek through the intricate design, but it doesn't feel vulgar. It feels molded to my body, outlining features that aren't necessarily good or bad; they just are. Until I take a step back to zoom out my focus, capturing the full image of myself all at once. With every flaw I thought I had, lacy framing adds a certain beauty to them I never cared to notice before.

The rising fire in my belly blazes.

"I… love myself in this," I whisper.

Amy has been stunned silent, gaping in awe. But with these words, she starts to weep.

"Oh, *A.*—" I flip around, desperate to soothe her.

But she's beaming. "Show everyone else. They're going to be as happy for you as I am."

Before I can second-guess it, I rush outside the dressing room with happy tears clouding my eyes. The moment everyone's stare lands on me, the room falls into complete silence.

Followed by wide smiles and happy sniffles. When even Celestia is speechless, I have trouble keeping my head up.

But my chosen family chimes in.

"Holy ship," Kira breathes, clutching Lexi closer. "Auntie Aliya is…"

"Pretty," Lexi whispers.

"Truly, Luna, you're so…" Rainn trails off, overwhelmed with emotion.

But her mother picks up where she left off. "Beautiful. Sexy. Confident. My son will be so blown away by his Luna. Our Luna."

My heart overflows with joy, forcing me to wipe more tears as they gush from my smiling eyes.

But Yas lets out a frustrated groan, making every head whip to her. "Dammit, I'm so jealous of Noah now!"

Everyone erupts into laughter.

But with my newfound confidence, I let myself loose. "With how well Noah treats me in bed, you should be jealous of *me*."

Everyone laughs again, and I drop my head to smooth my dress. I guess there's still a part of me that's forever unable to stop feeling shy. Maybe that's okay too.

Yasmine waves my words away with her hand. "Oh, *no*, Noah and I aren't right for each other. I'm way too aromantic for his mushy ass. Especially in bed."

My eyebrows raise, but inside, my wolf bares her teeth. "You've slept with him?"

Yasmine laughs. "I wouldn't go that far. We tried a best friend sex thing once at 17 and it was just weird. It's more than old news, it's dead and buried."

My throat burns, even though I know it's old news; if it wasn't, I'd sense Noah's attraction through our bond.

But what confuses me the most is how I'm feeling. What's with my jealous, reactive wolf today? Calm down before anyone smells it. I dated and had sex with multiple people before we met too. So why am I—

Kira glares at me, and my eyes widen further.

"Don't act like you and Amy didn't have *a little thing* in college, right before we met. I've always been jealous of that."

My face burns bright red, but Amy bursts into laughter. "You know you're my one and only, babe."

Kira's chest puffs, her sly smile appearing. "Yeah? Well, I'll never get tired of hearing that either."

Rainn tucks her hair behind her ear. "Listen, I—" She bites her lip, peeking into my eyes. "I won't lie, I've slept with Yas also. She's hot."

Yasmine's proud smirk makes us all laugh even harder, softening any jealousy I felt moments before.

"I can agree with that, Yas. You're hot as hell," I say.

Kira nudges Yasmine, and Amy and Rainn can't stop giggling with me.

I feel so free. Like I'm finally with my pack.

Before I can join back in on the fun, my wolf recoils into complete terror, sensing an oncoming threat before my conscious mind does. Everyone stops, staring at what must be pure shock and terror on my face.

A mindlink slices through my thoughts.

Celestial Couture Shop, huh?

31

I recognize his bitter quips instantly.

Mason Hart.

Would've thought you'd bring your Alpha along for protection from big, scary stalkers, he continues. *But I guess you Omegas really don't give a fuck about Alphas, do you? You just care about yourselves.*

I stumble backwards until my back meets an icy mirror. Tremors wrack my body from head to toe.

Kira is at my side in a heartbeat, her eyes golden as her protective Alpha musk drowns all other scents. "What is it, Omega? What's wrong?"

Yasmine rushes over. "I'm sorry if I freaked you out. I didn't mean to—"

I fight my panic, struggling to breathe deep enough to speak. I have to grip Kira's arms as Mason continues.

You went and whined about me to your Alpha, didn't you? Got me put on 24/7 surveillance. Tell him I'm here, waiting for him.

This sends me into full-blown tears.

Dammit, I want to be strong and angry. I don't want to be used like this again.

But no matter what I want, my wolf takes charge. And she demands I protect myself from harm at all costs. As she releases a potent, fearful scent, my wolf family dives in, immersing me in their worried, protective scents.

But someone else is worried about me.

Noah's wolf runs rampant in our bond. *Aliya, what's happening?!*

I know everyone else has the same question as Noah, but

anxiety has stolen my voice. I'll have to compromise, mindlinking everyone at once.

Mason is angry with me.

Noah's wolf bristles, his teeth baring. *What?! What do you mean? Where is he?*

He mindlinked me. Out of nowhere. He knows Noah isn't here with us, so he might be outside.

As Noah's wolf fades from our bond, I know he has already shifted. *Oh, fuck no. What's he going to do? Did he say?*

He's mad about the surveillance. Wants to see Noah.

Noah doesn't respond, but his emotions burst into flames.

He's probably on his way, but it's not reassuring. Even with Noah's speed cutting straight through the forest rather than using the winding road, it'll take at least 20 minutes for him to sprint here.

Anxieties come spitting out of me, rapid-fire. "What if Mason breaks in? What if he hurts everyone?! I don't want him to hurt you!" I shudder into Kira, my knees shaking. "It'll be all my fault—"

Kira growls. "He's not breaking in unless he wants to fucking die."

Amy gasps. "Oh, babe, let's not talk about anything too violent. Stalking and potentially breaking in is a huge trigger for her."

"Yeah, and that fucking bastard probably took advantage of that too. I'm going outside to defend us before my wolf destroys this shop."

"Agreed," Yasmine says. "Noah is on his way and giving me orders. Amy and Rainn, we'll let you know if we need you outside as backup. Luna, please protect our future Luna."

"And Lexi, please," Kira growls.

As Kira and Yasmine take off, Rainn and Lilian sit at my sides, nuzzling me.

But I can't smell them anymore.

All I see are Amy's wide eyes in front of me as she shifts poor Lexi's scared body to her hip. "Oh, God. I remember this look, Luna. She's maybe ten seconds from dissociating beyond our reach."

I can't really understand what Amy is talking about. In fact, I'm not fully aware of what *I'm* thinking about.

But my teeth chatter at the wolf eyes lighting up all around me, even Celestia reared up in defense. My mate feels the worst of all. He's not just stuffed to the brim with rage; he's terrified.

"I'm sorry!" I sputter. "It's my fault Mason's mad. I spoke up, and—"

"Shh, sweetheart. Come here." Lilian pulls my head against her chest, rubbing my back fast and hard. "Breathe all the way down to your toes and focus on the feeling of my hands on you."

It's only then that I realize it sounds like Lilian is speaking through a long tunnel, and I'm numb to her touch.

I close my eyes, fighting to take the reins on my own breath. As I deepen each breath, I focus on Lilian's hands, allowing them to root me back into awareness. Her cold fingers wrap around my temple and forehead, pressing me to her chest, and a strong hand on my back jostles my limp body.

But the more her touch brings me back to earth, the sicker I feel. I groan, hunching over.

"Shit, you're really pale. Are you going to throw up?" Amy asks.

My stomach recoils, threatening to spill with her words. But I shake my head, refusing to get sick. After a heavy swallow, I croak out a whisper. "I hate this. I want to protect you all too."

"You *are* protecting us!" Amy says. "You told us the truth, right away, even while you were worried you caused harm by speaking up. Please, don't let Mason bully you into victim-blaming yourself again."

Ugh, she's right. I groan, lifting off of Lilian to grip my churning stomach. "I want to protect Noah, but my wolf is freaking out. All I feel like doing right now is cowering in the corner."

"You just got hit with a pretty bad trigger, A. You sometimes throw up from all the adrenaline, and it's normal to go into 'flight' mode of fight or flight—or freeze or fawn, of course."

Lilian sniffs my neck, and just like Amy mentioned, I freeze in submission.

Our Luna softens her voice into a comforting purr. "You're okay, sweetheart. I'm just smelling you to see if I can sense what's wrong."

I relax, allowing Lilian to analyze my scent freely.

But Lilian's eyebrows furrow, taking another sniff. Then another. Soon, all three wolves are sniffing me.

Rainn's eyebrows shoot up. "She smells... Extra sweet?"

Lilian hums. "Rainn's correct. Your wolf isn't jumping to protect Noah because she's busy protecting someone else already. And if she's telling you to cower, that 'someone' is inside you."

My stomach drops. "Wait, what? What did you just say?"

Amy and Rainn meet Lilian's eyes.

"Mom, you think she's pregnant?" Rainn breathes.

My heart leaps into my throat, followed by a million thoughts at once. I knew I could be pregnant, but I didn't think anyone else would notice for weeks. The fact that both Amy and Lilian brought it up feels like truer confirmation than Noah and I have had yet.

But Lilian still hasn't answered. She furrows her brows, puzzling over a few more sniffs before shaking her head. "I genuinely can't tell. Maybe it's because it's super early, or maybe because she's a hybrid..."

"But I haven't missed my period yet. Noah would've noticed it on my scent, too."

"Let's follow your wolf's instincts, regardless. She knows what's best for you, whether we understand it or not," Lilian says.

My shock subsides into elation, my heart pounding as my fingertips trace my lower abdomen. The second my hand lands there, I warp into a weepy smile. I love them already, even if they don't exist yet.

Which means I cry even harder out of fear, wrapping my arms around my stomach. "Oh, God. No, no, no— I can't let anything happen to our baby if I'm finally pregnant."

Lilian gives my shoulders a steady squeeze. "Nothing will hurt you or your future pup. There's 20,000 wolves ready to make sure of that."

My stomach churns until my full body quivers. Rainn cuddles in closer, and I find comfort in her familiar scent.

"Are you upset you might be pregnant? Or just scared of Mason?" Rainn asks.

I swallow hard. "I... I need my mate by my side."

Lilian releases my shoulders, stroking them instead. "I know, sweetheart. But he's on his way, and we're here with you in the meantime."

I groan. "But I also don't want an abusive asshole to take another moment away from us. After all that hope and excitement, I feel vulnerable in this dress now."

Amy attempts her best smile. "You know what? That's just right now. I know you can feel confident in it again. Mason has nothing to do with the dress."

I nod, blowing out a slow breath.

Amy glances around the room. "And hey, even after ten minutes or so, it doesn't seem like Mason's busting in, does it?"

My shoulders soften, soaking in the complete stillness around us. There's only the wolves protecting me here. I can't bring myself to stop shielding my stomach, but I can breathe a bit deeper.

"I guess he's not," I say.

Amy offers her hand. "Come on. Let's get you out of this dress so Noah can still be surprised."

My shaking limbs refuse to function. I have to hang on Amy and Rainn as I remove the dress and slip on a robe. I double over in Amy's arms, dizzy from my over-anxious heart—until I feel Noah's pounding approach in our bond.

My fear evaporates into the background as a punch of adrenaline hits me in the gut. With it comes clarity.

I jolt upright. "Mason is taunting my mate."

As I make for the door, Lilian gasps. Petrified, wide eyes overtake her usual neutrality. "No, wait!"

I freeze. I almost forgot I don't have to worry about just myself anymore. But what if Noah dies, taking not only me, this possible-baby with him?

I can't think about that horrifying possibility right now; I don't have long to warn Noah, if I can convince him at all. Pressing against the shop's largest front window, I scan the forest for Noah's massive black wolf. *Noah, Mason is baiting you again. There's no way this isn't another trap. Mason always catches you when you're distracted by my safety.*

I don't give a fuck. I'll destroy him, and anyone he's with.

No, Noah, I need you! I need you right here with me before anything else happens. Let's solve this together, as Alpha and future Luna.

Noah's anger softens, revealing something much deeper than rage: primal fear.

Shit. I want him here primarily because I really think I am pregnant; my hand won't stop automatically landing on my stomach at the sound of Lexi crying in the back room. But if I tell Noah, he'll feel even more protective. I don't want him to be too impulsive.

I shudder through Noah's panic as I spot his wolf a few miles out in the distance, bristled fur making him larger than ever as he clambers up mountain rocks.

I-I can't lose you, Omega. I can't.

A sudden calm washes over me at the sight of my mate needing my comfort. *Stay focused, and you won't.*

To my right, Kira and Yasmine bare their fangs at nearby trees, their discarded clothes in heaps at my feet. That must be where Mason is hiding.

My wolf bares her teeth, despite my human form cowering into Lilian as she comes rushing up behind me.

But Lilian grabs me, dragging me behind a clothing rack in the center of the room. "*Why* did you do that?!"

For the first time since I've met her, I've never seen Lilian's fear so clearly represented in her anger. All I can do is open and close my mouth, shaking at the sight of her fear.

"You're a prime target! Not even the windows are safe. Don't you remember how your father died?"

I'm so horrified by her words that I sputter out an instinctual response. "I-I'm sorry, Luna, I— I wasn't thinking—"

We freeze. Lilian is no longer looking at me, her bulging eyes locking onto Mason as he emerges from the tree line.

I huddle into Lilian, terrified of what she could be so afraid of. What if she knows something about Mason's capabilities that I don't? The tighter she holds me, the worse my anxiety spikes.

But Noah's emotions twist in anticipation, warning me of his approach. When I spot his wolf overtaking a hill—only about a mile away now—his wild eyes are busy assessing everyone's position. When he spots Mason, he bares his teeth. *Aliya? I need to know where you are.*

I'm still hiding in the shop. Your mom and I are behind the first clothing rack.

Golden, electric eyes zip to the shop, bristling my wolf's fur in our bond.

Noah's ears flatten in relief. *You're okay. Thank you, Moon Goddess.*

Yes, I'm okay. But don't get distracted. If you're reckless and die, I'll die of heartbreak. Please stay as calm as you can so we can think through this.

Noah's wolf sneezes in irritation. But as he glances at the shop again, his ears slink back. *Okay, I'll regain my cool. Just do me a favor and stay inside with my mom, okay? My wolf is edgy as hell today and won't shut up about your safety.*

I shudder, wrapping my robe tighter over my abdomen in a protective hug. Does his wolf feel extra certain that we're pregnant too? I should wait to tell him, shouldn't I? But God, I want to.

Omega, I'm serious. Don't put yourself in harm's way over this bastard.

That's not what I'm thinking, Noah. I just want to say— My heart races so heavily I can feel it in my throat. *There's still a lot you want to accomplish as Alpha. Please stay focused. Not just on me, but on yourself.*

Noah's emotions ripple with anxiety. *Why are you saying this now? What's wrong?*

God, he knows me too well. *Sorry, I— I just meant— It's not just me you're protecting by staying alive. Taking care of yourself protects the entire pack. And even more than that... I need you to be okay. I can't do this alone.*

Aliya, tell me what's wrong. Something's wrong.

Nothing's wrong. I'll tell you what I'm thinking after we deal with Mason, but just listen to me that I need you to stay safe, okay? I can't do this without you.

Noah's anxiety heightens as he closes in on Mason, and I have to do my best not to feel guilty for being as honest as I can.

But Noah is filled with an intense resolve, steeling my heart with him.

Everything's going to be okay, my love. I'll hold you soon, okay? He mindlinks.

Okay. But don't sacrifice yourself. You're irreplaceable, Noah.

His ears flick in discomfort at my words.

That doesn't stop him from crashing into his classic skidding halt, soaking Mason with mud.

Ugh, are you fucking kidding me? Mason bares his teeth as he mindlinks us all.

Noah snarls louder than I've ever heard him, enough for the vicious sound to seep through the windows as he takes a swipe at Mason.

Mason scurries back into the cover of trees. *Shit! I just want to talk, asshole!*

Noah somehow gets even bigger, making Yasmine and Kira look like pups at his flanks. *You've lost your talking privileges.*

Mason shakes the mud from his coat. *Clearly. Which is why I'm declaring a pack split. I'm leaving Greenfield, and taking your strongest Alphas with me.*

Noah's ears perk up in surprise.

But before I can reel at Mason's declaration, Noah's sarcastic tail wag gives me goosebumps. Noah's nonchalance has the power to devastate anyone, but especially someone like Mason whose ego is his everything. I'm nervous it could throw Mason over the edge.

Yet Noah flicks his ear to the side, acting like he can't process what he just heard. *Uh-huh. My strongest Alphas. Sure.*

As other Alphas show themselves behind Mason, my instincts kick back in with a whimper.

Lilian squeezes me as tightly as she can, wave after wave of her calming scent burning my eyes. "Shh, sweetheart. I've got you."

There's such a sharp fear at the base of her scent, no matter how much she's suppressing it for me. It's scaring me more.

But Noah looks completely unfazed. Not only looks, but *feels* unfazed. Actually, he's calmer than he was when he arrived, as promised.

But we're horrifically outnumbered. Why isn't anyone else disturbed by this?

Noah's confidence relaxes everyone. He sits on his haunches, unthreatened but irritated. Mason takes it to heart, bristling until my teeth chatter.

Is this a fucking joke to you?! Some Alpha you are! Mason mindlinks.

No, it's just hilarious that you think my strongest Alpha is behind you. You've met my strongest Alpha, but you'll never admit it, Noah says.

I glance around, searching for this vital Alpha to be on our side. But who is he talking about? I don't think I've met Noah's strongest Alpha either.

Mason has no answers for me. His eyes flick from Noah, to my chosen family, to Celestial Couture's elaborate front door, and back again.

Noah's wolf shakes out his coat from head to tail. *Okay, Hart. List your reasons for splitting, and be on your fucking way.*

Mason's twitching tail pushes a growl from Noah, but Mason doesn't back down. His ferocious snarl stings in my chest. *You really need a fucking list? How about stalking me, for starters? If I didn't have a surveillance Alpha on my side, I wouldn't even know why you put me on it.*

And now I know exactly who let you slip past their watch today. First day as top Alpha of your Rogue pack, and you're outing your own pack members for treason. Great start, Hart.

A few of the treasonous Alphas' ears twitch, and Noah's sarcastic tail wags again.

What else?

Noah would be darkly laughing in his human form, but I'm gritting my teeth. *Stop provoking him! You're freaking me out.*

My mate shrinks with guilt, but Mason puffs his chest, thinking his scare tactics are finally working.

What else? We, the real Alphas, are taking charge over our inborn dominance again. We need somewhere Alphas can reign like the Goddess created us for. A habitat you failed to create. Mason stands as tall as he can. *Here before you stand the Hart Alphas, exiting your pack for being absolutely unlivable for our Goddess-given rights.*

Noah is surprisingly calm about this, rolling onto one hip and itching his ear with his back paw.

That's gross.

We all wait for him to finish itching, Mason tensing by the second. Finally, Noah stands.

Go on, then. Leave. Why are you still here?

Mason hunches into a defensive prowl, and I stiffen in Lilian's arms.

You're going to allow this to happen? I ask Noah privately.

Yes. I don't want him in our pack, or any other wolves that agree with him. This is great actually: I'm thinking he's the root of our region's Alpha domination cultist problem, but there's no way they'll survive as a pack on their own. All we're doing right now is giving them the space to band together stronger. Noah's fluffy chest expands by the second. *This is the best alternative, as long as them leaving doesn't mean they'll now terrorize neighboring packs. He'll just have to remember who his Greenfield neighbor is.*

With this thought, Noah towers over Mason, his fur bristling until he appears to hardly fit between the trees.

My hands grip Lilian so tightly that my fingers tingle. *What are you going to do?*

Tension ripples through the air, a complex mix of scents from beneath the front door giving off an overwhelming sense of doom.

Well, now that he's no longer part of our pack... Noah's lips curl into a four-fanged, drooling snarl. He reverts to mindlinking us all. *Another Alpha is invading my territory. Isn't that right, Hart?*

Mason's ears slink. The rest of his Alpha pack awaits his call, trickling closer in defense.

You better fucking run. Noah's chilling mindlink makes me cower, gripping the dresses beside me. Lilian shields me, hovering over me despite shaking herself.

But I can't tear my eyes away from Noah.

Charging at Mason in a single breath, Noah guns it after the pack in a mass of bristled black fur.

They're out of human eyesight and scent within a millisecond.

I flinch to chase them on instinct, but my muscles clamp tight in fear.

Lilian hugs me back to her. "It's okay, sweetheart. Stay right here. Amy and I will protect you."

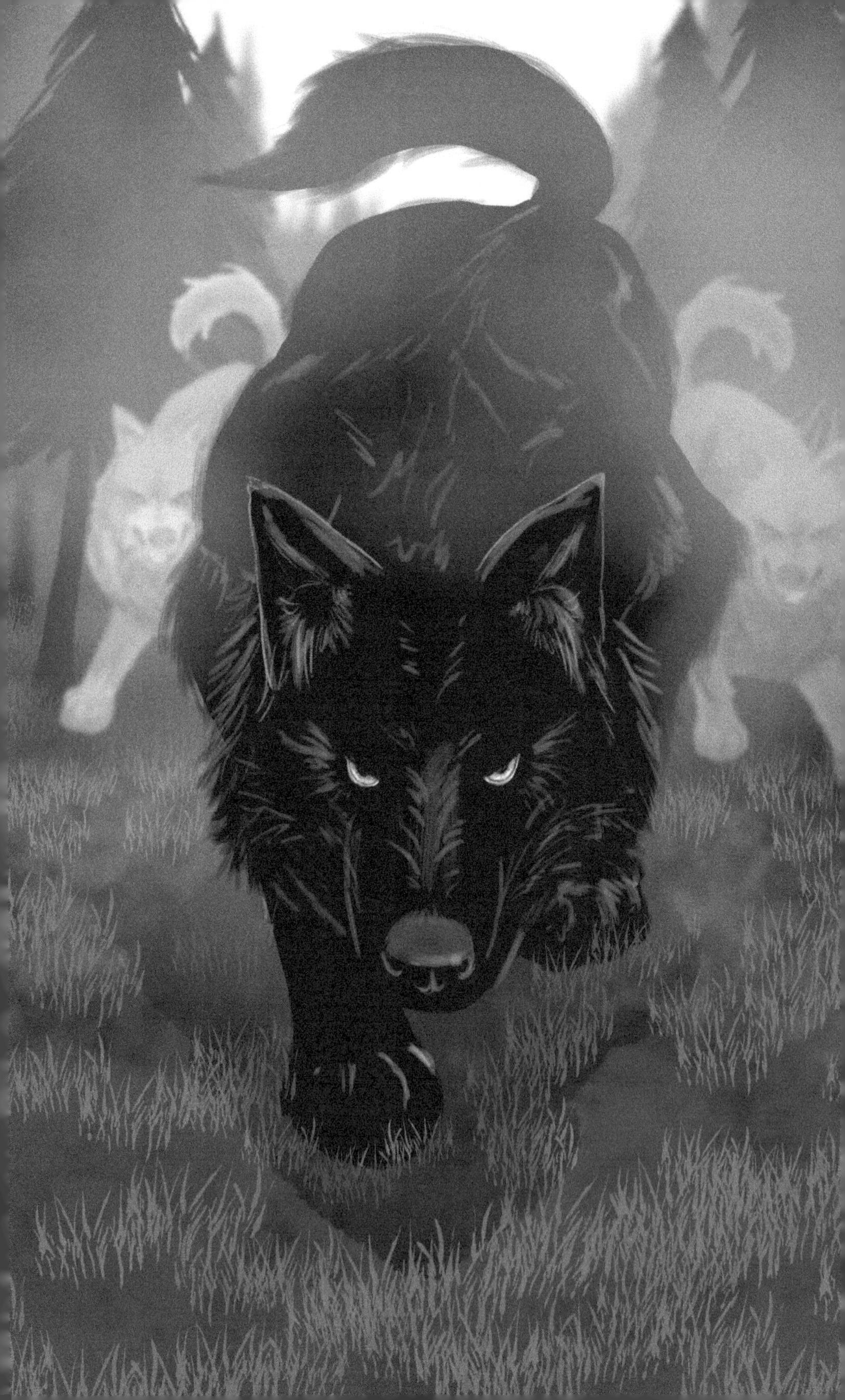

Now that I can't see Noah anymore to know if he's okay, panic burns my chest. "I'm terrified, Luna. I need him to be safe."

But Lilian's cool fingers guide my chin to the mountainside, her voice softening into a relaxing hum. "He'll be okay. Just watch."

Within seconds, Greenfield wolves stream from every angle, charging at Mason and his pack of treasonous wolves.

Mason's entire pack is forced to run for their lives.

The sheer mass of wolves who have Noah's back yanks me from my frozen state. I stand, gaping at the fierce stampede mere feet from the shop windows.

But a snapping sensation in the pack bond sucks the breath from me.

"Oh, my God! Please be okay, Noah!" I cry out.

But the shattering pieces of our pack bond aren't coming from Noah. Wolves howl in mourning across Noah's territory, echoing through miles and miles of trees. I feel each wolf in Mason's pack disconnect from the pack bond, spiking pain through my core, one by one.

I don't even need to see them to know Mason's Alphas are gone. That they betrayed us. I can feel everyone aching.

They escape from Noah's territory before I can even process their exit from the pack.

32

I can finally let go of my stomach. Lilian releases me, throwing open the front door to assess our surroundings from the porch. I follow close behind, gripping the iron railing.

A distinct howl absorbs my every breath. The song echoes through the trees until the birds scatter above the forest canopy.

"*Noah*," I breathe.

In his wolf's song, I hear grief, anger, and exhaustion. But mainly, relief. I grip my heart as it aches with him.

His howl is no longer alone, wolf voices erupting from every direction with their own emotional variations. Each subsequent howl lifts more and more pressure off of my bond with Noah, reminding us we're not alone.

But Noah's next howl is something else entirely. The second I hear it, I know it's for me. His giddy elation washes down every inch of my body.

My skin erupts with pleased shivers.

Mate, Noah says.

I hobble off the shop's porch on shaky legs, darting into the forest. *Mate! Come here!*

But Noah is already sprinting toward me. The second we lock eyes, he shifts into his human form, tackling me in the biggest hug he can manage, his arms encompassing my entire back.

I can't resist bursting into tears.

Noah gasps over me, gripping my head. "Oh, fuck. I'm so fucking sorry he did this. My sweet Omega, I—"

"He's gone!" I'm crying, but I'm also laughing. Noah pulls back, his eyes wide. "He's gone, Noah! We can enjoy our mating ceremony without having to watch our backs. We can have our baby, we can—"

Noah kisses me so hard that I have to cling to him to remain upright. Even as wolves surround us, we topple into the leaves, eager hands tugging at each other's hair.

Then Noah lets out a desperate whine. "O-Omega, I want to feel you closer."

I try to soothe him with my scent, but his Alpha musk frightens nearby Omega wolves into scurrying away. Noah wasn't kidding; his wolf is acting even weirder than mine today.

"Noah, are you about to slip into—"

He nips at my neck, and my whole body jolts before melting into his arms at the pleasure sweeping my core. Whether I want to or not, I moan loud enough for our onlookers to hear.

But when I hear rustling in the nearby leaves, my eyes snap open. "O-oh, God. Noah, um—"

Noah grips my back, licking and biting my neck until my hips buck into his. "I want you. I want to give you that baby." His eyes are a vivid yellow.

"Alpha, wait. I'm sorry, but I don't feel too well."

His hungry growls revert into whimpers. Softening his hold, he rubs his protective scent across my cheek. "Shit, I'm sorry. I've got you, my sweet Omega." Then he growls. "That piece of shit ruined your day right when you felt so happy. I should kill him, just for that."

I gasp. "Noah!"

He halts, his eyes reverting to their usual teal. Then he bursts into laughter. "S-sorry. My wolf is absolutely wild for you today. I feel like a hormonal teenager."

After today's stress, Noah's gentle smile restarts my tears.

Noah smooths my hair back before pulling my head to his chest. I nuzzle into his warmth, listening for his heartbeat. It's pounding like he's been sprinting for an hour.

"I didn't mean to make you so riled up," I sputter through tears.

"Shh, my love." He kisses me softly, his shoulders raising like they're desperate to cocoon me even closer. "I love you. You're so right, this is cause to celebrate. And I can't believe I'm about to be able to hold you like this as my Luna for the rest of my life."

I stroke his cheek, a luscious fire erupting in my belly from his smoldering gaze

"You're beautiful, Alpha. I'm absolutely dying to be your Luna." I pull back with a hammering heart. "But there's something else I need to tell you."

Noah's expanding ribs halt, his stare locking onto mine in anticipation.

But the more my heart picks up the pace, the more nauseated I feel. I swallow hard, taking slow, steady breaths.

I'm so nervous to tell Noah I might actually be pregnant now, especially because it's still too early to know for certain. I grab his hands anyway, determined to try my best for my mate. "Don't freak out."

His brows furrow. "Well, too late."

I let out a sharp, anxious laugh. "Really, Noah. I don't know if it's true, but—" I swallow hard, unable to look into his vulnerable, worried eyes. "Amy noticed something different about me. So did your mom. It might explain why your wolf is feeling protective. Mine has been too, all day."

"My mom said something to you? Amy too?" Noah's eyes widen, his sudden seriousness rattling me. He holds me by the shoulders, looking me all over. "What's wrong, Omega? Are you hurt?"

I halt his frantic search with a gentle touch on his chin, just before he starts sniffing me. "Nothing's wrong. That's the thing. It's so good, I don't want to lose any of it. Between mating with the love of my life, and now this…" I bite my quivering lip. "This is all I've ever wanted, right here."

With shaking fingers, I lift Noah's hands from my cheeks, placing them over my flat abdomen.

"I got really scared earlier when I saw a little blood." My heart races, but Noah remains still. "But Amy thinks it was implantation bleeding. And without even telling your mom, she said she thinks I'm pregnant, and—" The breath Noah draws steals mine, anticipation stretching every second tenfold. "And my wolf agrees."

But the smile Noah melts into makes me weep.

"A-*Aliya...*" His voice shakes as his hands can't decide where to land, finally settling on my cheeks. Noah takes short, desperate breaths, sniffing my neck.

He whimpers out a soft cry, kissing my mark. "Holy fuck. Y-you do smell sweeter than ever. This is— This is such a *good* sign, Aliya, I—"

As Noah blubbers through a watery laugh, I laugh through my tears, overwhelmed by wave after wave of emotion. Noah melts into me, meeting my soft nuzzling as he laugh-cries with me.

Smashing our lips together, we grip each other's shoulders closer until our torsos fall flush. This settles my tense shoulders, making me realize we're protecting our baby between our bodies.

A whine escapes me, making Noah release my lips.

"Goddess, my poor, sweet Omega under all this stress. We're okay now. I love you so much."

"I love you too, Noah. What if I'm really carrying your baby?"

"I'm so happy, my wolf could howl."

I giggle, his wolf leaping around mine in our bond between his heavy courting.

But my tears warp into fear. "Noah, don't get too excited. I haven't even missed a period yet, and anything could happen this early—"

Noah shakes his head, drawing my chin back to his lips. Kiss after kiss, his overjoyed pheromones hum in my heart. I soften against his chest, allowing him to nestle me into his embrace. "It doesn't change how I feel now. I just want to enjoy this moment with you, in case it's true. Will you let yourself be happy with me?"

I erupt into a smile, unable to stop the joy from pouring out of me. Noah giggles with me, nuzzling his nose against mine as my heart pounds into my ears.

When I remain quiet, Noah chuckles against my lips. "Okay, don't answer that. I'll keep carrying the happiness for both of us."

"No, I— I do feel happier than ever. Even though it's scary."

I gaze deep into Noah's gorgeous eyes, reflecting vivid green from the leaves surrounding us. Wrapping my hands behind his head, I draw his lips down to meet mine.

Noah breathes me in as our lips meet, parting for each other in an intimate dance that only we know. As our kisses evolve into a full-body makeout, hands gripping at each other's sides and backs, I'm hit with a desire so strong that I couldn't remember what year it is if I tried.

But someone clears their throat behind us. My nails dig into Noah's skin in fear.

Noah growls automatically, smushing me into his puffing chest. I whimper, sensing his readiness to attack.

Until we see who he's growling at.

Elder Alpha Frank scoffs. "Excuse me?"

Noah's eyes widen. "Oh, shit. Sorry, Elders."

The Alpha Elders glower back, and I shrink deeper into Noah's embrace. He's doing his best to stifle his defensive wolf, but his instincts are still on overdrive as I scramble to my feet; he rushes to keep me steady as if his life depends on it.

Elder Beta Terrence gapes with furrowed brows. "Are you… alright, Alpha?"

"Yes, I'm—" Noah huffs, shaking his shoulders to release their tension. He hugs me in front of him, covering his bare waist. "Sorry. My wolf didn't appreciate someone threatening his mate today. I'm doing my best to rein him in."

"That's understandable." Elder Beta Terrence nods. "We wanted to thank you for your continued efforts to protect this pack."

"Which also brings us to the Alpha Summit," Elder Alpha Aaron says.

Noah stiffens.

But his hands also lace around my waist, settling over my lower abdomen.

I've never felt something so powerful. Just his touch releases my remaining worries. Every instinct in me demands I protect my abdomen, yet I have full trust in Noah caressing the most vulnerable piece of my body. In fact, I think this is exactly what my wolf has craved all day.

The fact that my body craves Noah's touch because his child might be growing inside me is so gorgeous that it's almost unfathomable. I press my quivering lips together, struggling not to cry as my wolf happily whines against Noah's in our bond.

Elder Alpha Aaron smiles, not understanding my heavy elation wasn't in reaction to him. "We received word that the Summit is moving not one month, but two months in advance to August's New Moon. They want to strengthen our allyships as soon as possible. This includes celebrating the Greenfield Luna's arrival."

Despite his odd tension, Noah perks up. "Oh. Well, good. I'm looking forward to introducing my soon-to-be Luna."

My heart leaps, forcing me to bite back a smile. Noah chuckles, rubbing my back.

But Elder Beta Terrence still looks concerned. "Are you… physically prepared? Even with the Summit moving sooner?"

Noah shrugs. "I'm always prepared. Otherwise I wouldn't be a responsible leader of this pack."

The Elders glance at one other. My stomach churns. Something unspoken is said between wary, irritated scowls, but Noah didn't mention anything weird about the Alpha Summit in relation to the Elders.

Elder Aaron clears his throat. "Future Luna, this will be a great opportunity to strengthen your connection to fellow packs alongside our Alpha. We need our allies in case conflicts like Mason Hart's pack turn out to be a larger threat."

Noah and I sober ourselves, straightening for the Elders.

I smile. "Absolutely. I'm looking forward to meeting our allies and strengthening those connections."

"Good. And our pack is eagerly looking forward to your ceremony this week."

As the Elders excuse themselves, I lean against Noah's shoulder, basking in his warm scent. I get to be his Luna soon—in front of the whole world.

33

Amy combs my wet hair behind me as I settle my nerves, cradling my stomach.

"How are you feeling now, babe? Any better after your shower?" Amy asks.

"Yes, besides some bloating."

"Really? Do you feel any pressure or fullness like your ligaments are changing yet?"

My teeth chatter with nerves about tonight, and Amy stops brushing my hair to softly rub my shoulders.

"Is talking about pregnancy too much right now? Sorry."

"No, it's not. I've always wanted to tell you how it felt to be pregnant. I'm just... nervous. About tonight, and the possible-baby."

Amy sighs, gazing at the ceiling. "Girl, I seriously can't believe this still. You've wanted to carry a baby for as long as I can remember. I can't let my mascara run already." We laugh, and Amy returns to my hair. "But how did everything go with the Pack Doctor? You said everything was fine, but you didn't update me with details."

"I know, and I'm sorry I keep freaking out. But the Pack Doctor thinks I had implantation bleeding too... Which is a good sign."

"Oh, my God! So the doctor still thinks you're really pregnant?!"

My smile fades. "My hormone test results from the other day were still too low to be confirmed. She just told me an hour ago, and I couldn't stop crying."

Amy nods, stifling her excitement for me with shaky breaths.

"Don't give up hope yet, babe. But I'll stop asking in the meantime. You'll let me know when I'm going to be an aunt, though?"

My heart tugs with her words, threatening to make me bawl again. Amy shoots me an apologetic glance.

But I huff out a watery laugh. "Yes, A. I promise. And we don't have to stop talking about it. Jenny and I agreed that whether I'm pregnant or not, avoiding the truth will only give power to my OCD. I really want to enjoy it, even if I'm tempted to stay cautious."

Amy hugs me from behind, squishing her cheek against mine and smiling at me in the mirror above Noah's dresser. "Alright, then, I have plenty more questions. How's Noah with all this?"

Memories flood in of his hands on me this morning. I bite my lip, watching my cheeks flush in the reflection. "He's... excited."

Amy's eyebrows raise. "Girl, I can smell your horniness from here. Pregnancy hormones must be something else. How many times did you have sex last night? You hardly replied to my texts."

I giggle. "Well, I won't lie... We literally can't stop. I've never been this affectionate or lusty with anyone in my life."

Amy and I laugh, but a sinking suspicion tells me we're being watched. Glancing across the room, Amy yelps in surprise, and I jump in my seat at her reaction.

She grasps her heart. "Holy shit— Alpha Noah?! You're not supposed to be in here, especially not with those feral eyes on your bride! Human superstitions are serious business, you know!"

Noah's eyes are green, just like they were last night when I woke up with sex on the brain and jumped him. "I can't help it. I can smell my mate needing me from the kitchen."

As Noah barges in, Amy scurries out of the way, knowing better than to block an Alpha on the day of the full moon.

She waves her arms frantically to capture my attention. "You're not going to tell him to leave or close his eyes? I thought you wanted to follow more human wedding traditions."

My eyelids flutter as Noah's fingertips brush my neck, sliding lower and lower until they stop at my bloated belly. I grip his pressed ceremonial shirt, crumpling it with my desperation.

I give Amy a guilty smile. "I can't. I want him here. Just don't let him see the dress."

Amy cackles. "Why did I even try? I'm closing the door, then. Let me know when you want to get dressed."

I can hardly mumble a thank you before Noah presses one knee into the chair beside my hip, hovering over me. Hot lips clash against mine, just as feverish to feel my touch with a gripping palm on my lower back.

But Noah pulls back, interrupting our makeout. "Omega, you're shaking. What do you need?"

His eyes shift to yellow.

I bite back a smile at my doting Alpha. "I don't know. I'm a bit nervous."

"And I've still got you. I'll be by your side all night." He runs the cold tip of his nose down my cheek, grazing my neck until he gives my mark a delicate bite.

I jolt, knocking off my wrapped towel with a squeeze of my thighs.

Biting my lip, I peek up at Noah. "Oops…"

With a hard swallow, Noah only spends half a second gazing at my bare breasts before stroking my sore nipples. I flinch, gripping my breasts.

"Oh! Don't—"

"Fuck, sorry. Did that hurt? Oh, Goddess, you're so pregnant."

I burst into laughter, shaking his arm. "Noah…"

He growls at me, and I laugh even harder. But Noah is determined to tease me, his fingertips gliding up my inner thighs until a shiver runs through me. Lapping over my mark, Noah takes it a step further, circling his fingers over my oversensitive clit.

At the sound of my longing whimper, Noah's jaw clenches. "Fuck. No, we need to wait. I want everyone to hear that beautiful voice."

I shiver. Any and all nerves evaporate in an instant.

Noah's jaw tenses like he wants to pounce on me. I want him to look at me like this all night—in front of everyone. And I'm going to make sure of it.

I lean back, allowing him to get a good look at my swollen, ever-growing breasts. "Maybe I should help you now, so that it takes you longer to knot tonight. Get you warmed up and ready."

Noah purrs, his chest heaving as I slide off the chair. As I kneel in front of him, he groans. "Feisty isn't a strong enough word for you, Omega. You're going to kill me."

"Do you want me to stop?"

Dropping to his knees, he scoops me into his lap through a heavy kiss. As he grinds into me until I let out a soft moan, Noah grins. "No. Don't stop. You're right; I want to take my time with you later. Maybe enough to get my cute little Alpha to come out to play too."

My heart flips, but my wolf rolls over in our bond, enthralled by Noah's challenge. Noah's rough growl loses its playfulness, unleashing a wave of heat through my chest. I settle my open lips against his, breathing in his every exhale as I free his shaft from his ceremonial slacks. Noah sucks in a sharp gasp at my touch. The soft, desirous sound squeezes my core.

Taking his length into both hands, I shudder as he huffs into my mouth, gripping my bare hips for more. I work him from base to tip, giving the dripping head extra attention until Noah whimpers into my throat.

As his hand slips between our bodies, skating far past my lower abdomen, he purrs through my kiss at what he finds.

"You're dying for some love down here, aren't you?" He toys with the wetness between my legs, already lubricated enough to make slick sounds throughout the room. "Even after I mated you into the headboard all night?"

His golden eyes shine so bright that I fawn for him, exposing my neck.

As his fingers softly pulse against my dripping core, his tongue on my mark brings me to the edge.

But Noah isn't satisfied with this, leaning over me until my bare back meets the icy wooden floor. His burning tongue keeps me flushed and writhing as his fingertips stimulate my inner wall, curling over and over again until my hips squirm against the wood.

"Noah—" I gasp, struggling to contain my breath. "You feel so good, no matter how many times we do this—"

When my back arches, squeezing his fingers inside me, Noah lets out a helpless whimper.

"Fuck. My gorgeous— Oh, shit—" Thrusting deeper into my palm, Noah's muscles ripple above me until he comes across my chest. With shaking breaths, Noah's full focus turns on me. "Omega, look what you do to my body."

His piercing stare warms my cheeks as I writhe on the edge, his fingers beating faster and faster.

He's staring deep into my eyes. And soon, everyone will be staring at *us*.

"Ah!" I drop my head back, allowing the sensation of my mate inside me to overcome me. Noah pounds his palm against my clit as he thrusts his fingers inside me, massaging out a heavy orgasm while my legs squirm beyond my control.

As I continue to moan through every breath, shivers run up and down my body. But my groin aches for more as Noah eats me alive with his gaze.

Even as he delicately cleans my chest with my dropped towel, his yellow eyes tell me he feels the same.

"Good thing that was just a warm-up," I mutter.

Noah chuckles as he drags his nose up and down my neck, squeezing our chests together until I hum in delight.

But then he breathes a deep lungful of my neck to analyze my odd scent—just like he's been doing all week. I give up on reassuring him before I even try, allowing him to do his thing as I catch my breath beneath him.

Except this time is different.

Noah's muscles flex taut beneath my hands until his wolf has me effectively pinned.

"Oh—" He sniffs me again, digging his nose into my neck as he breathes faster and faster. "Oh!"

I flinch at his ticklish attack, unable to keep from laughing. "Noah, you big puppy! What's going on?!"

"No, Omega, I'm serious—"

I laugh even harder as his wolf smashes his head into mine in our bond, his happy tail zipping every direction like it wants to fly off his butt.

But Noah's wolf eyes regain my focus, his eager hands tightening by the second. "Aliya, I promised to stop saying this until it was true, but you're pregnant. You really are."

My head spins so hard that I have to grip Noah's shoulder, my nails digging in on their own. "Noah, I'm tired of repeating myself—"

"No, really!" He looks deep into my eyes, unable to catch his breath. Then he breaks into a gushing smile. "Your hormones hit another level. Like, way more than enough to make a test positive. You have to believe me."

Before I can speak, Noah digs into his pocket with shaking fingers, pulling out a crumpled pregnancy test box, smushed like it's been stepped on a couple times.

I burst into hearty giggles. "Oh, my God, what did you do to that thing?"

My racing heart makes me lightheaded as Noah pulls me to my feet.

But I don't have to worry about falling on my way to the bathroom; Noah hoists me into his arms, making me shriek in laughter as he dashes through the living room.

Amy's jaw drops as Noah carries me down the hallway—butt-naked and laughing too hard to speak. "I'm not going to ask!"

By the time we reach the toilet, my heavy laughter threatens to empty my bladder without my permission.

I wave frantically at Noah. "Oh, no, oh, God! Give me the test before I pee!"

"Shit—" Noah scrambles to open the pregnancy test box, yanking on the top so forcefully that he accidentally ejects the stick across the room. It comes to a spinning stop against the bathtub.

I gasp, dancing with my knees pinched together. "Noah!"

He scrambles on all fours after the test, thrusting it into my hands with the sharpest athleticism I've ever seen.

I pee on the stick just in time. For a solid few seconds, Noah and I stare at each other, our brains still catching up with the rapid succession of chaos.

But as my sudden, bellowing laughter disrupts my peeing, we have to lean on each other as we laugh so hard that we fall silent.

Although, I get the feeling Noah's eyes are watering from something else. He bounces on his heels in a squat, hardly able to wait for me to finish the test, let alone for the results to show. My heart aches with love for him. He really wants this baby.

I groan. "You are so damn cute! Your baby might kill me if they're even a fraction as adorable as you."

This warps Noah's eyebrows even further, sending him into full tears. "Omega, t-that's so sweet to think about—"

"Oh, my *love*..."

As we huddle in for a kiss, our lips wobble against each other as our tears combine against our cheeks.

Burrowing my fingers into his hair, I kiss him between deep scratches over his scalp. *Tell me what's going through your mind.*

Noah shakes his head, breaking our kiss to rub his eyes with a shy laugh. "I-I'm just— I'm *so* happy for us. Happy doesn't describe it. After all we've been through— After what *you've* been through... Goddess, Aliya, this is just—"

I can feel my face warp into the heaviest ugly cry. We erupt into laughter again.

Noah whines at my contorted face in his palms. "My sweet Omega. I love you so damn much."

"I love you too, my shy Alpha. I really do." I lean over the toilet, throwing my arms around him and squeezing as hard as I can.

With a fresh towel around me and Noah's mussed clothes reorganized, Noah and I fall into a silent, rocking trance, holding each other in the frigid bathroom as we wait for the test to reveal itself. He drags his fingers through my damp hair from root to tip, each strand cascading down my back like gentle raindrops. My eyes flutter shut.

Noah kisses the top of my head. His deep whisper rumbles against my cheek. "No matter what happens, I'm so grateful we're here together."

I have to breathe deeper to keep up with my throbbing heartbeat, especially as my instincts scream louder than ever.

Gazing up at Noah, I whimper through fresh tears. "I think I really am pregnant, Noah. I've been too scared to admit it because I want it to be true so badly, but I think you were right. Deep down, I felt it too: a little drop of something different in our bond. It's been there since my last day of school—the second you mated me."

He stares at me for a long minute, cradling my head in one palm as his heart races faster and faster against my ear.

Noah releases me in a rush. "Fuck, I don't care if it's too early. I'm looking at the damn test."

I bite my thumb as Noah snatches the test from the countertop, drawing it only a few inches from his face. He doesn't speak for a long time, green irises flickering between the result and the test key.

I clutch fistfuls of my towel, afraid to move. "What does it say?"

I can hardly breathe as I wait for Noah's response, his eyes still darting like he's struggling to grasp what he sees. I genuinely can't tell if that's good or bad, and I'm too scared to ask.

Finally, Noah mutters, "I-it's really faint, but—"

Noah bites his lip, shaking his head.

I tug on his wrist until he shows me the results.

It's faint, but it's clear enough to me: there's no way a negative test would have two lines.

I choke out a heavy sob as I meet Noah's eyes, but I'm not the only one; his palm covers his lips as his shoulders shake through tears.

Noah bends to wrap his arms around my waist, rubbing his wet cheek against my chest.

But then he drops to his knees, steadying my hips in his hands. As he kisses my belly through my towel, I suck in a sharp, sobbing breath.

Cradling his head to my stomach, I'm stunned as I meet my eyes in the mirror. They're a hot, irritated red and my nose is swollen, but I look so in love.

Dropping to my knees with Noah, I smash my salty lips to his, inhaling his hot breath.

As he holds me, I can't stop smiling, knowing tonight will only get better. "The best days of my life have all been with you, Noah."

His smile breaks our kiss. We rub our foreheads together as we hold each other.

By the time we can stop crying, Noah and I have done our

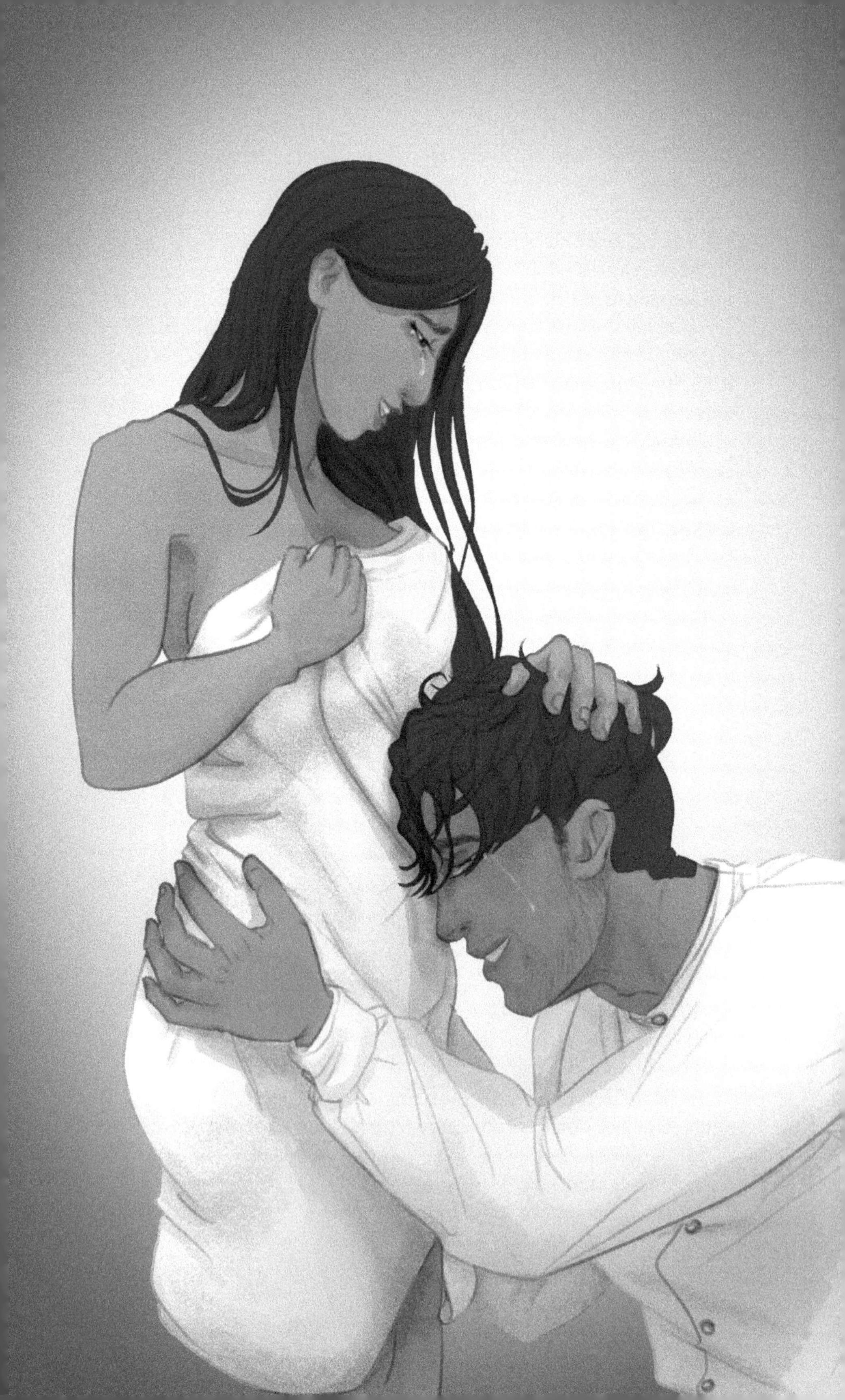

best to splash our faces with water and untangle my frazzled hair. When we finally make our reappearance in the living room, Amy's eyes widen when she sees my irresistible grin.

"You two look like you've been through hell. But happy hell?"

Bursting into laughter, I reveal my positive test to Amy's eager hands. "You're going to be an aunt, A."

Amy screams, sending Kira and Yasmine rushing into the room.

"What's wrong?!" Kira asks.

Amy blubbers over Kira, gripping her arms. "I'm going to be an aunt, babe! So are you!"

Within seconds, Yasmine is playfully slapping Noah's arm as he covers his bright red cheeks, Amy and Kira have me in a hug sandwich, and Rainn is sobbing happy tears in her mom's arms.

I brush my fingertips along my aching abdomen, my cheeks hurting from smiling.

I love absolutely everyone here, even this little speck of our baby beneath my fingertips.

34

I'm too delirious with happiness to feel nervous by the time I step into my Luna ceremony dress.

Everyone has given up on the human tradition of separating Noah and me before the ceremony, especially since Noah is glued to my hip. We've compromised by draping one of Noah's massive ceremonial robes over my shoulders, hiding my dress from Noah with dark blue velvet covered in embroidered, celestial embellishments. Noah's hands are already up both the robe and my slit skirt, but not for the reasons they will be later.

Noah has been stroking my belly in the back of Dave's car, and my wolf has taken over my senses.

"I've been so scared we wouldn't have this moment," I whisper.

"Shh, I've got you both."

The more he holds me and our tiny dot of a baby, the closer I huddle against his arm, loving his touch.

"My heart feels so much calmer when you hold me like that."

"Yeah? Good. Thank you for letting me know."

Dave clears his throat, and I know it's from the downpour of mushy emotions we're unloading in our collective scent.

Let yourself relax, my beautiful mate. We have a long night ahead, Noah mindlinks.

My eyes close as I hold his palm to my abdomen, allowing my body to soften in his arms.

But the second Noah guides me by the hand into the forest's ceremonial clearing, everything becomes more real.

Eyes bore into us for miles—half the community shifted into their wolves from all the excitement in the air. I shiver as Yasmine,

Dave, and Noah's advisors neaten his ceremonial gear and Amy and Rainn remove my robe to fix my dress.

When our dearest friends and family step away, allowing us to turn and see each other in the moonlight for the first time, I'm stunned by Noah's regal beauty in the moonlight.

The vest he's wearing shines unlike any of the regular embellishments I've seen on his monthly ceremonial clothes. Vivid stones shimmer on top of every embroidered moon and star. Jewels drip down his wide form, cascading down his shoulders and chest from thin, bright silver chains that hug his wide form. I had no idea the body jewelry Lilian and Rainn draped over my shoulders would be worn by Noah as well, but they suit Noah better than anything I could imagine him in, allowing his inner beauty to shine on the outside in a way that twists my heart.

And he's looking at me just the same. The moonstone he gave me glitters as I draw a shaky breath. The wind caresses my skin through my shimmering, sheer skirt, its embellished lacy edges softly licking my bare legs, but I don't feel cold; a fire ignites in my chest, barely quelled by the see-through, lacy bodice hugging my torso down to our budding baby.

Neither of us move as Noah's eyes roam down my body, skimming over me twice before landing on my eyes. His eyebrows flinch, and my heart tears as he dissolves into a soft, weepy smile.

"Aliya, I—" He shakes his head, striding toward me. His fingertips trail down my arms as my breathing rate rises. "In all the years g-growing up that I knew I'd be top Alpha someday, I could never imagine I'd be mated to a Luna as e-elegant, sweet, or loving as you. I don't know what to do, except t-thank you. For existing here, w-with me."

Tears escape down my smiling cheeks. I choke out a delighted laugh, leaning into my mate. "Thank you, Noah. After all that suffering in the past, I never thought I'd experience this pure bliss beside someone, let alone with a sweet, shy Lycan."

Melting into a soft smile, Noah takes my hands. He draws me closer for a delicate kiss. Grazing over my lips, Noah leaves behind a lingering warmth in my heart, reminding me I don't have to face anything alone anymore.

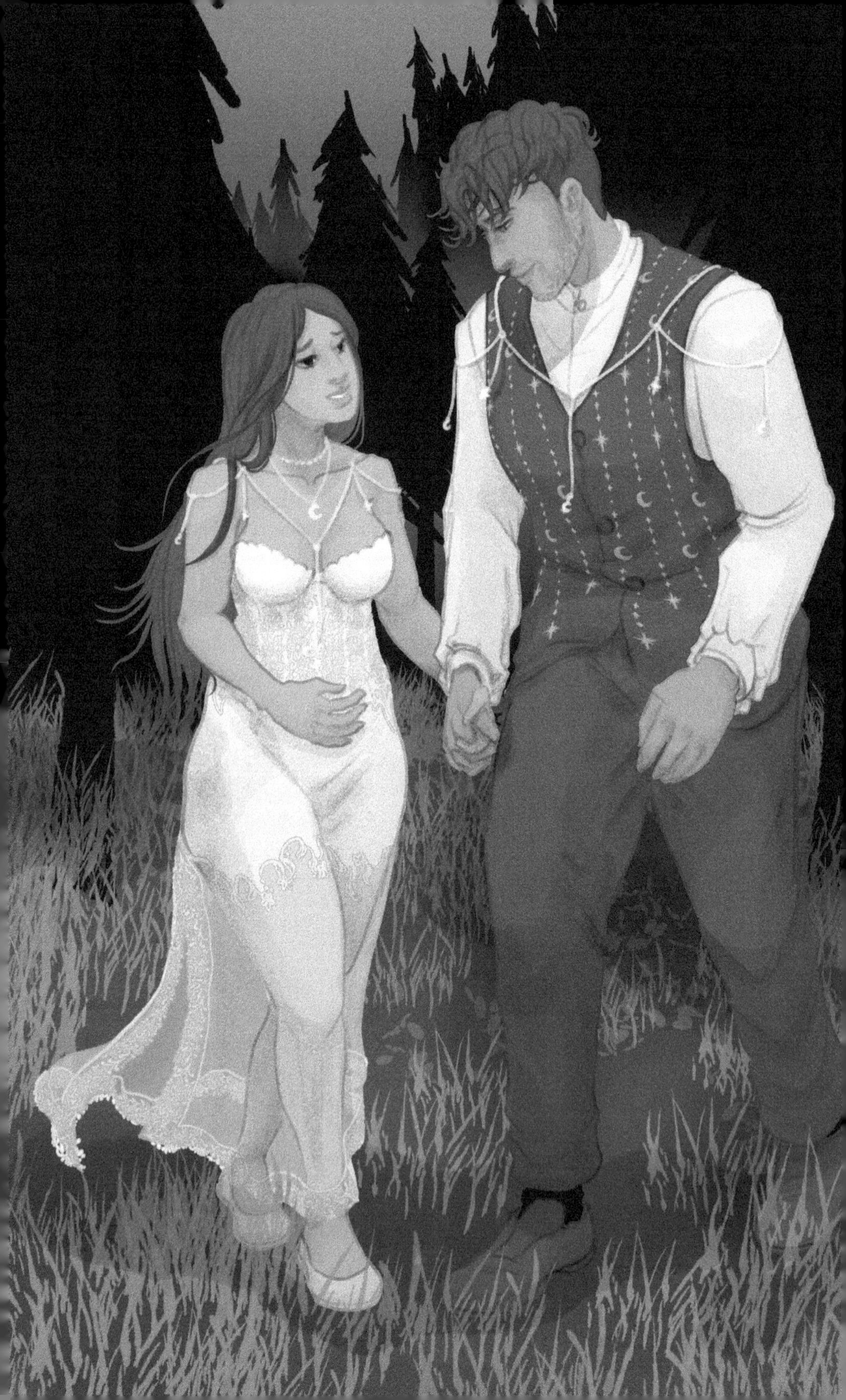

As we pull back to gaze into each other's eyes, Noah softens his shaking voice. "Ready, my soon-to-be Luna?"

My lungs shudder at his words, an uncontainable smile mixing with my gnawing anxiety. "No, I'm still nervous. I care about this moment so, so much."

Noah nuzzles my cheek, releasing enough protective pheromones to soothe an army.

I purr, rubbing myself all over him as my wolf takes over, high on pheromones.

Noah bites back a smile. "Oh, shit. Sorry, I got a little excited."

I giggle, taking a few extra breaths to calm my nerves. "Okay. I'm ready."

Taking Noah's hand, I stride deeper into the forest. The full moon shines between enormous treetops to light our way, but glowing eyes surround us, wolves gazing in wonder. By the time we reach the ceremonial stage, the tranquil river protects us from behind, but more wolves than I've ever seen in my life stand before us. This time, they're not just here for Noah and I as a mated pair; they're here to witness me vowing myself to every single one of them.

Nerves shake my bones, but I stand tall at Noah's side, even as the breeze whisks through my translucent skirt.

I want this. I want to be Luna.

And I want to seem proud to stand by Noah's side, but it's more than that. I want to seem proud to step into a nurturing role I've always dreamed of.

Dropping my hand, Noah addresses the crowd, his deep, rumbling voice echoing through the trees. "My father and mother's ability to lead Greenfield attracted me from a very young age. Not because of the power, but because of all of you. I could see how much it meant to you to have such loving figures at the head of the pack, and I wished for nothing more than to find a mate who would desire to step into the same role with me."

Noah drops his head, taking a deep breath.

"But as I grew older, I knew that was unrealistic. The care that your current Luna and our late Alpha put into this pack extended beyond their actions. It was their open, generous hearts that held the pack together, and that lifetime commitment can't be forced. But then I met your future Luna."

Noah pauses, his breath shaking as he turns to me, staring directly into my eyes. He opens his mouth to speak, but he chokes up, dropping his chin to his chest.

Oh, my sweet mate. Rejoining Noah's side with a teary-eyed smile, I grasp his hand, giving it a soft squeeze. *I've got you too, my shy Alpha.*

Noah meets my eyes with a weepy laugh. His wolf's intensified love for me washes goosebumps across my body.

My mate keeps his gaze on me as he addresses the crowd in mindlink, unable to speak aloud. *When I met your future Luna, she was already a Luna in heart and mind. I swear she was born to share the purest love I've ever felt, but it's more than that. She feels it with her full soul. And she wants to share it with you.*

Noah clears his throat, kissing my forehead as tears warp my expression.

He protects my head from onlookers with shaking hands, tilting me to face only him. "S-sorry, I just— I just can't help myself. I love you so much, and there's no way to truly express it all."

"I love you with my whole soul, Noah."

As I draw him in for a tender kiss, the pack bond buzzes with excitement.

Except strangely, all I can focus on is Noah. He closes his eyes, taking his time to hold me despite the entire pack waiting for the ceremony to continue.

After drying my tears, I nuzzle his nose. "It's okay. I'm ready, even if I'm crying."

Noah's grin fills me with so much warmth, I could sob again.

But he releases me just in time, holding my hand as he faces the crowd.

After a deep breath, Noah's calm voice extends across the forest. "It is the honor of my lifetime to present to you your next Luna."

Okay, here it is: I'm about to show them how I feel about becoming the Luna of their pack, and with wolves, every body gesture matters.

As I step forward, I soften my shoulders and keep my smile loose, showing the pack I'm not a threat.

The crowd falls still, entranced with my every movement. I scan the forest before me, searching for the reason they're gawking. With such a massive crowd, it shouldn't be possible to hear the slow wind whispering through the leaves. Am I doing something weird?

But Noah stares just the same, his eyes locked on to my face in awe. Even his wolf falls still.

When no one voices a complaint, I realize they're not disturbed, concerned, or angry with me. They're giving me space to speak.

But all I can see are desperate eyes staring back.

Shit, I hate being the center of attention, and so much is riding on me. If I'm a disappointment to them, I don't think I can stomach it.

I cover my belly on instinct, feeling vulnerable for the first time tonight.

But when Noah steps closer, his scent cocoons me in his familiar sweetness. I straighten my shoulders.

No. I can do this.

Clearing my throat, I try my best to speak up, even if my voice quivers through every syllable. "H-hi, um—" I place my palm over my heart, steadying my breath.

As I look at my muddy shoes, I have the sudden urge to remove them, sinking my feet into the mud. The second I do, my feet press into the soggy earth, and my eyes are lured up to the Moon Goddess, herself.

She's gleaming tonight. I've never felt her so clearly, her massive nightlight steadying my heart until all I can feel is the deep pull of fresh air in my lungs and the aching, sugary love in my chest.

My wolf steps forward, speaking with me. "In human culture, we say our vows to our spouses as we marry them, committing ourselves to them for life. But I've always seen it as more than that. It's a commitment to a combined lifestyle, including welcoming everyone they love. Today isn't just about your top Alpha and I, it's about all of us as a pack, coming together as a family, which is something I've felt every day since I arrived here."

I take a deep breath, struggling to keep finding my voice. There's a deeper reason I want to be Luna, and sharing it exposes more than I've been comfortable with for a long time. But as one sweet woman wipes her smiling tears in the front row, my heart swells with protective love. I know what I have to say.

"I-I know how it feels to feel unsafe at home," I choke out. "Which is why I want nothing more than to be a home for you to return to. As my vow to you, I vow to represent unconditional, maternal love in every action I take as Luna. I promise to cherish each of you as my own, through life and in death, so that although we might not know each other personally, you'll never truly be alone. It's an honor to love you, Greenfield."

When I glance back at Noah, he's not the only one crying. Lilian is rubbing his back—the most intimate I've seen the two since we've met. Tears streak her cheeks, yet she hands Noah a tissue from her dress pocket.

But before Lilian steps forward to continue onto the next ceremonial step, I blurt out, "Wait."

My heart hammers into my throat as everyone falls into silence. Noah's eyebrows lift with my rising nerves and Lilian frowns, but I extend my hands to Noah.

Melting into a smile, Noah grabs hold. We stand facing each other, the entire pack awaiting my next words. But as I gaze deep into my mate's eyes, his pure, doting trust stirs a magnifying excitement in my heart. I've never felt more ready to confess my deepest love for someone in front of others.

With a shaking voice, I pull Noah closer. "Noah Greenfield, my sweet, gorgeous mate."

He bites his lips. The emotion in his eyes stings mine hot. I hug his hands to my chest, struggling to stifle the rising, aching longing in my lungs.

"I'd first like to thank you for allowing me to walk alongside you. Our marks connected us down the soul, but I feel like our souls were already connected—maybe for lifetimes. Every second we've spent together, I've gathered a deeper understanding of what it really means to feel loved, to love, and how I can love myself. I can't think of a greater gift, and I only hope that I can share even a fraction of this gift back with you."

I take a deep, shuddering breath through Noah's rising emotions. His tears spill over as he drops his head, leaning in closer. Releasing one of his hands, I catch his tears with my fingertips.

"I vow to be your lifelong witness. No matter how horrible or wonderful life might be for us, I'm here to share your pain, your love, and your peace. I vow to nurture the mind and body of that beautiful black wolf who nurtures all of Greenfield—" Noah drops his head, and I place my palm over the left side of his chest. "And I vow to protect this big, generous heart that holds everyone in its loving safety. I'll be there to hold you in return, and defend you to my last breath. I love all of you, Noah."

Cupping my cheeks, Noah drops our heads together. His hot, tearful breath brushes my lips. "*Aliya—*"

All at once, I spill over. I whimper through hot tears, and Noah's creased forehead settles with his soft, joyous laugh.

"I love all of you too, and more— I—" Noah clears his throat, snuggling me closer. His deep voice softens into a gentle whisper against my lips. "I love everything you are, everything you wish to be, and everything you're not. It's a gift to simply know you. But to also get to share my soul with you is so— So *healing* and fulfilling, that I—" Noah shakes his head, chuckling as we dry each other's gushing tears. "I can't imagine myself enjoying my life anywhere else but by your side. Goddess, I don't even want to stop holding you now, but I will. I'm dying for you to finally become our Luna."

My heart flips as Noah leans in to softly kiss me. Humming against my lips, he strokes my cheeks with his thumbs as I brush down his mark. He pulls away with a weepy smile, and I let out a bright, giddy laugh through my tears.

Even though my interruption wasn't part of our ceremony plans, let alone traditional, Lilian gives me a genuine, proud smile. She steps forward to meet me as Noah steps back, and I know it's time to offer her my hands.

I can't stop shaking. Lilian meets my eyes, her sadness pouring into me even before her scent hits.

"*Luna,*" I breathe, my lip wobbling with hers. "Oh, Goddess, your poor heart—"

She breaks into a smile, shaking her head. "I'm happy. I promise you, I'm happy."

She's not. She's grieving so badly that I'm nauseated.

But before I can soothe her, Lilian addresses the crowd, her powerful voice startling me with a jolt of my shoulders.

"Nurturing each pack member from pup to elder is no easy task, and the next Luna before you knows this." She readjusts her hands in mine, bouncing them to emphasize every statement she makes as if it'll send their weight further into the crowd. "I have never been more confident in another Omega's ability to lovingly take on the world."

My heart flips.

Lilian takes my cheeks in her palms, kissing my forehead before placing hers against it.

"It is an honor to pass on my title to you, Luna, by the Moon Goddess's grace, and your Alpha's permission."

My heart rate sprints, hardly allowing me to breathe.

This is it. I'm about to become my Alpha's Luna.

Lilian steadies me as I wobble, remaining by my side as Noah drops to his knees in front of me.

I gasp, teetering in shock.

He wasn't supposed to do that; he's putting himself into a submissive position, surrendering himself below me in front of the whole pack.

Anxious wolves rustle through the forest, but Noah holds me by the waist, redirecting my focus.

"Breathe with me, Omega."

I stare deep into his eyes. They're so light in color that I know his wolf is fully present.

In his eyes, there's no fear.

I've never seen anyone so brave, so secure in who he is, submitting himself with so much riding on his shoulders.

His protective pheromones surround me, but this time, they're laced with a hunger that strikes me in the gut. I can't find my breath, but my belly finds its fire, boiling throughout every molecule of me. With it comes a confidence that leaps higher than I've ever felt, widening my chest until I embrace my full self.

I don't want to hide anymore.

Yes, this is right. This is where I'm supposed to be.

"By the Moon Goddess's grace…" Noah licks my palm in preparation.

His protruding fangs catch the moonlight. I shudder, his desirous stare piercing my heart.

"I pronounce you Luna of Greenfield."

He sinks fangs into the meat of my palm. My nerves send a shockwave throughout my system, wobbling my knees.

But Noah makes it as quick and painless as possible, more like a heavy pinprick. As he licks the blood clean from my palm, I weep in joy; wolves howl across the forest for me. My eyes flutter shut.

Each and every pack member becomes vibrantly clear in our pack bond, flickering like little candles blinking to life in my heart.

I'm both so in love and so terrified that I sob, the weight of each being within me feeling too important to hold alone.

But I'm not holding them alone. Noah's presence touches every single candle, providing the oxygen to each fire.

Noah stays on his knees, immersing himself in my scent as he nuzzles my belly. When I lift his chin with both palms, aching to see my mate's face, the crowd falls silent once more.

Nothing I can do could compare to the honor he just granted me, but I want to show Noah how deeply I love him by baring my body to him. In front of everyone.

I drop to my knees, shivering through every wave of emotion in our bond. He holds my cheeks just like I hold his, his enamored focus flicking between my eyes. When I let out an uncontainable whimper, Noah rolls his forehead over mine. He strokes the back of my hair like he needs to hold all of me, hugging our baby against his body as he crushes my nose to his.

"I feel like I exist on this earth to do exactly this, with exactly you," I say. "Thank you for existing here to do this with me. I love you."

Noah dips to wrap his arms beneath my butt, tugging me against him until I'm in his lap. I whimper as Noah nuzzles into my chest, his wide hands dragging up my back until we press together as close as we can.

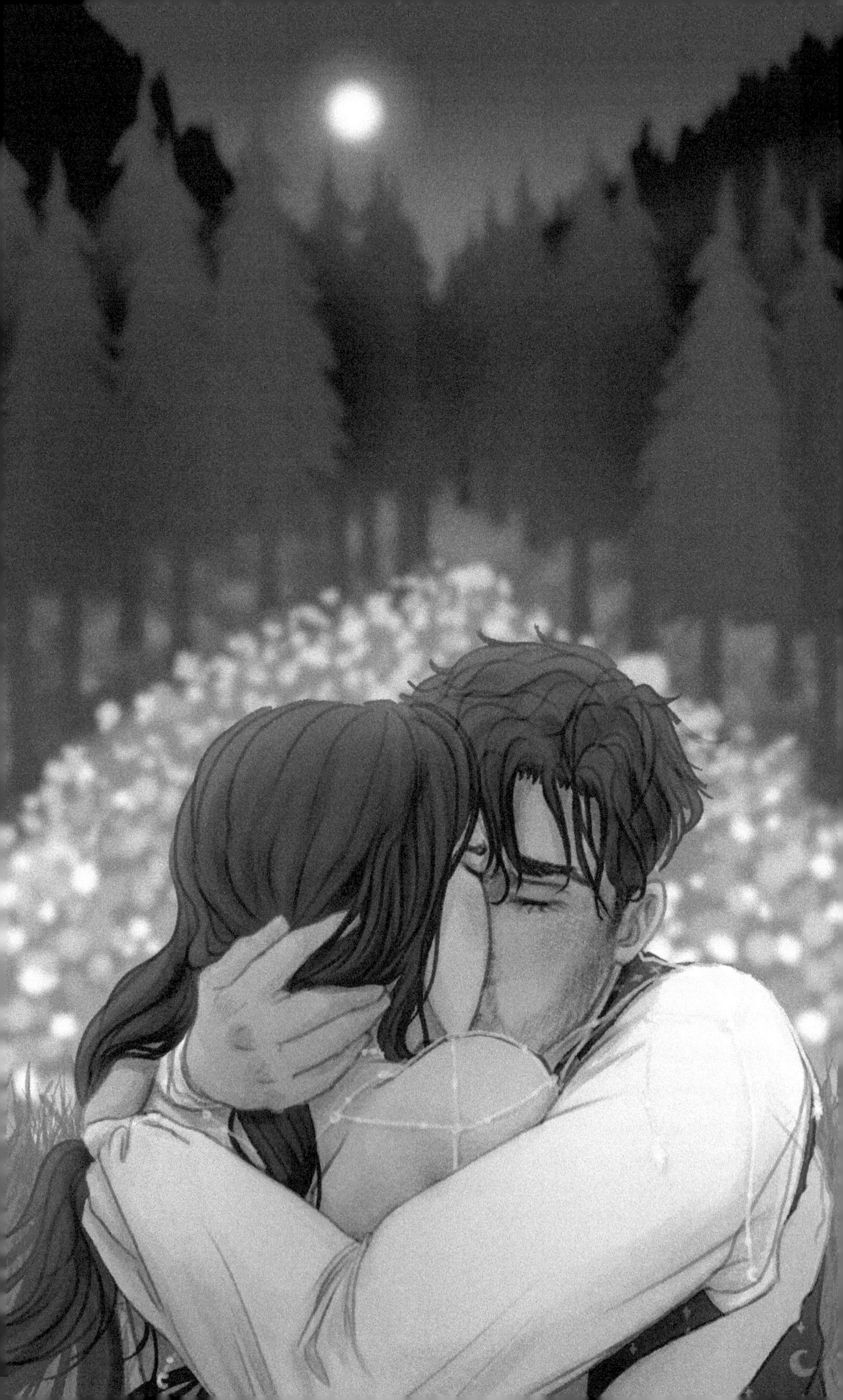

His voice comes out rough and wet. "I-I love you so fucking much, I—"

He smashes me into a full-body kiss. Thousands of wolves erupt in howls. It intensifies the bond between Noah and me, reverting my focus into something else entirely.

As Noah's whines deepen into mating growls, my body tingles with his every sound, knowing tonight is about to take a drastic turn.

35

Our limbs tangle on their own, just like they do in our nightly cuddle balls.

But neither of us are as relaxed as we are in bed. There's an urgency in the speed of our frantic breaths, electrifying the gaps between our bodies like it's daring us to meld into one. Noah's grip seems to consume me, pleasure erupting from my mouth when his nose meets my mark.

"Ah!"

My breath tightens into short rasps; I just moaned in front of a crowd of thousands of wolves.

But when I look to our side at our pack, I've never seen anything like it. Every single soul is enraptured with Noah and me, analyzing our movements. Some already strip bare, figuring we're getting the mating ceremony started.

And as Noah focuses on my pleasure, first and foremost, there's no denying I'm at the center of it all.

Oh, fuck. This is intense.

"I'm starting to freak out," I whisper.

Noah growls, his wolf threatening to break through to protect me.

But that's not what I want.

Before it's too late, I grip his hair how he likes it, burying myself into his lips to redirect him. *No, Alpha. Don't hold back for me. My fear is just fear, and it's only here because I care so much about this moment with you. Mate me. Mate me in front of everyone.*

My wolf's demand only excites Noah's wolf more, his resurging fangs accidentally pricking my lip. He licks the drop of blood clean for me, cradling my head until I'm aching for more of his lips.

I pull back. "Enough. Kiss me again."

His eyes ignite with a newfound fire. He draws me in, his deep voice rumbling against my lips. "There's my feisty Alpha."

Noah happily obliges my demanding wolf, moaning into my mouth as he meets my tongue. *When you stepped forward tonight, it blew my fucking mind. You were already my Luna. Everyone could see it.*

I whine, my body dipping against his as our frantic makeout quickly edges into something more. *I wanted so desperately to be your Luna. I always have.*

Noah growls into my throat, sliding his hands down my back until he can rock my hips over his cock. Pleasure rises higher and higher in my groin, inching up my spine until I can feel it swirling in my chest.

"A-ah! Oh, Goddess, that's good."

"Good girl. Tell me what you want."

Oh, God. If we don't stop now, we'll want to mate right here. But we planned on mating in the field, as per the usual tradition.

Our wolves have other plans.

"More," I gasp. "I want more. I don't want to stop."

Noah's breath hitches at my words. When he groans through his exhale, it comes out as such a deep purr that I shudder.

Noah licks my neck, a spike of pleasure penetrating my core even though all I'm doing is rubbing up on my mate. Gripping fistfuls of my ass, Noah flicks his tongue across my mark, and I know it's over for me. With each lick, my core clenches like he's inside me.

"Alpha! Ah!" My fingernails dig into his back as my knees spread, allowing him full access to my soaked panties.

Holy shit. The sensation is so strong from all the emotions we're feeling, that I'm already about to come.

As Noah's hard shaft mercilessly stimulates my clit through my clothes, my voice comes out in breathy gasps.

"W-wait, stop, I-I'm already—" I meet Noah's yellow eyes. "We're not— in the field—"

Noah yanks his hips back just before I come, prowling over

me with rolling shoulders. The longer I writhe in desperation to finish, the more Noah comes back to his senses. "Fuck. Sorry. My fucking wolf took over."

"I want him here, don't resist him. Please, I'm so close—" My wolf whines through me, and Noah winces.

His hands shake as he strokes my head and face, halting my wriggling hips with a hand over my belly.

"But you don't want to come just yet, right? Hold it in, my love. You can do it." His eyes flicker an even brighter yellow as he eyes my squirming body up and down. "Hold it in, so I can make you come ten times harder than this in the field."

This only arches my back more, failing to subdue the pleasure in my groin.

"Can you hold it, love?"

I gasp as it hits me anyway, unrelenting heat pooling between my legs. "I-I can't—"

Kneeling between my spread thighs, Noah glides his hands up my slit skirt in a heartbeat.

Two fingers slip into my panties, penetrating me in one, tender push. He curls his fingers, rocking my hips with just enough pressure to make me grip his wrist for more.

I can barely choke out my words, my approaching orgasm fuzzing out my breath. "A-ah! *Harder*—"

He adds a third finger, prodding my inner wall so quickly that my legs jerk with pleasure.

Noah was right; my orgasm hits me harder than it would've the first time, field or no field. He collects my moans with hungry lips, his wet fingers slowing into a gentle pulse as I shudder. My nipples harden in the cool summer night, gasping through the lasting effects as I gaze into his eyes.

"Fuck, that's my good girl. You did it, Aliya."

My heart spikes into my throat when I realize what he means; I just came in front of *everyone*.

I almost can't believe it. That it's physically possible for me after all I've been through, and that I'd also love it so much.

And I know it's because I'm doing this with Noah. Even if it's only my boosted hormones, the fact that they're boosted means just as much; I wouldn't be carrying Noah's baby without him loving my heart to safety either. God, I can't believe we made it here.

And now that we're here, I'm craving more.

I whimper, my thighs squeezing Noah's arm hard enough to let him know what I want. "Hurry. Take me to the field."

Our bond erupts with anticipation as Noah's face hardens into lust.

"Fuck," he breathes. "I'm not sure I can handle how good this is."

All I can do is moan, my legs twitching with leftover pleasure as he slips his fingers from me.

Noah helps me to my feet, doing the work for my shaking knees. But then his scent surges with something primal, stopping our forward progress.

In a split second, Noah is behind me. Holding me up with hungry hands, Noah caresses my breasts, sides, and belly—suggesting to mate from behind with hungry, low growls. The mere sound of it tells me he's all instinct, urging my wolf to the surface.

I drop my head back, moaning with every kneading slip of his touch over my stinging nipples.

"Alpha, *please*— The field. Or else I'm not going to last."

He gasps. "Fuck! S-sorry." As we stumble deeper into the forest together, Noah groans in frustration. "My damn wolf is out of control—"

I stop him mid-dash, rubbing my horny scent all over his chest. "Stop forcing him down, Alpha. Let him out with mine."

With a desperate huff, Noah kisses me all over, urging me through the trees. As he guides me to the field, I'm aware of a large mass of wolves following us. Watching us.

My heart pumps harder than ever from their stares, but since all I can see and smell is my hungry Alpha, each heartbeat feeds into my pulsing groin.

I whine, and Noah nuzzles me even closer, dragging his nose along the most sensitive spots of my neck.

"Mate. My gorgeous, sexy mate. I cannot *believe* I get to be with you for the rest of my life. I can't be this lucky." Noah's locked stare is so intense that I can't stop shivering. It's a painful effort to keep from tackling him.

But as we court each other to the middle of the field with clashing lips and eager hands, the last of my fear evolves into excitement, knowing he's right here with me. And I'm right here with him.

Only paces from the largest tree in the field, Noah strips his ceremonial robe, revealing his flowy undershirt and embellished vest, glittering in the moonlight with his every heavy breath. I come to a halt, facing him. His fierce stare sweeps my body.

"I want you." The depth to Noah's half-shifted voice spikes a thrill through my core. "...My Luna."

That's all I can take before I grip his vest in both fists, cinching our bodies together. When he succumbs to my grip in front of his entire pack, my neck erupts in goosebumps. Every slip of our tongues taste like our combined pheromones, pushing my wolf further to the surface until she's all that's left of me, purring and writhing against my mate.

Noah growls, gripping fistfuls of my ass as he rubs his bulge against me, but that's not enough for him.

"You smell so good, Omega. You want it that bad too, huh?"

"Yes, Alpha." My voice comes out airy as I nuzzle his lips, seeking more of him.

"Then how about I prepare you to mate?" He purrs against my lips. "Tell me, Luna, should I use my mouth, or my hands?"

My heart hammers into my throat. He's ridiculously skilled with his tongue, enough to have me squirming at the thought of it. Noah takes note of my rolling hips, his eyes devouring me with want.

"Your mouth," I whisper. "You're too good at it."

His gaze lands on mine. We hold our stares, excitement rising in our bond with each passing second. But Noah doesn't dive between my legs yet; with one big, eager palm gripping the back of my head, he dives for my lips. Each kiss Noah places on my mouth steals my breath. Not only is he working my lips so hard that each press sends a jolting ache through my heart muscles, but I'm constantly aware of the eyes on us. Staring at our every move.

Can I really handle Noah going down on me in front of everyone?

But as Noah's hand slides past my lower abdomen, his fingers prod my clit just as he slips his tongue back into my mouth.

Every concern melts away as I release a sharp moan against his lips. The soft fabric distributes Noah's touch across the entire base of me, each rub tightening my grip on his shoulders with how luxuriously deep it hits. I rock my hips into his wide palm, kneading every bit of pleasure out of him.

He releases my lips with a tender pop. "That feel good, Luna?"

I squirm at the sound of my new title, heightening Noah's growling purrs.

"I hope it feels good." He prods me faster, making my knees dip under the weight of his touch.

But when I give the tip of his shaft a massaging squeeze through his pants, Noah growls.

"Don't. I want to outlast you at least twice."

My heart trips over itself. "O-oh, my—"

Noah steals my words, dropping to his knees to plant heavy kisses across my groin. Parting the slit of my skirt, his fingertips brush my thigh. We lock eyes. I shudder as his stare roams across my face.

"Beautiful." Noah's whisper tickles between my thighs as he drags his nose up my clit.

"O-oh, God— Alpha—"

Noah kisses my wet core through my lacy white panties, his hands skating behind my thighs. I dip against his lips with every kiss he plants, his pressure increasing with each shy whimper that escapes me.

Until his lips close around my clit.

"O-oh!"

I want you to feel it. How fucking good you make me feel, just watching you enjoy yourself, Noah mindlinks.

My focus latches onto Noah's emotions through our bond. His pleasure in reaction to mine has a domino effect, expanding in my groin until I double over his head.

I can't hold back the loudest moan I've had all night as Noah keeps his promise, preparing me to mate with the full pad of his tongue between my thighs. Suckling my clit through my panties, Noah grasps my hips to keep his hot mouth on me. My knees spread as my fingers dig into his scalp with a grateful massage.

When my cheeks burn hot enough to make my eyelids flutter, I grip Noah for stability. "A-Alpha, it's too good—"

He hums against my clit, gripping my panties' fragile waistband, and I groan.

"Oh, *no*, I—"

No? Noah's ravenous eyes flick up to mine, shooting a knee-collapsing jolt through my groin as his tongue rests just above my bare clit.

He stopped.

My hips jerk into his tongue, threatening to drop me to the floor with how weak his hot tongue makes my knees. "Ah! Not 'no!' I can't stand up, Alpha! I'm going to come *hard*—"

He eases my melting body to the floor, ravishing me with weighty licks the whole way down. Settling on my back, I no longer have the words to describe my pleasure, my hips bucking into his lips as Noah's tongue glazes my bare flesh.

My ankles hook behind his shoulders on instinct, pulling him closer. Noah purrs, dragging his tongue up and down my labia.

But just when my back arches in delight, rolling the back of my head through the dirt, Noah pulls back. His golden eyes brighten with every breath. I blink, and he's tearing at his pants.

"Mate— I want to—" He grunts, unable to unfasten his pants button with how massive he's grown; tenting is impossible with how thick he is. "I want to really give it to you. I want to feel you come around me."

My heart flips at how bold he's being, but my pussy flexes faster, gaping wider for him by the second. I scramble to free him, but neither of our shaky hands can untangle the throbbing mess he's made of himself.

He gasps. "Fuck, I want to help you so badly—"

When Noah winces in pain, my protective instincts take over. Gripping the top of his waistband, I yank hard. The button whizzes past my shoulder. But I only have one focus, diving to soothe him with my lips.

"Holy—" Noah groans as my tongue meets his throbbing tip, flexing rapidly against my touch.

He takes my cheeks into his palms, drawing me off him. "Not like this, gorgeous. I wasn't done spoiling you."

Within seconds of tender kisses on my mark, he has me splayed on my back. I can smell how much he adores me. Heat burns my cheeks down to my neck as Noah's heavy-lidded eyes lock onto mine.

My knees widen as he rubs his bare shaft along my dripping pussy, coating himself.

I grip his thighs, unable to stop my hips from squirming. "Alpha—"

"I've got you, Luna."

As Noah smashes our lips together, he reaches between us to grip his shaft in one hand. I squirm as he slips his tip against my clit over and over again, pushing higher and higher moans from me. Fistfuls of dirt do nothing to stop my rising orgasm, pressure building in my groin. I tear my lips from Noah to cry out to the moon.

"Alpha! I want you inside—"

He slips into me all at once, my soaked pussy welcoming his engorged shaft. When he bottoms out inside me, my knees squirm beside my shoulders from how full I feel.

"*Oh!* I'm—"

Noah drags the entire length of himself back out of me, his heaving breath tickling my nipples through my sheer top. It feels like his shaft extends forever, tugging more and more pleasure out of me until he plunges in one more time, pushing a gush of fluid from me.

I'm not just panting, I'm mewling for him with every breath. I writhe in the dirt as Noah gradually speeds faster into me, my pussy squeezing him so hard that he moans.

"Shit— You feel so fucking *good*—" Noah rubs my clit as I cry out in pleasure, his thick cock leaving no nerve untouched.

"*Noah*—"

Every muscle in my body squirms as I come, burst after burst of fluid from my core washing me in a tingling warmth.

As I whimper in bliss, rolling my head and hips through the

grass to indulge in more of his slow strokes, Noah's flexing cock prods my cervix, still clinging on for more.

"Gorgeous. So fucking gorgeous."

"Mmm, Alpha, thank you."

Noah hovers over me, dipping his rippling frame to give me the softest kiss he can manage. It's not until his lips soften my moans that I realize pleasure-filled cries echo all around us, hundreds of couples mating in the most passionate mating ritual I've seen.

Noah nuzzles my mark with a calming blanket of his scent. "I'm so fucking proud of you. Because you let yourself go, they did too. Your pleasure is powerful, Luna."

My heart leaps into my throat. I can't believe this, but he's right. I just screamed my Alpha's name and came in front of thousands of wolves.

And they loved it.

My heart gallops as bodies tangle around us, burning brighter in our pack bond as their own bonds strengthen.

And I'm feeling braver than ever. Loose and delirious enough to crave more, now that I've had a taste.

I want Noah to feel how ridiculously in love I am right now. He's the one who inspires so much pleasure in my life, even when we're not having sex. I want Noah to feel wanted.

Gliding my fingertips down his neck, I trace his faint scar from my mark. His body's resulting pleasure hits me straight in the heart through our bond.

He loves it.

I kiss his mark this time, relishing in the little shiver he gives me. "It's your turn to be pampered, gorgeous. Let me take a turn on top."

Noah freezes, nervous anticipation racing through his side of our bond.

Oh. Maybe it's because we're being watched. No matter how much he loves it, me being on top puts him in a submissive, vulnerable position. I'd be making him into a prime target.

But that doesn't seem to be Noah's main concern, stroking my cheek as he gazes into my eyes. "A-are you sure? I was going to keep treating you."

But his heavy cock prods inside me for more, and his emotions whirl with excitement.

I inhale his yearning, sweet scent. My eyes are tempted to roll back from how delicious he smells. "If you want it, I mean it, my big, shy Alpha. I want to show you how much I love you, with my body. Let me nurture you."

Noah's shy stare softens his massive frame, but his cock flexes harder, intensifying his breath.

Oh, my God. A dominance is emerging from within me from seeing him like this.

But is that safe to express in front of everyone?

I test the waters, stroking Noah's mark as lightly as I can with a slow drag of my nose.

Noah shudders, pulling in and out of me with an automatic buck of his hips. His yearning grip tells me enough, but then his scent explodes with desire—and my wolf takes over.

"My shy Alpha," she purrs. "You like it when I hold you during sex, don't you?"

He buries his face into my shoulder, hugging me tighter.

Then he nods.

My heart flips, but my wolf puffs her chest. "Sit up, beautiful."

He obeys me, and the pack notices. My heart hammers, but it's nowhere near as vulnerable as Noah's—so raw that he's hardly able to hold eye contact.

And here I am, not even minding we're being watched anymore. It's all thanks to Noah. I want to make him feel as safe to mate in public as he's made me.

"Don't worry about anything else in the world but us. If you're uncomfortable, or even unsure, we'll stop. I'll protect you, Alpha. You're safe."

He huffs out sharp, desirous breaths, but they're laced with fear. "I-I feel safe with you, but this side of me, it's— It's different, it's—"

I shake my head. "I *love* this side of you. He's just as gorgeous as every other piece of you. Let me play with him." With my soft lick on his mark, Noah huddles closer. "I want you to feel good."

Noah's heavy breath shifts to one small, pleading whimper.

A cascade of desire drips down my spine, urging my hips over him as he sits back on his heels. I cup his cheeks, staring straight at him as I ease myself back over his cock.

"Oh—" Noah's eyelashes flutter, his voice a shaky whisper.

He grasps fistfuls of my hips, aiding himself inside me until he prods my cervix.

But Noah freezes, his eyes wide. It startles me into halting in place over him.

"Shit. I-is it okay to be so deep now? If you're— If you're carrying our—" He swallows hard.

Our bond erupts with emotions when I realize we're not mating for the same purpose anymore: we're already pregnant.

"The baby will be fine, love. They're tucked away and safe." My smile erupts from me as I whisper these words, threatening to send me into tears.

Noah cuddles me closer, kissing me as deeply as he can through his smile. His breath pulses against my cheeks, fingers embedded into the roots of my hair as he rolls my hips over him. I control the speed, easing him to the cool earth as my breasts press flat against his chest.

"Relax, Alpha. Let me mate you too. Set your wolf free with me."

Noah whines louder than he has all night, his scent bursting. But it's not his usual musk; his scent blooms with a flowery submission.

My eyes shoot open, but Noah's lust-clouded kisses remain fully in the moment, even as my Alpha-like musk flushes his cheeks.

He likes it. He likes when I'm dominating him.

An excitement I've never felt before crashes through me, urging me to drop my ass over him over and over again, crashing down on his lap. Noah exposes more of his neck to me, and the last of my self-control evaporates.

Dropping myself down on him and staying there, I rock over his cock, craving the soft, shy moans escaping his lips.

"*Luna...*" His pleads send tingles up to my belly button with every thrust, his shaft hitting everywhere I love at once.

"Ah! Alpha." I lift myself back off him, only to lower myself in a slow, agonizing press of our bodies melding.

With longing whimpers, Noah tugs my ass down over him until I flood the space between us with wet heat, squirting over Noah's pelvis. Each pump is accompanied by my frantic wolf licking Noah's mark, the urge to re-mark him stronger than ever in my chest.

Noah suddenly hugs my hips in place, freezing his. "Stop."

He shudders against my chest, whimpering and gasping.

I cup his cheeks. "Noah?! Are you okay—"

"No, I need this to last forever. I don't want to knot you yet."

Instead of relief, his words set a tumultuous fire in me. I want to fuck myself over him even harder, squeezing the pleasure into my thoughtful, gorgeous mate. I rub his scalp, dropping my head back as Noah trades to kiss my mark.

His heavy cock has grown so thick that just his flexing feels like he's digging deeper, tempting me to keep bouncing over him.

"Love, just let yourself feel good," I say.

"But you want more too, I can feel it. If I knot you, you'll have to wait too long. And I can't help but feel like your wolf needs something."

As we kiss each other, nuzzling and squirming in an attempt to hold still, Noah suddenly sucks in a gasp.

When we meet eyes, his wolf leaps out through his deepening voice. "You want me to lose myself in you, don't you, Luna?"

I whimper, crumbling against his lips as his claws prick my skin.

"Yeah? Turn around for me."

I gasp as he exits me, leaving me gaping and cold. But my shaking limbs manage to keep me upright long enough to turn around, my skirt sliding back over my soaked thighs.

Noah peels the fabric up and over my hips, baring my ass for the whole pack.

But I love it. Kira mates my best friend against a tree, Amy's busty mating dress proving more useful than ever as Kira tongues Amy's nipples. Yasmine steals a gorgeous Omega woman's attention for the night, her casual partner seeming to enjoy herself as much as me with gasping, high-pitched moans. Dave passionately mates with his mate of ten years, kissing as if they're teenagers again as their hips frantically collide.

And I've never felt freer.

I'm shocked back into my body as Noah grazes my shoulders with his fangs, his sweating chest brushing my bare skin.

"I love you so fucking much, Luna. I've never been this turned on."

And I can feel it, his tip far larger than normal as it prods my entrance.

"Oh, God, it's too big, Alpha."

Noah rubs my clit in slow circles, kissing my mark as his tip pulses against my entrance. I squirm, rocking my hips back over him until he finally slips in, stealing the air from our lungs.

"Fuck," Noah hisses.

By now, Noah struggles to hold back, his huffs morphing into desperate moans. But his pleas mix with grunts, his shaft stimulating my insides in both depth and girth. I'm so wet that he glides in and out easily, as if we hadn't even changed positions. But that only means he kneads me deeper, this position allowing him full access to me.

"A-Alpha! You're so big, I can feel you in my—" I lift my chin to the sky, crying out with every wet slap of his hips into my pussy.

"Where can you feel me, gorgeous?" His growling voice makes me jerk with pleasure, his cock hitting every nerve in my core so tenderly that tingles climb to my face.

But I can't explain it to him, my face threatening to get mushed into the dirt as my arms turn into jelly.

Noah lifts my chest until my back presses against his wide form, his wolf locking me in place with an arm beneath my breasts. He pounds faster, bouncing them over his forearm.

"Ah! Alpha!"

Toying with my sensitive nipples, Noah only stops when my cries turn too desperate.

"Not yet." He rubs my bloated belly, and I nearly explode. "If you weren't pregnant, I'd make sure of it tonight. I want to give you everything."

My hips have lost all rhythm, squirming for every last drop of affection he'll give me. Noah slowly restarts his hips, emphasizing the end of each thrust with an extra snap. His wolf nips my neck, and my whimpers never want to end.

Noah pants against my cheek heavier than he has all night, his hips speeding faster. "Fuck, I can't hold back any longer. I'm going to knot."

Settling me back on the ground, Noah's hips remain stationed deep into me, shifting his thrusts into pulsing, luxurious presses against my G-spot. My claws dig into the dirt, shaking legs and rock-hard nipples only worsening from the shivers he's cascading over my body. He pounds into me with his claws in my sides, pheromones burning my nose as he licks my neck over and over again.

"I can't stand it, Noah!" I moan, slamming my hips back over him. Noah grunts, and heat gushes through my core as he fills me with fluid.

"Oh, Goddess," he whimpers. Noah crumbles over me, his knot expanding as his hips continue to jerk.

He's whining too heavily to speak, but I can still feel his ecstasy through his mindlink. *I want you to feel how much you mean to me. Can I mark you again?*

My body instinctively bares my neck and ass, allowing Noah to pump a few residual bursts into me. It hits so deep that my back arches on the edge of release.

His fangs clamp into my neck so hard that I yelp, but my resulting orgasm shakes through me. Noah overwhelms me with pleasure, kneading my clit as he rocks his tip into my crowded cervix, his knot giving me the most filling hug I can imagine between my legs.

"I-I love you—" My cries are whispers, but I know Noah can feel it. I love him too much for anyone to not smell it for miles.

By the time his hips still, we're both whimpering through tears. I can feel how committed he is to me through his fresh mark, letting me know he's here to stay. He feels more in love and sure about my status in his life than ever. This shatters the rest of my composure, breaking me into sobs.

Noah stops my mark from bleeding, caressing my belly as he holds me upright. "Shh, gorgeous Luna. Breathe deep."

I nuzzle against him, never wanting to let go.

He plants soft, tender kisses all over my neck, cheek, and shoulder. "I'm sorry, gorgeous. I didn't mean to be so rough on your neck."

"No, I loved it. I loved it so much."

"Good. I've got you, love." Running his hands over our baby, Noah urges another sob from my lips. "You're so fucking beautiful and brave. Thank you for doing this with me."

"I wanted to. I just love you so much, Noah. So much that I can't stop crying. I can't believe we're having a baby."

I trace his arm down to my belly, holding our pup together. As we share a weepy kiss, my heart won't stop flipping.

But then Noah's eyes flicker open, analyzing every approaching wolf.

My stomach drops when I register the sheer mass of them that have been witnessing us. Except they're not just staring anymore. They're heading directly for us.

I whimper, curling into my mate as protective instincts rupture within me. "A-Alpha!"

"Oh, my poor sweetheart." Noah coos over me, his scent exploding with reassurance. "It's okay, gorgeous Luna. You're safe."

My shoulders loosen, but that doesn't stop me from being confused. "What are they doing?"

Noah breaks into a shy smile, tracing gentle circles over my belly. "Since you're our official blessing holder, they want to return the favor whenever the Alpha and Luna mate. They're going to ask the Moon Goddess to bless us with pregnancy."

"Oh. How sweet." I bite my lips through fresh tears. Noah chuckles, kissing my fresh mark until I liquify in his arms.

"There you go. Good girl." His humming breath makes me squirm with leftover pleasure, my enamored scent billowing from my pores. Noah takes a deep whiff, humming with delight. "I love how you smell. You're so pregnant."

I erupt in giggles, but when he flexes inside me in response, I nearly topple over from exhaustion. "Oh, God, Noah—"

"Relax, Luna. Drop your whole weight on me."

I do as I'm told, leaning back against my mate's chest. His arms encompass all of me, holding me in as tight as they can while gently protecting my belly. I feel so good to be held by him that I can't stop moaning in pure comfort.

But as he gives the surrounding wolves the go-ahead to approach with a nod, my heartbeat hammers once more.

"Noah, won't they smell I'm already pregnant?" I whisper.

He stiffens, and all approaching wolves freeze in place. "Shit, you're right." He's silent for a long moment. "Did you want to tell them?"

"Well, I *want* to—" I swallow hard. "But it's still early. What if— If I—" I shake my head at the thought of losing the baby beneath our palms, my heart threatening to shatter right here.

"Hey, hey, hey— Don't blame yourself for that before it even happens. If it ever will." Noah kisses me with a gentle purr, sending a shiver down my over-sensitive spine. "Wolves see pregnancy in the Moon Goddess's control. They'd want to grieve with us as much as they want to celebrate."

My heart flips. "Really?"

"Absolutely. Even after 33 years, we celebrate my big sister's passing day, along with any other pups. If wolves lose a pregnancy, we say the Moon Goddess had greater plans for their pups as stars, helping her bless us."

I suck back tears, gazing at the starry sky enveloping the big, beautiful moon.

I choke out a sob. "That's sweet. And sad."

"Stay right here in this moment with me, okay? This has nothing to do with us right now." He covers my belly with his full palm, cocooning me in an extra hug. "Right now, I'm holding my mate and future pup. That's all we know."

I swallow hard, absorbing his words. I want to celebrate. To be happy to the fullest without anything holding me back. I just don't know if I want everyone to have to hurt alongside us if that happens.

But that sounds like a very familiar fear.

My heart picks up the pace as I cup Noah's hand around my belly, coming to a decision. The more I lean into it, the more excited I feel.

Each word shakes as I gaze up at Noah. "I'm a little scared, but something you said when we first wondered really stuck with me.

If everything goes to plan and we have this baby together, I want to enjoy it with you the whole way through. I want to celebrate this pup with you, right now, in front of everyone."

Noah bursts with excitement, smashing his nose into my cheek just as hard as his wolf nuzzles me. "Y-yeah? We're telling them?"

I giggle, stroking his cheek as I draw him in for a slow kiss. "I love you, adorable Alpha. Yes, let's tell them."

He holds his breath. "N-now?"

I break into laughter. "Yes, now! They're waiting."

Noah's kisses are filled with pause, his mind whirring. It only makes me giggle harder.

His words come out sweet and soft. "Fuck. I'm shy."

I smash my lips against him, giggling at his cute grin.

Let's tell them together. Through mindlink, I say.

He nods, adjusting his grip to cuddle me as tight as he can manage.

By now, the wolves circle, gazing from a distance with heightened curiosity. I can't hold back my smile.

Your Luna and I have news to share, Noah mindlinks. His chest thrums against my back, anticipatory anxiety bursting through our bond. It only makes me smile wider.

But Noah doesn't announce it. *Your turn, my gorgeous Luna. It'll be your first mindlink to everyone as their Luna.*

My heart stumbles over itself. As I gaze into the moonlit eyes around me, I feel it: they really are my family, and I'm about to tell them I'm carrying another new family member.

I choke out a laugh through my tears, smiling so wide that my cheeks hurt. *We're pregnant with our first pup.*

All at once, the pack erupts into howls.

I jump, but with how elated the pack becomes in our pack bond, Noah's scent overflows with the purest joy. It smells so decadent and comforting that the rest of my tension falls away, melting me in Noah's shaking hands as he caresses my belly.

Noah purrs over me, kissing my cheeks, neck, and heavy-lidded eyes until I'm coated in a fuzzy warmth. My giddy laughter is watery, an endless stream of tears gracing my cheeks as Noah's eyes pool over.

"I can feel how happy you are." His voice quivers as he nuzzles into me. "Like you love them already. Just as much as I do."

My heart throbs at his words. All I can do is stare at him. After all the years I agonized over having children someday, at times hating how much I craved it since it only worsened my gnawing, empty heartbreak over all those wasted years struggling to recover from Steven's damage, I'm here. Except I never imagined it would be this beautiful. I never realized I could feel a love this strong for my partner, and that I'd have the honor of witnessing how much they love our budding baby, long before they've even arrived.

My tears slow, leaving me with a smile so bright that my cheeks ache. As I pull Noah in for a kiss, I press all the affection into his lips that I can, silently thanking him for sharing this dream with me. Whether he can feel it or not, he takes a deep breath like he's breathing in the love I'm pouring over him. The sweet, touched arch of his eyebrows tells me the happy ache in his heart hits just as deep as mine.

As we pull away, I've never felt more joined as a unit.

Noah blinks slowly, unable to look away despite mindlinking our pack. *Okay. Feel free to approach, but be gentle with our Luna.*

The wolves approach slowly, one by one, many of them in their shifted forms. With brushes of their sides, nose boops from shifted wolves, and careful nuzzling, I weep.

"Their love is so pure, Noah." My voice comes out soft and wobbly.

"Good job, gorgeous. Take it in."

As I stroke the back of Noah's head, cradling him to me, he weeps too. I feel so accepted. So taken care of.

Noah nuzzles away my tears with gentle kisses until I steal his attention with my own lips. Our breaths quiver through our kiss, but we can't stop smiling.

"My sweet Luna." Noah beams.

My body buzzes with joy at my new title, never believing it so intimately until now. As I huddle into my doting mate, I allow myself to feel it; we're safe.

To Be Continued in Book 3

In a thrilling conclusion to an epic love story, every secret, mystery, fear, and joy comes out.

Snarling teeth, bitter reunions, and a thirst for dominance brew tension between global pack leaders at the Alpha Summit. But the more Summit traditions Aliya and Noah experience, the more secrets Aliya uncovers behind why her fated mate's rejection of Alpha domination is so frowned upon... and the more Noah attempts to hide his inner truths.

Hunted into a corner, the fated mates are left with the ultimate choice: they can follow the old pack ways, or they can rebel, choosing to love themselves for who they are.

Acknowledgments

While I don't write about my direct life experiences, I do push myself to write about topics I relate to that I keep nested deep in my heart. Writing this way directly combats my OCD and PTSD, leaving me feeling like I've undergone some sort of internal battle, only to come out a bit more victorious by the end of each book.

After publishing webcomics for multiple years, one thing that continued to surprise me no matter how many times it happened was that readers related to the smallest aspects of my characters' experiences. Oftentimes, these aspects surrounded topics I previously thought I was alone in.

I wrote Freeing My Alpha with this concept in mind, once again terrifying myself by writing about deeper, vulnerable concepts. However, I know in my heart that these fears are my signal that this is what matters to me most: sharing authentic survivor stories in the hopes that you can feel less alone in your experiences. Thank you for continually teaching me that I'm less alone in life than I thought, as well as joining me on this journey.

No book can be created alone. I want to thank the many people in my circle who brought Book 2 to life.

Kayla Vokolek not only kept me sane during the editing process of such a massive book, but also had me laughing through to the end despite pre-publishing stress (which is a true feat)! Thank you for your willingness to work with me and put your heart and energy into it every time, no matter how wild the subject matter.

In the early days of this series, when Book 2 was simply the middle chunk of a massive script, Julia Aniella was there brainstorming and laughing with me the whole way through, which I will always treasure. Thank you so much for sharing your love and thoughts about these characters with me.

Lukas, thank you for donating your time and excitement to Freeing My Alpha as its alpha reader! I so appreciate your readiness to dive into my stories. I feel so lucky to have a friend I always know I can share them with, thanks to you.

Thank you so much to my loving family who perched their hardcover copy of My Shy Alpha on top of the piano, warming my heart each time I see it. Mom, I'm so grateful for how you've taught me to treat my fellow human beings with such tenderness, allowing me to imagine the sides of Aliya and Noah that readers tell me they love most. Dad, thank you for calling me in to show me your excitement over getting notifications for my upcoming releases and taking the time and utmost care to review my cover artwork, helping me take it to the next level. Blake, thank you for rooting for me in every way, hyping up my books and so generously helping me drag them to both the slowest and busiest events without expecting anything in return.

Ren Rice, the owner of the beautiful Romance Era Bookshop has been such a genuine and thoughtful supporter of me and my books, starting with Book 1. What an honor to have My Shy Alpha be featured in not only my first book signing event, but also yours!

Speaking of being lucky, what great fortune I had that Helen happened to be my work buddy during both the cover's first pass and its final touches. Thank you for your kind support, thoughtful critiques, and generosity always, including making some of the most stressful parts of art the most fun by matching my style of an uncanny level of suddenly deep conversations.

Pam, Jessa, Sam, and friends at Fated Promos, thank you so much for your guidance and support in helping me reach more readers. I truly appreciate the time and care you put into figuring out the best steps to boost my work, and am so grateful for the difference it's making.

My friends are truly my found family, and they uplift me through every book launch. Layla, thank you for truly being my sanity whenever I feel like an alien (since at least we can be aliens together in this weird world). Jamee, thank you for always sticking by my side and rooting for me no matter which direction life takes us. Thank you, Karla, for laughing with me about the absolute rollercoaster that is the publishing industry. Thank you, Michelle, for relating on so many levels with me as an artist, helping me feel far less alone. Briar, thank you for always showing up to support my books with such excitement and encouragement, continually bringing a smile to my face.

To my Patrons on Patreon—Lukas Kazmirski, Katy, E the cat caterer, Anonymous, Mitchie, Phokoro, Stacie, Cass, Jennifer Belveal, Courtney Madison, Drask, Leyth, Kim Warren, Jason, GenderBender LLC, Sarah Rodriquez, Aaa Bbb, Pinkalien_99, and Valerie Miller—thank you for both your invaluable generosity in supporting my work, and for doing so even before seeing its final product. What an incredible opportunity you've given me to continue doing what I love!

Beta and ARC readers, thank you so much for generously offering your time to read this book early. Likewise, every reader on Inkitt, Wattpad, Patreon, and Tapas, as well as readers of the original visual novel, thank you for showering the unedited draft with so much love from the beginning. A special thank you to readers who also went the extra mile to directly support the book with tips on Tapas and reviews on Inkitt. You continue to inspire me to create better stories for you to enjoy!

I want to give a special thank you to the Shy Alpha Hype Team on social media. Your voices have amplified my stories' reach farther than I could ever do alone.

I'm so grateful to every reader I've been so lucky to meet at book signings and conventions. Each time you share what my story means to you, your words stick in my mind in the best way, reminding me why I love to write.

And to you, dear Reader, I wish I could properly explain how much your presence matters to me, other than that you being here to witness Aliya and Noah's story means the world to me. I love having the chance to share their ups and downs with you, especially the parts that resonate with your past or present struggles. You're not alone, and I'm always rooting for your well-being. I hope the best is yet to come, and I can't wait to see you again for Book 3!

You matter to me. If you or someone you know is struggling, please flip to the following page for mental health resources.

Resources

You deserve support and free access to knowledge. Please utilize the resources below whenever you need them. The world needs you here.

International OCD Foundation
https://iocdf.org

International Society for the Study of Trauma and Dissociation
https://isst-d.org

RAINN (Anti-Sexual Violence Nonprofit)
https://www.rainn.org

Psychology Today - Find a Therapist (International)
https://psychologytoday.com/intl/counsellors

Trans Lifeline
https://translifeline.org

The Trevor Project
https://thetrevorproject.org

International Association for Suicide Prevention
https://www.iasp.info

More by River Kai

BOOKS

My Shy Alpha
Book 1 of the Steamy Shifter Romance Series

Unraveling with You
A Steamy Contemporary Romance

Soul Survivors
Book 1 of the Psychological Romantic Thriller Series (Fall 2024)

Book 3 of the My Shy Alpha Series (Spring 2025)

COMICS & GRAPHIC NOVELS

Resonance
Space Gays Vol.1

What-Sexual??
Vol.1

What-Sexual??
Vol.2 (Winter 2024)

About the Author

As a bisexual and transgender creator, River Kai specializes in LGBTQ+ Romance, Sci-Fi, and Fantasy with mental health and disability representation, creating stories for readers like him to see they're not alone. While he writes in multiple Romance sub-genres, his stories share three recurring themes: empowering character arcs about healing from trauma, authentic representation of transgender or bisexual main characters with depression, anxiety, PTSD, and OCD, and a sweet-but-spicy emphasis on consent.

For current updates, follow River Kai on social media
@riv_kaii   *@riv_kai*   *River Kai*   *River Kai Art*
or sign up for the River Kai Art newsletter at
riverkaiart.com

Milton Keynes UK
Ingram Content Group UK Ltd.
UKHW010613130624
443933UK00013B/175/J